Rupe
For the
Bookshop, x

The Sca

E.B. Lurie

Lots of
love,
Lill xx

Zed Books Ltd.

The Scaffold was first published by Zed Books Ltd.,
57 Caledonian Road, London N1 9BU, UK, and
171 First Avenue, Atlantic Highlands, New Jersey 07716, USA,
in 1986.

Copyright © E.B. Lurie, 1986.

Cover designed by Henry Iles.
Printed by Biddles of Guildford, UK.

British Library Cataloguing in Publication Data

Lurie, E.B.
  The scaffold.
  823[F]   PR9369.3.L/

  ISBN 0-86232-600-1
  ISBN 0-86232-601-X Pbk

From A to Z

I

"KNOW ALL MEN WHOM IT MAY CONCERN..."

The senior official read from a document ivory with age. His elbow lay nonchalantly on top of a bubble-gum vending machine in the Indian shop. Ginger short-back-and-sides rested against a shelf of sub-standard pilchards in tomato sauce. " 'that blah-blah-blah appeared before ... Registrar of Deeds ... the said Appearer being duly authorised...' " He grunted. "Shit, what a load of bull."

"Here, let's have a squiz." His assistant stopped fingering oranges and avocados, leaned across to assess the watermarks and seals on a Deed of Transfer. The words sounded sour, sucked from lips narrow as a slash on a lemon-skin. "...which power witnessed in accordance with law was this day exhibited etcetera truly and legally sold on the so-and-so day of ... in the year'. Shit" he repeated.

"What's biting you now?" asked the elder. "We been through all this before, let's see." He glanced at the cover of the folder. "Nine times already, this our tenth friendly little visit, so what's up?"

"You know what? Comes month after next by the time Transfer goes through, be a hundred years near as dammit from the day those original Naidoos grabbed this place. What was it again they forked out for it at the time?" He turned the page and whistled. "Hells-bells, can you beat it? I keep forgetting it's so, so next to nothing, only four hundred, just four tiny little hundreds. That's not bad going hey, getting dished out four thousand now, just like that, cash on the table."

Arms spread, the Indian shopkeeper braced himself behind the wooden counter. His fingers gripped the brass rule screwed at the edge as border to a maze of scratches on the varnish. "What you want? Keep keep coming. Who send you, who you call yourself?"

"Look man, as far as you're concerned we needn't even have names,

1

it's the Department you're dealing with."

Two buttons were missing from the convex bulge of the waistcoat behind the counter. He could not tell which official had spoken; the manila folder masked their faces. As the mahogany head swivelled in indecision the sheen of hair-oil gleamed under a bare globe. "For why you say every time I must sell? Sell? Why? For what you say it?"

"For all of the four thousand the Department's willing to cough up. You don't believe me? Here, it says so, you can see for yourself." The senior official thrust the folder forward in an offer of inspection and waited, using the nail of his little finger to dislodge a sliver of breakfast trapped between two teeth. "All right? That's one hell of a lot of money you know. Only wish I had even half that in my pocket. You won't believe it, true as I'm standing here you won't, I'm telling you the likes of us we can't even afford so much as a packet of curry powder these days." He sniffed, inhaling the mystery of pungent oriental spices past the hairs inside his nostrils. "Not on what they pay us. Not a damn."

"You can say that again." His junior nodded, grabbed the folder, slapped it shut and tucked it under an arm. "Look, if he wants to play hard-arse that's his look-out, only I bet you, come crawling back later try blame us. Now listen hey, Mister ..." He inspected the cover; the pause separated title from name. "Naidoo, yes that's right, Naidoo, listen, jokes apart, what's it really you've got here in actual fact? Can you in all honesty claim it's a, what they call a commercial site of any real value? Now can you?"

The elder official nodded slowly, his head heavy with the wisdom of middle-aged experience. A frown denoted that each word to be uttered had been weighed and found worthy. "I'll be quite open with you. In all truth more like slum property so to speak. We'll simply keep on coming, time and the law's on our side remember, no two ways about it. Unless you'd prefer it otherwise, there's always ways and means of getting you people see sense, make no mistake about that. Up to you my friend, take it or leave it. Tenth time now I'm telling you all this, just to put you in the picture. It's only a question of sooner or later."

"Ach leave him, waste of time letting him know nicely, let's bugger off" pleaded the younger man. "Send in the papers, haul him up in front the Compensation Board, stick in a Request Voluntary Transfer, stamp the Confirmation Order and finished."

"These youngsters, impatient." From a head cocked over to the side, the voice of a kindly uncle confided to Naidoo. "Listen, you've got experience same like me on my side, you know your business inside out.

2

So let's face it, after the rest of you people have all been shifted, where your customers going to come from? From round here? Have a heart, there'll be not a one left in any case. Expect they'll trek all the way from hell-and-gone?'' He shifted his weight from left leg to right. ''Mustn't for one moment think we don't feel hang of a... okay, a few little hassles to begin with starting up where you're going to, so what? Look, we don't make the rules, we've got a job to do and you can't turn round and say you're not being treated fair.'' He stopped suddenly, as though realising that words dribbled too quickly dilute their effect, eased the folder from his assistant's arm and flipped it open on the counter. Fumble fingers creased flimsy after flimsy sheet. The search slowed, a licked forefinger turned thicker pages with a rustle, hesitated, pointed in triumph. ''Here we are. You sign here. We'll be the witnesses.'' He unclipped a ball-point from the breast pocket of his safari jacket. ''Must be in black ink on white paper. Don't ask me why.''

''What you want to buy? What?'' Glitter-eyes burning, the owner glared from the two officials to a gang of barefoot urchins that had sidled into his shop. He could have been confronting either group. On tip-toe at the counter, each child reached up to slap down a palm-warmed copper coin.

''Nothing to be ashamed of living with others same like you yourself... in the long end, come round to realise what's good for you, what side your bread's buttered on.'' The officials were ignored by all except a knee-high figure wary on a crept journey to the bubble-gum machine. An undersized hand tried its luck with the handle; even without a coin... sometimes. Not today. He joined his chitter-chatter mates clustered temple-to-temple before a display stand which reflected their faces. Behind the cracked glass lay a mound of pink and white and yellow marshmallow fishes stuck together in tail-curled chaos. ''Portion 13 Remainder Lot B Plot 666, it's not even properly zoned according the latest Town Planning Scheme.''

Arms waving behind the counter, in a voice now an octave shriller and multidecibels louder, the accent thicker, Naidoo shouted ''What you want? What you do here? You get away, away.'' Again, he could have been attacking either target. He swept coins from the counter into the drawer of his cash-register.

Only the urchins obeyed him. They snuck out as though ashamed of their very existence, each stretching a fish between teeth and fingers as they trailed bare feet across lino cracks. Twin shoulder-blade ridges marked the back of each shirt.

Naidoo lifted the counter-flap to stump round towards the officials. Three inclined heads formed a close conspiracy of adults against children, then recoiled; oiled comb rakes from beer and bacon, ginger stubble and lank blond strands from betel-nut and garlic.

"Steal, right out my own shop. Must watch all time or take away belongs to me" he complained. "Not safe, even here behind counter, not safe any more."

"Not so in the new place." The words bore the stamp of an official assurance.

"Street-lamps, roads, water; sewerage they'll be putting in later. Might still look a bit on the raw side, come back in a year's time and you wouldn't recognise the place. I'm telling you."

"Spending millions. Shopping, parking, even set aside ground for a mosque, the lot, you just name it ..."

"They've all signed out their own free choosing, Gool and Pillay and Naidoo and Essop." Acid lips spat out the names.

"Just hang on a sec, not so fast, not so fast."

"What's up now?"

"No man no, this here's Naidoo. The others, they're for this afternoon."

"Not safe here anymore" Naidoo continued, the interruption disregarded. "Police? There'll be lots police? Here you never get."

The officials shared a quick glance. "Police station, man, what you think? Most terrific, should only see it, really beautiful. And big, hell, like from here right away to the corner over there. Very first thing gets put up in all new townships."

"Four thousand, cash down. Compared with what your people picked it up for in the old days, paid peanuts. I reckon it's a good thousand more than what the Compensation Board, if you decide to let it get so far as that."

"Yes, some buggers have all the luck."

Naidoo waved a forefinger under the officials' noses to silence them. "Say I want sell shop, house, plot next door, then who's going pay revenue stamps? Expect me put up for transfer and lawyer and... on top of...?"

He in turn was silenced by a wagging finger. "Drive a hard bargain hey? Look, if you dig your heels in we'll just have to organise something. Don't worry yourself on that score, there's ways and means to wangle exemptions and so on and so forth. Just leave it to me, won't cost you

4

so much as..."

All three turned to face a moving shadow at the back of the shop. Mrs Naidoo shuffled forward from the passage behind the counter and re-arranged the limp folds of her sari; the shapeless chalk-blue cloth was held bunched by a ruby brooch red as the dot of lipstick on her forehead. "What they want, these men, what?" she snapped at her husband as though he was the neighbour's dog, and glared at the two strays in her shop. Sharp sounds in a tongue so foreign that the officials giggled— how could those others talk without words, only barks and snarls?

Naidoo waved his wife away and again the three heads came together in conspiracy, now of males against females.

"Women" snorted an official, "they're all the same, give us men a hard time."

"She know nothing." Naidoo shook his head. "First she ask, will be safe there? Stupid woman, know nothing about new police station. Then, who'll pay lawyer, stamps? She forget, she think I never sell a property before. Then when I tell she ask me why haven't signed already. She worry I'm not going to sign." He shook his head again, sadly, in forgiveness of the frailty of all women.

Naidoo, now the shrewd businessman with gold-capped teeth, used his own fountain-pen to scrawl his signature decisively, with a flourish.

"Here" said the senior official, "this copy's yours. The cheque, just try to be patient, it'll take a bit of time. All these papers, this whole pile every single one... " He flipped the pages in the folder and sighed. "Must be cleared first by the Local Office and only then get sent up ... man, you just don't know even half the fuss and bother." He turned at the door to acknowledge the satisfied nod and smile Naidoo could not keep off his serious face.

Outside, two bunched fists, each grasping a packet of curry powder, saluted back to a brown hand fluttering under the faded signwriting across the facade.

At their car the officials saluted again, laughed, slapped their thighs and called out an almost friendly joke General Naidoo Dealer would not hear above the traffic noise. They saw a portly figure framed by the door-way of his shop, still smiling and waving, flanked by the criss-cross burglar screens on the windows either side, dwarfed by the chipped coca-cola sign and the peeling Lexington giant grinning at a king-of-kings size filter tip. The car springs yielded as they eased themselves into the front seats.

5

It took six weeks for Transfer to be lodged on a Thursday morning. On Friday Naidoo was served with a Final Notice to Vacate.

Early on Sunday cars and cars and delivery vans began parking outside the shop and adjoining house. Men of the family grunted as they loaded furniture; women tripped over sari hems and squashed rolls of bedding on to the back seats. Pots and crockery piled up on the pavement. Small children dashed up and down the garden path in bursts of excitement. Schoolboys staggered under the load of cardboard cartons tied with string; one burst open and packets of long-grain rice spilled into the road; talk, talk. Neighbours watched silently from the other side of the street.

Trips. More trips. A final trip.

In mid-afternoon Naidoo made a last round of inspection—all clear. He locked the front door, slipped the key into a waistcoat pocket and patted it.

II

Two minutes past midnight and an angle-poise lamp.

In yellow light, sealed in a Persian rug and plate-glass study elegant with Penguin shelves and hi-fi, the sharpened point of a 2H drawing pencil hesitated over the third item in the second column, changed a 5 to a 6. No, better not risk it. Balfour fumbled a rubber, gripped it for a single stroke and re-wrote 5, big clear and dark. Click-dammit, click-flare: hollow cheeks sucked the flame of a 9-carat lighter towards the tip of another cigarette; tremble fingers brushed ash from the previous one off the page, then played over the keys of a pocket calculator.

Time and place defined him. Overworked and comfortably suburban. Certificates on the imbuia veneer of his walls proclaimed the details, their frames protecting the seals and signatures that protected his professional status. Bachelor of Science in the Faculty of Engineering; Associate Member of the Institution of Civil Engineers; Master Builders Association; Post-Graduate Diploma in Construction Management; Fellow of an exclusive and semi-secret brotherhood. Dates hinted at an age of forty-odd.

There was room for one more stub in the ash-tray. He check-added the summary of CONCRETE SHUTTERING & REINFORCEMENT and turned back to EXCAVATOR. What did it really mean "... to a depth not exceeding... grade & compact to 98%"? Only a high priest of construction could interpret the mystery concealed behind the cryptic language, and have the courage to translate it into numbers. Why the discrepancy between that area and 'Premix Paving' under SITEWORKS?

Worry about it, worry while changing the pencil for a ball-point to address an official envelope. 'The Chairman, The Tender Board, Tender for Proposed Commercial Training & Community Centre, Due 11 a.m.' The final figure would be written with this pen, it felt heavy, eighty-

7

four grown men with their families plus the four apprentices seemed to be leaning on it. And only he could decide if it should point towards the queue outside the Labour Exchange or to fifteen months of slavery.

Say Atomic Welding could be played off against Cape Steel, offered monthly cash with no retention for an extra 2½% discount, that would come to say eighteen hundred, no wait, more, one thousand nine hundred and thirtyseven, then...

A hiss of tyres from a speeding car pierced his cocoon of concentration. Then, silence, intensified by the single bark of a watchdog three or four gardens away.

Who would be in such a hurry, so late? A power-failure in another suburb? Jammed signals in the marshalling-yards or a harbour pilot summoned to a drifting tanker? Night-workers, slit-eyed in cold midnight vigil, nursing the city's heartbeat while its citizens sheltered in the warm security of blankets. Tonight he too another lonely member of this sect, still alert at... nearly one a.m. already.

If say half the two thousand odd was loaded on to the rate for that undermeasured Premix paving, then when the area was remeasured for Final Account the profit would be stretched to... how much? As much as that rubber band between the paper-clips on the inkstand could be pulled in tension....

"You're still at it?" It was an accusation, not a question.

Balfour pushed back his chair the fraction that showed he was nearly finished and stared at her with the blind eyes of a husband who hardly notices his wife. "What? Well, what is it? I didn't hear you come in."

"Should I make tea now?" She rested her forehead against the doorframe.

"Please. You know... I'll join you in a minute." He blinked, heavy-lidded in a haze of smoke. "I've just thought of something. You wear that old dressing-gown and pale face to show how late it is. For the supermarket it's all bright make-up and a floral print."

"Well, I can't sit up the whole night waiting for you."

He crumpled an empty carton of Lexington, flung it into the wastepaper-basket and scratched open the cellophane wrapping of another. If the total of the sub-sections on the Final Summary page agreed within ½% with... Nearly, nearly finished. This was the worst part, the decision.

Easing himself out of the green leather chair needed a weight-lifter's effort of grunts and flexed muscles and leverage. Stiff from hours of sitting, he shuffled to the kitchen.

"You would've slammed the door" he said, "if it wasn't for the

8

children sleeping.''

She answered by keeping silent, turning her back on him and pretending to prefer the fridge. "You're always like this" she sighed to the milk-bottle heavy in her hand, "the night before a big tender. Can cut this strain in the whole house with a knife. Especially Boyboy, he feels it worst, impossible the whole day. Others seem to have such good jobs with the council, with your qualifications and experience, they're crying out for…''

"For heaven's sake we've been over this so often. Every time it's the same."

The tea-pot in her hand seemed to tilt over from weariness. The steam mesmerised her. With the glazed eyes of an entranced oracle she whispered "I know that feeling, from always before a really tricky… say like a neuro or a… the whole theatre staff, even the cleaners… Want anything with the tea?''

"What've you got? And please, don't try to palm off any more of your mother's stale dropscones. Not again.''

Her head twitched as her neck became rigid. "I tried some new recipe instead of just waiting up for you. Almond. From Larousse.''

He followed her to the pantry alcove and as she stretched up to a shelf his claw-fingers tested the muscles of her buttocks. The flannel of her dressing-gown felt rough and warm, but under that a slippery film clung to her flesh. "Don't complain." He forced out a half-laugh. "With a backside like yours you could've trapped any man you wanted. Even a goods-yard assistant foreman.''

"If I've told you once I've told you a hundred times, we were never officially engaged, he just happened to be in Daddy's darts team from the Recreation. In any case I never let him, at least not properly.'' She sniffed. "Which I bet is one up on your so-called lady friend, that brainbox, change-the-world.'' She rattled a biscuit tin and slid it across the formica surface of a built-in kitchen unit. "I simply couldn't believe it that time you pointed her out to me. That flat-chested buck-toothed little bitch with the string hair and all so hoity-toity.'' She minced a fancy waltz across the foam-backed floor, palms aflutter at her hips, "With acne on that stuck-up nose of hers.''

"Nose? What about nose?" He hugged the tin and wrestled off the lid. "These smell all right to me. You'd rather I took a dark one or a light?''

"Please yourself. There's a few got a bit burnt on the outside. I'm still not used to that eye-level oven yet. Besides it wasn't your crooked snout that hooked me. Just remember the first sight I had of you young man, it wasn't your face but that thing of yours dangling there on the operating table next to an appendix fit to burst and I still can't for the life of me decide which looked the more inflamed.''

"Not bad, not bad at all.'' He nibbled away the corner of a biscuit with small and careful bites, squinting up to the ceiling to show that this was only a tasting, not serious eating. "Bit too much vanilla.''

"You think it's worth repeating? Yes, but I always stick exactly to the recipe first time I try anything new.''

"Here's your answer.'' He swallowed the biscuit with one bite, took another, and another.

She leaned across the deep-freeze to watch him, chin propped on cupped palms.

"Nerves. Whenever you eat too quickly I know there's something. What's it you're sweating over now?''

"Last one.'' His Adam's-apple jumped and he brushed crumbs off his lapel. "Commercial Training Community Centre thing, big one, really big. Have to land it, must, otherwise what do I do with the men? As it is I've already put half-a-dozen on cleaning windows and ... next week I'll have to start laying them off. And I can pull it off, I know I can, I've been watching all the tender results like a hawk these last three months and there'll be only one other firm really interested. I've judged exactly what figure they're going to come in at. Grind them into dust, like this.'' He leaned his whole weight on to a rigid thumb and pulverised a biscuit crumb.

"You'll never grow up.'' She looked down on his stocky figure crouched over the tin, sandy hair curly with the chaos of an urchin's mop, waiting for the scolding. While the kitchen clock jerked its second hand through another arc of time to twist still tighter their bond of married years. "Then when you do land it then what? Another year or so of being tied to a block of concrete or some crane that's always breaking down. Hardly a husband.''

"I don't perform my marital duties often enough, is that it?'' He grinned, panther-glided past a copper jelly mould to grab her, slide in a hand and tweak a rubbery nipple. She shook him away; her hair trembled, brushed the lace collar of her gown and settled back into style. The bleached strands were darker at her scalp and from the corners of her eyes furrows radiated in the pattern of a map of dried water-courses. "No, stop it.''

He chuckled, "That's exactly the way you used to say it whenever

10

we used to wrestle in the old station-wagon, remember? Parked there on the Marine Drive with yellow lights reflected in the bay from all those blocks of flats across the water and wondering which one we'd set up house in. A pair of youngsters in the mother city that spawned us. And now we're here. Hell, we're nearly middleaged already.''

''I often feel I look it. Were you really planning to marry me? Or lead me on, all you wanted… never dared allow myself even to hope for this much, not in my wildest dreams. For myself, some small place and then when Daddy finally retired, help them, you can starve on a railway pension.''

''Yes, I know, I know. It's late already.''

''You forget that year's class medal and practically in charge of the whole orthopaedic theatre. Still… double-storey right slap-bang here in the best part of Claremont…'' The sweep of her arm, wide sleeve flapping, blessed the chimneys and the shutters, the lawns with banks of massed hydrangeas, the maid asleep in the servant's quarters, her own car in the garage. ''I don't want that swimming-pool, honestly I don't, I don't want another trip overseas, it all means nothing to me, nothing.'' She shivered, drew her lapels up, clutched them below her chin with white knuckle-bones and crouched in an old-woman's posture. ''That's all from you the earner, not you yourself. You're hardly here at all… you've never really given yourself properly to being married, always there's that, like some space fenced off inside you… nobody can ever reach you.''

He finished his tea and took another biscuit. With full mouth he mumbled ''I should be doing better y'know. Right kind of school, enough meaningless letters after my name, not lazy. With a father it didn't pay to become a judge and my mother, what she pulled in later with her graphics, how far have I got? Not even a director, only area manager of some medium-sized construction company, the do-everything man for that semi-literate cockney at the other end of the country.''

''You never could stand him. I don't know why you put up with… all the time, he could be right here in this very room now, between us.''

''Former head of a big London firm… bullshit, more like an odd-job handyman in the East End slums. There's that something missing in me, no bloody good at a dinner party, people bore me and useless at things like club committees. Each time I hear that cockney whine over the phone I want to puke, but somehow he manages to slither his way into…''

''I can squeeze another half a cup, or should I make fresh?''

''You haven't seen that new mansion of his, all from my brains and sweat, mine. And what really gets me up to here, there's no bad taste

11

there, not a single drop of kitsch, not anywhere, he's got enough ready cash to call in the very best of interior decorators. Opulent yes, huge, even an original Matisse and not a single Tretchikoff, not that he'd know the difference anyway. No, that's enough, just a drop of milk or I'll have to get up in the middle of the night to piss.''

"It's morning already.''

"So it is. I've got to phone his highness at the palace at eight with the final price before I fill in the Tender Form. You should see this fleshy-nosed rat in his marble study, crouching there at a huge antique desk, uncomfortable as... and in a waistcoat, I ask you, but perfectly tailored. And to top it, theodolite and tripod propped in the corner to impress visitors. He wouldn't even know how to set it up.''

He looked up to watch her stroke tender fingers over the embossed patterns on the tiles above the dish-washing machine. "Actually you're a very clever man with no faith in your own... just look here at these, how you worked in really leftovers from that bank job and then went and booked down the last cent against your account. Next year maybe we should put in one of those extractor fans, it'll only add to the value if ever we decided to sell. You know...'' Hands on hips, she proclaimed a formal statement. "This must be the most beautiful kitchen I've ever seen. You could take a colour photo and put it in any of those magazines.'' She tidied the drape of her dressing-gown with a gesture of emphasis.

"Don't cover up those legs of yours, they've still got that racehorse colt shape.''

She lifted her hem to examine them. "At least I've managed to avoid middle-age spread. I'd die if ever I got varicose veins. It's a horrible op for a woman, those scars, they can look ghastly. I must get my hair done next week, I'm sure I look a fright. You're still calculating in your head aren't you, all the time. It shows in your eyes and the way you keep on counting with your fingers. It seems like only yesterday how I took time off for a blow-dry rinse and set before I even dared go in there the first time just to have a peek what kind of face you had, though I had no business really to be there at all in the ward. And you didn't even notice all I'd spent you were so sedated you looked ghastly, mumbling away a lot of nonsense all about that lady-friend of yours I could've strangled her right there on the spot. I bet she still goes round hugging a great big pile of pamphlets instead of a man. Politics my foot.'' She sniffed.

He jammed the lid back on the biscuit tin. "Wasn't ever really part of that crowd, or even one of the beer-drinkers in the rugby team. There's the one thing I did envy them, not their crackpot ideas but the way they burned, they absolutely quivered with sincerity. Me? There's not a single time or place I've felt so much a part of anything to forget myself. That must be real luxury, absorbed into something bigger than your own skin, say like a monk in the cell of a mediaeval cloister. No friends, no hobbies.''

"You're yourself. All the fifteen-odd years I've known you you haven't changed, not that much.'' She snapped her fingers so close before his face he had to squint to focus on the gleam and flash of gold and diamonds. When he cringed back one step, forefinger pressed against his lips, she copied him. For half-a-minute, a minute, they tried to breathe silently.

"Did you hear anything?'' he whispered. "Or was I imagining?''

She shook her head. "It must've been the wind, or maybe he's gone back to sleep again. A child that age, he shouldn't still be getting those nightmares, he should've grown out of it by now. Nerves, it's this terrible strain in the house, it's destroying us all. What job did you say it was this time?''

"I told you, but you weren't listening, as usual. A Commercial Training Community Complex, not five minutes away, convenient as...''

"For one of the chains?''

"No, official, or partly... one of those vague semi-government development boards. At least the money's safe, not like that time... And he had the bloody cheek to blame me for it.''

"Where? Right here in Claremont?''

"I suppose you could call it that, or more like Lansdowne really, or even lower Crawford or upper Athlone. Royal Road, that area. Somewhere near your former part of the world isn't it?''

She admitted her past with the pride of a raised chin. "You know I practically grew up there. This housing scheme the railways used to have, but that's from before the days Daddy got promoted Works Inspector and we moved to that three-bedroom. Didn't I ever show you?''

He forced up his eyelids and frowned a pretended interest.

"Not a drain-cover in the whole Royal Road I didn't use for hopscotch. Pinch coloured chalk from school. All the kids, from both sides of the line we'd all troop together, there was this Indian place there on the corner...'', vibrant with the breathless whisper of an excited child, lisping, her blue flannel dressing-gown simple as an illustration in a story-book. "Acid-drops, those were my favourites, they lasted longer than the bullseyes.''

"That's all coming down, the shop, the house next to it.''

"Well I never." She sighed. "Well, I suppose you can't stop progress. You going back to the study or should I switch off? Come, leave it, you're practically out on your feet."

He grunted agreement. "Yes, done all I can really, calculations I mean, last bit is judgement, guesswork. Still haven't decided yet. Got to do my teeth."

His feet dragged towards the door. A finger hesitated on the light switch, almost too slack to press it. He turned to look at her crumpled on a chrome-and-leather stool, untidy, forehead on forearm on flawless enamel. "You coming?"

Her whisper carried the loneliness of all deserted women, all widows. "So, for another year, and after that?"

He left her sighing in a sterile wilderness of gadget efficiency and clung to the banister rail to haul himself upstairs and stumble through the nightly ritual—toothbrush, swirling water and pyjamas.

Blankets up to ears, eyes closed, pretending to sleep when she joined him, he felt the mattress deflect, rebound as she plumped her pillow, settle to the shape they had imposed on it over all their thousands and one of shared nights.

Now only leaf rustle from the avenue of oaks as though they too stirred in restless twisting. Pins and needles pricked him into turning over. What was it, pride? tact? sheer stupidity? forced him to breathe deeply, evenly, in the rhythm of sleep. Eyes open, staring at the dark. He knew that she knew that he knew.

She knew he was awake. "You can't sleep?" she whispered. "Want me to help you? You always sleep better afterwards."

"I'm not at all... I'll drop off in a moment."

She reached over, fumbled inside his pyjama trousers, found his secret, encircled it with thin fingers and squeezed. Her rings felt cold. His legs twitched. "It's all right, don't worry, I'll be all right, honestly."

"I'll come over" she insisted. He felt from the way the blankets tugged that she was pulling her nightie up to the hips. A pair of warm legs wriggled in under him.

A deep breath and he gave himself to her, sensing the exquisite satisfaction that she, the understanding wife, would draw from not being satisfied.

There was only himself and one other. All the rest could be ignored. That job had to be done, had to.

But at what level? Coming too high—just wouldn't go. Rather lower down, the lower the easier, almost too easy to slip in.

Yet not too low, that would spoil it, rather add one thousand and one and one, add two thousand, two, two, three and three, four, four and five... enough.

He rolled off her. "I'm all right now" he panted, "I've settled on the tender figure. Definite."

And was asleep by the time she had scrambled back to her side of the bed.

III

The alarm only added to the turmoil. Boyboy was refusing to take peanut-butter sandwiches to school, he had already used that naughty forbidden word twice, once to his sister, once to Nanny. Did he need discipline or love? Freud disagreed with Spock. Father snapped at Mother. A bathroom door was slammed. Nanny mumbled when Madam swept into the kitchen and stormed that Master's coffee...

Balfour folded the Times at the Financial page. How had marmalade got smeared over the sports page? The latest quarterly report of the Bureau of Economic Research predicted tighter conditions in industry for the next two years. Construction in particular, the value of building plans approved by the major municipalities—the graph dipped. The toast was burnt. If the children didn't stop their nonsense and hurry hurry hurry they'd be late. Seven forty-five.

"You're cutting it rather fine" she reminded him, "if you're still going to phone from the office at eight."

"No, I'll phone from here. If, if I can find two minutes of relative quiet."

"Well, I can't bring up the children and run the house all on my own you know."

"You think I haven't got enough to... you try looking after nearly a hundred grown toughs... to keep even some control over only two children... now stop it, once and for all stop it."

A schoolboy in short grey trousers kept on swinging his satchel at his sister's knees. The metal lunch-tin in the corner made it hurt even more.

Balfour threaded his way towards the study, through slaps and tears and a young lady's protests of offended dignity. Two minutes later he was back.

"I can't get through" he announced. His household ignored him.

Another half a cup.

He drained it. Only when he was chewing on the bitter dregs did she respond. Offhand, over the shoulder while she re-tied the ribbon in her daughter's plait, "well, try again in a few minutes."

A cigarette on the side terrace. It was twelve paces long from north to south, thirteen from south to north. Two slabs in the slate paving had come a bit loose, the fuschia needed pruning. He lit a second from the stump of the first.

"But Mommy, the concert's only three weeks away." A high-pitched plea pierced the french doors and blended with the purr of a neighbour's Mercedes reversing down the driveway.

The answer was too soft to hear the words, only the lower calmer tone, soothing, gentle as the swish of the pink négligé she wore in the mornings.

She was kneeling, arm around her son's shoulder. "You've got your exercise book?" Nod. "And your crayons?" Nod. "You've put seed in the budgie's cage?" Nod. "You remembered to... what's the matter, my darling, darling what is it? Oh my God."

Balfour stroked the moulded architrave at the doorway. The children stared slack-jawed at him, saw their mother offer a shiny sleeve of support, shrank back from the anxiety in her voice. "Aren't you feeling well? You're absolutely grey. Here, come sit down."

He suffered himself to be led shambling towards a chair, then shook her away and said "I can't believe it, I just simply cannot believe it." He lit a cigarette. "I gave him the figure and he said... he told me to load it by a hundred thousand. Ordered me."

There was relief in her laugh; she used the breath of it to release the pressure in her chest. "Is that all? You had me worried for a moment. Come here my girl, let me put your hat straight" and she set the brim of a straw panama exactly level. "There." She stood up radiant with pride, beamed rays of warmth at blazer and cap, at a pastel-blue tunic unsullied by the shadow of a single crease. "Now off with the pair of you or you'll make me the disgrace of the lift club."

Only then did she turn to her husband. "What are you making such a fuss about? He's the boss, isn't he? He must have a good reason. Surely."

He sat with an elbow on the dining-room table, hand pressed on the top of his head, wondering if he was using his fingers to tidy the hair, or the hair to steady his fingers. "It doesn't make sense to me. It just simply doesn't make sense."

17

He slipped into top gear and realised that he was using the frame of daily habits as a refuge. The time expended rushing to the storage yard was protected from doubt by urgency. Twenty minutes behind the shelter of a schedule.

So had his moustached and helmeted heroes in adventure books used the reflexes of musketry drill to defend the stockade; arrogant without compunction, had laid the foundations of their empires and raised the marble pillars of their monuments. Balfour parked under the barbed wire strands and broken bottles on the yard wall.

He tripped over a bent column-clamp propped against the diamond-mesh fence, ducked under the hoist of a rusty concrete mixer and skirted stacks of surplus pipes to fling open the door of the pre-fab office. The week's wage-sheet was in a mess but where the hell had the time-keeper got to?

At twenty-two minutes to nine he banged on the corrugated-iron sheets of the watchman's hut. Banged, banged. Shouted. Waited, foot tapping, till the overture of stirring sounds inside led to a solo of creaks from the door. Opened only a crack, still hooked on a strand of wire and a bent nail. "It's me, the boss." Never since doors had been invented had one opened so slowly. Patience.

Patient nods to the figure in reject army greatcoat, a length of steel pipe in one hand and transistor in the other, who crouched on a warm morning over a punctured paraffin tin of coals. The timekeeper? Yes, timekeeper. Oh, the boss means the timekeeper, maybe, maybe he... At eleven minutes to nine it was decided, well, either on toilet or gone down to shop.

Allow no more than ten minutes in the office; for cramming into the wastepaper-basket a day's accumulation of junk-mail and a half-dozen explosive phone-calls about only the more outrageous of the wrong deliveries. Three minutes to get rid of an insurance tout. A registered letter from the bank—a complete fuck-up as usual. That overdue report from the Portland Cement Institute, that would have to wait. Oh shit, ten past already.

Only thirteen minutes usually on the new freeway nearly half-way across the city to the site. Last week one wrong turning had led all the way back—to the waste of a journey started all over again.

One wrong tender and... if... the wasted years of starting a career all over again; there must be easier ways of weaving skill and energy into the fabric of society. Friends, neighbours, relatives, their lives seemed to roll evenly on a level path.

18

A roller blocked the access path to a not-quite completed structure, the road-works sub-contractor had arrived on site at last, only three weeks late. But something looked wrong, the base course must have settled, alignment of the pre-cast channels wavered. He called the foreman.

"Dougie, can you check the levels? I just haven't got the time and stop that cowboy before he..."

Around each power-point in the finish-painted walls, the electrician had left five black finger-prints. Guilty. The painter's leading hand pleaded innocence, it wasn't part of his job to clear up every bloody pig's mess.

Artisans begging for instructions tried to pluck his passing sleeve, labourers waylaid him begging for loans—later, later, this afternoon, tomorrow.

No, it was too late for the architect to change his mind about the mortice locks. The feature alcove under the main staircase stank of stale piss.

Twenty-six past ten.

His car flowed into one of the streams converging on the city centre. The third red traffic-light must have stuck. Two minutes.

Three minutes, while the drivers on either side smiled contentedly ahead and drummed finger-tips on the window ledge in time to Forces Favourites. Even the truck-driver grinning into the rear-view mirror seemed happy to have his body jellied by diesel throbs. Pedestrians strolled at leisure, housewives dawdled and settled to the unhurried ritual of endless gossip.

No other driver ever got pipped so often at every vacant parking lot. Once more around the block. Coins for the meter had spilled all over the glove compartment; his watch was one minute fast by the City Hall clock and showed nine minutes to eleven. Perfect timing.

Outside the official building the Flag was flapping at half-mast in the sun; some forgotten politician had died last night.

Balfour could not hold himself from spring-bounding up the granite steps, away from the throb of traffic which kept on coursing through one-way arteries across the heart of the city.

Inside, quiet shadows submerged him. He let himself be drawn into a system of corridors complicated as the channels of bureaucracy. Each numbered door was closed, each notice board had arrows pointing in both directions and when figures glided past their outlines seemed more blurred than their reflections in the polished lino.

Podium, Concourse, express lift up the Tower Block.

The foyer at the back of the thirtieth floor was crowded. Balfour edged himself sideways through the crush towards a row of wooden boxes and peeped through the slot of No 7—plenty of envelopes already in. He licked the flap of his own, ended the lick with a kiss for luck and held it suspended. Even with the load of a hundred thousand there was still one chance in a million.

His rival jostled him, acknowledged his nod, and when Balfour opened his fingers to let his tender drop the rival copied him and quipped to other figures crushing them against the varnished panels guarding their secrets.

More nods to peers; the graduates recognised one another as a class, windbreaks and suede ankle-boots were their uniform.

Balfour side-stepped an oily paint salesman who was smearing his way from snub to snub. "Keeping busy? Good, good. You'll use our products if you have any luck today, won't you?"

The rival? Where had the rival gone to? So, pretending to study the notice board. Looked nervous but quietly confident.

More confident than a loud group whose superior dress denoted inferior status. Too smart in polyester, black briefcases with silver bands, they exchanged the triple-million boasts of their employers as though all was due to them; office-boys playing at the junior executives of ads.

Who else? The usual crowd. That painfully respectable young Muslim from the estimating department of a multi-national; a thick-lipped Hollander with hair on the back of fingers clamped on a half-smoked cigar; an excitement of Italians clustered in the corner, paunches pressed together, fluttering hands before one another's liquid eyes and interrupting, "si, si, quattro mille due cento."

Five to eleven.

Balfour felt the muscles of his stomach tighten, there was a sour taste in his mouth. He lit a cigarette and noticed that the rival was watching him between the bullock shoulders of a team of local stolids. Both forced up one corner of the mouth into a shape of minimum politeness. Three edgy youngsters who were trying to start up businesses on their own rescued him with small talk and hints of cut prices. The talk grew smaller, faltered, petered out at two minutes to eleven.

Now even the Italians whispered, and as though drawn into the vacuum of semi-silence, or willed by a collective yearning for the security of a weekly Wednesday morning ceremony, three grey figures materialised next to the tender boxes, distilled from the vapours of chance and hope that had brought the tenderers together.

The Chief Clerk (Admin. Sectn. Tender Div.) plus his two assistants waited blank-faced till the last note of the City Hall chimes had reverberated into a memory of sound, then suddenly ducked down to the tender boxes, rattled and exchanged keys, banged doors, stacked and scattered envelopes across the table, muttered; so busy-busy-busy they refused to be interrupted by a disturbance at the back.

A man stood on tip-toe, waving above his head an envelope clutched in panic fingers. A newcomer to the tender market had got lost in the labyrinth. Too late—the crowd jeered in a release of tension and pressed closer towards the table.

Balfour listened to the sound of tearing paper as envelopes were ripped open.

Dust was thick on every slat of the venetian blind, everything so orderly, so normal, each 'Invitation to Tender' on the notice board at his shoulder proudly crowned with a coat of arms. There was as much connection between this room and the brutal urgency of a construction site, as between a panelled court-room and a prison.

Sweat beaded the Hollander's upper lip and the tip of his cigar trembled.

An Italian jaw, swarthy as burnt toast, ground its teeth. A youngster starting-on-his-own chewed gum.

The Chief Clerk cleared his throat. Even the hisses of whispers stilled.

Above a muted background chorus of laboured breathing the voice was flat and dry. It was routine for him to announce "Tender Number One, Complete Repairs and Renovations to Official Residence…" and read out the results. Behind his back Balfour heard a voice exclaim "They're mad. That's sharpening the pencil too much, nobody can ever come out at that price. I cut mine to the bone and look…"

"Tender Number Two. Replacement of deep-pile carpeting in Council Chamber."

"Tender Number Three. Supply and install air-conditioning unit in Director of Services office."

Balfour smiled. Only a few taxpayers were present here this morning, the rest too busy working to pay off their assessments.

"Tender Number Six. Additional accommodation at clubhouse and improved storm-water drainage to rugby fields at Departmental Sports Centre."

He forced his way right up to the table. It was covered with a litter of jumbled papers. The junior clerks were sorting tender forms, the senior's face was grey as his alpaca office jacket and the lips waiting to pronounce sentence had been soured for years by hourly cups of tepid liquid from the tea trolley. One junior whispered to the other and they giggled, poked elbows into each other's ribs and laughed. At this moment,

21

two lowly paid youngsters were so free they could afford to laugh. Authority intervened with a frown of annoyance and impatient gestures. The Chief took over the sorting himself and Balfour felt each heart-beat throb against his ribs. A burning slime welled up inside his throat.

"Tender Number Seven. Proposed Commercial Training Community Centre for Board of Coloured Development. Lowest tender received…"

My God! Made it! Can't be true. Was true. What the hell was going on? The rival, exploding in the centre of the crush, using one hand to force apart the bodies before him, the other to smite the air in protest.

The Chief Clerk, bored, balanced himself between the calm of experience and the ratty nerves of constipation. After sitting out decades of seniority in the service, he'd come across it all before. "Well, if you go stick your tender into the wrong box don't blame me. You know the Regulations just as much as what I do."

"But I didn't, I didn't." A middle-aged master builder quivered with the passion of a toddler's tantrum. "I put it in number seven, I can prove it, I've got witnesses."

Balfour heard himself call out "yes, I saw him, I'll swear to it if necessary." A few voices behind him echoed in support.

The Chief Clerk hesitated, consulted his juniors, shook his head. "Look, I'm not saying that you did or you didn't, all I said… anyway, look, yes, here's your tender, man, with all these papers…" He flicked a hand over the mess on the table. "All right, all right, I'll open it, I'll read it out, but that's not to say it's being admitted. That's up to the chairman of the Tender Board. Okay?"

The difference—ninety eight thousand four hundred and fifty. Spot on.

Waiting for the lift Balfour heard the sing-song voice chant through the weekly litany. "Tender Number Eight. Repair vandal damage to single classroom at Red River Primary School for Coloureds. Lowest…"

Stuck above the lift buttons were two notices. "Lunch Hour Service in Staff Canteen. Hear the Pastor of our Land expound the Word of God and reveal the power of his Faith", and "Annual Dinner/Dance in Staff Canteen. Couples R5-00 Singles R3-00. Live it up to the music of Purple Disasters. Please bring your own liquid refreshment."

As the lift dropped he felt his guts rise inside him.

Balfour crouched over a pine kitchen table in the yard office, one leg doubled under him on the plastic seat.

"Can you speak up please, a bit louder. What? I can't make out what

22

you're saying. No, of course not. What? I think we've got a bad connection, hang on, I'll try dialling naught. Is that better now? Put down, I'll phone you back.''

"Balfour again. Can you put me through please?''

"I was waiting to be put through, I think we got cut off. I'm still waiting. No, I won't get him to phone me back, I'd rather hang on. Yes, I'm still there. No please, come on, how can he be out, I was speaking to him not a minute ago.''

"For heaven's sake, this must be the tenth time, what's going on there at the switchboard? It used to be quicker with trunk calls before direct dialling, or d'you want to send a runner with a message in a cleft stick? Yes, yes I'll hold as you say. Ah, at last... to continue... yes, I realise you've been waiting nearly half-an-hour. I was trying to explain, their tender has been put on the official list, that means it has been admitted, I phoned up and asked the girl in the office the name of the lowest, and later I went back to town just to make quite sure. The results are up on the notice board, it's there in black and white, we're second, officially. Half-a-dozen others taking flyers, none of them really need the job. Yes, I am fully aware that admitted doesn't mean accepted, you know government departments, they always wait till the last minute of the thirty-day option period. Yes, I know, I know it's a standard Condition of Tender, 'the lowest or any tender will not necessarily be accepted, nor need any reason be given for the acceptance or rejection of any tender.' This isn't my first time you know, I'm not a tender virgin, I've been at it over fifteen years, I know what I'm talking about, I say forget this one. There's that telephone exchange due next week, I could just about manage it if I stuck at it over the whole week-end. After that only a few odds and ends of rubbish to go for, shit little jobs, but we could pick up a couple of small ones just to keep ticking over and keep the key men only, like Dougie and Manie and the brickies. No, I don't really know him personally, nodding acquaintance. Seems a steady enough type. How old? Might have a few years on me, experienced all right, done several jobs for the department of nearly the same size, I don't see what's this got to do with... No, he's well qualified, been going for years, about the same size as we are down here, one of those one-man one-job-at-a-time careful firms. Look, if we land that exchange we'd need the BP 1000 self-erecting crane rather than... would it be available? What's that? No, he won't be put off by the difference between him and the rest, his tenders are always on the mark, reputation's first rate, quality of work and credit-wise, everybody knows. Look, I think we must cut say one-and-a half or even two percent for the exchange, just to make sure. Why do you keep on harping... their plant? What about their plant? They've got every bit as much as we have down here. Repeat that please. You sound unusually calm if you don't mind my saying so but don't you realise it's practically panic stations? If we miss out next week it's either coming to a virtual stop or at best bits and pieces till next year's crop with the budget. No, just the usual crap from all quarters still we should manage First Delivery on this present one say eight, maybe nine, make it ten weeks to be on the safe side. The weather? Weather's all right. Beach? Why the beach, you're thinking of flying down for the week-end, I could fetch you from the airport. Who, me? I don't follow, you know what I'll be doing the whole weekend. Yes, she's all right, the kids are fine. What? Do you want me to be quite frank, I can't make out your line of thinking but thank heavens that's not my responsibility if... let me finish... if it grinds to a complete halt. D'you want me to put that in writing or have I made myself quite clear? Impossible, I think we're talking at cross-purposes, let me state the position at the moment all over again. Of the six carpenters..."

Shaded by the oaks, the compost heap was rich with a smell of damp fertility. Balfour scattered over it his offering of grass cuttings and inhaled the fresh aroma. Only a few weeks and they too would be brown and rotted, ripe to be returned to earth in sacrifice for the spring planting.

From the far end of the lawn, striped by the mower, the children's voices... or did it come from the birds who peck-pecked amongst the flower beds? Or the long-tailed ones fluttering behind the leaves on the lower branches?

He followed the path to the front terrace and inspected the yellow cushions on the set of cane garden furniture. Yes, the chaise longue, that was the right shape; he tried to force himself to relax. Now that the wind had dropped towards evening, with the sun half-hidden by the mountain, green looked almost blue.

Still he fought the energy pulsing through the muscles of his arms and legs. He sat up to watch the red-and-yellow ball that bounced bounced bounced and rolled across the lawn. Jump up and pounce on it? Instead he called "where are you, you two?"

"Daddy, he's cheating."

"Come here, it's time to switch on the sprinklers."

He patted the seats of the chairs on either side in invitation to the two panting figures. "Sit down, I want to talk to you."

"One can't play with him anymore. He's a crook, he keeps on..."

"I wasn't, it was you. It was you was crooking."

"You."

"You."

A fatherly frown, a burlesque of menace in the eyebrows that made the children laugh. At least it stopped them bickering long enough for him to say "look, it's time you started growing up. I don't want any more... no more performances like yesterday. Right? That's a promise? Because I'm going to be terribly terribly busy for a whole year and I can't afford to waste my... we're starting a new job in a few weeks and it's... it's huge."

"How huge is huge?" they asked together.

"Colossal. A community centre with super-duper-market."

"It'll have chocolates and a toy counter" Boyboy decided, "and we'll come and help ourselves. Peppermint creams and bicycles...." He listed all his favourites.

"Where?" A sensible question from a sensible little lady.

"Quite near, but it's not the usual... not just a place for people with money to spend it there. It's for the so-called underprivileged, where poorer people can come and learn how to improve themselves. You know, not everybody's got a house like this with a garden and next year we'll be putting in that pool at last."

"Daddy, Daddy, there's a boy in our class, he's got a pool you can dive into and a tennis court."

"I'd hate to be poor" she said, and winced. "All those rags, and the dirt. The way the children beg and the grown-ups they're always drunk."

"Not all, and there are reasons they can't always help why they behave like that. Let me explain." The children put on their bored "daddy's-lecturing-again" expressions.

"We live in what's called 'society.' That's, well everybody all together. And there's plenty we get out of it, new cars and holidays and..."

Boyboy bounced on his seat. "Where we going at the end of the year? Ooh please, please let's fly to the marina again. Please."

"We'll see. Well, you can't just take take take, you've also got to put something back. And if I for instance know how to build, I'd like to build something that... to help, so there won't be poor people, or less of them, or at least not quite so poor. So the government, which is, like in charge of everything, they've decided..."

"We got told all about it at school." She leaned back in the chair and tidied her hair with a gesture copied from her mother. "There's this new teacher, she takes us for a course called civics. She's absolutely divine and her clothes... you know she wears a different dress every day. She said all those, those others they must start looking after themselves because they can't go on being helped for ever. She's gorgeous. Showed us slides, how much gets done for them and then all they..."

"What's a... what you said?" Boyboy used his question to interrupt and claim attention. He had to ask something. Anything. "A community centre."

"Where people can get together to do interesting things. So they won't hang around on street corners and get up to mischief. There'll be a library and an information centre, with spaces set aside for hobbies like electronics and making furniture, pottery, indoor games and dressmaking... you know... a hall for club meetings. Chess or snakes-and-ladders. Play music, have parties..." Balfour stopped, the children no longer listened. Swept by the flight of his vision, they stared at the clouds and floated on the gossamer wings of their dreams.

"Daddy" she whispered, "it sounds heavenly. They'll really want to go there, all the way from those new suburbs with the lovely houses teacher said we're building for them."

"There's another reason too, why I particularly want to do this job." On either side slender forearms were crushed by the power in the fingers that gripped them. A current of feeling poured into the children, so intense they were flooded into silence. "I want to build something to be remembered by, not only me but all the men who'll work there, our sweat and tiredness that'll shorten our days. Don't ever put up a memorial for me, I'll construct my own so one day, when you have children the same age as you yourselves now are, you can take them there, show them how straight up and strong that central column stands, say 'my old man, he built that.' " He released their arms; with head bowed in respect for the eternal mystery, almost ashamed, he murmured "I won't always be here you know."

"Where you going Daddy? Daddy, where you going?" Did the child need his adenoids seen to, he always listened with his mouth so open?

His sister blushed for her baby brother. "I'll... I'll go and help Nanny." She stood up, brushed down her skirt and in a few moments returned ballet-stepping behind Nanny's waddle, carrying a salver of olives and pretzels. "Thanks Nanny." Balfour pointed to the table; laying down the tray made her short of breath. "Did Madam say when she'd be back?"

He did not understand the mumbled answer, could only stare at the huge pair of receding buttocks bouncing away under a pink overall; kept on staring, now at the bubbles clustered on the translucent lemon slices.

"Let me taste."

He laughed as a freckled grin twisted into bitter disgust. "I hope I'll never pull a monkey-face like that" he said. "You thought you were in for a treat, and then... that was a dirty trick to play, wasn't it?"

"You wait" warned his son, "you just wait, wait till somebody does it back to you."

"That's not a very nice thing to say to a father."

The boy's face darkened as shadows poured their pools of moisture round the sprinklers. Now only the apex of each jet was still striving up to catch the last moments of the sun, in cascades of dripping diamonds. A car purred along the driveway and stopped. The children bounced up and raced away to help their mother with the parcels.

Balfour watched his wife's high heels and shiny calves of elegance prance along the terrace. The dutiful peck on cheek and the family arranged themselves around the glass-topped table to tear off wrapping papers and peek into enticing lumpy packets.

"Here" she said to the children, "you take these things inside" and shooed them away.

"You'll be furious." She laughed an apology. "I don't know what came over me. One of my extravagant sprees, d'you mind?', and shyly, face averted, bent down to open her bag. Another parcel, another garment; she stood up to hold it by the shoulder-straps in front of her, stroked the soft cloth and with a flat palm draped it against her curves. "Like it?"

"Love it."

"But do you love me?"

"You'll let me show you how much, in the only way that really counts? No, of course I don't mind. With my percentage of the profits you could treat yourself to half-a-dozen provided you're prepared to earn them."

She sat close to him. "Big talk. As though you'll have any go left in you with a job that size on your hands. I'm pleased about it only for your sake."

Balfour leaned back and closed his eyes. "I still can't make it out, how they came to pass over that other crowd's tender. Got something against him. It shows, you can never read another man's book. You see firms, they seem solid as a rock and then.." He snapped his fingers. "I don't know and I don't want to know. Should I fetch you a glass?"

"I'll share, if you don't mind the lipstick smear. Well, cheers, here's to the new job. If you can't beat them, join them."

"Maybe he's about to fold but I doubt it. They must have some very solid reason." Balfour topped up the gin and tonic. He slid in another slice of lemon and it clung to the others floating in the fizz. "You know I'm hardly starry-eyed with admiration for the powers-that-be. Still, call it only window-dressing if you like, pandering to outside pressure, even trying to draw in overseas investors, at least it's some small movement in the right direction."

She pushed away the glass. "One little drink and it's gone to my head. It always makes me want to cry, especially… whenever I see other families say on the beach, all together, plain relaxed. With us it's always serious, take everything so heavy work work. Now you want to look a gift horse… to examine its tonsils."

"These fellows in control, they can't be all bad" he said, "even if they'd want to. It's only in the middle ages things were either clearly black or white. Nowadays it's more complex, streaky tones of grey. D'you know when Saint Augustine went into…"

"I really must go inside and see what the girl's up to. I'm worried about her you know but I can hardly move, I've been on my feet since…"

"What girl? Maid or daughter? It's Boyboy's adenoids…"

"Stop worrying, he'll grow out of it." Firmly, with the maturity of a mother advising a son she said "it's time you did a bit of growing up yourself."

Balfour nodded. "You're quite right, I do worry. Even that directorship, it'll either come or not come. Mind you, with a job like this to my credit I'll be reasonably confident." He added another half a tot and only a splash of tonic.

"Listen." She pressed nail-varnish against lipstick. "Those birds. All they need to build a nest is any old twigs and a few leaves. You're full of ambitions but they're the ones are singing."

"I can't wait to get cracking. I'll write a paper for the Journal, I've got some marvellous ideas for a whole-day non-stop cast and how to waterproof those basement retaining walls. It's a crazy design." He stroked her knee and the stocking creased under his hand. "Imagine after the pair of us have gone up the chimney in smoke, I tried to tell our two, when they're as old as we are now, how they'll drive past with their families and point out to their children in an offhand sort of way, 'You see that huge ugly block over there, the one that looks like a fortress with the steel-blue face bricks where every perpend lines up dead plumb, you know he built it' "

"You're a dreamer" she murmured, and felt his hand.

Fingers entwined, they sat close together in the evening calm. Inside the house a chandelier blinked on its lamps, the radio woke to a thumping march; the news was all disaster, the weather looked like rain. It did not matter. Nothing mattered. In the garden all was bloom and blossom.

IV

Balfour drove past a row of vacant semi's and parked the fourwheel-drive at the field behind the abandoned shop that had been Naidoo's. Standing in the middle of the street, in his hand a rolled plan imperious as a marshal's baton, he signalled to the company's truck to pull into the kerb and park behind him.

Even before the wheels stopped the foreman had already sprung from the cab and was snapping with the nervous energy of a terrier "get a move on, come-come-come." Bovine with dumb resentment, to emphasise the stiffness induced by a ten-minute ride, the men dropped slowly over the tailgate in ones and twos and threes. Those still crouching under the olive-green canvas shelter on the truck body reached down to pass on the tools—sledge hammers, shovels, picks and forks sharp as weapons. The men settled their helmets and the cluster of uniform khaki overalls blocked the pavement; the company's name stencilled across their backs marked them as foreigners in the area.

A rearguard of the locals who still inhabited the neighbourhood stopped to inspect them. "Man, what's this going on here?" "Looks like a bloody invasion." "They act like the place belongs to them", and from the bristling housewife offended by the lumps of phlegm in the gutter, "there's some needs a lesson in their manners."

Balfour hauled himself up on to the truck's running board and started counting heads. Three missing. Count again, while another few drifted off to the take-away at the corner and a pair of youngsters at the back edged nearer to the bus-shelter, where a batch of factory girls smirked and giggled at their wolf-whistles. At last, "Now listen. This is the new job where we're going to be for about a year. There'll be a bulldozer shortly to help you and a blaster to break up the rocks so I don't want a single living thing... make sure you clear the whole place properly.

When you get inside, all in a line, about so far apart and move across from one end to the other. All clear? Dougie, you've got a crowbar? Let's get a bit of that fence down."

In answer, the foreman raised an arm with fist clenched around a steel bar in a gesture that could have illustrated equally well either progress or destruction.

"One thing more" Balfour added, "when you're through that, you can move into the shop and the empty house at the back and for ten minutes I'll pretend not to notice anything that disappears. Right, let's get cracking."

Panting and grunting while he ripped corrugated iron sheet after sheet from the fence, the foreman only half-listened. "Dougie, you know last week there was a whole settlement of unauthorised... squatters' huts just overnight from nowhere. They should all have been cleared by now except for the odd drunkie or kid playing. Even a dog would get killed."

The foreman flashed pliers from the back pocket of his overalls. As he snipped the last strand of wire Balfour called "Follow me," waved a stiff arm and with the spring and bounce, the slightly muscle-bound rolling gait of a former varsity second-team scrum-half, led his men through the gap.

They kicked their way across the field, through knee-high grass and weeds and spiky bushes. "Close up, close up there on the far side" he ordered. "Move over, you're too bunched here. Now forward, all together."

They advanced step by step. A few temporary deserters slipped back into line, others left it to piss against the fence and the row of picks and forks hacked and stabbed at damp cardboard tyres cartons rusty tins bottles wire charred stumps more bottles a broken pram squashed plastic containers and a terrified cat that broke cover and scampered to safety; bypassed the solitary tree, forced a way through a screen of bushes into a clearing, surrounded a squatter's shelter and halted.

Outside it a woman's long skirt formed a tent from hips to ground as she bent towards a paraffin tin brick-supported over a fire. White steam emphasised the darkness of her arms. The men shuffled nearer. She stirred the mess inside the tin.

Her infant toddled closer to her. Pot-bellied, naked except for a filthy vest covering his shoulders, the cheeks of his bare bum were dimpled. Twin runnels of dried snot, grey and scaly, made his eyes seem even moister, larger as he stared from face to face, from the scrubbed tan of one man to brown to black. Balfour hesitated. The woman went on

31

stirring.

"When did this spring up? They can't stay here" he said to the foreman. Still she stirred. "For their own safety, they'll get hurt." Unhurried, round and round, but now he sensed she was pretending to ignore him as though if only she kept on patiently enough he and his men and the menace of their presence would evaporate like mealie-meal steam. "Does she know she's got no right to be here?"

She had to answer—with a flash of white teeth and a stream of tongue-clicks. Un-understandable. He beckoned to a migrant worker in his team. "What does she say?"

Again the verbal torrent, now longer, now spat out with passion. The labourer listened with his head inclined, bored, sheltered from involvement by the stamp on the permit in his pocket. "She say, this woman she say, her man, her man he come back just now."

Balfour closed his eyes in pity, for himself and her. All so predictable.

If only when he opened them the site and his conscience would be clear. "Tell her she must go before the bulldozer, now-now-now."

His sentence was translated, paragraph by paragraph. Speech after speech, the woman and her clansman parleyed. At last he said to his boss, "This woman, she say she got paper."

"Let me see it."

Her glide from the pot towards the rusty sheets and cardboard patches bore the slow dignity of a tragic queen. Minutes, minutes later she came out with a roll of crumpled papers in her hand and handed them to the labourer. He passed them to the foreman, who with fingertips he later wiped on his tunic, passed them to Balfour.

An elapsed tramways weekly, a receipt for a deposit on a lay-by, a hospital admission card, a pamphlet for the Evangelical Church of Zion.

She started gathering her life's heritage; the dented fibre suitcase, the primus, the child's doll with both arms missing, the shiny black transistor gently cradled on folds of dull grey blanket; all performed with the formal grace of what had become a tribal ceremony.

Balfour tried to move away but he had to speak, to some one, anyone, had to. "Dougie, you know it's to help prevent things like this that we're going to build this place."

They did not even need to use the hammers. A few blows from the pick were enough to flatten the obstacle, and all that remained was the smell of wood smoke and paraffin and musty bedding that cigarette after cigarette clung to Balfour's nostrils.

"It's all here" he said, "concentrated. What the sociologists write reams about and politicians rave and economists sprout mountains of drivel. And do you think they won't be back tomorrow somewhere else?''

"Look, look" the foreman answered without turning. He dived into the debris and rummaged. "Bottles. Come look here for yourself how many. They were running a filthy shebeen from here. Pigs. And you still feel sorry for them. Move on, move" he yelled to the men.

"What's so wrong about that? Why should Drinque-o-rama and the Farmers' Distillery be granted right to operate a monopoly? Why only them and not her?''

"What about her?" The blaster burst through a bush behind Balfour's back. "She's good for a quick one, whoever she is? Now where's that mountain of stone you were talking about on the phone last week. No, the week before last. Man, I've been hunting high and low to find this place."

Balfour led him to a rock outcrop in the north-west corner. They studied it, stroking their chins. Fissures invisible to a layman's eye were clear as roads leading to the rock's destruction. Their chalk crosses looked like a children's game, they argued with juvenile intensity, rubbed them out with the flat of their palms and remarked a different blasting pattern.

"Look" said the blaster, "your idea, not mine. Can't play around with iron-stone, not the kind you get round here, I'm telling you it's harder than a kaffir's head."

They used the fourwheel-drive to manoeuvre the compressor into position. It was routine for the crew first to brew tea over a fire, only then, leisurely as a pastime, run out the hoses and lay black snakes from the grease-streaked yellow machine across the trampled weeds.

Curious what's-that urchins were drawn to the gap in the fence. Fascinated, goggle-eyed, the bare feet of those in front were forced to shuffle forward through the dust by increasing pressure from behind. Taunts and jeers drove them even further, to the daring journey of a few hesitant paces into forbidden territory.

The compressor coughed, belched out a puff of exhaust, shuddered and settled to a steady throb. Testing the jackhammers produced a burst of tingling rattle that scattered the children. Their faces no longer tan or beige or fawn, now chalky-grey with terror, they fled out to the street.

Balfour let himself be seen in a token of authority. Too late, already they had dissolved into the neighbourhood, were no longer human, had faded to mere memories of nuisances like the plastic bottles and wrapping papers the wind swirled into the gutter.

On the pavement a bigger crowd had assembled. None spoke, their pressed lips told him whatever he chose to interpret. Mothers with small children crouched in the shelter of doorways; bent old men with skull caps stopped hobbling on sticks towards the mosque; straight-backed schoolboys in sloppy tracksuits, their books on display, high cheek-bones sharp with resentment; loafers who slouched, mouths curled in chronic sneers; heavy-buttocked schoolgirls in black gym tunics with box-pleats, their peppercorn frizzles plaited in rows; and through the tight net of tension, sauntering with the arrogance of conquerors, squads of khaki overalls converging on the one remaining shop.

Balfour shouldered a way through the press. Bodies cringed back from the strangeness of him. Hand on its shoulder, a mother drew her child away from his path, from the bustle of his colonial energy. In the shop he snapped and barked "get back to your places" and "this isn't a bloody holiday', escorted his men back into the street.

There not a body stirred, they could have been an arrangement of models, then all heads jerked in the same direction as though twitched by the strings of a master puppeteer.

A labourer with a red flag marched down the centre of the empty street. Behind him, huge and menacing on a low-bed trailer, the bulldozer seemed out of proportion to the single-storey buildings, its curved blade shining almost from lamp-post to lamp-post.

He watched his men drift back to their posts and felt the onlookers watching him in turn as he waved out a semaphore of signals to the driver of the trailer. A wave of foot shuffles rippled through the crowd, mutters of resentment swelled and broke into curses as newcomers flooded in from the side-streets and stretched up on tip-toe at the back.

Inside the fence the blaster motioned to Balfour who nodded. The drillers leant on their hammers, old sacks tied like aprons to their waists. As he watched their bodies blurred out of focus, vibrations in forearms spread up necks and their heads trembled. He heard the compressor labour, the noise of the jackhammers assaulted his ears when he came nearer to assess the speed at which tungsten-carbide bit into ironstone. Double the time reckoned on.

Sweat rolled down the drillers' faces, clear globules so transparent the black skin seen through each droplet glistened in the sun. Migrant workers denied their celibacy with rape of the earth itself. Virile males pressed their weight on to rigid rotating metal shafts, pierced round wounds into a body that could protest only by refusing entry. Still they thrust, shifted stance and thrust again, limbs quivering in an ecstasy of effort. Slowly, slowly around each hole piled a circle of spent and sterile powdered rock.

34

The foreman was beckoning to him—come quick. The sharp way the arm jerked meant—urgent.

Balfour hurried across the field. "What's it now?" There was impatience in his voice when the hammers stopped for a change of drill bits.

"Come look here" said Dougie and pointed to a bundle of rags under a bush. Sniggering men surrounded it, their picks and forks grasped ready for the hack or stab. A tremor fluttered through the cloth as wind twirled a dry leaf which settled on an ear. Hesitantly, feeling for an unseen predator in hunt of prey, fingers stirred, fumbled the ear and brushed away the leaf.

"You think he might be ill?" asked Balfour and his subordinates mocked him with guffaws. He bent closer in inspection and gagged at the reek of sour yeast.

An eyelid twitched, a bloodshot eyeball rolled in random directions and settled to a hazy stare at the intruder's face. A sighing effort of groans brought the bushman head a few inches from the ground. Thick lips cracked with sores prepared to speak. "Fuck you."

"Come on, up-up-up." Balfour realised he was imitating a policeman. Degrading, not unusual enough to make any impression on the subject, the object. He switched to a minor key.

"You'd better get out of here before the bulldozer comes. You'll get hurt."

Only his workmen heard him, only they reacted, with shared glances and sniggers. The head had sunk back on its pillow of leaves and branches, it lay crowned with thorns and twigs. The foreman stirred the body by rocking the toe-cap of his boot against the ribs. Now the man half-sat with straight legs and trunk propped on elbows, blinking at his attackers; the outcast of a desert tribe trapped and surrounded by the enemies of nature. Instinct led him to single out the leader of the pack and Balfour recoiled from the attack of his defence.

"And what the bloody hell d'you think you doing here?" the vagrant slurred. "Bugger off, go on, bugger off, you got no right to be here. I'm watchman in this place. I'm here long before you so I say, I say fuck off." He struggled to lift an elbow from the ground to impose his authority with a wavering arm, and again collapsed. He seemed to have no bones.

Two other descendants of a common ancestor laid down their picks and hauled him to his feet. He lurched and staggered, staggered towards, staggered first to Dougie, then Balfour, then… a slap on the shoulder set him facing the gap in the fence. A push in the back saved him the trouble of finding the energy to walk. Another push, another few loose-kneed steps.

"Master must listen to me nicely now. Master. What more the master wants from me?" he appealed, then accused "what you all doing here in my place? What you doing to my place, it's me belongs here, it's mine. You're just piece of shit, shit." They hardly heard his solo above the jackhammers' chorus. The foreman nodded to the two labourers. On either side flat hands were thrust under the stinking armpits, cruel fingers crushed each wrist. With his feet bent down in desperation to maintain some contact with the earth that once had supported his clan, now had spawned and rejected him, they rushed him to the gap in the fence, and heaved.

When Balfour arrived there the man had gone, sunk like a flung pebble into the wave of hostility that swelled out of the sea of brown faces. But whether the resentment of the crowd was against the vagrant or against himself, and whether for being heartless to a harmless victim or for thrusting a despised element into their respectability....

"I can go now?" asked the trailer driver, offering his booklet for signature. The dozer had snorted and wriggled its way off the trailer and stood panting just inside the fence. All the blaster shouted was "Okay."

Now Balfour rushed with frantic energy. "Clear the street" he ordered and supervised a detachment of labourers who moved down from corner to corner, pushing the crowd back with shovels and pick-handles held out horizontally before them.

"Keep the dozer here to block the entrance. Surround the field." Red flags waved, whistles blew. By the time the men had returned from the street to stand at ten-pace intervals right round the fence, at least half the crowd had drifted back again.

The earth merely shuddered a single protest. The explosion made less noise than the bulldozer's idling engine, a brief puff of dust that the wind soon dispersed. The disappointment of the crowd which had risked return matched Balfour's. Only the top crust of rock had splintered but the blaster was delighted. "You wouldn't listen to me, now see."

"Did you put in the millisecond delays like I told you?" asked Balfour, nauseous from failure and from the stench of gelignite fumes.

"That's rubbish" said the blaster. "All those newfangled fancy gadgets. There's only one way and that's the right way. You couldn't perhaps let me have a little cheque could you?"

"Have to try again. When?"

"When the cheque or when try?" said the blaster. "I've got plenty sticks left, magazine's chock-a-block but it'll take three weeks to get the permit to transport any. You think I can call round tomorrow?''

Several glances at the watch and as many promises still could not get rid of him. The bulldozer operator saved Balfour with the abrupt rudeness of a serf whose boss was absent; he didn't work for this white man, he was here on hire and shouldn't be kept hanging round the whole day on standby. Push over that one tree? Was that all? Childsplay claimed the blaster, who did this explosives stuff only as a sideline, in actual fact he was somewhat of an expert on pushing over trees, he'd flattened more oaks, bluegums, pines, poplars, you-name-it, there was sweet fuckall anybody could tell him about trees. One white man spoke to another as an equal. The operator sniffed at him in mid-sentence, clambered up to his perch and made the earth tremble.

The machine wheeled round on to the line of attack. Bush branches were snapped and torn. The tracks left twin trails of flattened vegetation and when the huge blade raised and lowered, raised and lowered itself in anticipation there was such implied force and terror in the test that everywhere small boys scampered in random panic from their hiding places.

Ten paces from the tree the bulldozer stopped for a short rest, then lowered its blade and started gathering momentum for the charge. Even the urchins cringed back a step or two, before jumping forward in admiration as it jerked to a sudden halt.

Each slouching step was deliberately slow, with feet dragged along the ground in the teenage insolence of a sideways sidle. He sauntered in front of the full length of the blade and the way he ignored both it and the shouts of the operator and Balfour and Dougie and the gasps of awe from the smaller boys, showed how aware he was of his moment of power greater than a bulldozer's. He stopped to roll a cigarette, shaking shreds and grains from a flat tin, and when at last he licked the paper, balanced it on his lower lip, lit it and flicked the match away, the smell of crushed leaves and diesel fumes was sweetened by cheap perfume.

"Dougie." There was a note of helplessness in Balfour's appeal. "At three hundred an hour does he know what he's costing us?"

"Him, that gutter-rubbish. More than he's ever likely to earn."

Clear at last. With clanks and rattles the bulldozer reversed back to its starting line, paused to suck air and fuel into its engine and moved into the assault.

As the blade thumped the trunk the tree shook its branches in annoyance.

At the tip of each twig blossoms trembled with fear while the engine revved, the clutch slipped, tracks lost their grip and spun.

It backed off in impotent fury, repulsed. From a wound in the bark, resin oozed. The boys lost interest and started playing cops-and-robbers with the tree as den, till that too bored them and they imitated bulldozer-versus-hero.

The operator switched off and jumped down to earth where he and Balfour argued with waving arms. The crowd from the street was now clustered at the gap in the fence, no longer silent but so chattering with excitement that their arms too swung in circles or raised clenched fists of emphasis.

The engine restarted easily. Balfour back-stepped behind the machine, beckoning "further, further. Still more. Now go."

Changed tactics; the advance was more deliberate, more intricate. First the blade bit into the ground and a rolling wave of soil curled up before it. Earth that had lain at peace since the creation was torn into a sudden age of mathematics and metallurgy, of a curved blade and its alloy edge.

The brute reared itself up on to the mound of its own creation, hydraulic arms raised its blade and cautiously, seemingly afraid of getting hurt, it nudged against the higher branches.

Wood snapped, crack after crack. The tree creaked and yielded to a sick angle. Now the machine pushed, pushed harder, harder. Jerk by jerk, the trunk came over. Branches on the far side became entangled with low thorn bushes, then with weeds. Blossoms were crushed into dust, into dirt. And still the roots clung to the earth. The machine reversed to an earned rest.

Balfour had been standing further off than any of the children. As he came forward he heard the crowd cheer and noticed how the mountain would now have been clearly exposed but for wisps of mist across its face that gave it the demure mystery of a veiled bride. The scenery could wait, would wait for ever but that tree had to be shifted now, this very minute. He called the bulldozer forward to approach from a different angle.

A single mechanical snort and the tree slewed round in a horizontal plane, its hidden parts displayed in obscenity. Insects crawled out of crevices as the boys whooped and jumped on the trunk with less respect than prehistoric hunters on the field had shown to a felled mammoth. Balfour looked down to the hole that had sheltered and nourished the roots, at the wound where the earth had been done a great injury, that he would heal with learning and concrete, with treatment as scarring as facial surgery. The bulldozer operator came to join him and for a moment they stared at the outrage they had dared commit.

The blossoms would bear no fruit, only a blob of spit as the operator cleared his throat to ask "Well, what's next?"

All vegetation to be cleared from the entire site and piled in that far corner over there. If any of the kids got hurt, well, they'd had enough warnings. Right, get cracking. And also, that rock outcrop, have a go at it with the ripper.

Push and reverse, push and reverse; at the end of each run a track of stripped ground stopped at a tangle of churned bushes. Push and reverse, till the foreman blew his whistle for the lunch-break and retired to his sandwiches and thermos in the truck cabin, well isolated from the labourers.

They had separated into groups, brown from black, one black tribe from the other, helmeted figures crouching over the fires that dotted the field, some roasting on shovel blades moles that the bulldozer had killed, others tearing at hunks of bread or slurping tea from jam-tins with the lids bent over as handles. Balfour stopped to watch them, his tired men, their lethargy, to focus on an image he could cherish later of their loyalty on a devastated field. No, already a haze of drifting smoke obscured the harsh reality, gave the scene a romance found in the blurred and faded illustrations of a secondhand book-stall history of some obscure campaign.

Rather seek it in the last moments of a building condemned to die. Seek it? It? What was there to look for? For a torn poster of the Taj Mahal in the passage? There was nothing else left, nothing; looters had ransacked the shop and adjoining house. Even switches had been ripped from walls and twisted wires poked out of the conduits. The shop seemed tiny; incredible they could have packed in there everything a household needed, all the food and crockery and cleaning aids, even the amusements, newspapers, magazines, a pin-table or video game perhaps. Also incredible that these few small rooms had surely bred another of those families that spilled out of big black American cars at picnic spots; the sari women, children, brilliantine men with shirt-sleeves held up by silver bands, more children. Now from the blackened ceiling-boards in the kitchen a twirl of flypaper dangled from a drawing pin, its victims doomed to a second death by demolition, and where the stove had probably stood a pile of turds with a blue fly buzzing on it. What was a life but a brief visit to a house of strangers?

Was that why warders pulled a hood over the head of the condemned trembling on the scaffold? Not to spare him the sight of his executioner, rather to save the hangman looking into the eyes that still perceived the waste of it, the waste. Balfour wandered out of a building as bare on its last day as on the day it had been created. For a moment sunlight on the white walls dazzled him. Even the advertising signs had been torn off to reveal a balanced symmetry of Georgian geometry.

No time to admire its dignity of form, rather assess the walls for signs of weakness, decide from which direction the bulldozer should approach, the height and angle of the blade. He paced right round the building—not a single crack. Came round a front corner and noticed how the crowd had thickened. People spilled off the pavement into the gutter and when the foreman joined him and they tried to wave the spectators back, he overheard remarks about the tree... "made a lovely job of it" and "fixed it a treat."

A middle-aged Indian ventured to bustle out of the throng and clutch at Balfour's sleeve. He jerked a thumb towards the structure. "My place" he boasted, "my business."

"It's a beautiful example of, one of the last... yes Dougie, what is it?"

Naidoo and the foreman stood on either side of him and spoke to different ears.

"... profitable, oh yes, very, comfortable living..."

"You'd better come, I think there's going to be a fight. With picks. I told you, you should never have allowed them a free run through the place."

In the passage two labourers glared and muttered at each other. The Taj Mahal had been reduced to shreds of curling paper. "Out, out. Come on, get out" the foreman ordered and chased them shambling to separate exits.

"Send them to opposite sides of the site" Balfour said. He went out into the street again, to a flood of excitement that stirred even slippered matrons to flap their aprons and hop on swollen feet, swept more and more and even more children scurrying from nowhere, from side-streets and doorways and the windows of abandoned dwellings.

Unordered, almost, Balfour felt 'in response to popular demand', the bulldozer left off clearing the site and lurched towards the target. He turned to wave the crowd further back, heard the machine begin the manoeuvre that would bring it into position, did not see the operator misjudge the turn and the edge of the blade nick a corner of the building.

All he heard now was the crack of splintering timber and the dull rumble of collapsing masonry, then a moment of exquisite calm and quiet ruptured by a great cheer from the crowd. All he saw on turning was a swirl of dust and when that cleared, rubble and... this was so bizarre, at home they would hardly believe it when he told them, on a shelf tucked into the only corner left standing as a pair of jagged triangles, a home-made draughts board with the bottle-top counters still in place.

A mound of rubble, scored by parallel depressions of twin bulldozer tracks, sun-dried bricks and clay mortar, quite unsuitable as hardcore under the basement slab or even the paving of the parking area. What had been architecture and a social focus, home and business, landmark, was now an awkward transport problem. For say six eight-ton tippers, what size front-end loader? If one was available, and from which plant-hire firm, and at what rate per hour? Naidoo pestered him again, bristling with pride of possession. All those others cheering on the opposite pavement, they had no right to approach so close. "Look" he said, "was old building, very old. Not strong, no, not strong at all."

The bulldozer operator switched off and clambered down, from seat to caterpillar track, to ground. If that Indian could go on wasting the contractor's time it was almost safe for a coloured man to risk a sharper tone of voice. He waved away the very air before his face as though offended by the absence of diesel fumes and snapped "Listen, I can go on with the bush clearing but you can't expect me to work spot-on without proper level pegs."

"Haven't been given any definite levels yet" said Balfour, "but I'll try and work out something for you. Suck it out of my thumb."

The peace of it, the finesse in the midst of brute power and savagery and destruction, to caress with sensitive fingers the adjustments of a delicate precision instrument. He chased away a toddler who brushed against a tripod leg and forced him to re-set the level's bubble.

Pegs A1, A2, A3 in place. B4 checked with C5 to within a hair's breadth. Balfour relaxed in the sheer monotony, till he glanced at his watch... oh no, the day nearly over and the work hardly begun. Time for one more row.

Bisected by cross-hairs on the lens he saw a plump and stocky figure stump through the gap in the fence. Naidoo's first few paces still had the confidence of rightful ownership, of familiarity. Now watched through open sights he picked a wary way along caterpillar track-marks, past crushed bushes, strands of barbed wire, over a field that no longer belonged to him or to the neighbourhood, had been ripped raw to become a construction site. A foreigner on foreign territory, he balanced step by careful step on the points of dusty patent-leather shoes. Balfour buttoned his breast pocket over a Land Surveyor's diagram of the plot and wondered if Naidoo's blue striped suit had ever been tailored with jacket as well, or only trousers and waistcoat.

The fingers that clutched his sleeve were short and squashy as the raw sausages that they sold. "Good piece of ground. Fine area. But lot of trouble, nothing but trouble."

"A vacant plot give trouble?" It wasn't easy not to be abrupt.

First Naidoo nodded. "Plenty trouble." Clearly there was more coming. Why fling away the advantage of unshared knowledge in a few seconds, rather draw out the relish of it by fiddling with a silver buckle on the strap across the shiny back of his waistcoat. At last he granted a confidence to that sunburnt man who seemed to be in charge. "Rates. Health Department. Inspectors looking for... that woman and that man with the child, they think I don't know they haven't got papers? I take the risk. You know what they can fine me? Me! But to get rent out of them..." Each point was confirmed by a series of emphatic nods. "Big trouble every week to collect. Excuses. And I charge them nothing, next to nothing. It's good, it's good you cleared, I do them favour, I don't need their money, a profitable business." He pointed to the heap that had supported him. Balfour tried to move away. Naidoo skipped clumsily round an oil drum to detain him. "Fine place you put up here. You put up very fine place. I know." That secret they shared, it set them apart from those inquisitive bystanders out there in the street, the workmen, everybody. "They show me the plans. Very fine place you put up here on my ground."

The sweep of his pudgy arm indicated boundary beacons there, and there, and there. It pointed to a corner towards which all were running, Dougie, every labourer, the bulldozer operator, streams from the street.

When Balfour reached the spot the youngster was not even sobbing, only shivering with shock, but whether from the sight of his own blood or whether from excitement at all the attention that he drew... did it matter? More urgent to get an ambulance. Twenty voices gabbled together to report, yes, somebody had already phoned from the shop. A chorus of thirty, forty versions gave fifty explanations, but after the first Balfour realised he knew as much as he would know after the hundredth.

They formed a semi-circle around the casualty at a respectful distance, pointing and whispering.

His playmates cringed together, further off, their chins tucked into breasts from embarrassment, eyes fish-goggling with awe for he, he who a minute ago had been only another of the gang was now transformed by a pulsing trickle of red and a slice of raw meat to something remote

42

from themselves.

A man, respectable in Islamic Sports Club blazer, collar and tie, bristling with importance, bustled forward with the confidence of a course in First Aid. He examined the wound. "More than ten stitches" he diagnosed, "twenty, but mustn't let them do any cutting", while the boy kept sucking in great lungfuls of breath as though surprised at still being able to.

The moan wail moan wail of the siren sounded different, not the usual impersonal dirge of disaster but now a soothing song of comfort as the ambulance nosed up the street and stopped at a point where the crowd parted. The attendants strolled casually across the pavement, assuming that the three-minute efficiency of the service allowed them to be languid.

Balfour watched the bare feet below matchstick legs, the scabs of neck boils above a torn shirt be led away from dirt and anonymity towards the luxury of starched and sterilised sheets, a balanced diet fed by fussing nurses, the minute attentions of teams of specialists peering at X-ray plates, discussing cardiograms, encephalograms... "Dougie" he shouted, "get them back to their places. Come on, move, there's nothing more to see."

The men had been drained by the excitement of an accident after a long day; they dragged themselves back to lean on their tools and chat. The foreman's whistle at knock-off time was merely a confirmation.

Now silent, they trailed in single file towards the truck and were driven down a suddenly deserted street. Balfour hurried through a last round of inspection, settled watches for the night, ordered patrols. What else had to be done? He paged through his notebook—it wasn't the items one remembered that were important but those forgotten. No, nothing vital.

Nothing but rubble and devastation, Even the only bright spot, the crimson pool of urchin's blood had dried to a caked smudge of brown. The field was bare, they must build quickly, build, or weeds would sprout from that one corner where it had been fertilized and over-run the place.

Already it had produced a crop of images, of caterpillar tracks and barbed wire, of toppled bricks and dust, a line of helmeted men advancing through smoke, an explosion's shudder and a siren's lament, refugees, blood and a body in rags, confusion, exhaustion—an adventure story attractively presented to entertain the children on a winter's night, warm beside the heater with the telly in for service. If they'd be interested. If. He turned the ignition key.

Traffic, bath and langoustine à la provençale.

Balfour sipped his Green Chartreuse.

"Had a good day?" she asked and turned a page from Household Hints to Holidays Afloat.

"The usual, the usual. Nothing special. One does whatever it is has to be done. Mind if I put on the last movement again? What I love about Haydn, he's so exquisitely civilised."

V

It took the exact number of working days Balfour had allowed to clear the site completely. He forced each operation to conform to a schedule relentless as the passing of time itself.

Every morning when he arrived freshly shaved at dawn, the first object the sun lit was the squatters' shelter re-erected on a different part of the site; each time smaller, the corrugated iron sheets more buckled, the construction more rickety. Day after day the watchman's explanation piled further complication upon confusion till Balfour no longer wasted time and authority on the incident, merely nodded to the foreman and watched through the site-office window how slowly the woman stacked her things together, balanced them on her head and glided out of sight. Not once did she look back to see how easily her home was flattened.

On the seventh day—no upright sheets as wall, no roof, only a pair of shutter panels taken from the stack and propped leaning against the fence. In the cramped triangular space the woman crouched, her child asleep on a pile of straw. That day no vapour of steam from the paraffin tin she used to cook the porridge thickened the early-morning mist. Balfour shuffled his dew-damp boots and spoke to her, slowly, gentle as the sun's new-born warmth, then called an interpreter; she must understand, Clause 1A of Section 2 of the Schedule of Quantities, 'Site Works', stated quite clearly "Clear the entire area of all existing structures, vegetation..." She should feel sorry for him having to do this heavy thing.

She looked down at her bare feet and did not answer. He never saw her again.

Yet the shadow of her tenure remained, the sight of fire-blackened bricks scattered over the site darkened the start of his working days as he felt vaguely disturbed that she was no longer there to disturb him. Time, and the urgency of minute by minute lack of time faded the impression of her to the memory of a memory; she was revived whenever some unknown drifter was noticed trespassing vaguely past the 'No Unauthorised Entry' sign. "Yes, what do you want?" either Balfour or the foreman would bark and in answer get a mumble, another mumble about "no, nothing. That woman, she used to be here." 'And what do you want with her?" A further mumble, something about "business."

"Dougie" Balfour said while they watched the mound of rubble from the shop and house gradually decrease, "often we must not hesitate to hurt in order to cure, or am I being dishonest with myself and looking for excuses? I can't make up my mind."

"Well, you're the boss. You're the one who decides."

"No, I'm not. The job is the master, it's all-powerful, it controls us all, even my thoughts when I'm asleep."

"We coloured people, we can't afford to think like that. It's a luxury. D'you still want all six trucks for tomorrow?"

Balfour timed the loading cycle. The front-end loader bit into crumbled bricks and clay, shattered glass and snapped-off doorframes, tore out heaped mouthfuls and fed them on to the backs of patiently waiting tippers. A few urchins still interested enough to risk the lash of the foreman's tongue scampered away from the wheels as each truck reversed out with its load of shards and relics. Rubbish that once had been prized was now a nuisance, a problem of transport and time and budget, would again be prized by future archaeologists scratching through the midden of a municipal dump for evidence of nomads who had been forced to move. Six minutes per truck. Say about thirty loads. Not much left.

From the door of his site office he could look right over the shoulder-high pile of debris, across a barren acre to a row of abandoned terrace cottages, all the way to the slate roofs of dormer-window mansions further off, right up to the mountain.

Its rocks and ravines veined with shadow now dominated the site, nature pure and raw coldly superior above half-finished storage sheds and trailing pipes and cables and a notice board—'Commercial Training & Community Centre'; all reputable names proclaimed in sans-serif, the area connected with water, electricity, telephone to the metropolitan network, yet exposed to wind and grit and loneliness.

Thirty times six minutes—three hours. Tomorrow the demolition team could be split, half to stay and tidy after the loader had left at nine, or half-past; half to reinforce the gang excavating the main column base.

Only heads showed above the spoil-heaps surrounding their common pit. Picks rose, poised, glinted in the heat, plunged. Shovelfuls of dirt were flung up in cascades of dust that the wind swirled across the whole suburb, into the plastic mug of Balfour's thermos, between his teeth. His hair felt dirty.

He rubbed his palms together and revelled in the sweat that lubricated his joints and muscles as he bounded towards the excavation. The nearer he came, the quicker the picks were raised in salute.

Squatting, hands on knees, the boss looked down on his labourers, up to them for advice; no full-of-himself crap about this whitey. "How's it going down there?" He made it sound as happy as a song.

The men stopped and shook their heads. "No" they panted, "it chops hard my boss."

He jumped from the top of the spoil-heap, a leap that jarred the back of his neck, grabbed the nearest pick out of a labourer's grasp and hacked at the earth. "Come on, it's child's play. Easy. Look."

A dozen arcs of power and hardly panting. No time these days for squash at the Club and chit-chat over drinks, no need even.

Fit. Busy. On top of it. Confident enough to descend below the level, down to stand amongst the lowest and lift their drudgery to excitement and a raised profit. "Not much more to go. Only so much deeper." He stretched up on tip-toe, patted the top of the tallest head and grinned back to the laugh he had earned from the underlings whose names he all knew, except for a few.

The week before, to mark the start of the job, every worker had been issued with a new overall, an improved pattern with company name across the back in a brighter red and (a good touch this, proud of the idea) badge on breast pocket. He watched the khaki figures round him stoop in effort, labour had its own smell, listened to the grunts that greeted each thud of their picks. But why were only three, four, yes four, khaki? The rest blue or dirty white, a couple of dark green CITY ENGINEERS DEPT. WINDOW CLEANING SERVICES was shovelling out what COASTAL MARINE hacked loose. Rage or pretend not to notice?

He was only another member of the cast, play-acting the role of leader, a figure in a charade where every face was turned away from its neighbour. Did they know nothing of her winter costumes and his four suits hardly ever worn? That cashmere sweater birthday present whose colours clashed? Or the Harris tweed jacket with lapels that…? Only at night in their hovels, heads of peppercorn curls close together over a candle on a fruit-box, could they whisper of a suspected vision of jewellery and tiled bathrooms and holidays at the Marina. A convenience, a convention, tact—to pretend their lives ended each day when they

47

stacked tools after the time-up whistle, that the world was contained inside the planks of the setting-out profile surrounding the building area. So many pairs of hands, bodies wrapped in cast-offs crammed each night into huts or the repeated rows of sub-economic housing, men who deserved the compliment of a human rebuke. ''Stop that loafing. Right. Get cracking.'' The sharp tone of voice was meant to carry the sting of a master's whip; no more than he expected they expected from him.

The shrill summons of the phone in the site office made Balfour jump to its demand. A few springy steps and he was there, now another man, his being changed as easily as a driver slipping into a smoother gear.

Cool, remote, the efficient employee, he reported ''No, you couldn't have reached me on the other site in any case, phone's already disconnected, breaking down sheds, First Delivery next Friday, then I'll concentrate everything here except for those couple of minor works... yes, you'll usually be able to get me either here or at the yard. Under control, site just about clear, started excavating but still no detail drawings and still no official handing over of site. Yes I have, dozens of times, swore they'd send someone later today. No, seen to it already. Sub-contractors? All been confirmed, went into the post last week. They're keeping well thanks. 'Bye.''

Half-past-three. Time for paper, to unroll plans, flip through piles of delivery tickets, check time cards, use the back of an old specification to calculate lengths and volumes and quantities, the mass and pressure of man-hours versus money.

He crouched on an uncomfortable stool, feet hooked round the legs till a cramp in the calf and a salesman with a grin as glossy as a colour-printed brochure gave an excuse to stand. Yes, the truck-driver could use the phone if his diff had packed up. All right, all right, you can go and look for your son, for the last time, be careful where you walk and for heaven's sake just keep him away in the future. No Dougie, the Council said they'd clear latrine buckets on a Tuesday. Cement Sales had promised delivery for tomorrow and here was Manie from the shed-erection team, burly and grumpy... run short of sheets to finish the roof and the wind turning. Impossible. Asbestos didn't grow legs overnight and walk off on its own. This needed a cigarette but the carton was empty.

Out from the shadows of his office Balfour quick-marched across the road to the take-away. The sudden glare of the sun made him sneeze and through his tears he noticed the usual onlookers; loafers sneering at the fools who let themselves be worked like that; scab-kneed urchins; the grey man who could have been a retired official, grey face, grey dog

48

on leash, grey raincoat even today; the dodderers with cheeks the colour of shrivelled raisins, worked whole lives in the building, mumbled it was the wrong way to tackle a job like that; half-a-dozen youngsters' goggle eyes clustered round a scarlet sports-model squatting insolently at the kerb on its bulbous tyres.

And obviously the driver of the car, tall with pale face and spindle legs tight in corduroy, who stalked towards the office. Balfour intercepted him. "You're looking for me?" Careful, this intruder was too languid.

"You are the foreman here?" A suitable voice, it condescended down from a camel head balanced on a shaft whose Adam's-apple was protected by a cravat of silk batik.

"I'm in charge. You can speak to me." Balfour remembered to unclench his fists.

The Architect announced himself to this bristling and aggressive little fellow. He fanned a hand of flutter-fingers towards the notice-board; art-nouveau cuff-links seemed to hold the starched bones of his wrist in place. "Just by the way, it's spelt with a K, not a C. You'll see to that won't you? You've had much experience of this type of work?"

Balfour rushed into a list of contracts completed, recited with the pride of a roll of honour. "You can ask the Quantity Surveyor about me, ask the Consulting Engineer. We've worked together on the…" The whole region was littered with their efforts. "Look, we've got problems on this one, a list of queries long as my arm, the levels to begin with, they just don't work out."

The Architect answered with his eyebrows only.

"If you compare the existing Council sewer with the grading of the basement parking area…"

A raised palm silenced him. "Most unfortunately, I'm here in a strictly unofficial capacity. The Department insists…," he stressed the word, repeated it with separated syllables, "insists all dealings with my office to go via the proper channels, I notice you've got only part of the facebricks on site. I particularly included a clause in my specification you know, all facings to be…"

"Oh that" said Balfour, "that's in every departmental job, it's in their standard spec. In any case, impossible to comply with, never enforced. We're lucky to have got any at all, only because we're old customers who pay on time."

The Architect stepped back a fastidious pace from grit and churning tyres as a truck reversed past them. Balfour jerked a thumb towards it. "From the demolition. Rubble. Dust unto dust, that's how it all ends and only last week, you should have seen it, alive with dignity after those hideous advertising signs had been ripped off for souvenirs. So simple, there was a beauty and a balance to its shape. The last one round here, a pure little gem, plain, those proportions had a kind of perfection to them.''

"Oh quite, quite, naturally if one appreciates the aesthetics of..." He paused while a truck bounced on its springs when the front-end loader rumbled a bucketful of muck on to its back. "I've introduced certain elements of architectonic tone values in harmony with the traditional vernacular." He peered down to Balfour with the interest of a crane inspecting a cocksparrow. "Definitely seen you before but simply cannot place..."

"Weren't you at the opening of my mother's retrospective?"

"What did you say the name was? I didn't quite catch..."

"She worked under her maiden name. Last month, at the National Gallery. Look, I've put down provisional level pegs but..."

"Of course." The slapped thigh, the affable laugh; a cold hand groped towards a warm handshake. "Those lineal concepts. You know..." Confidentially, in a whisper, "I managed to pick up a couple before she became so sought after. Recognised the potential. Almost embarrassing, the way the value's appreciated."

"This job." Balfour rolled up his sleeves another fold and waved a tanned forearm towards the excavation. "I've got a theory. Places like airports or a community complex like this, they're the modern equivalent of cathedrals in the Middle Ages, where people congregate, feel together and get drawn nearer some vision of perfection that the public relations experts..."

He stopped, realising he was alone. The other had strolled away towards his car and Balfour stumped after him on legs that hurried like his words as he blurted "those detail drawings, we're still waiting for them. Working in the dark."

The Architect answered over a houndstooth shoulder. "Yes, those old places, they do have a certain interest to them. Stylistically."

"The dozer hardly had to touch it. Collapsed, like a set of my son's building blocks."

Now the tall figure dominated all the admirers respectfully silent round the Model RX7, Mark III. A toddler stroked the chrome fender inserts while the driver jangled his keys as though trying to remember something.

A mere afterthought. "By the way... strange I haven't come across the name of your firm before. You go in for other work besides this type of thing?"

"Mainly structural stuff" said Balfour, "like reservoirs and…"

"You have a property development division I take it?"

"No, spec building's a bloody racket."

The Architect wriggled uncomfortably low in his bucket seat. "Most construction setups do have these days. From a tax angle. Look, if ever, and it's a question of design…" He started the engine. Purr. "Those Fernwood town-houses, snapped up before the roof trusses erected."

"Those levels" said Balfour.

"Well, when you do get round to it. Can always side-step the professional scale of fees." Beachfront apartments, sectional titles, holiday houses—inaudible while the engine revved with a snarl and he spun away.

His place at the kerb was taken by a white Volkswagen beetle with Government Garage numberplates.

"Thank heavens you've come at last." Balfour greeted the driver. "I've got a list of queries for the Inspector of Works long as my arm."

"So this must be the contractor himself" said the Inspector. "Man, me I'm like the jewboy's hamburger, without the ham. Burger is the name." Exactly as expected, safari suit only slightly frayed, long socks, the clipped moustache and sideburns all standard as a departmental specification. The pads of forms (Weekly Reports in triplicate, Site Certificate in duplicate), rolls of plans under the arm, he would have seemed indecently exposed without them.

"All I've got so far is the lay-out" said Balfour. "No details, there's nothing to define the level at the north-west boundary."

Burger hardly glanced at the unrolled plan. "You talk about define. D'you know what's the latest definition of a virgin?"

Listening to a slower rhythm in the beat of the pick-thuds was more important than the answer. "That's a good one" said Balfour. He forced himself to smile. "I must remember it. I've been trying to work out and I can't…"

"No man, now you're trying a fast one. If you couldn't work it out…" Burger mock-punched him on the shoulder. "They say there by the office you're supposed to be just about the smartest bugger from out the whole bang-shoot of the bunch contractors. Now let's see how clever you really are, you explain me something for a change. Tell me, what's the difference between a whore and a nun?"

Balfour felt his cheek muscles becoming tired. He watched Burger stamp the ground to punctuate the punch-line, let himself be staggered by back-slapping.

"You know what?" said Burger, "I reckon we're going to get on like a house on fire. You'll be surprised, there's not that many floating around with a sense of humour to appreciate…" He eased out one of the rolls of plans cradled under his arm.

"No" Balfour exploded, "not again. The same balls-up as on the last job we did for you people."

"What's up now?"

"Wrong plans."

"That's nothing" said Burger "to lose my sleep over. These kind of places, they're planning to stick them up left right centre. Bloody smart too, even coloured tiles in the shithouses but you mark my words these blue-arse baboons, they'll have them turned into pigsties. In no time. Matter of days. They're all the bloody same."

"The centres or those you call baboons?" asked Balfour.

"Both. Same difference. The buildings all off a type plan. There's this bugger there by the drawing office. Smart, I'm telling you, just as clued-up as any of those graded draughtsmen gone through the Tech. He drew it." Burger pointed to the Front Elevation. "Good, hey. These private architects, they just get dished out the type plan. All they have to do is bugger it around a bit to fit onto each site. And collect one hell of a big fat fee."

"Surely I can't work off wrong plans." Balfour heard that his voice was an octave too shrill.

"Blame these girlies in Records, they keep making the god-almighty fuckups. Good for the one thing only, but who in his right mind would ever want to ram it up one of those bitches, beats me. You'll have to write in about this, you've got the reference number. You know what?"

Burger screwed up his eyes, head cocked to one side. "Man, I've been saying to myself all this time, but I know that face from somewhere. Just hang on a sec, hang on, didn't you do that new boiler-room and coal-bunkers there by the Alexandra Institute?"

"Yes, years ago. You weren't on that job were you? I can't even remember any more the name of the Inspector, but it definitely wasn't you."

"You see I was right after all." Burger slapped his thigh. "No, that old bastard, the one with the limp, he's gone on pension now two-three years ago, he used to handle all those Alex jobs. Now just fancy it, and all the time it was you I used to note stuck up there on the scaffold."

"What a terrible place. It's the most depressing…"

"Gets you down does it?" Burger shifted his weight from left leg to right. He rotated a stiff little finger in an ear, withdrew it carefully, examined the blob of wax on the tip, rolled it into a ball and flicked it towards the excavator team. "I've got to go there quite often."

"I'm lucky" said Balfour, "you didn't mistake me for one of the hundreds of mental deficients they keep there."

Burger blinked. "That's not bloody funny" he snapped, "just cut it out will you. Here, you must sign the handing over of site certificate." He tried to open a pad on a raised knee. The wind teased the carbons into curls.

"Let's try here" suggested Balfour, and they bent over the bonnet of the four-wheel drive. "No, you put the firm's name there and the date goes at the bottom."

The ballpoint would not write; the gutter was the proper place for it. A pencil's point first was licked, then snapped by excess pressure. "Look" said Burger, "don't you come along and try tell me how to do my job. I've been filling in these forms since before you were sitting there on your arse with your nose stuck into some book up there by the university or whatever fancy place.. Let's get the one thing straight, right from the beginning."

"Yes?"

"You do your work right and I'll do mine. You've got fifteen months for the job as from today, no tomorrow, I put down tomorrow's date to give you the extra and I'm telling you sure as I'm standing here now in front of you, the big boys up there in Head Office, they're anxious. Don't say I haven't warned you."

Balfour nodded.

"Now so far as what the actual work's concerned, here's ten copies of the spec and ten of the bill, so you've got no excuse. Just see you stick to it, all of it, even the commas and the fullstops. Then we'll get on without you getting your nose put out of joint. I've made myself quite clear? OK?"

"There's the question of levels" said Balfour, "and the correct detail drawings."

"I told you, but you wouldn't listen, you must write in. And by the way, on this job, not so long as what I'm Inspector of Works here, not one single facebrick gets laid till the last one's on site. And these column bases, not so much as a dollop of concrete till I've okayed each and every one."

The Volkswagen's engine fired at the third attempt.

The door of the double garage closed with a click and Boyboy raced across the lawn towards his Daddy.

"How's my boy?" Balfour picked up his son, held the wriggling body in front of him at stiff arms-length and twirled round a few times.

"Let me down, let me down, I'm not a baby."

He dropped the boy and knelt down, make a mock serious face. "I've done that to bigger ones than you my young man, to the biggest giant that ever there was."

"You didn't. When?"

"Playing scrumhalf for the Varsity second team and against us was this human bull, he later became famous and scored a try against the All Blacks."

Hand in hand, they sauntered into the lounge.

"Any messages?" he called, glancing at the day's post. "Any messages?" he repeated.

She bent lower over her darning. She stabbed the cloth with a needle and pulled the thread taut till it snapped. A pair of trousers flapped down on to the Afghan. Tension arched her spine as she pointed. "Look at it, just look at it. I'm sure even your labourers dress better than you do."

"I don't need to bother" he said, "not really, it's not expected of me. Not like that architect. He honoured us today, all flared waistline and airy-fairy frills. Typical. The Inspector too, a run-of-the-mill mass-production model."

"So after five minutes you know all there is to know. Labelled as typical and finished. That's typical of you I'd say, a mind set from beforehand..."

"You seem in a hell of a mood. Now off with you juniors, go set up the wickets, I'll be with you in a minute." He crumpled a few circulars of Bargain Offers addressed to the Specially Selected Houseowner. "Don't we all choose to see and hear only what we expect? I know them more than I've let them know me."

She pressed her lips into a straight line; each corner seemed to be sucking on a sour edge.

"Something's upset you" he said.

"Why do you say that?" she snapped. "In order to upset me? To prove you're always right?"

"I only asked if there were any messages. Please."

"He phoned." With a sigh, she regarded a tear in the sleeve of a windbreak. "Your lord and master. I can see now why you can't stand him."

"What time was this? What the hell did he want?"

"About four. Tea-time. Asked for you but somehow I've got a feeling it wasn't really... No wonder that red-head walked out on him. I'm sure she wasn't actually his wife, I bet they weren't even properly married. Now he finds himself short of a hostess for all those overseas functions."

"What? What overseas functions? What on earth are you talking about? But I spoke to him at half-past three, he knew I wouldn't be here."

"You don't even know what's going on in your own firm. It's the grand tour if you please, trade mission or something, with some Minister or other. Whole crowd of them. Conferences, conventions, London, Paris, ending up in Switzerland. Ten days at a resort. Am I fond of skiing? Me! Suite in five-star hotel. Don't I need a break? The bloody cheek of it. Or d'you thing he was just... not meant to be taken seriously?"

"Joking, or at least trying to. Not that I've ever known him to as much as smile."

"On and on. Couldn't get rid of him. Masses of entertaining. Nanny could manage the children, you'd help her, so capable even though you'd be so busy with the job and now all the extra duties on top of..."

"Oh go on." Balfour perched himself on the edge of a chair, palms on knees. "You're just making this all up. You're just trying your damnest to bait me."

"And next you'll pretend you know nothing about becoming a public company with quotation on the Stock Exchange. Look, I don't want there to be secrets between us but all that hint-hint talk, if that's what it needs for you to become a director..." Red spots burned on the prominence of each cheek. She stood up with a twitch of the shoulders, tugged down her hem to a level of modesty and blazed "What the hell does he take me for? Some dockside tart who'll lift up her skirt for him at the drop of his fiver?" and stormed raging into the kitchen.

Silence round the dining-room table. "You booked for the Festival Series?" asked Balfour, topping up his goblet of cabernet.

She nodded. "And I sent that blue suit of yours to the cleaners, seeing that everyone will be dolled up. That's the only one you ever wear. Boyboy sit up straight and stop behaving like a piggy-wig. Look at the mess you're making."

Seconds, but no thirds of strawberry dessert for the children. No, definitely not, if Nanny went to all the trouble of making it she was entitled to her share.

"You know," Balfour crumpled his serviette, "I never expected I'd be able to get as much as seven-and-a-half percent discount out of Atomic

Welding. Do you realise just how many thousands extra profit we'll clear?''

She pressed a warning finger against her lips and rolled eyes to glance in Nanny's direction as the dirty dishes were stacked clattering on to the tray. Only after the pink overall had waddled out of the dining-room did she whisper "You shouldn't talk like that in front of her you know."

They trailed towards the lounge to become the typical family; children on the carpet, daughter finishing homework, son struggling to assemble plastic units; wife and mother watching and listening; husband and father still obsessed by work.

"It's a crazy design" he said. "This huge central column supporting a dome over the main concourse, like some modern cathedral of commerce."

"I can't for the life of me remember" she said, "if there were columns in Saint Peter's. That's the biggest one of all isn't it? Now who was it again? Not Leonardo that other one. Yes, Michelangelo. Michelangelo" she repeated clearly, so that the children would hear and perhaps remember.

"You're not thinking of Saint Paul's are you? We've never been to Rome."

"Well, in any case I'd like to see it one day" she murmured. "Maybe when the children are a bit older. Time flies. When did you say the programme's coming on?"

"Another twenty minutes" he answered. "I'm looking forward to this, I've never before had a contract featured on the telly. Let's polish off what's left of that cabernet by way of celebration."

She crossed the room in a flurry of curves to fetch the bottle and dribble out the dregs into Stuart crystal; her pleats swished against his leg as she twirled on polished calves reflected in the polished floor.

A sip and a nod. "It'll be beautiful, when we're ready to cast the main base. This deep pit resting safe in mother earth herself, with all my reinforcement bars lined up like a giant geometric puzzle or some modern abstract sculpture or monument. Pity to bury it for ever and ever, pity we can't turn the whole building upside down."

"You'd like to turn the whole world upside down, wouldn't you?" She perched with crossed legs on the arm of his club-easy.

"Yes" he agreed, "yes, I would. It's topsy-turvy as it is. I wouldn't mind twisting the whole bloody lot if that's what's needed because everywhere it's the rotten side held up and admired."

They watched a preview of coming features flicker on the screen.

56

"It's all a load of bullshit" he decided. "Trade mission my foot, just another name for a prolonged booze-up at the public's expense."

The discarded politician who had died last month glared down at them, stern but wise; revived by death and a shift in the caucus. Conscripts with reversed arms protected his gun-carriage and his honour; muffled drums proclaimed his posthumous promotion to a Son of the Soil and a Father of the Nation.

Commercials jingle-jangled. They saw the ideal family reflected in sharply focused colour. The model/wife/mother poured for her mate from a bottle with label of gabled estate facing the audience. "Before he used to adore me more, now his thirst comes first."

Lost as orphans the children on their magic carpet floated in a paradise where parents are perfect. "When I grow up" whispered Boyboy, "I'm going to drink..."

"Ssh", hissed with all the severity of adult discipline.

The family tensed themselves into more alert postures.

"It's the Minister himself" she whispered.

"But it's completely slanted."

"Ssh" the others silenced him.

Balfour fidgeted. "That's nonsense" he blurted. "There's not one single word of truth, there's no connection... a load of crap."

Ringed fingers tried to soothe his forearm. "Not in front of the children. Please. It's only a television programme, for entertainment."

Gripping the arms of his chair, he forced himself to endure it for another minute, then jumped up shaking futile fists at an overblown front elevation. "This is more than I can stomach. It makes me want to puke" and marched out to the terrace.

From leaf rustle and the moist aroma of cut grass, from the crescent moon and the milky way he returned to an underworld of squealing tyres and revolver shots.

"Why those lies? That cheap propaganda? What for?", and with troubled eyes the others regarded him as though he were some alien come to mock their customs in a foreign tongue, destroy their idols and spread the germs of epidemics.

57

VI

"Daddy", in a spellbound whisper, face upturned, eyes aglisten with pride, "why didn't you tell me your picture would be in the paper? All the other girls are madly jealous, they say you look fabulous and they all wish they had a father like that so I said that actually you're much better looking than in the photo so then they all..."

Boyboy was not impressed. The picture wasn't half as big as the heavyweight scowling on the sports page.

Her parents came on a hesitant pilgrimage to remind the newly-appointed director's wife how they used to change her nappies.

"That phone again" she exclaimed, "it must be the millionth time. Thank you, thank you but it's not me who deserves the congratulation. Yes, I'll tell him, when I see him." The 'when' emphasised. "No, it won't really make any difference to us", a giggle of mock-modesty, "except I'll be seeing even less of him than before. He's absolutely... up to the ears." She replaced the receiver with a sigh of self-pity for the overworked receptionist and the undercherished wife.

A printed card from the bank; in the bottom right-hand corner a short handwritten note from the manager, with pamphlet enclosed to remind him that the Personal Financial Planning Service had been specially tailored to suit his individual requirements.

An unpromoted Burger, still only an overlooked state official, defended his self-respect with disrespect. "Man, once there's this hang of a big-shot director, so he sends his old lady out to go get herself another few fur coats and a couple bagfuls really nice pieces jewellery and no sooner she's out the door he goes charging into the kitchen and there's this kaffir-girl down on hands and knees scrubbing away like mad at the floor so he says, just like that, 'Annie, how's about it you and me...' "

"Congratulations" said Dougie with a remote smile and a hand extended to span the distance from a realm where a man put himself through a proper apprenticeship, learnt a solid trade, did a full day's work, married in the Methodist Church and set up home in a decent suburb like Grassy Park, saved and bought a secondhand Datsun, enjoyed an annual holiday under canvas somewhere up the West Coast. And is lucky to be chosen foreman; and that was that—no directorships of public companies in Grassy Park. At least not this generation.

"Being quoted on the Stock Exchange won't really affect us" explained Balfour. "I mean, not here on the site, not for the time being anyway. Later maybe we'll be able to tackle even bigger jobs."

Neither Manie nor any of his carpenters read newspapers. Or at least pretended not to. Or maybe did and did not feel obliged to mouth the expected arse-licking phrases; or wanted to and could not find the words. Or—there were more urgent matters than politeness.

"I wouldn't stand quite so near the edge if I was you" called up a gum-booted Manie sloshing through the mud and pebbles and slime at the bottom of the column-based excavation. He pointed to the embankment, a wound in the earth frighteningly deep and raw and wetly exposed.

"Then better get out of there" Balfour advised.

"No, I'm all right."

"Don't be stupid. What if it caves in, we can't take chances like that. Bring your whole gang up." It was the boss giving an order.

Manie scrambled up to stand panting at Balfour's side, leather nail-bag at the hip, claw-hammer choked in a fist. "It's those steel-fixers." Burly, his paunch heaved with blame. "If only the bastards had come on the Monday like they'd promised. Now, it's the ground-water, look."

Just above the bottom of the excavation, bleeding at the level of the water table, mud oozed in, sluggish and relentless. The pumps slurped and gurgled. A clod plopped down with a viscous splash. Balfour could almost feel the pressure of damp earth on his shoulders and annoyance with a brain that should have jumped to a quick solution.

"I'll try and work out something" he muttered. "Maybe get that old sheet-piling from the yard and start all over again. In the meantime, carry on and finish off the sheds."

He skirted the excavation the long way round to reach his office sooner by avoiding the Council Electrical Inspector who probably wanted the crane's switchbox re-earthed. No luck.

"Yes, I know it's dangerous. I'll get it seen to."

At last—on his stool, pencil scribbling figures on a sheet of scrap. If the pressure increased with the square of the depth, then the bending

59

moment...

"Look" said Burger, dark in the doorway, "that's one hell of a big bloody dog's-breakfast of a mess down there. Me myself, I couldn't give two stuffs one way or the other but that old shithouse of a senior inspector, he might rock up any moment and then there'll be all merry hell to play."

"We'll get it all cleaned out before we start casting."

"I don't fancy the looks of it." Burger sniffed. "Not one little bit."

"I said we'd get it one hundred percent. Maybe by lunch."

"I should fuckingwell hope so." Burger shuffled forward half a pace. "Man, you haven't got one of those coffin-nails of yours for me by any chance? I don't usually smoke but today I just somehow fancy."

Then the phone shrilly insistent. "Who?" snapped Balfour. "You want me to place the order for aluminium roof-sheets with your firm? But for heaven's sake, you people got my confirmation at least a month ago. No, it wasn't you I spoke to. It must be floating around your office somewhere, please check up on it, I don't want another balls-up like that other time."

Would force produced by mud be nearer the figure for dry earth or for water? Balfour went back to the excavation to assess—but why wasn't Manie and his team busy on the sheds? Where the hell had they got to?

He peered over the edge, down to figures high-stepping over or crawling through the cage of reinforcement, and Manie driving home four-inch nails with vicious hammer-thuds and grunts. A few dozen reject scaffold-boards, some four-by-threes left over from the sheds, a bit of rusty corrugated iron here and there, wire borrowed from the fence, an ugly and untidy mess—in half an hour or so it would be reasonably safe.

"You've got some good men there" said Burger. "I can see it. Know their onions all right."

"Well" Balfour grunted with relief, "there aren't many problems on a job can't be solved with a sledge-hammer and a string of four-letter words."

The latter phrase inspired Burger. "You buggers" he yelled down to the men, "you like it deep and wet, hey. That's the best kind hey."

One man gaped undecided to see how the others would react; one man laughed because he seemed to find it funny; another forced out a noise because he felt it was expected; a couple ignored him; a few giggled at that stupid bastard making an arse of himself up there; some shook their heads and grumbled; and one man carefully straightened himself through the criss-cross mesh of steel bars and glared upwards with eyes that sparked with the hardness of struck flints.

"It's nothing, cool down, get on with it" an aloof Balfour called, for the man to know that really he was calling the Inspector to order, and for the Inspector to know that really he was sparing him a public rebuke.

Burger adjusted his shoulders inside his suddenly uncomfortable safari-jacket. "You haven't maybe got another of those kill-me-quicks? You know, when I was in training I never used to touch it, but I don't know what's come over me today. Nerves man, it's a bugger, gets you down."

The foreman joined them.

"That should do the trick" said Balfour. "We can start swinging over the chute into position for concrete."

Dougie's silence was long enough to be deliberate. He pointed, then spat out each word like an insult. "Why does that stupid put those four-by-three bearers on flat instead of on edge? He should know better by now, he's older than I am."

"The what by what? Did you say bearers?" asked Burger, and for answer Dougie measured him carefully by eye.

More diplomat than civil engineer, Balfour suggested the following items needed a skilled foreman's urgent attention; the crane's earth-lead, the chute, stone and sand piles shovelled nearer to the mixer, so many sacks of cement brought out, a drum of plasticiser diluted twenty-to-one.

The two white men waited; one till the too devoutly christian foreman was out of range from the too devoutly muslim leading-hand; the other till the too clever-by-half shortarse little crossbreed was out of earshot.

Balfour allowed himself the luxury of a sigh.

Burger allowed himself the luxury of blurting "I've got the hell in today. This whole bloody scheme, fucking waste of good money if you ask me. You really think they'll be prepared to dish out busfare, those that haven't got fancy cars, to trek all the way here? That'll be the frosty Friday. Don't you believe it my friend, they'd rather lay out their cash for booze. I'm telling you, I know what I'm talking about. This whole thing gives me the screaming shits."

The gentlemanly contractor, the professional graduate, in his calmly educated voice explained "I'm not so sure. In any case, they didn't choose to go and live all the way out there, did they?"

Hands on hips, the Inspector inspected a typical example. "It's all right for you to talk, you people from those big houses up there by the top part of Claremont. Listen, those coffee-and-milks, they've got to live somewhere I grant you, but not so long it's in my own backyard. Let them keep to their own. Give them half a chance and they'll flood you out.''

Balfour replied neatly, with a half-bow. ''You must excuse me now'' he murmured, and approached a busy-busy-busy Dougie with a polite ''if you can spare the time.''

The foreman's dry smile united them against time-wasters, officials and labourers.

''I think'' said Balfour ''we could start clearing up down there ready for casting soon after lunch. It's the most horrible untidy mess I've ever seen but a case of now or never. A damned awkward job, creeping round inside the cage. Send someone small, one of those young loafers.''

Earlier that morning the south-easter had surged its clouds over the rows of the municipal sub-economic housing scheme, whined into every pair of red-brick semis all identical as grains of dust, where on kitchen dressers stood saucers with coins ready for the funeral insurance or the instalment on the hi-fi. Theirs had come with gilded handles and one free LP record. The youngster slammed the door of No 487F Acacia Way on his mothers screams and curses. To hell with school. A load of shit.

He dawdled past the chain-link mesh around the pre-fab classrooms and listened to a class recite that faded holy sing-song, faded as the net-ball stripes on the gravel playground. All right for kids shoved fifty sixty in a room two to a desk where if you so much as, they'd haul you out and swish a stingy cane across your arse right there in front of all those goody-goodies half your size.

Rather lean, make it look comfy, against an electric pole, take the whole morning to untie the strings of the Herald poster—HOODED MONSTER STRIKES AGAIN. Only grown men had time to spare, like those few others in the street also finished with school, you could pick snot from your nose or gob into the gutter and nobody took not even that much notice. Not even when the wind head-over heeled the poster into the dirt together with those other bits of paper trapped flutter-flutter under the Coloured Education notice by the gate where some stuck-up prefect still waited for the latecomers. No, not near there.

Along a short-cut footpath through the bushes, over that sand-dune where last weekend, the neighbour's pigtail daughter, a whole gang of them they'd got her. Only neither the Spoilers nor the Jesters, they wouldn't want a bugger who still goes home each night early to his mother. Not that lot, they'd piss themselves with laughing if you said straight out from school, mess you up, make you feel hang of a spare. And they usually hung out there behind the autolot, so better turn left.

Past the Forthcoming Attractions at the Palace Luxury Cinema. It took, must be ages, to watch a whistling cheerful on a step-ladder brush-paste the world's most famous complexion next to a man-size smoking automatic. But when you looked close-up, that nose, hell, just a mess of dots like blackheads. Now to clear out a bank guards-and-sirens underground, should make the whole damn double-feature out of something real like that.

Under the outsize advert board over the railway. It made you feel small just to look up to it, buggers so much bigger than yourself but he must be barmy that grinning muscle giant in the middle with the drops water on chest and more drops on the bottle. Wasting his time sucking out a straw with a couple blonde birds round tits both side. Rather push their long legs apart, they only had bikinis. All three happy, a speedboat must cost a stack.

A bloke really needed money. Those two notes still left over from that dropped purse there by the supermarket, they crinkled in the back pocket with each step. One for Ma, one to last till first pay-day and then... ah-hah. Even old whats-his-name and him only a half-cripple they'd stuck him a treat there in the hip with a chopper, he'd cleared up the jackpot one month and then not a week later goes and hits the double and he'd gone limp and all up to his boss and when the whitey starts to scowl him out tells the bastard he can stick it.

Nothing doing at the factory where they smoked fish or something. And bloody rude too on top of it. Why they want to shit on you like that when you haven't done them nothing.

A 'No Vacancies' tied to the gate by the timber yard.

Baldie's head, not one hair on it and just a single shake there by the petrol station. Too much trouble even to look up.

That other place—just barbed wire and a mad barking watchdog. They couldn't even be bothered to send somebody to tell you to bugger off. Fuck them.

Workshed kind of place where they fixed up the trains, with a sour old bastard in a glassed-in coop like for a chicken. Sign on for some sort of learner? Who me? Go to classes, at night, in a bugger's own time, he must be off his bloody head.

No, not even anybody to talk to. When you so much as stopped to ask the time all you got was half-past ten. If you was lucky. Otherwise that hot-eye stare and the tight lips and a side-step like an invite not to disappoint them with a grab and run straight into reform school.

Shit no, not like him there in a khaki dustcoat behind the handlebars of one of those three-wheel delivery scooter affairs. You could pedal all the way right round the world like teacher said in geography, maybe school wasn't so bad after all, and land up here in the same place. Old, legs heavy with the work and the years, lips saggy with the rest of your teeth pulled so you couldn't even whistle Top of the Pops. Like those old buggers over there, the way their trouser legs flopped when they slop-slopped and the paper carriers hanging down too heavy from their fingers. Easy, there's some bad ones as would risk it even here in the open street.

In a shop window protected by automatic alarm system—6 months budget account wear while u pay post free anywhere within... anywhere within some smart office, behind a big desk with pens and things and one of those fancy contraptions to give out any numbers you want just like that, with the check suit over there and the stetson to match you could rake in plenty every week.

Nothing to lose by wandering into those older streets where they seemed to be shifting the people out. Half the buildings empty, enough to give anybody the creeps, the Vampire or the Werewolf or even the Dreaded Killer who could crush you dead, they might be hiding anywhere here. A bit lost. So what, who was scared?

Not for kids like those babies still in the classroom, you had to be real tough to last it out on a building site but they said the pay was better than the council. A man's wages for everybody, young same as for old. That foreman looked one of those real little shithouses running around pretending to run the whole show when his face was every bit as dark as. At least he noticed you, he shouted. It makes a bugger tired just to watch him and still more that half a day to go.

"Okay, okay, I'll pull off my jacket. Unemployment card? What's that?"

Cleaning wheelbarrows for chucking cement and whatnot into that big hole, even more boring than school. Didn't they ever stop to eat? And they must be screw-loose in the head, the whole bloody lot of them, in some wild panic must get it done today. Why just today? Mad.

Really mad. First he says wheelbarrows, a fukken mountain of them and then when you'd done two sort-of-clean he says leave it, go down the hole clear out papers and odd bits of shit. Then no sooner you're down, deep under the ground no better than some kind of corpse in the graveyard, he blows the knock-off whistle. Up again. Sun and wind can make you feel a bit more alive.

That white man just standing there doing nothing outside the shed, he must be the big boss to judge the way he yelled to that arsehole of a foreman, "Did you send one of those youngsters down to clear out?"

Dougie pointed to the spindly figure trailing listless steps after the other men hurrying to the take-away.

They crowded him away from the service hatch. Behind it two women dashed and twisted, bumped into each other and jerked arms in frantic bursts of energy; whisked flat pads of sizzle from the hotplates on to opened rolls, dipped ladles deep into cauldrons and gratefully leant their weight against the black handles of stainless-steel urns for a two-breath rest while the container filled. In steam and smoke, in the hot stale smell of oil and pre-cooked fastfood, they rammed grease-soaked wrappings into paper bags.

The back of the queue swung its tail of stragglers into the road where dark hands with pink palms patted the fenders of each passing car. With catcalls and jeers from doughnut lips, their popcorn eyes fizzed at a passing head of aluminium hair-straightening combs. She minced away with a smirk and left him stranded at the counter.

"Er... how much then did you say the soup was?" Most of the others seemed to go for the soup.

A weary arm pointed to the price-list.

"And what's a hot dog?"

The woman used a forearm to sweep strands from her forehead. Her armpit was dark with sweat. She sighed "Yes?"

"All right, I'll have soup then."

"Then why didn't you say so in the first place."

"And chips. Give me a packet chips. Yes, with vinegar."

So then she goes and spills the salt for hard luck like in that picture on the classroom wall, Our Lord's Last Supper.

"Here." She slapped down the parcel. "Anything else sonny?"

In a man's world, an earner could afford to talk smart out the side of his mouth like that outsize cowboy up there in the picture, demand a 20 filter, yes the yankee blend brimful with flavour and ultra-smooth with king-of-kings-size filter. "And also." The jumbo coloured notice ordered him to come alive with cola.

Outside in the street, un-noticed, a neat black-and-white board prohibited him from spitting in a public space.

Squatting, bum warm on the kerb, feet in the gutter, knees well apart to show that a man had a steady job, just like those others from the site. He copied them, refused to drain the polystyrene cup but flung out the dregs in a freearm libation to the gods of plenty; for an instant a parabola of squandered soupmix hung curved across the street, then collapsed on the tarmac with plops of shredded cabbage and whitened shin-bones and bits of chicken skeleton. What the hell if there was only a single coin left over from the note.

He slurped down the last of the lukewarm strips of half-raw potato and folded back his sleeves in preparation; better another fold to make quite sure. Paper was something not to be trusted, it was the stuff of school reports and court orders and medicine you had to get from the clinic. Carefully, his hands nervous with suspicion, he smoothed out the crumpled newsprint and shook crumbs and salt-grains from the creases. Yes, paper it could be dangerous all right, but also with the right piece of paper, with the right letters on it and the right numbers, you could strike it hang of a lucky like old limpy with his winning tickets. Letter by letter, lips moving, he spelt out in a whisper all about the terrorists and accidents and things, there was this cabinet minister and the fashion queen on the one side.

Blow-all on the other side. Only some list of names and numbers next to. And right here in the middle, the name of this same crowd as was building here, whatever it was they were putting up. Across the top, what did it say? "Big Profit Clean-Up On Construction Opening Issue." Cleaning-up was a shit job but what was this hey? Just take a sight of this.

Respectfully, proud to be connected, he smoothed gentle fingers over Balfour's oil-soaked face. It was shiny, wet with grease, right there close in front of you, you could stroke it, such a friendly smile, not at all like that faraway frown from the boss by the office you hardly ever saw.

With pinching finger-tips he eased out the picture. Into the back pocket, next to the one coin and the one note, to show Ma tonight.

He was patting his seat to make quite sure it was still safe, when the whistle blew.

Back down again, into that hell-hole. Teacher said in Scripture how sinners, they got stuck down there in hell for ever. And those big-time crime merchants who crooked out the millions, they got put rest of their life in a cell with bars on door and window just like this cage here. Anyway, it was worth it, there'd be a decent pay-packet to take home every Friday, so long the Spoilers or the Jesters didn't grab. Pick up the bits cardboard and plastic bags and scrape the mud because that foreman and him up there, they were looking down on you, only not at all like in the picture, cross and tired.

"Dougie" said Balfour, "those few youngsters we took on, don't

66

bother to sign them on. We can lay them off tomorrow, just book them as sundry casual labour."

"Yes sir, they're all useless anyway. Takes a bit of a half-human rubbish to clear out the other rubbish. Look, crouching down on all fours like some baboon in a cage at the zoo."

"Anyone born into one of those townships" said Balfour, "they're trapped in a cage of circumstances till the day they die."

Dougie nodded. "That's just about the heart of the problem."

"And a heart, isn't that trapped in a cage of ribs? Protected maybe, but it can't escape. No man can escape from himself."

"It's the eternal soul of man" Dougie lay-preached, "that's what counts. The heart, it's only a pump."

"I'm worried about the pumps" said Balfour, "they're barely holding their own. Get him to try and draw the water towards the sump and break up those bits of wood. Then he can pass the timber offcuts through the mesh."

The foreman sniffed. "Manie and them, they should've cleared up their own mess after them when they'd finished with the shoring. Those bearers, I still say they should've been on edge. You think it'll hold?"

"At least for today. That's one reason we must start casting soon. I wish to hell that damned Inspector would come and give his go-ahead."

"I've seen better jobs" said Dougie. "The whole lot hanging on a few nails and a couple of bits of wire. Once anything starts coming down..."

"He'd be quite safe as long as he stayed inside. I'd go down myself if I thought there's any real risk. He'd be trapped for a while, but well protected by the top reinforcement. Look, here comes the chute."

Above them, dangling from the crane's jib, swung an assembly of scaffold pipes clamped round curved steel plates. They waved it into position, no, a bit to the side, a bit more, the concrete would slide down it into the foundation, right. It dropped, shuddered, settled as the wire rope went slack, the top secure on the embankment, the bottom pointing at the centre of the excavation. Dougie clambered up and freed the hook which swung in the wind like a question mark above their heads.

"You don't think a bit nearer the mixer maybe?" asked the foreman.

"No, that's just perfect. Remember the concrete will be very much on the dry side, it won't run like porridge. We must keep a tight quality control, watch that team there at the mixer when we start."

"I just hope you've got the level right."

Balfour shrugged. "That's what it says on the latest plan they gave us. I presume they've made up their minds at last.''

Width times breadth times depth equals volume, allow an extra two percent for compaction by vibrator, so many gauges of concrete, so many sacks of cement to be brought from the shed, at two-and-threequarter no say three to be safe minutes each, so many hours, better test the floodlamps.

They parted, Balfour to the Inspector's site office, Dougie dashing from the tangle of cables at the switch-box to the dust of the cement shed, to the gloom and chaos of the tool-store where he dragged out the two medium vibrators.

The youngster looked up to see if they noticed how hard he was working. Gone.

Time for a break. He tore off the cellophane wrapping that preserved the vacuum-packed goodness of fine rich Virginia and tossed it behind him to the area he had already cleared. A flicked match followed—there were heftier chunks of wood they'd spot from up there. And hang... what was this? Who'd want to chuck a half-full bottle... it wasn't water, too yellow, and why piss into a bottle when it was easy to even crap there in the corner like this morning?

The label, smart hey, a real tit of a smart, they called those things on the big house gables. Sniffed more like vinegar than piss, but the taste of the pick of the vintage, fucking awful.

Still, if you got stuck into your job in a real rough place like the building there was a way to do it, like you could see on Friday nights there by the clump bushes behind the smuggle-house. Whole bottle in one go and this only a half. The empty, there in the corner they'd never look. Those chunks wood, heavy, even the small ones, they weighed, not so easy to hold. Not so easy to see neither with all criss-cross irons just over the head couldn't lift face up to look proper. Soup and flop chips, the grease, maybe bad or something. He up there, he wouldn't be cross if one of his men, if a grown-up got sick. He'd smile, in the picture he looked, he looked like what? In the back pocket, the button, the button was, no here, pull, no fuck it, blast it, that bloody coin, fuck that bloody coin, it must go roll itself under the bottom irons, over there, a little more, crawl a bit like a baby couldn't stand, stop and breathe deep, if only a bugger could see proper there was all those hook affairs on the end of the irons bent over. Oh shit, oh shit, oh ma, ma, the terrible pain, the pain and the sick just over the eye here on the side. Flat hand against helped nothing but no blood so couldn't be that bad, just a little rest, under that whatyoucall stuck over couldn't see under from the top and he wouldn't mind, just a few minutes rest, he would forgive the sin, if you worked that hard then you deserved to rest in a bit of peace.

Crying with the helpless sobs of a newly-born, he tried to crawl, crept in little reptile wriggles towards the earth embankment and nestled, a womb-curled foetus, against the primeval ooze and slime and ordure from which he had evolved.

Burger sat slumped over his table, staring at the coy nude on the calendar.

"I was sure" said Balfour, "one of those big induced-flow pumps would've been able to control the water-table. Now two of them can barely hold it. If we can't start casting now-now-now... You must come and have a look, everything's okay."

Morose, the Inspector looked heavier and flabbier than usual. Strangely silent. Only a sigh.

"Mister Burger, please you look upset about something. Have I said anything? Or any of the men?"

Slowly, the head turned to answer him; the movement appeared to twist the thoughts in it from some private curse to a public one. "Well, so what if I am befucked? What's that to you?"

"I'm sorry." Balfour hesitated. "You seemed on top of it all earlier and now..."

"And when did I say I had the needle in for you? Or your crowd for that matter? There's some of them like that foreman of yours, Dougie, or Manie as well, there's some as is even quite respectable."

"I hate casting at night under floodlamps" said Balfour. He tried to read the time upside down on the Inspector's watch.

"It's a bugger hey." Burger tried to shake pain and confusion out of his head. "You battle like all merry hell to get the one thing right, and then... nothing doing. Not a damn."

"It'll be easier" said Balfour, "once we're over this hurdle of a main column base."

"You talk about hurdles" Burger answered, patting the bulge of his safari jacket. "You won't believe it but true as what I'm sitting here now, I used to clock fourteen point six for the hurdles. But the wife, couldn't get her to run, not a stuff, not two steps, for her only the field events. She chucked a beaut of a javelin. One year, there by the provincial championships, I'm telling you she would've..."

"It'll take at least five hours" said Balfour. "You know we need your official go-ahead.''

"Now I haven't run for years, not even this latest what they call it now? Jogging. You talk about running, it reminds me... once there's this bugger he hadn't crapped for a whole month so he grabs a bottle castor oil glurk-glurk-glurk all in one go and he starts running... no, forget it, I'm not really up to spoiling a good story when you're not in a mood to tell it properly.''

The foreman hovered at the doorway. He tapped with the respect of a court retainer hesitating outside the throne room.

"I'm coming Dougie" Balfour whispered. "Go and make absolutely sure everything's ready." To the Inspector he spoke with emphasis on every word and a more emphatic pause between each one. "Mister Burger, may I remind you the contractor has a certain right to organise his ....."

"Wrong is right." Burger banged a fist on the table and pencils rattled. "Organise a place properly" he sneered. "You spent all those months there by Alexandra and you think that place is properly organised? Man..." He gripped the table edge. Knuckles tensed white in the red beef of his hands. "The child... the child, it's in there.''

"I'm sorry" Balfour murmured. "I'm sorry" he repeated with all the embarrassment of a sincere sympathiser.

"And in Ward D. Dammit man, I ask you, did it have to be D ward, did it have to?''

"I didn't know." Balfour patted the Inspector's shoulder. "I never guessed.''

"Now you know why the wife, why she carries on like that. Gin usually, otherwise brandy, anything goes. Every night, till two three in the morning. And they got her at last, they grabbed her there by Woolworths. With the things stuck half in half out her bag. Must've been watching out for her. Man, you can't try swipe things when you're three-quarter way arseholes pissed, now can you? And still hope to get away with it.''

He slapped the table, then turned his face up towards Balfour and tried to smile. "With another royal blue tracksuit. Another one, she's got a whole bloody wardrobe full of royal blue tracksuits. It's all for the child, she tries to give them, nearly every visiting day she tries but the child... man, it can't even hardly walk properly.''

Bent-spined, Burger panted with the exhaustion of a defeated athlete after a marathon. "They take them out the ward on a Tuesday and every second Friday in the summer, in a long line, make them hang on hand-in-hand with those attendants on both sides. Down to the flower bed, twice round it, then back again. Now they've laid a charge. I tried to talk to them, and then to the Prosecutor. Nothing doing.''

Pools of shadow flooded over the site. The sun was drowning itself in black and silver waves that the south-easter swept in a pall of wind-driven cloud across the mountain face. The ravines drew more purple into their veins and the pine forests lower down flourished to a darker green. A single gust rattled a loose sheet in the Inspector's roof. From far, far away across the open site came a few shouts, a metal-on-metal hollow clang, then silence, followed by a pattering of sand and grit against the steel-framed window.

Dougie unblended himself from the shadows and stood in the door-way, tapping his foot impatiently, drawing whistling breaths between clen-ched teeth. "When?" he hissed.

"It's the innocent who catch it" said Burger. "The really bad, if they're bad enough, they always get away with it. A child, if it's not bright in this world of ours, then it's better off dead.''

Balfour squeezed his shoulder. "Don't say a thing like that. Don't ever wish death of a defenceless child.''

"When?" Dougie repeated.

"Now" Balfour answered softly, then firmly he commanded "Get cracking.'

Outside the Inspector's site office Balfour turned up the collar of his windbreak and trembled, more from excitement than from cold. He felt the wind tease his hair and his exposed ears tingled when a few loose stones rattled in the hollow mixer drum as it started revolving. A thump, followed by a dull rumble; another thump, the sound deepened to a sloshy grind as stones, sand, cement and water churned together in exact proportion.

He crossed the site to watch the first gauge of concrete spill from the mixer into the crane bucket. Good, a stiff mound, anyone who knew anything about concrete could see it was good, it had that luscious half-earth half-chemical moist aroma, grey-green, a delight. He signalled and the crane's hoist motor sang out an electric chord of power, up, up; the jib swung over with another motor's tune and he watched the bucket drop, drop, halt jarring just above the chute. A jerk on the release lever and down slumped a solid ton of it. Beautiful.

Again, again, the cycle was repeated. Behind the mixer the loading team was working up a good sweat, they always shouted when stirred up at the beginning of a big cast. Who didn't love a challenge when you knew you were going to win? He waved to Dougie, who answered with a thumbs-up.

A small knot of spectators watched from a gap in the hoarding which now screened the site from the street. The urchins were all at supper except one little fellow who gaped from behind his mother's hip, the grey man with his dog and Naidoo the Indian shopkeeper who still dropped in every day just to see how things were getting on you know.

Four minutes ten seconds per cycle, slow. Four fifteen, four ten again. Not good enough.

Burger dragged himself across the site with a curt nod to the grey man as he passed. Chin on chest, he sheltered in the company of Balfour and Dougie near the mixer. They watched the loading team tip in their wheelbarrows with guts-wrenching heaves and grunts, then rest panting for a few seconds and start their frantic shovelling again, again, again.

Four minutes five seconds. "Too slow" said Balfour, "the team's unbalanced, there's one man short on the sand."

"I know" Dougie answered, "I had to pull one off from there. One of those young loafers must've just floated off into thin air. Concrete, at the first sign of hard work... the lot you get today, all the same."

"Don't worry." Balfour laughed with the joy of a problem solved. "I've got an idea."

"Yes." Dougie spat out his disgust. "I've also got an idea comes pay-out on Friday he'll be there all right whining for his back-pay."

"And if he never comes to light again..." Balfour shrugged. "So what? Look, if we use the big vibrator instead of the two medium ones, that'll save one man. It'll do the trick."

He stepped forward amongst his men, beckoned one come here, another go there, re-arranged the team with pushes in their backs and by grasping biceps and leading others to new positions. Dust grated between his teeth when he clenched them.

Three minutes twenty. Better, Three fifteen. They were settling down but wouldn't be able to keep it up at that rate till the end.

Again three fifteen. Again. The loading, mixing, transporting and placing cycles all balanced. No bottlenecks. Over and over and over, the process seemed to run automatically, carried from gauge to gauge by its own momentum.

Three twenty-five. The men's strength was fading with the light. Their brown faces no longer distinguished one toiling body from the other, all had become part of the dark. Only white eyeballs rolled with fatigue and teeth flashed in grimaces of effort.

"Lights on" Balfour called to his foreman, and suddenly the shadowy places became black as glare brought a hard and theatrical unreality to the tableau at the mixer. Motes of cement dust spiralled up the beams towards the floodlamps.

Burger blinked. Now he was exposed. He twisted away his face from the activity as though every hurrying man still had time and energy and interest enough to read the hurt on it.

Balfour slapped him lightly on the shoulder. "No stories?" he quipped. "Come on."

As the crane swung another load into place Burger too changed direction towards all who could hear him. "Listen, you heard the latest one?" A mimic of himself, a plucker of sleeves, he played himself into his role under the lamps, slapped his thigh, bellowed the punch-line and repeated it with the forced gaiety of a circus clown.

Balfour disengaged himself from a guffaw that rattled hollow as the momentarily empty mixer drum. He joined Dougie at the excavation and they peered over the edge.

"Can't see very much down there" said the foreman. "I'll run out a lead-light."

"There should be enough in by now to absorb that big one." Balfour supervised the vibrator team as they lowered the long flexible cylinder into the column base.

A high-pitched whine; the concrete jellied and contracted, air bubbles rose and popped. The earth quivered and from the soles of his boots to the top of his head Balfour thrilled at knowing the whole suburb would pause in the middle of the evening meal to ask 'what's that?'

"Did you say something?" Dougie yelled, and pointed the lamp downwards.

"What?" Hand behind ear.

"I thought I heard... "

The lumpy surface of the concrete levelled itself; free water floated in pools. Enough. Switch off. Silence, but their half-deafened ears still hummed.

"It goes right through you" said Balfour, "into your very core. With a, like a scream, it sounds almost human."

"Did the trick all right" the foreman noted. "Squeezed the last drop of air out. D'you notice how much more bubbles it brought up than with two mediums, and we didn't even miss him."

"Who in hell ever would?" Balfour took the lamp and played the beam backward and forward across the excavation. In the corners and under the chute deeper shadows seemed to move and squirm in anguish as the light tried in vain to explore their secrets. "Dougie" he asked, "you're a church-going man. Tell me, is it right to think that down there is a part of me, of all of us, preserved for all eternity?"

The chute shocked and shuddered under another load as Burger joined them.

"Looks a bit funny to me" he said, "but so long as you're happy."

"It's that big vibrator" Balfour explained, "it brings up even more laitance than usual."

"Laitance" Burger repeated. "What's that?"

"The scum that always rises to the top of concrete."

"Oh that." The Inspector sniffed. "That's fuckall, it always does."

"It does look a bit different" Dougie observed. "Somehow greener and more slimy than usual. It must be the light."

"You talk about scum rising to the top." A Burger joke was about to be launched. "You can say that again, in more ways than one."

Another hour, another seventeen gauges. Balfour zipped up his windbreak against the night chill as again the vibrator's wail keened through the empty streets with a howl of lament.

Twelve left to finish it. Balfour strode amongst his exhausted crew and held up only six fingers to show "six to go". When these had been done he repeated the trick, misled and led them to the point where the team at the column base stood up and waved the cross-arm signal to show "enough."

A full bucket dangled from the crane's jib while the men crowded, weary, round the tap at the lean-to outside the tool store.

"I can't make it out" said Balfour. "I can't for the life of me understand it. There's a whole gauge left over. Now where in heaven or in hell can we dump it?"

He turned to the Inspector. In a conqueror's stance, feet planted on the earth as firmly as the concrete he had planted in it, hands on hips, he declared "Mister Inspector, you can tell your Department the whole structure will be resting on a pretty solid foundation."

VII

The great central column and its satellites poked row after row of rectangular fingers above the corrugated iron hoarding that surrounded the site. Grey stood proud and plumb over buckled rust. Near the pre-fab offices and sheds a gap in the metal sheets drew trailers and delivery vans and tiptrucks with spinning tyres that scattered grit and dust as they bumped over the gravel access path; a stream of material poured on to the site, was dumped and stacked more or less at random, then re-arranged in planned and measured order. Check and re-check with dumpy level, theodolite and tape; refer to plans and specification and schedules; arrange and record men and their skills in labour-hours; deploy and maintain machines with capacities rated to do the job. From the outside, there was a glimpse of figures, some hurrying, some dawdling; a discord of whining motors and shouts and bangs, thumps of heavy weights dropping, clangs, clatters, never the sound of the quiet voice that tried to control a force that had generated its own momentum.

Time itself became constricted by tightening rounds of phone-calls, calculation, reports, meetings where he fidgeted, kept glancing at his watch and pressing the Senior Inspector or Architect or Consulting Engineer for decisions, decisions. Even his tours of inspection were hurried into a series of rushes from column to basement excavation to footing walls. At least the brickies could be trusted; with the flicked wrists of experts they smeared out precise dollops of mortar and settled each facebrick firmly on its bed, edge exactly level with the taut nylon line.

"We'll be in the soup" said Balfour, "if the other loads don't match but we couldn't wait. They said the next kiln tomorrow, which means the week after."

The structure grew on its own as he nursed it with all the devotion of a fussing parent, force-fed it with supplies and labour and finance and plant—his own children he saw each evening at the dinner-table, then coffee in the study and struggles with reluctant problems behind a closed door. Work even at the week-ends, with his stress bearing the extra load of having to be polite to in-laws over Sunday lunch. He forgot to comment on the new mohair curtains in the lounge.

One morning as he parked in the shadow of the tower-crane that dominated him he sensed a difference in the surrounding streets. No longer was the neighbourhood part of a coloured suburb from which a few families had been moved, but now mostly abandoned buildings where a remnant of inhabitants still sheltered .

Days? Weeks? Later as he crossed the street from his site, his realm, to the take-away he noticed that the foreign territory outside the hoarding had become more foreign. Spec builders were tearing out rotting window-frames to leave gaps like missing teeth. Walls that had flaked and peeled with strips of tired dirt now dazzled out a 10-year guarantee of sparkle white. Venus posed in a pre-cast niche, Roman urns bloomed pretty with geraniums and brass knockers happily polished the sun. Across the road carefully groomed sub-agents in tailored costumes led hesitant couples up the paths of compact gardens, through patios, into the temptation of character and atmosphere and an ample bond for any holder of a credit card.

And over there, half a block away, a corner shop had re-opened, a one-rack boutique with a shelf of hand-made dolls, in the window scotch-taped posters of pottery classes and vegetarian cooking.

Most evenings Balfour stayed on the site long past the knock-off whistle, to persuade or trick or order certain teams into overtime. "This section of basement retaining wall, it must be cast now so we can strip the shuttering on Monday and carry on. Otherwise we're stuck."

Then as he drove away he noticed the pride of new home-owners watering their freshly planted hydrangeas. Under a glass-fibre roof, a car-washing bridegroom bustled with energy, the excitement of a promising middle-management career reflected in sea-blue surfer's eyes, his surf-board firmly clamped to the roof-rack. Through a replaced sash-window, varnish glossy, Balfour saw the aproned bride tidy her blond hair-do in an open-plan kitchen.

Hour after day after week behind the hoarding—with curses and noise and dirt, the massed tons of bricks, steel, concrete had to be pressed and moulded into the form of a structure. Girl-mothers wheeled their high-sprung prams past the access gap and turned away from all those uncouth men and that horrible mess. The sheer brutality of it. Rather re-arrange the fringes on the canopy and exchange breathless tips about absolute bargains in yellow-wood kists and antique carriage lamps.

Sometimes Balfour overheard them compare dailies with live-ins.

"She's inherited an absolute gem from her mother."

"And how does the gem take to a change of madam?"

"Well, you know she's become practically one of the family. Besides that older generation, for them a non-white is hardly human at all."

A delivery scooter, 'Pharmacy—Urgent', parked at the gap. Foot on the kerb, tune through the teeth, the driver watched roll after roll of orange plastic sheeting being offloaded and dragged across the access path to the storage shed.

Balfour charged down the steps outside his office. "Dougie" he yelled, "for Christsake, see they pick the stuff up and carry it." He stormed at the brown faces gaping at him. "What happens if there's a nail on the ground? You want tears in it? There mustn't be so much as a mark. Come, two by two, both sides. Bend your knees, don't use your back to lift. Ready? Uh-huh. Come, next one."

The scooter dawdled away. A young mother hesitated in its place. "Excuse me."

"You got hold of the details yet" asked the foreman, "for those GPO inlets?"

Balfour shook his head. "That crowd's impossible. And by next Tuesday we'll have to cast in the conduit pipes... nothing, I can't get sense out of them."

"Then what about the waterproof sheeting? We daren't cut later, that's just asking for trouble. It'll leak like an absolute sieve if we don't allow for."

"Excuse me" she called again, with a schoolgirl's lisp.

Impossible to ignore. Balfour pointed a thumb at his own heart and drew a nod from a head of sun-bleached strands.

"Can I help you?"

It was the way he said it that flickered her eyelashes and lifted her pomegranate swellings with a gosh of surprise—so very much the gentleman, such polite manners with his head bowed in attention and the voice, really educated—charming too and working in a place like that; it just goes to show, you never can tell.

She moved her ringed fingers from the bar of the pram to renounce the role of mother by fussing her pleats into the more attractive flare that fitted the private secretary or junior teacher she had been. "I hope I'm not disturbing?"

"Not at all."

That little bit crooked smile—fabulous, but weary. "I've been meaning to ask, but whenever I pass you're always so busy."

"There's a lot to do. Yes?"

"Yes, I suppose there must be. You'll think me stupid or something, but..."

"Not at all." Balfour expelled from his lungs the fumes of petrol and sweaty men and too many cigarettes, to inhale the softness of her perfume.

"It's just that I wondered." A loose-collared blouse exposed shoulder-blades that invited a line of little bites along the ridge. "You see." She pointed at the notice-board displayed above them. The sun warmed to gold the down on her forearm, blue veins marbled her bicep and the armpit was shaved to nudity. "It says there 'for Coloured Development' but this is now a white area isn't it? When we bought, the agent, she said..."

"I don't know."

"Oh." Pretty pert-lips rounded to a void circled by crinkled lipstick. "You see, we've sunk everything we've got into... our last bean. Even had to borrow from my folks."

"Be careful."

"You should only see our place. It's got such potential. We've got all sorts of plans for later."

The voice of male experience sounded grave. "Plenty of these cottages, I can see it's only the pretty wallpaper holding together a basically unsound structure. All very attractive for a year or so."

"It's a real shame." She too could be serious. "How these others had to move, but if a place is standing empty in any case. You know, this housing shortage, it's simply terrible." She tinkled the little silver bell of a giggle. "Besides, we've already signed on the dotted line," then remembered the pram. "It's just that I wouldn't fancy her growing up amongst, you know."

"A girl?" Balfour leant over to inspect the mound of pink bunny blankets under a plastic mobile.

"Only the undesirable sort of element" she said. "We've even got some coloured friends, well, not really, more like acquaintances actually, from my husband's work. He's in insurance.

"I really don't know" said Balfour, "why they should site a coloured community complex precisely here. I'm only building the place."

She waved to a friend across the road while saying "Listen" to hold her audience captive, then turned her blonde-fringed and only slightly buck-toothed face to announce "Well, it doesn't make sense to me."

Balfour managed to hold back his words in time. It would have been the third time he had confessed that he did not know. Instead he said "Excuse me" and deserted her to seek certainty in the chaos and discipline, the music and ear-assaulting noise of the basement parking-bay excavation.

He nodded in passing to the grey man watching from his usual post and quick-marched around a stack of bricks. Burger intercepted him, grabbed his arm and hurried him back to the access point.

"Look, look" said Burger. "Man, but I fancy that small one there in the pink slacks. See it? Just note that little arse of hers, how it goes oops-oops the way she walks. Shit, it's bad for a bugger's blood just to watch. Hey, hey." He clutched Balfours's arm and the fingers squeezed it to pain. The Inspector's polished brogues danced a tap of agitation on the gravel path as he panted "Just take a sight of... that other one there in the mini-skirt bending over the pram. Man, she's got next to sweet blow-all on underneath, just a tiny triangle only so small, beats me why they even bother at all, you can still see all the hairs and everything."

"All comes off the lingerie counter at Woolworths" said Balfour.

"Woolworths" repeated Burger. "Man, that one word, it keeps coming back to cut me right in here, like a knife, it's still going to kill me, I just don't know any more what way to turn." His nod to the grey man was curt and sour.

They watched him stoop to pat and fondle his Alsatian's neck, then straighten himself up as each young woman passed. He seemed to force his dentures into the shape of a smile, fangs wet with saliva, and to every chestnut and sun-lite and golden-glo head he lifted his grey hat. And from every face that was turned away, from every upturned nose, he stooped again to the savage companionship of the dog's snarls. "Shut up" he snarled back to it.

"You know him?" Balfour whispered to the Inspector.

"Know him? Who, Botha? I'm bloody well related to the old so-and-so. Sort of. But don't blame me for that. Look, hey, now what was it I was going to say? Yes, those shutter panels you're using there on the basement wall, are they oiling them or something? I noticed like kind of dirty you could say."

"Something new on the market we're trying" said Balfour as they strolled towards the temporary sheds and offices. "A shutter-release agent. Seems to work, the concrete's stripping absolutely perfect. At least it does no harm."

Burger screwed up his eyes in puzzlement. "A what? Man, I wouldn't fancy it one bit if those walls started leaking.''

''That's got nothing to do with keeping out external moisture'' Balfour explained. ''It's the Hyperlastic sheeting's the problem. I hope to hell that Postal bloke turns up this time, he's already half-an-hour late. I must get away early because I won't be here tomorrow.''

Burger hesitated, poked him in the ribs and winked. ''Girl-friend hey? Take the whole day over it?''

It was difficult, but essential, to smile responsively. ''There's a meeting at Head Office. I've got to fly up.''

Dougie rushed between them. ''Now the fur's going to fly.'' His overall shook with little vibrations of fury. ''That new electric impact drill... '' The force spat into each syllable served to describe the machine. There was no need to complete the sentence.

''The big one?'' Balfour sighed. ''It cost a bloody fortune and the insurance won't.''

''Manie doesn't look after his things. It's one of that...''

Now Manie thumped towards them. ''He mustn't come try blame me. I didn't even have it last, it was there in the store...''

Each explanation was interrupted by an accusation. Always it was some 'other man' who haunted a site to dissolve tools, make supplies evaporate, lose essentials and mark out a trail of burnt-out motors. Five hundred down the drain.

''So there you're hiding.'' The fog-horn bellow of the Chief Superintendent (Building) from the Postal Central Depot boomed across the basement excavation. The giant crossed the site with a few seven-league strides. Behind him, strung in an obedient line, stepped five grey-flannelled assistants each with a manila folder tucked under an arm. A florid face, heavy with bone, hung over Balfour's head and blotted out the mountain. Above inflated jowls, a scarlet nose coarse with open pores and a maze of blue veins. The pig-eyes twinkled. ''So it's you after all. Man, what's all this fuss about?''

Over a handshake vigorous as an exercise, Balfour murmured ''I'll order a replacement'' to dismiss his two men and followed the others into Burger's office. The Super throned himself on the stool, palms on knees, while the five assistants stood so silently against the walls the mere possibility of any ever speaking was precluded.

''The problem's where the basement waterproofing membrane is pierced by those conduit pipes for the GPO inlet'' announced a worried Balfour.

80

"Coffee" answered the Super. "You come on to any other job and there's the coffee ready waiting. Milk, sugar, the lot."

"There's a take-away across the road, I'll send..."

A hand of oversize beefsteak waved out a signal of dismissal. "Don't bother" he said in a way to imply the opposite.

"Unless we know exactly" Balfour continued. "Full details, then we could pre-cast a block with PVC centre-bulb waterstop and..."

"Cake." Multi-decibels rocked the cramped pre-fab office with a Richter-scale tremble. "When you strike it lucky it just happens to be somebody's birthday, there's the cake as well." He twisted round on his stool to beam at his assistants. Five blank faces stared straight ahead. Now frowning, he leaned forward and confronted Balfour. "Listen my friend, let's face it, you're just chancing your arm. What you're really after is for me to go sticking my neck out. Now you tell me something for a change. Exactly how many telephone exchanges is it more or less that you've built so far?"

"That's precisely what I want to know." Balfour burned cold with desperate patience. "Must the basement of a training complex be treated the same as the cable vault of a telephone exchange?"

"You haven't answered my question." The Super copied Balfour's tone to show that two could play the game.

"What question? I'm asking the question of how we're expected..."

"How many exchanges?"

Balfour counted on his fingers. "Five. No, there was Table View as well, six. No, seven, if you count the additions to... "

"Seven." The Super nodded. "Seven. Let's even say six-and-a-half to be on the safe side. And you're trying to tell me you still don't know how... no man, no, have a heart. You're not going to get me to swallow that one."

"Then I take it" said Balfour "that we're to stick to the standard type lay-out. I think I've still got some copies of the detail filed away with the old job records. Will you please confirm... "

"Now when did I say you must use an exchange cable-vault detail?" A finger wagged under Balfour's nose. "Trying to put words into my mouth."

"Mr Burger" appealed Balfour, "you're supposed to see that.."

The Inspector shrunk back into a corner. "No" he protested. "You leave me out of this. I'm Community Co-Operation, I've got fuckall to do with Postals."

The Super paused at the doorway. "Go ahead by all means and use the standard details if you insist on having your own way. I'll be the last one to stop you but let's get the one thing quite straight, it's off your own bat and don't ever try make out I said so." The five assistants moved to follow their leader.

They listened to him pass prolonged judgements on the rugby tour, on how to catch the biggest fish and the best way to do chops on an open fire.

His handshake of farewell was even heartier than his greeting. "That's one hell of a place I see you're building here. Enjoy it hey."

For a moment Balfour drooped over the table in his office, head in hands, before phoning home.

"Nothing special" he said. "I might be back a bit late, the three of you eat without me, don't wait. I've still got to do the bank, auditor, the usual."

"You sound tense" she remarked. "Problems?"

"Of course problems, they're my bread-and-butter, without problems for me to solve I wouldn't be here. Doctors need the sick and Lifeliners their neurotics."

"Relax, learn to take it as it comes. I've also got... "

"Not that it's anything that couldn't be set right with a bottle of whisky put into the right hands, only I don't play the game according to those rules. And I don't want to know how many porcelain dishes Nanny has dropped today."

"For tomorrow, should I put the key of my chastity belt in the bottom right-hand corner or will you keep it in your wallet? By the way, Boyboy nearly howled when he heard we weren't going to the airport. Hullo? Are you still there?"

"I'm coming, I'm coming. Sorry, an interruption. No, it's really not practical. First flight up and last one back, I'll simply leave the car in the parking lot. Yes, I'm coming. 'Bye."

The knot of sullen labourers refused to look him in the eye, rather stared at their feet, their answers mumbles of resentment.

"There's nothing wrong" Balfour coaxed them, "in taking off shoes and socks. Look I'll do so myself. This whole place." He waved an arm to define the extent of the basement. "It's got to be tanked out with this plastic stuff. One little tear and... water. So what if someone has a nail in his shoe? Or tramps on a stone? All that work for nothing. Come. I don't mind going barefoot." Coy as virgins at a river pool, the men took as long as possible to pull off their boots. Balfour led them down to where Dougie was already fidgeting impatiently with trouser legs rolled

82

to below his knees. They showed how to spread out the rolls, then stood back to watch grown men hesitant with shame.

"There's a couple of trouble-makers amongst them" advised the foreman. "I'm telling you sir, you mustn't swallow cheek from them. Once they feel they're getting their own way, they'll be all over you."

"I think it's cultural" said Balfour. "Professors can afford to stroll around in open sandals but for them shoes are a symbol of sophistication."

"Hey" Burger shouted down from the top of the embankment. "I reckon I should've brought my bathing cossie along with me but how's about laying on a few dozen bikini girls?" He slapped his thigh.

Balfour scrambled up to stand beside him. "That payment certificate" he said. "Have you filled it in yet, the bank will want to know. It should have been in yesterday already."

"Yesterday" Burger repeated with the hiss of a deflating tyre. Limp, he hung on to Balfour's arm and squeezed the elbow. "Yesterday the summons arrived. They've set down a date. Long way ahead but that's something to look forward to, isn't it?"

Not smoking, his seat-belt clipped, Balfour waited for the take-off.

At the start of holidays this had been the exciting moment to hold hands and pity the blasé businessmen idly turning pages of the Financial Times or skimming through confidential reports. He ticked off another item in the Schedule of Quantities open on his lap. Foundation brickwork virtually complete, say 90%; so many thousand facebricks for superstructure cavity walls...

A thrust of power, vibrating momentum pressed him back against the seat-rest. The jet soared above midget cars crawling along a toy freeway, over a pattern of red roofs impersonal as a lay-out plan below retracting flaps. The wings settled to the shape of routine; the captain's drawling ritual, a tray off a trolley, polite remarks to left and right, descent on schedule.

This aircraft was still the same in either of the towns, its passengers unchanged, the terminal buildings identical. Could distance really have been so easily demolished? Briefcase-heavy, he drifted through the Arrivals lounge.

An overgroomed young woman minced towards him, each step a feat of balance. "Mr Balfour? I'm the lassie from PubRelPro" she elocuted from lipstick prominent as capital letters. "Your Public Relations and Promotion hostess for today's little do. Stay right here, don't dare move or I'll scream." She chirped and twittered while gathering her brood about her as the various flights homed in. "Ten minute delay on three-oh-seven, bugger it" she announced, lighting a gold-tipped filter with a competent flick of the wrist.

Competent too was the way she weaved the mini-bus through double-lane traffic as deftly as she weaved double-meanings into every single line of patter. With scarlet talons aflutter, she pointed out the firm's phallic skyscraper erections on the sky-line.

Thirty floors up in the Conference Centre, Balfour followed others along a deep-pile corridor where the air-conditioning was scented, into a teak board-room with a buffet side table more elaborate than the agenda-sheets and notepads at each seat. He sought a lonely corner and looked down through a plate of tinted glass to ventilation shafts veined with drain-pipes and tiny yards cluttered with spilling dirtbins, piles of coal and cardboard, and a rusty bicycle frame with a single buckled wheel.

"Come, come, you must meet the others" invited the chairman.

Balfour pointed downwards. "From here you can see what really makes a city", and suffered himself to be eased into a round of handshakes and murmurs.

"Gentlemen, have you all partaken? Should we make a start? I see Item Number One is listed as 'Chairman's Keynote Address', but all I want to say is..."

He read from typewritten sheets in a monotonous whine. After forty minutes Balfour glanced down to his pad and saw that the only note he had taken was "Project corporate image."

Drone after drone, with hesitations at the longer words. In mid-sentence the lassie jerked her mask of cosmetics round the door and interrupted with "the toast in ordinary bubbly or a sparkling red? The red would show up better on the press takes."

The chairman sucked in his lower lip to consider the matter with due regard. The safe conservative, he advised "The usual, the usual."

"And just the one round of applause after the announcement and another at the grand finale, or you'd prefer to be interrupted?"

"Just the one would be sufficient I think, but if there should happen to... Maybe a few... spon... spontaneous, wouldn't do much harm would it? Where was I? Oh yes. Thus the induction of an accelerated cash-flow is an essential parameter..."

Tea-break in the Venetian Room. Gondolier waiters glided trolleys between visitors striving desperately to seem at ease. Into each strained pause all in turn forced remarks designed to impress.

"Somebody must be paying for all this" said Balfour. "Is it the poor bloody shareholders or is it me?"—offhand, flicked lightly up to the ceiling, to the Grand Canal and palazzos of the room in general.

His question seemed to hover, be kept suspended by cups half-raised in hesitation till the chairman's "Quite, quite" pierced the silence and the incident fell dead.

Back round the table, constantly alert to appear interested, they endured a silver-templed economist from Federal Financial Management Consultants. "Gentlemen" he baritoned, "let me put it to you in terms that professionals with your somewhat technical backgrounds would appreciate—a structure of confidence fabricated on a solid foundation of liquid resources."

Luncheon in the Roman Senate Chamber, Guests of Honour and Directors at the Head Table and the hundred other places formal with carelessly scattered roses and a feature menu crowned with the company badge. Starched serviettes were folded into the shape of tower-cranes.

"Ladies and Gents" began the chairman. "...and in conclusion it is both my pleasure and my honour and my privilege to bid you all to charge your glasses and rise and join with me in toasting a resolution passed at this morning's meeting of your Board. The declaration of a special interim dividend..."

At the back, the hostess from PubRelPro jumped up, held her hands above her head, and clapped. Press photographers crouched and jostled one another before the chairman's smile, crying "Hold it" and "Again please" and "Turn a bit to the left", before blinding the room. Reporters scribbled on their pads.

Balfour turned to his co-director (Northern Area) at his left. "I can't remember" he said, "that we voted on a resolution."

"They say a four-page spread" was the answer, "in next week-end's Business Supplement."

The Director (South-East and Midlands) at Balfour's right whispered into his ear above the applause. "What's this he said about a resolution or something?"

Menus were passed along the table to be autographed. Hot competed with cold in a baked Alaska and Curaçao with Havana.

Now bloated, drowsy with wine, they trailed back down the corridor and heard the chairman introduce the experts before excusing himself. At the door he added "There's some kind of portfolio or what-have-you been put together. All the brochures and pamphlets and so on, with full transcripts of this afternoon's. And a sort of frame affair for your signed

85

copy of the menu plus some other forms and things to fill in.''

Graphs of projected expansion climbed up a portable screen, their slopes propped by the proviso of pursuing an aggressive marketing strategy. Slides showed neat arrangements of coloured blocks and arrows for channels of staff communication, and an Associate Professor from the Graduate School of Business explained that construction contracts should be analysed along critical paths rather than merely built. Words concussed them, the wall clock was surely slow.

Afternoon tea in the Florentine Room for a dozen dull men glancing at their watches. If the mixer wasn't turning by now they'd never manage to finish the day's cast. And had Manie remembered to put in extra stays this time and Dougie to check the Hyperlastic sheet for tears and to block out for the cable inlets?

Balfour dragged his body back to its boardroom seat. More words poured into his ears, his eyes were glazed by tabulations. His mouth accepted a few dainties of supper snack and his head shook to decline the caberet—his flight was the longest.

A silent hostess drove him back to the airport, handed him her business card and left him with a grimace and a cursory ''You'll be all right?''

On the last flight of the day the cabin staff was too weary to comply with the regulation welcome; his wife sucked her husband into home and marriage with a full-lip kiss.

''It's funny'' she said, ''how I've been missing you, knowing you're so far away, different if you'd been for so long on the site near here.''

''Any messages? Little ones asleep?'' he grunted and slumped into his favourite chair in the lounge. ''Oh hell, dammit.''

''What's the matter?''

He clicked open his briefcase and flipped through its contents. ''Must've left it on the plane. Doesn't matter, only a collection of junkmail. Could've shown you the menu, even reading it's enough to make anyone want to throw up. So over-lavish. Waste of a whole day, some cheap publicity stunt, what did they need me for.?''

''But you're so capable.'' She shifted some ornament a fraction and stood back, ear on shoulder, to admire the arrangement's balance. ''Not only the kitchen, look what you've done in the garden, the pergola and the trellis as well.''

''Anyone phone? Anything urgent? Otherwise I'm going off to bed.''

''Nothing urgent.'' Settee, rocker and easy-chair, she jerked round the room plumping up the cushions. ''Nothing that can't wait until tomorrow.''

''Come on, what is it? I can see there's something.''

"Nothing. Why?" she asked, suddenly static, eyes too open. "What makes you say a thing like that? He phoned, that's all. I said nothing important."

"Who phoned?"

"His majesty, that's all."

Balfour closed his briefcase and stood up. "What the hell for? I was with him practically the whole day. That's nonsense."

"Just I should remind you, you were in some meeting or something, he didn't want to disturb you. Something about chasing up the monthly payments in time."

"Next thing he'll remind me to toilet-train myself. And his trip? He talked about his trip did he, because the whole day, not a mention."

"Not really." She stroked her husband's sleeve. "Well, just the once I seem to remember, sort of in passing. You know..."

Balfour shook himself free and paused at the door. "There's something not genuine about the whole... He's a bit of poison. But don't worry, we'll get a picture postcard of the view from Zurich, full of spelling mistakes."

"Aren't you being a bit hard?"

"I'm going to bed. Good night."

"You're exhausted."

"It's all right, there's no need for you to tell me that."

There was an early-morning nip of damp to each breath as Balfour stood on the step outside his site office. Sniffing and sneezing, the men drew their tools from the store and dragged off to their posts. Phlegm rolled in raw throats. A petrol engine coughed coughed and spluttered. Late-comers, eyelids still gummed with sleep, hurried up the road and tried to slip in unnoticed. "Boss, the train, it was late. I get up half-past five but you see..."

Naidoo's words were visible as scented puffs of condensing vapour. "Generator" he explained. "Eleven year I got it through uncle, no trouble, none, now... radiator, tyres, all together. You know what they ask second-hand generator?"

"Good morning" said Balfour. "You're early."

"For whole week... I see a big advance, very big. Back from wife's cousin at retread place, an arrangement, must be early. So now I drop in. Wife also, she's... not good." Little head trembles of emphasis served as punctuation.

"Sorry" Balfour murmured, his eyes following the bucket as the crane swung the day's first gauge of mortar towards the bricklayers. "Sorry" he repeated, both to excuse his inattention and to sympathise with illness. Another "sorry" as he made to move away.

Flutter fingers plucked his windbreak sleeve and when he returned he read anxiety dark in the Indian's eyes.

"Not a good understanding of time, a woman, how it takes time. To settle nice, you follow? Takes time to build up new business. The customers, they must get know you first. Have some very good lines, fast sellers, cotton print, ready-pack spice all variety, Benares brass, all good quality, good. You come along any time, I'll make special..." Naidoo stumped away past an incoming truck, two short legs pounding the gravel path with more force than his eight rattling cylinders. Only the tip of his head showed above the steering wheel.

A load of crushed stone avalanched from the tipper's body with a roar of dust. Heavy engines pulsed as they dragged ton after ton of sand to be spilled on the heap. Brick lorries manoeuvred past the setting-out profile round the building area before the team crouching on the platform jumped off, and with bits of old inner tube to protect their palms, banged down red-hards and hollow blocks and facings.

The right material of the right quality at the right price in the right place at the right time. At least more or less. Balfour hurled his own efforts into the stockpile, demanded that others too pay their extravagant tributes—while the tyrant absorbed its due, swelled with the greed and grandeur of an overlord. The bulk ruled them all and its servants were too busy to feel proud to serve their master. It was acquiring a personality, hard, dominating and oppressive.

"What the hell d'you think you are doing?" Balfour, hands on hips, confronted the driver of an articulated trailer. Or tried to, shouting up to the cabin where the driver went on reading his newspaper. "Look at it. Just look at it." He pointed to the pile of aluminium roofing on the ground as the offloading team let another sheet slither down and clatter on to the stack.

The driver folded and refolded his paper, put it away. Only then did the door open. There was a long way to clamber down. It all took time. "What's up now?" aggressively defensive.

"Look at these corners. Look. Completely fucked up. This one's bent, and this one. Come over here, on this side. Now can you see?"

The driver shrugged. "That's how we always. Nobody's ever before. You can phone the office if you like."

Dougie intervened. "Where that screen wall butts against the corner column, it shows a rebate only on the one plan but then the hoop-iron ties... "

To the foreman Balfour snapped "All right, I'm coming I'm coming" and as he left barked over his shoulder "Tell your blokes to take it easy, for heaven's sake."

There were too few minutes in the hour. He hurried back to the office, looking ahead to a remote figure and felt he was rushing towards some future image of himself fifteen or twenty years on, another middle-aged reject grey with vacant time. Worked-out, a discard with whole mornings to waste by standing, just standing while grains minute as seconds trickled through the hour-glass of empty years, striving to suck morsels of interest from dust and sand heaps and the activity of others.

In a voice slimy as the grease of eggs fried on a gas-ring in a lodging-house room, the grey man asked "So they're keeping you busy are they, keeping you out of mischief? Tell me, just by way of interest, what you planning to use them for? What are these, you know, this sheets I mean?" and found comfort in comforting a sore on his dog's neck.

"These? Single span aluminium roofing sheets."

"Thick, why so thick?"

"Yes, rather pricey. That's what's specified."

The urgency of his need to talk talk talk moved the grey man a pace to block Balfour's return. "Tell me, a person can use them, they'd be all right on a ordinary house say? Or too, like you yourself said, I heard you really lay into them, too buggered up? Listen, listen you could advise me... "

"Expensive way of covering a domestic roof." Balfour tried to side-step neatly. "Careless, no real damage, minor, unnecessary that's all."

The dog strained towards him on its leash. Its owner dragged it back. "Sit. Sit. You can't ever get it right again? It means they're worth, say next-to-nothing now?"

"Aluminium, it can be bent back easily enough, besides, corners fall under laps." He watched the dog settle on to its haunches. "Just being a perfectionist. Wasn't that the phone?" and he slipped away.

An elderly labourer waylaid him with such experience that the phone despaired to silence.

"Boss. Boss you see, well, there's something," muttered with a childlike innocence hiding behind the embarrassed cunning.

"What is it?", as though both were ignorant of the lines to follow. There was a tradition in the roles they had been cast to play.

"Boss, it's like this, there's... what's happened... I'm a little bit in the trouble." It was always said squirming, looking down at the ground. Calluses and broken nails made his fingers fumble with the button on the breast pocket of his overall. A rolled-up bundle of crumpled papers. "A hundred boss. You can take off every week."

In the office Balfour sorted lapsed permits from final warnings from letters of demand from an unfilled application form for subsidised housing. "Let's start with name and address. Your full name, I know only your nickname."

"Fifty boss. Fifty would do me. You can take off... ". The confidential whisper, the nod of acceptance that inclined the head of grey hair to one side, tried to trap Balfour into conspiracy.

He should have been smiling on a rocker in the sun, grandchildren playing at his feet. Instead, usually he struggled panting with a loaded wheelbarrow or endured the sneers and sniggers of easy jobs like sorting and polishing. A foreman's charity was dispensed with curses. "Forty" he hissed, "all right, make it forty" and settled the matter with a weary wave of the hand.

"Full name and address" Balfour repeated.

"Tigervalleyestate" rushed out in a single word up to a corner of the ceiling.

"No, your name."

"George."

"Is that your surname or your first name?"

"Solomon."

"Is your name George Solomon or Solomon George?"

"Primrose Lane" he blurted. "Thirty-six" he admitted with the bravado of a captured highwayman.

"The name first." Balfour sighed, exasperated.

"From the forty I get weekly ticket and also... ". He licked thirsty lips in anticipation. "The boss asks me where I stay. There past the farmstall. It's not the first road, you take the second turn to the left."

With the skill and patience of a dentist, Balfour extracted item by item from the reluctant sockets of the man's confusion.

"Your age."

The labourer considered the matter before replying. "The boss means how old I am?" A long pause. "Forty-one" he decided.

"Oh come on, you'll never see forty-one again."

"All right, then make it thirty-two then." A number was a number, one was as good as the other.

"Children?"

"Yes."

"How many under the age of eighteen?"

"Eighteen? Yes, six," a bit hesitantly. "No, seven."

"You're sure?"

"Yes boss, I said six. Forty's all right, so long I get it today."

Balfour laid down his pen as though its weight exhausted him. A few deep breaths of recovery before he pleaded "Listen, now listen, please I'm not a bank, nothing before pay-time on Friday. You'll always keep landing yourself in a mess, at least see your children learn how to manage. That's what we're both working here on this building for, isn't it? That's their chance, grab it, help them to help themselves."

"No boss, no. The boss mustn't say things like that." The man cringed back as though accused. "I don't know nothing about this grab and help yourself business. It's those others there, some in Manie's team."

"This isn't nice" stormed Burger, barging in without knocking as the labourer crept out. "Not one little bit bloody nice at all. Now they come shit all over a bugger from a dizzy height. It's that firm of yours. Look, I've got nothing against you personally, I blame your Head Office. They get on to our Regional Representative's crowd down here, and look, look what it says here, 'Please expedite overdue certificate.' Overdue my foot."

"Well." Balfour tried to make it sound soothing. "It should've been posted over a fortnight ago, we've budgeted on getting in at least a hundred thousand by now and the bank..."

"It's those rich people" Burger exploded. "What do they want money for? They're the ones got plenty. Now they come along try blame me not handing in my PW7 Requisition in time. You come show me in the book of words where it say so, how many days after."

"There is a clause. Here, nineteen stroke i. Couldn't you at least put in an urgent interim for say a half? Even fifty thousand would help."

"Just hold your horses a sec." Burger licked a finger and turned over a page. "No man, don't come along with stories, there's not one single word in there anywhere it says."

"On page six, towards the middle. At least forty thousand."

"Well not in my copy in the Prelim and General there isn't."

"In the Standard Conditions of Contract. Here, look. I promised the bank we'd deposit at least forty thousand today."

Burger grunted. "Ach, then they must've lost the file somewhere in the Payments Office', and shambled out muttering "you'll have to get on to one of them about it. Out of my hands brother.''

Balfour jerked round the dial to a wrong number. At last... but no answer from the Payments Office; The Senior Inspector knew nothing about, try maybe in the Contracts Section—where a girl giggled at the joke of anybody getting so worked up just because nothing had come through to her from Registry.

He went out to prowl round the site. The brickies knew their job, the facework was beautiful. They discussed minute adjustments to edge the spacing a fraction closer to perfection. Under a lean-to shelter outside the sheds, surrounded by coiled hoses and sacks and oil-spilt drums, the elderly labourer was rolling himself a cigarette.

"What are you supposed to be doing here? You'd better come with me, let's finish off that application of yours.''

The man licked the paper with maddening care. "You fill him in boss. Boss. Make it thirty boss. That foreman, he says fix up all this spade handle. The whole lot.'' There were at least six. The way he crouched made it seem the most difficult task on the site.

They would need every spade next Wednesday—the whole dome and ring and radial beams in ten crucial hours. Gothic cathedrals took a thousand years to rise from the earth, and now in a single day a mountain ancient as the earth itself would vanish behind concrete. Sunlight blazed a random pattern of glare on its rock outcrops, mist trailed formless from the peaks behind the rigid geometry of Hyload towers and pipe stays and girders at regular centres.

Balfour scrambled up the scaffold. High and lonely, exposed; far below the earth-bound workers crawled round the structure with the swarming servitude of ants ravaging a carcass. They were sheltered from the wind that up there cut him to shivers. He zipped up his windbreak and called to Manie "Bring up shutter panels with the crane. Start laying from over there so then the adjuster plates...

Manie picked a cumbersome and dangerously careful way across the framework. "We'll make it in time if the electricians get a move-on. Fine like this, the whole bang-shoot in one go.''

"Pumpmix from that side'' said Balfour. He felt the wind tease his hair and gooseflesh prick the skin behind his ears. "Then Readymix can rig up their conveyor between the... and our crane and mixer for the shell itself. Bit of a gamble but should work. I'll go down and try jack up those bloody sub-contractors.''

Somehow, a mammoth was rising out of the morass of chaos and confusion, the shape was forming, already a skeleton of walls showed where it would be fleshed out with plaster and paint and plastic. Providing the bricks and steel and services arrived on schedule. Even hours were in short supply, lost in a waste of detail. He took a short-cut down through an intricate pattern of criss-cross scaffold-pipe stays.

Hardly time to be a father or a husband. That last half-hour each day, slumped in his favourite armchair under the standing lamp, he usually grunted across the lounge "Little ones all right? Seemed lively enough. And you?"

"Nothing special." He watched her bow lower over her book or macramé, deeper into isolation. "And yourself?" she murmured.

"Interruptions, one after the other. Non-stop. The work's nothing, I still enjoy it, if only people would either leave me alone or make up their minds. We'd better move over to the study. Some forms to be signed." Behind his desk, he sorted papers from his briefcase. "Just one example, every single day I have to waste so many minutes on old Botha."

"Botha?" she asked. "I've heard that name somewhere before. Who's he?"

"One of the regulars. They all stand and stare for hours through the access gap in the hoarding."

"What's he want?"

"Nothing. He's grey all over, complexion, hat, long raincoat, dullness itself. Even a grey Alsatian to match, it slinks against his grey legs like a part of him. You know those retired officials, that type, there must be thousands of them. Desperately lonely, can't smile, can't make friends. You think I'll also land up like that?"

"At least Daddy manages to keep himself busy the whole day long. Now he's on to racing pigeons. You should see that coop he's building in some old pal's backyard. What's this about signing?"

"They sent a courier from Head Office" he said, unfolding a printed form. "Those papers I left on the plane, there were things to fill in. Here, this one's for you, the house is in your name so you'd better sign it. Down at the bottom, next to the pencil cross. Yes there. These others are for me."

She scrawled carelessly, hardly looking, and shrugged her indifference. "I must say all this is utterly beyond me. Me myself, and the way I was brought up, you worked at your job and at the end of the month."

"Directors always guarantee a firm" he explained, frowning. "It's only a bank formality and if you can't trust Barclays. I mean, we've got most of our investments with them in one way or the other. Besides, d'you see tonight's Argus? Look what our firm's shares are standing at today."

She shook her head. "Those things don't interest me. No, I'm not being.. actually they terrify me. I can't explain."

They heard the kitchen door click as Nanny closed it behind her. The house was strangely silent, no sound of children, no TV. Book-stacked shelves enclosed them with facts and fictions distilled from the wisdom and experience of centuries.

"I know nothing" Balfour decided. "I thought that Head Office splash was, well, so much bad taste, nothing else, but here are the results for you, they're real all right." He squirmed on soft-sprung leather. "Still, isn't it all too easy?"

"You've worked terribly hard. Then when you get everything you want, you want nothing. Some days I also wish, why can't it be, like, more simple?"

He signed his name a few times. "I know what you mean, I also can't help... too complex. As when I was chatting today to, who brought these papers, office gossip I suppose. Seems three or four of the directors are going on that trip and rumour has it another couple are all set to resign."

"I wish you would. We've got more than enough. Surely by now we have?"

Hands clasped behind his head, he leaned back and asked the bronze candelabra "Why didn't anybody mention a thing that whole day we were all together? All right, I know I don't mix easily, I can't, you know, present myself. All the same. So many things I no longer understand."

"It's beyond me," She craned her neck forward as though searching the future and seemed to wilt in the chair—a drooping petal become weary with the burden of seasons awaiting her, when dry and wrinkled and arthritis twisted, elegance and ornaments would have become futile.

"Nothing makes sense" he said. "Why plant the complex just there, slap-bang in the middle of those Chelseafied streets, and not anywhere else? And why have we, why us, we've got so much and there's this old labourer, he's so pickled in alcohol he can't ever get really sober, all he's been allowed to know is an hour or so of oblivion. At least he can get what he's learnt to want out a bottle."

"For them it's easy." She clutched together the lapels of her lamb-swool cardigan under her throat and diamonds sparkled above knuckles whitely gleaming. "We should be dancing on the clouds with champagne corks popping. We don't know how to live you know. Maybe that boss of yours, maybe he's got the answer."

"And I've still got work to do." Balfour adjusted the angle of his lamp and selected a pencil.

VIII

Monday would be loud with the clatter of reinforcing rods clanging on steel shutter panels; Tuesday to set up the bolts and pipes to be cast in, runways, final checks, all shouts and curses as teams rushed in panic through last-minute urgents; Wednesday a ten-hour hell of deafening crisis; but today, Sunday, the hours dragged him with holy slowness between lethargy and discontent. The one car rolling down the secluded suburban street to beach or forest seemed unhurried, its engine idler than the usual week-day rush to work. A day given for relaxing, for the family and garden, in a sabbath costume of loose casuals and secateurs. Balfour tried to fill the quiet valleys of stillness between each gong of the church bell with a snip and leaf rustle as he trimmed his hedge.

The street was almost dead with desertion. Only a few girls brightly pink and yellow between straw hats and straps of patent leather on glare-bleached socks; an older couple, sombrely charcoal and beige shapeless, their lips tight and dry as frigidity incarnate; and a young man meticulously scruffy in denim and ginger stubble, arms awkward as he shuffled towards some vision glittering in eyes reborn to see the light.

"Come here." Balfour beckoned to his wife. "Look at them, just look at them. Loveless." He massaged her thigh, skirt hissed over stocking. "Sins of the flesh. Can you imagine any holy-holy really abandoned, all gasping and writhing?"

"Don't be so crude. Maybe they've got a different kind of love. Nobody says you've got to be athletic to feel you belong somewhere."

"Exhausted lovers with sprawled limbs don't moan with hymns. Or drag themselves off to some ugly mock-gothic little barn."

"Oh I don't know. I used to go every Sunday morning, would you say it did me any harm? Besides, you're too hard, on yourself especially, they're only people. If it helps them."

"At least that dome we're going to cast Wednesday, no renaissance masterpiece, still it's some kind of latter-day equivalent. Where a community can congregate and be vouchsafed, that's the right kind of word they'd use isn't it, a glimpse of the better life."

She ruffled his hair. "Give that head of yours the day off. Oh hell, my sauce, it must be burning', and she hurried away.

He ambled to the garden shed, deliberately slowly, trundled out the lawnmower and played with the levers and controls of an adult's weekend toy. As advertised, on special offer for one week only, guaranteed to do the job in half the time, it spluttered, settled to a coarse roar as he relaxed in the luxury of sweat and muscle strain. Gone the quiet, gone the matins bell, off with the weeds and tips. He inhaled fumes more aromatic than a fresh-cut lawn; row after row, order after mess, only another half-hour to go and the engine stalled.

Fuel tank nearly full, spark-plug clean, filter clear, what the hell could be the trouble? Leave it, leave it, on Monday the agents might honour their 12-months warranty ticket tidy in the top left-hand drawer of the study desk, if it was where it was supposed to be.

The children would be waiting, aimless, anything to fill the void of their Sunday boredom. Week after week before tea on the terrace, the hour used to ram values? culture? prejudices or judgements? into their innocence, habit pressed into the form of ritual. Yet what else? What else but a call of duty to call "Come. Where are you? There's a new record I've bought I think you might like."

"Peter and the Wolf, Peter and the Wolf." The plastic cubes of a construction set were scattered across the Afghan by a little boy's knee with its inevitable scratches.

"No, a new one, a piano concerto. A whole huge famous orchestra with, oh, he must be the world's best pianist."

"Then I don't want to listen." A sideways kick sent an orange triangle skidding against a Queen Anne leg. A moment later from the garden came the thud and bounce, thud and bounce of a tennis ball hurled in some lonely self-invented game of deliberate defiance.

"Daddy, why are concertos always in three movements? It's stupid." She slipped the ribbons off her plaits, to advance herself from schoolgirl to young lady with potential talent.

"Tradition I suppose. I don't really know. So many things, we get used to them the way they are. Too lazy or afraid to doubt."

Skirt-hem neat on the study floor, her head leaning against the wing of his leather chair, she asked "What record is it?" with words slightly clipped in the voice that a schoolgirl felt an adult should use.

"Greig's Piano Concerto. It's very much you, my Alice." He caressed delicate adjustments to silver knobs and fiddled with a new gadget that forbade the existence of dust.

"Don't call me that, I hate it when you call me that. I hate it even more than my real one. It's you gave me that horrible name, I didn't choose. As soon as I'm old enough I'm going to change it."

"But you look exactly like her. You know those illustrations, it used to be your favourite story book."

"Maybe last year, maybe then I did a bit before I changed my hair. But my nose has always been a different shape, thank heavens for that at least. I'm going to... I haven't quite decided yet, either Genevieve or Minerva."

"Then move over a bit and let me sit down, either Genny or Minnie."

The tattoo of a pair of fists drummed against his knee-cap, stopped for a faint hiss more intense than silence, the prelude before a diamond splinter oozed honey-dipped notes out of a plastic groove. His fingers combed her hair, silk smoother than a violin string, did not need to coax her temple against his thigh as an adolescent mirage of romance coaxed from her eyes the slight dampness he could feel soaking through lightweight pure new wool.

At last, again the silence of a hiss. Her predictable sigh and shiver. In a whisper, "Daddy?"

"Yes, my girl."

"Can I ask you something?"

"Absolutely anything."

"And you'll promise to be honest? Not give me a father to baby answer?"

"I swear it."

"And you promise not to laugh? Nor ever ever tell anyone what I'm going to ask?"

"I swear again. Now take a deep breath, close your eyes and ask quickly, before you change your mind."

"Do you think I'll ever be able to play like that?"

His fingers explored the bone structure of her shoulder, the shape of his own making. "There are some, some who have a sharper sight to see under the surface, but they've still got to be ruthless with themselves to drag it out."

"Sometimes, like now, I feel I've got it." An open confession. "What's going to happen to me?"

97

His own questions, his own image reflected. He whispered to himself, "There's the dedication, hour after hour, all the drudgery of endless practice, and only if you're lucky at the end, maybe..."

The door opened too quickly for a day of rest. Energetic hands re-tied a bow with jerks to emphasise that she was wearing an apron. "Sauce Hollandaise." She spat out the words, each syllable a separate lump. "If it curdles just once more I'm going to scream and you'll get ready-made tomato out a bottle and jollywell like it too." Hand clamped on to hips. "And what are you young lady doing sitting there on the floor like some mermaid statue? You know very well what your teacher told me at that PTA and the Eisteddfod only just round the corner. An easy gold with practice, now off with you."

The parents watched their daughter shake her hair loose as she left, listened to hesitations and stumbles up and down the scales.

"Sometimes I wonder" said Balfour, "if we're right to try and suck nourishment out of a dried-up Europe. You know, Greig, French sauces, Eisteddfods. Without the crudity and ugliness of here I'd probably just drift along, flabby and complacent. I should learn to revel in it rather and not be so itchy with resentment."

"So what are you going to do about it, except for words? You make me old."

"Play cricket" he said, "or maybe leggy-leggy", and levered himself out of his chair. "I'll manage to lose as usual, but do you know when my old age will really be confirmed? When I try to win against him and still lose."

"What made me feel absolutely ancient" she answered, "that other night at the PTA. To see, all bent and wrinkled, girls I was in the same class with."

On the lawn Boyboy condescended to sulk "Oh all right, but we play for reals, not just play-play. And between the lemon and the peach counts for four."

Balfour ruffled his son's mop. "Clever. Just because it kept landing there last week."

"On purpose", with shrill insistence, "I did it on purpose."

They spun a coin with the solemnity of international celebrities surrounded by cameras.

Bounce and crack, rush, shout and pant.

"Nearly" said Balfour. "You nearly got it right, left elbow up more. And your grip on the handle, the thumb like this. Smooth, keep balance. There." he clapped. "A beauty." They went to inspect the damaged branch on the lemon tree.

"Not a beauty" Boyboy mumbled, "doesn't even count, not so much as one. Don't want to play any more." A deep breath pumped manly courage into his chest. "Fuck it" he managed to say, said it to his own Dad.

"Yes, I agree" his father answered in a voice so disappointingly level that the little shoulders cringed away from an absent slap. "I've also had enough. As you said, fuck it."

Balfour wandered along a gravel path that meandered aimlessly past the birdbath, past the sundial. Leaves discarded by their branches drifted down in apathy, in alternating light and shadow, the clouds seemed undecided. He squinted up towards the sky—from the south-east, unless it switched suddenly, unlikely at this season, no change for at least three or four days. Wednesday, Tuesday, Monday. Sundays were always grey days, flabby and formless as the cutworm he squashed with a toecap. In silence, a creeper strangled an ornamental and brushed against his trouser leg, a bed of agapanthus trailed tired leaves over a few weeds. Restless with nothing to do, too vague to do anything except stare down at the garden furniture. Surely killing time was criminal as murder, the minutes lingered. Twenty to eleven.

Invalids reclined like this on cushions in the sun, feeling warmth on their eyelids, limbs drooping. Rest-days sapped a whole week's stamina; snooze late, slip on a loose shirt, maybe smoke a pipe, say "Tea, ah good."

Sunday was filled with the soft sound of sluggish 'S's'—sleep and slippers, slacks and sweaters, rope-soled sandals slopping across the sun-terrace, scones and silver on a starched tea-cloth, with the heirloom patina of Georgian silver ashine in the sun, a breeze playing with the cloth edge and a bee on the strawberry jam; foam rubber seats on a cane chaise-longue—soporific, slack, slothful.

"Another cup?"

"I suppose so, Thanks."

She performed the tea ceremony in strict sequence; the milk, the heavy pot, the light relaxed remark. "So you've become a two-cup man."

"Have I? Really? Hadn't actually noticed it myself. Only on Sundays, strictly Thermos during the week."

Hands competent, she tidied the tray with the care of a theatre sister laying out instruments for an operation. "You should take a few days off."

"Don't be silly. With the big cast in three day's time. Here they come, on the dot."

Polished to deny its vintage, the little car chug-chugged up the driveway, hands waving through the windows. Always Granny and Granpa stood blinking for a few moments after their daughter's peck-on-cheek, to see her clearly here before teak shutters and chimneys and lawns, not framed on the mantelpiece of their pre-war flat near a suburban station.

They came into the house slowly, slower than their fit and tough years called for, with the slowness of respect that led them to shuffle around, not over that carpet and heavens alone knew what it must have set back their daughter and that man of hers. As though Nanny couldn't keep polished the whole parquet floor, glazed like a mirror, the bit of it you could still see.

Granny stumped forward on dumpy legs active under a body built up from spheres. "Here's a little something to make life sweeter." and she offered a pyrex dish.

"Let me take it to the kitchen" said her daughter. Three women crowded round the stove, experts clashing and interrupting; the men heard exactly how it should be warmed. No, not in the oven, under the grill. A new infra-red, what for?

"So" said Grandpa and examined the calluses on his fingers that he would carry with him to the grave. He'd worked in his life, hell how he had worked, a breed that had died out, all anybody needed nowadays were some letters after your name and a lot of that spindly old-fashioned furniture, dangerous with sharp corners. Those things, watch out, a bump on the hip and you'd know all about it. He drifted out, arms hanging, with furrows of puzzlement across his forehead. Nothing made sense any more.

Shoulders loose and sagging, slashes of folded skin cutting his cheeks, he fiddled with a spanner over the lawnmower now dismembered in the garage. "Here" he wheezed, "then she'll be as good as new. The metal they use these days," and held up to his son-in-law an oil-soaked spring cupped in a horny palm. "I must go show the old girl she'll be tickled pink that's all it needs."

At first under supervision, then thankfully alone, leaning on the spade, Balfour trimmed and re-trimmed the edges of his lawns blade by blade and made it last till lunchtime. He came to the dining-room table to find the others impatient, watching Granny tuck chins into her scarf and grimace. "You ask we've seen anything nice lately? Only horrible."

Grandpa flapped open his serviette with a flourish that put an exclamation mark before his first word. "Disgrace. Now they've even got negroes and japs and what-have-you jumping around there on the screen. Anything goes. Jeanette McDonald and Nelson Eddy, they just don't make pictures like that any more. Balalaika and Rose Marie and that other one about, I forget now what it's called.''

Granny dabbed at a corner of her eye. ''Yes, Rose Marie, we've seen it nine times altogether so far and each time, you know I still cry. Now that's what I call beautiful, really beautiful.'' She dabbed again.

''If that helping's for me'' said Grandpa, ''fine just as it is. You don't spoil a plate of good food by pouring grease all over it. That's for bearings, not for joints.'' He winked to his grandson's stare. ''You catch on? Bearings on axles, joints of beef.''

''But Daddy, it's sauce Hollandaise.'' His daughter sighed her disappointment.

Leathery fingers grasped knife and fork with a firmness fit for weapons. ''Well, I'm not going to let any Hollander or German or Frenchman tell me what's good for me. We managed all right before, before all this, this from outside. We knew how to live all right. Work and play. Dancing, Saturday nights there by the Recreation, how we used to throw streamers and pull those, like, you know crackers with paper caps and things inside. And then that one year at the Rotunda, you remember Ma? Yes, we really went one year to the Rotunda, honestly, cost me close on a whole week's pay-packet, to celebrate something or other. Yes kiddies, yes I remember now, it was your mother's confirmation and you know what? Your Granny, you won't believe this but it's true, it's true Ma isn't it? You won some kind of a prize for your fancy dress. Honestly, you can ask her.'' He stabbed and hacked a slice of meat, masticated with denture clicks and nods that confirmed as gospel each word of his wife's response.

''A picture album, the kind with a padded cover. You know I've still got it. Yes, at the back of my wardrobe and sometimes, like when I'm feeling a bit, well, out of sorts or with the pain from that trouble I had last winter, so then I take it out and look what a really pretty baby your Mommy used to be. I should have entered her for shows and things but her Daddy didn't want, said it was making yourself cheap.''

''Yes, you know them.'' Grandpa glared through the tufts of his eyebrows. ''You know what they are, they'd only use the picture for some advert in the paper or on a label or something so then any coolie or hottentot out the gutter could use my baby's face to wipe himself if you'll excuse me talking like this at the table, you know what I mean.''

While the children bent over their plates and giggled, he clamped emphatic jaws on a last half-potato, swallowed fiercely and his Adam's-apple jumped between parallel ridges of sinew and loose crinkled skin. For a moment he bent in disbelief over his empty plate, then leaned across it to pat his son-in-law's shoulder. "You haven't got much to say for yourself, have you? Yes girlie, thank you, I don't mind if I have a bit of a refill. But we used to work hard, make no mistake about that, none of this press a button and bobs-your-uncle stuff. Like nowadays just picking up a phone and ordering so many lorry-loads of concrete."

At the last word, Balfour jerked straight in his chair. "Sorry" he said, shaking alertness into his head. "My thoughts were a bit astray."

"Thanks my girl, that's plenty. Like I was saying, I watched them laying a new ramp there up to the loco shop right next door to me. A whole huge gang of raw... I know you're not supposed to use that word any more these days specially not in front of the children, but still in their blankets and sweat, they had to really work in those days, not like now. And you had to watch which way the wind was blowing, smell them from a mile off. But I'm telling you, they were a damnsight happier then than... what's this latest thing they're all talking about, in the papers, over the radio, TV, all over, some newfangled council or other? Well in those days they used to sing. You ever hear any of them sing nowadays? Not on your life, it's all this rock-and-roll or... I'm telling you, it's a public disgrace, you can't even walk so far as from here to there but one or more of them, the whole pavement, as though they own the place. You know I don't even let the old lady even to the Post Office for her pension on her own." He shook his head to defy the changes; even those fancy patterns drawn by the lad's mother they kept stuck up there in frames on the wall, even they seemed to alter each time you moved your head.

"It's too terrible" said Granny, "simply terrible. I don't know what the world's coming to. No respect."

"Can we go now?" asked the children, scraping their chairs back. Balfour reclaimed paternity with a wink.

"Aren't you waiting for dessert?" Their mother's voice hurt them with her own hurt. "You know Granny's made a rice pudding specially for you. It isn't easy for her to stand there over a hot stove."

"I hate rice pudding" Boyboy grumbled and slumped down again, pouting, chin on cupped palms.

Granny tapped his forearms. "It's not nice to keep elbows on the table" she whispered, glancing towards the head of the household. 'You must eat nicely. It's only good manners" she explained, "your Daddy wouldn't like it.''

"What? Did somebody say something?" Balfour blurted at the abrupt end of a journey from far away. "Was I keeping my elbows on the table? What's wrong with that?"

"It's got eggs, it's got vitamins, it's got good." Granny nodded wisely at the count of each value. "All things that are healthy for you."

"One thing about my old girl" boasted Grandpa, "she makes the best rice pudding this side of the equator."

"Mommy." Balfour's daughter stared at him while she spoke, too wide-eyed for innocence. "Mommy, aren't you supposed to be on diet? And you know we don't have to wear school uniform for the Eisteddfod so, oh please, all the others..."

"It's delicious" said Balfour. "If I had a sweet tooth I'd finish it and even ask for a helping."

"You're sweet enough, are you?" said Granny, watching her husband dig in his spoon. "As it says in the Bible, that out of the strong shall come forth sweetness. You've started yet taking the children to Sunday School?"

"I never have and I never shall" snapped Balfour. "We've been over this before, I refuse to discuss the matter any further. I've got my own principles, that's all."

"I'm sorry, I'm sorry." Granny bowed her head in reverence over the silver rim of her plate. "This a new dinner service, isn't it?" she asked her daughter. "It's so plain, you can hardly see the pattern and thin, terribly thin, you're sure Nanny won't break each time she washes up?"

"Mommy, really, for heaven's sake." A spoon tossed on to a tray clattered with a percussion of anger. "It's all right kiddies, you can go now. Do you always have to go on trying to make a, a, out of me in front of my own children? It's the best bone-china money can buy, I've got nothing to be ashamed of."

Balfour counted on his fingers. Three weeks ago that Sunday had been bad, twenty-one days; Monday would be difficult, Tuesday worse, Wednesday impossible with tension, the twenty-fourth a day to bring down the curse of hell.

"Ashamed? You should be proud." Granny waddled round the table collecting plates. "You've got two such bonny little ones and a beautiful house and a husband who loves you. What more could anyone ask of the good Lord?"

"Hear hear" said Grandpa as he handled his spoon to try and scrape away the glaze on his plate. "Now that's what I call a really good tuck-in." He fumbled a button on his hand-knotted cardigan that had burst open under pressure. "You were talking about Sunday School. Well, let me tell you something." A wagging forefinger pointed out how privileged a listener was this young man who needed the wisdom you wouldn't find in not a single one of those books of his that anybody could just walk into a shop and buy with money. "At first we had to drag her there kicking and screaming of a Sunday morning, till she got used to the idea. Then she even sort of got round to getting, you know, used to the idea. They enjoyed it, those kids, they had fun, things like little plays, picnics."

"That picnic, that one year at the river. Daddy, Mommy, you remember?" A shriek of laughter called her parents and their shared years closer, the skin puckered at the corner of eyes that twinkled, and Balfour looked along the length of the littered table at the shapely, over-excited woman who happened to be his wife, the mother of his children. She used the knuckle of a three-carat finger to wipe away a tear. "Coffee? Anyone for coffee?" she chirruped. "Thanks Nanny, you can clear the dishes."

Grandpa creaked upright and stretched himself to the point of bone-clicks. He started the weekly shuffle towards his favourite chair in the lounge and slumped down at ease; it always took an hour or two and a decent meal to feel at home with the size of the place, fancy ornaments and pictures, high ceilings rich with bronze and crystal chandeliers, tasselled pelmets over the french doors. Much too quiet, even a coffee cup replaced on a saucer made a noise.

"Well well well, I shouldn't complain, should I?" he sighed.

No contradiction from his son-in-law, who seemed hypnotised by the view of the garden that stretched and stretched away in tones of green.

"People complain too much these days" Grandpa declared. "That's the trouble, they think it's smart to knock down anybody in charge a peg or two, that counts as one up for themselves. As though they'd do any better." He dozed off for a few seconds, then snorted "Like it says in the paper. D'you see this morning's Sunday Times? The authorities, they must have pretty solid reasons for doing what they do, they know things that you and I don't get to hear of." He jerked his thumb towards Nanny's bustling, tunelessly humming overall in the adjoining room. "And then people, overseas, other places like that, they've got the blooming cheek to come along and criticise."

"Who's criticising?" demanded his daughter, guiding her mother towards the rocker. She turned to her husband. "I suppose now you'll say it was wrong to serve Hollandaise with a roast. I bet you didn't even notice the mustard and the herbs. I don't give a damn", and she crossed the room, skirt swishing, to stand behind her comfortably settled parents.

"I think I'll lie down outside" said Balfour. "Take it easy a bit." He slipped out of the net of tension that had stretched over the room to pull its possession away from him.

Three pairs of eyes watched him wander across the front lawn and drift into the obscurity of overhanging branches.

"What's up with him?" Grandpa jerked a thumb towards the french doors. "Never seems satisfied and never says anything."

Granny squirmed into a position of greater comfort. "Maybe he's worrying about that lawnmower of his or, or even, even for not taking the kiddies, on a Sunday morning I mean, like he knows he should." A few little sighs and a grunt, she fitted her convex shapes deeper between the plump and squashy cushions. "You know what men are and he's not an easy man. Let him be, that's my advice my girl, it's really his home just as much as yours."

Her daughter perched on the arm of Grandpa's chair and examined her nails. "I'm not all that sure" she said, "that it really belongs to us any more. Actually, well I suppose it does really."

"What you mean?" her parents asked in chorus.

"Don't tell me" said Grandpa, "surely, I mean, I thought he was doing so well."

"That he is. Make no mistake about it. Just we signed a security or something for the bank. Don't let it worry you, it's nothing, only a formality you know, all to do with becoming a director."

Two grey heads nodded in reassurance. Grandpa's exploring tongue discovered a remnant morsel of beef or rice and he chewed, jaws working steadily, while dredging through all his years in the world to sift out a suitable comment. "Banks, insurance, that kind of thing" he pronounced, "they're only out to get you. Look, I've never actually owned any property myself, but look how it said there in the paper that time, "See your friendly man from the something-or-other." Fix you up nicely for when you go on pension, no worries. All my savings, and where would we be today if it wasn't for what you put aside from your time there by the hospital and so on? You tell me?"

"Daddy please, I've told you before, it's not me you owe the thanks."

Grandpa stabbed an agitated finger against his daughter's thigh. "In the gutter, that's what I'm telling you, in the gutter."

"We knew you'd never let us down" soothed Granny. "Not after all we did for you, the measles, chicken-pox, your going-on that time with... all right, I won't ever mention it again. Maybe he's not all that fond of rice pudding. I'll try an apple crumble for next week."

"Mommy, for heaven's sake. All right, you make it. Make two, make three."

Granny creased a double chin with a nod of satisfaction. "The little ones, they like an apple crumble. Otherwise things are all right between the two of you?" She leaned across her chair and whispered "You know what I mean, we girls mustn't be shy between ourselves, men can be difficult that way, they don't understand what we women... "

The parents watched their child bounce up from the arm of the chair, stride across the room to stare at her husband's body lying slack on the grass as he idly picked at weeds.

Balfour managed to ease over on to his back, surprised at his own groan. He surrendered himself to idleness, to the uncomfortable feeling of doing nothing definite, to the close examination of an elbow criss-crossed red by a pattern of grass.

Above him arched the dome of infinity. What should have been perfect and blue and all-enclosing, was flawed by wind-driven cloud and a jagged outline of mountain, by the precise bulk of terra-cotta tiles. Sun and shade accentuated the ridge and valley folds of his roof; ivy on the chimneys, two weather vanes (a bronze cock and Father Time); ground-floor shutters striped alternate bars of varnished teak and shadow.

A bird wheeled in freedom, soared and dipped with easy wing-flaps to defy the pull of gravity, higher than the steeple at the bottom of the street. It could circle above it, squawk derision and enrich the sacred emblems with encrusted droppings. And then? Then what? Return to nest and the rearing of its chicks, still bound to the treadmill cycles of its evolution.

Upstairs a pair of curtains jerked apart, a window opened, an arm waved and a child's voice claimed him.

He wagged the fingers of an extended arm in answer. Silence. When a cloud drifted past the sun glossy leaves on evergreens darkened with a wash of gloom and reflected the rich fertility of his soil.

Week-end. His home, his possessions that owned him. Bond-free.

The sun burst clear and he laid a forearm across his eyes till the skin became clammy. It felt hot on his exposed cheeks and throat and arms, grass blades prickled through his shirt. He turned over to stare into the open areas and vast stalks of a grass forest where an ant picked a hesitant

106

way between towering green trunks. Down there was a damp mat of yellow humus, all obstacles and brown earth craters that trapped it in a maze of no-escape. Natural environment or fate? Certainly not choice.

He straightened a stiff leg, rolled over to his side and muscle by muscle, forced himself to relax. It was a duty to relax on Sunday afternoons. Sprawled with cheek against lawn, he sighted across the surface, coarse and undulating, towards his home.

Where a pair of brown arms flung washing over a line in the side garden and clipped pegs in time to a wailing dirge. The latest craze of golden disc, or tribal? The dark feet showed their pink soles as the maid reached up to the line, then settled flat and broad-toed, seemed to grip the earth in fierce possession. Around her neck was looped a skein of wool and out of her overall pocket hung a half-finished square of knitting with a clashing pattern of zig-zag stripes.

Which meant? An end-of-season sale by some discount chain or remnant scraps of madam's Beehive Fingering? A knitting pattern found on a torn-off page in the kitchen sink, potato peel scraped off; or traditional, the secrets of its cryptic shapes whispered over a ritual fire encircled by conical huts of cowdung and clay? Or these the colours for some future day of barricades and sirens and plumes of smoke from blackened mounds of rubble?

The song wailed louder, swelled with the menace and the pulse of drums. Hypnotic. Balfour felt a vein throb in his left temple, and he sat up. To notice the imitation-leather case of a transistor propped against the trunk of a wise old English oak.

The confusion of those discordant notes. Progress.

But why was the maid still working on a Sunday afternoon? It should have been her ''off'', these hours bore a deadness with them that imposed a rule of rest. Of course, of course it was her own washing she was doing, getting her costume ready for the evening service in one of those cement-block chapels dotted in the townships; hard wooden benches, the drone and wail of hymns all undulating quavers and a preacher fervent with Jerusalem and Bethlehem. Nothing to worry about.

A formless scud of detergent foam swirled from the washing line with the aimless white drift of a ghost in search of eternal peace. It sank softly, weightless, was punctured and held by stiff grass blades. He watched the rainbow bubbles pop in slow succession, the green was hardly wet where for an instant they had played with iridescent jewels of colour in the light.

He stood up, brushed clippings from his trousers and strolled towards his house. Twenty to four already, time for one side of an LP before tea. How had Bach spent his Sunday afternoons in the days of wigs and patronage?

Boyboy was lying tummy-down on the study floor, shoes in the air, nose against a page. His son ignored him when he asked "What's it you're reading?"

At last, for answer, the cover was turned over to show "The Mediaeval Structures of Western Europe."

Back to the open page, the fascinated stare. "D'you mind Dad? I found it on the shelf."

"Of course not, as long as your hands are clean."

A grubby finger pressed down the ceiling of King's College Chapel. "Dad, Dad, why is it the roof doesn't fall down?"

Balfour slipped Bach from the protection of polyethylene, matched baroque on to a stroboscopic turntable. "They had some experience from simpler ones already built and such enormous hope, a certainty it would still be standing now."

Tousle-mopped, intent, open-mouthed and freckled, the little head nodded.

"It took hundreds and hundreds of years, fathers, grandfathers and sons, they couldn't help themselves, this hope, this being certain, that's what kept them going."

"I don't understand."

"Nor do I. Nor does anyone today. It's called faith."

"But Dad, Dad, your roof..."

"Today we have to calculate, it's different." He turned a knob and notes fluttered their dove-wing beats in blessing over father and son and mood.

Granny stumped into the room. "Tea-time" she sang, "time for tea. That's church music, I can hear. You listen nicely Boyboy, then one day you'll play as good as your sister. Your mother, what didn't we spend on her for ballet lessons', and she padded away humming improvements on the Berlin Philharmonic.

Balfour endured the family tea in silence, while Grandpa sighed "Well well well" between slurps and Granny observed how quickly time flew, another week gone by. Cups were passed and re-passed.

Even the rattle of crockery yielded to a pause so stifling Grandpa felt compelled to clear his throat. "That place you're building." He kept on waiting for a response. "You know there used to be a coolie shop there on the corner. Suppose it must've been the father in those days.

I'm not going so far as to say he's actually a, well, in their own way of course, but only after the money. You know for a bread, just an ordinary wholewheat, when now you can walk into any supermarket and off the shelf help yourself, what's up now? He shouldn't still be crying, not at that age."

Boyboy had limped into the room, sobbing out the story of a splinter. His mommy knelt beside him but he edged away and leant his forehead against the wall, shoulders convulsing with each sniff. Granny knew exactly how to but Grandpa was the real expert, the splinters he'd removed, nobody's business.

"No, Daddy must."

The whole family crowded into the bathroom and watched Balfour ease it out to hisses and gasps of pain.

"Hold tight," he whispered. "Nearly, nearly, here she comes. There. You see, anybody who's got a big garden must expect a thorn or two. It's part of the price."

His busy-busy wife indulged herself with cotton wool and antiseptic, while Granny plucked her son-in-law's sleeve and panted "You know a properly trained sister, there's many a time she knows even better than the doctor himself."

"Just going to drop in at the site for a quick look" Balfour growled and went to shrug himself into his windbreak in the entrance hall.

His wife swung sharply round the corner. He could predict exactly the force and direction of her storm.

"And you couldn't even find the common decency in you to stay for another few minutes till they left. You know what it is? I'll tell you, I'll tell you what it is, you despise them, don't you?"

"Not in the least, they're thoroughly decent people, it's just I don't have much in common, that's all."

"Yes, that's all. They just happen to be my parents."

"I won't be long."

The sight of Naidoo's heavy black car was no surprise. Through the windows shone some vivid, some pastel saris, more bobbing heads of children and children.

"Only chance I get to show family. Week-ends. They can't believe, so big, big. Very busy this week, I make sale. I see straightaway shops out there all too much the same so I clear cotton print, I clear spice, rather I specialise. The denim jean, record, cassette, all good music. Sitar, jazzband, folksing, only the latest."

Outside the watchman's hut Balfour glared down at an unknown man so concentrating on adding a few sticks to the fire that distractions were made non-existent.

"And who are you?"

Another stick, another minute. "Aaaii." He rotated a head of pepper-corn curls through arcs of infuriating slowness.

"Where's the watchman?"

"Yes" said the man. "No, the watchman." The story was too involved to follow. There was a cousin and a sickness and a mother looking after and another brother fetching something, and this other brother's other wife, her permit, the watchman, he'd be back, five, ten minutes, one hour.

Balfour picked his way through a litter of debris into the dimly-lit forest of props that supported the shuttering. Row after row in absolute align-ment, stayed and cross-stayed, the perfect pattern of their assembly would be tested on Wednesday, dismantled ten days later. He clutched at a prop and nearly slipped when a bottle rolled away under his foot. A pair of urchins scampered away out of the half-light and their sniggers echoed between bare concrete floor and metal roof to mock him with derision.

A teenage couple, smug and smirking, strolled out hand-in-hand.

A vagrant staggered away.

Ahead, far to the right, a dog barked, barked.

Alone, deeper into the gothic gloom, now the drum-beats of his footsteps rang hollow against the hardness of steel pipes and plates and clamps. They enclosed him in their multi-thousands to uphold the loads of his careful calculations. Double that the number of their bolts, multiply beyond infinity the weight of guilt should a single one be loose, yet was it possible to check them all? One had to trust.

The dog barked again. He was being watched; a pair of fire-points burned red, blinked a jungle warning of cruelty and vanished. It smelt damp and metallic, stale piss, stale air. Balfour turned and watched the vagrant stumble clear of the ring of outer stays into the faint glow of the day's last light. He turned again, drawn to the darker dusk at the centre where the solid column stood steady on its base. Here the stresses would be concentrated, here the major ordeal of the design.

Behind him he heard the pad-pad of the dog's approach, spun round to imagine, to glimpse a shadow of grey vague as a swirl of cloth. A raincoat? An elusive figure with faceless head under a grey hat? When he hurried to the spot there was nothing.

Nothing but his own supports rising so far above his bare head their tops could only be assumed. Twilight-dim already, high-tensile bars enclosed him as he groped to escape from the trap. It was getting dangerous.

IX

When Balfour drove up to the site at half-past six on Wednesday morning he could not park in his usual place. Three truck-mounted mixers blocked the street, their obese bellies slowly revolving with sloshy rumbles. Behind the hoarding, petrol engines were already throbbing impatiently; about half the labourers had arrived from their squatters' shelters in the bush, from township cottages and council flats alive with crawling babies, flapping washing-lines and graffiti on the stair-walls. The rest were drifting through the gate every few minutes.

"You're early" he said to the drivers.

Smart in white overalls and berets, each with a gumbooted foot on the running-board, they dragged on their cigarette stumps, dropped them in the gutter and stamped. "Okay" said their leader, "we're ready whenever you are."

"Dougie" Balfour shouted, "let's make a start, even if we're still short-staffed." He hurried up to the deck for a last-minute check; dew-drops clung to the reinforcing bars, the steel shutter panels glistened black with wet in the pre-dawn light.

He leaned over the edge and called "Come come come', watched far below him on the ground the mixer drum roll round and round, the skip rise to load it. The placing crew climbed up alongside him, yawned and shared an early-morning hand-rolled cigarette. Suck, inhale and pass-along, they waited silently, trained and experienced.

"Better test the vibrator" said Balfour.

Sleepily, a man bent down and pressed a button. A whine deafened the suburb. A nod, okay. Again silence.

One by one, differing noises made their entry into the chorus of construction. Now the truck-mounted drums spun urgently, the pump gurgled, the conveyor rattled and the mixer sounded full, the crane's hoist-motor howled out a paean of power as it lifted the day's first batch.

Balfour watched the bucket swing dark against a rose-pink flush in the sky and drop in front of him, hang trembling elastically at the end of the cable before a jerk on the release lever dumped a ton of concrete at his feet. The steel plates of the deck shocked at the impact, steadied. Fine, the mix just a bit on the wet side. Maybe dew had condensed on the stone and sand heaps overnight and the next gauge would be as dry as it should be. More concrete churned upwards along the conveyor, the pipe kept on vomiting in spurts. So far so good.

The beams were filling steadily, so packed with high-tensile steel and service pipes there seemed hardly room for concrete; the ring right round the outside deep and heavy, the radials more delicate, fanning from the centre. Extend their lines and they would spider-web the city with himself voracious at the core.

"I'd like it faster" said Balfour as his foreman joined him.

"It'll be better from now on, nearly up to full-team. Not even properly light yet."

Mist on distant hills delayed the sun, clung in the hollow of the quarry so densely tippers left there for the site with headlamps yellow. At the sandpit near the coast the front-end loader had its fuel-tank filled for a busy day. The cement factory geared itself to overtime. In diesel depots and power-stations digits multiplied and spilled over into balance-sheets and banks. Men and their families would eat full meals that night.

It was coming quickly now, three minutes ten, water content just about spot on, only a couple of absentees. Balfour looked round for something to give an order about, to justify his presence, to mark the point in space and passing time at which he found himself.

Now he saw the radial beams as converging on the central column with himself no longer predator but prey, trapped into place, an instant. At this moment the harsh harmonics of machines composed a coda to all remembered music, cot-side lullabies, school hymns and varsity sing-songs, the day's finale predictable. He watched an orange sphere, unstoppable, surmount the bank of ground-mist on the horizon and sparkle a rainbow spectrum from a dewdrop trembling as it clung to the underside of an electrical conduit; the thump and shudder of a further batch shook it loose, another replaced it, the trill of the vibrator dislodged that too as the sun warmed and dried the pipe, lit the roofs and traffic of the suburb.

Down in the street he could see husbands and career-girls lock, safety-lock their front doors and hurry, hurry to the bus-shelter where they waited, shoulder-to-shoulder, 65% man-made fibre to 35% cotton, impatience blending with routine. Their transport was part of the bumper-to-bumper crawl-cars, tippers, cars, buses, loaded truck-mixers passing the empty ones leaving the site, and a beige panel-van with a blue lamp on the cabin roof revolving revolving as it circled the streets.

"Watch it" said Balfour. "Watch what you're doing. That beam's so packed with metal there's hardly room for concrete, work it in, underneath especially."

"It's easy to put down on paper." Dougie sniffed. "They can draw anything, all separate, plumbing, electrical, the lot, one crowd doesn't know what the next one's doing and we're expected to stick it all together."

One hour, two hours, the tide of concrete kept on flooding, relentless, scheduled, monotonous. Balfour left the deck, he could afford a plastic cup of thermos coffee.

Could afford to relish the prospect of relishing the wetting of a dry tongue, while he strolled around the site letting himself be seen, forcing his presence to be noted with a nod to the crane-driver, a double thumbs-up to the mixer team.

Even a 'Good morning' for Botha, who with his Alsatian heaving and bucking at the leash, stood fixed in a stare of fascination at the neat stack of aluminium roof sheets.

"Always at it." said Botha, "even on the Lord's day of rest I seen you, in under there, checking. You keep check on who's under you and I keep check on you', and he turned towards Balfour the grimace of a friendly tease. The now strong sun reflected off his glasses and made him seem blind. "I see plenty going on here, I could help you a lot you know, provided you... But I better hold my tongue, for your peace of mind as well as mine. But anytime..."

"Quite, quite" murmured Balfour, his gaze roving the site. Well organised. He spotted a bustling Naidoo who refused to be avoided and stretched up on tip-toe to hiss a confidence.

"Listen, listen. You should see mister, how I change my idea. This time, it give high profit, very high. Two video game. Later maybe, pin-ball machine, I can get, good condition. Plenty room in the shop, plenty, because the selling goods, not any more. Too much cheap stuff out there, no selling, oh no. Entertain, that's it." He nodded, emphatic.

Kept on nodding even after Balfour had evaded him and stepped into the shelter of his office shed, into seclusion, quiet, shade.

There was time to inhale the steam drifting from the coffee cup, to glance at the banner headlines screaming disaster across the front page of the Times, light a cigarette, listen to the steady rhythm of sounds that sang a song of profit. Nothing special on the Financial Page, Wimbledon as expected. Phonings? No, nothing. Another half a cup.

Balfour stood up and stretched himself. Luxury, beyond lazy boating mornings at the Marina, to discover leisure in the middle of a major cast. He strolled across to Burger's office.

"Look at this" said the Inspector, and rapped his knuckles against the pages of a folded-over paperback. "A thousand jokes, supposed to be, but you know what, I counted them, there's only nine hundred seventy-seven. These days, only shows you, you just simply can't trust nobody. It's not funny anymore. Nothing's funny anymore."

"Not funny? That's the biggest joke of all" Balfour smiled. "Count it in as an extra one. Nine seven eight."

"Come again." Burger squinted up at him, head cocked in puzzlement. "Hang on." He reached for a pocket calculator. "Hundred sixty-two pages, say about six on a page, makes." He fiddled with the buttons. "No, you're way off, it gives nine seven two, plus the one you say I must add. Nine seven three. You see, you see, even bigger crooks. Look at this, what those Japs make these days, clever little buggers."

Balfour inspected it dutifully. "Very neat" he said. "Seems a good quality plastic case. Look, what I really came about..."

"Plastic." Burger stared at his calculator as though slit-eyed midgets and magicians concealed in its intricacies might breed some permutation of numbers to solve his problems. "Plastic's rubbish, it breaks. Plastic toys, to try keep it amused. You know I have to buy the toys there by the, by the, the baby counter. Even then, a minute, two minutes, no interest, nothing. That's my week-end. And I'm so tired, so blooming tired I can't hardly... shit, after a big-size cast like this we're all going to need some rest."

"At the moment I'm fine." said Balfour. "Maybe it'll hit me later, delayed reaction. You been up on the deck today?"

"There's those test-cubes I've still got to take" Burger answered, "then I'll give a look-around. Not that I'm really in the mood."

"It's where the radial beams come together all supported on that central column." Balfour rough-sketched a diagram on a sheet of scrap. "A mass of pipes, fire service, electrical, we're battling to pack the concrete in and still don't know if any air-conditioning, ducts and so on, how they'll affect them. That's a separate Departmental contract remember. Hardly expect beams collapsing in a gale but all pretty dicey."

115

"Make it wet" advised Burger. "Wet concrete flows nice, then you can get it in proper.'

"And what if you take your test cubes on a wet gauge and the result flops? I'd look pretty bloody silly then, wouldn't I? Especially on a mix designed in the Institute laboratory."

Burger fought against the inertia of weariness to stand up. He squeezed Balfour's shoulder, partly to support himself, partly to emphasise his message. "In all the years I been with this fukken department, not once I've got anything but top-class results. You know how? I'll tell you, practical, experience."

He tapped a forefinger against his temple. "You take just a handful extra cement and mix it in with, right there in the cube mould. No trouble. Come, I suppose we'd better have a look what's cooking."

They emerged from a cramped box of ply panels into a wide space of sun glare and dust and louder noises. The Inspector moved towards the mixer with a suddenly officious bustle; his arms waved, his jaw wagged, legs stamped with all the energy and authority of a man so free of distraction he could dedicate his life's effort to efficiency.

Balfour wandered in under the shuttering, into gloomy half-light, and clambered through the maze of props and stays supporting the deck. Drip drip from the joints between the plates trickled cold and wet on neck and ears, the shock and shudder of each fresh batch dumped above his head thumped a load of headache into his skull. The vibrator screamed its shrill lament, right through his body, down the central column, into its base and its support, into the earth—a tingling, a quickening, a high-frequency pulse of life.

The design seemed sound enough, at least so far, based on standard loads and stresses. Still, for a man with wife and children to place himself under here at risk, forcing them to share a faith in the principles of his profession... the theory of structures was his gospel, not theirs. He spotted a minor deflection.

Out, up, up, on to the deck. "Manie" he shouted, "a couple of wedges", and explained where and how. "Otherwise just about perfect, holding beautifully."

Only ten minutes behind schedule with nothing amiss, nothing urgent to do. Production depended on monotony, experts always made it seem easy. Housewives dawdling towards the shop hardly glanced at the morning's busier routine, the surrounding streets were almost free of traffic.

Only the beige panel van with its winking winking blue light that kept circling the area, one street, another street, nearer and nearer, then

116

hesitating at the access gap in the hoarding, leaving slowly, cruising, returning to nose its chrome radiator grille up the gravel path, to a halt alongside the stone pile behind the mixer.

Balfour saw a blue uniform elbow relaxed on the sill of the driver's window. Nothing happened. Another gauge, another. An empty Ready-Mix truck tried to reverse, manoeuvred, reversed out past the van to be replaced by a newly-arrived loaded one. The next radial beam filled; he made sure it was compacted with special care and the ring beam advanced a further span. Bucket up, bucket down, jib clockwise and anticlockwise, the crane's routine was a metronomic bore. A slight slow-down, the wheelbarrows of stone were having to divert around the van.

Now the passenger door opened, and still nothing. The slab could do with a bit of smoothing here and there, but not too bad, theory was being proved practical.

When next Balfour glanced down to the ground he saw a young policeman stand hesitating as though overwhelmed by all the technical complexities surrounding him. The parallel knife-edge creases of his trousers seemed too neat in the mess and busy confusion that in Balfour's eye reflected perfect order. Below the flaps of the blue tunic a looped leather strap dangled loose and floppy and a hand stroked the bulge above it as though to draw courage for another pace into dangerously foreign territory. A youngster with a shaving rash, adolescent pimples, probably a mother up-country, his advance was tentative as the spelling mistakes and corrections of his weekly blue-notepaper letter to her. Mouth agape half-open, part adenoidal, part awe, his polished round-nosed boots shuffled through sand and grit as he approached the labourers one by one. All shook their heads; installations dwarfed him, impersonal machines ignored his brass badges. The crane was the biggest of the things that threatened him. He edged towards it with a swagger of unconcern before tugging down the hem of his jacket into a line of smartness, patting his collar into regulation place and shouting up to the puny human form that directed all that force and power.

The driver crouched in tense concentration over the control panel. With split-second timing he guided the bucket into position while the policeman's neck flushed scarlet and inflamed. Balfour watched the mouth open for another shout before the blue figure clambered up on to the ballast box, careful to keep his tunic clear of the heavily-greased bearings and bitumen-sticky cables.

Now the driver crouched differently while the bucket was being received, steadied, secured by the placing team high and distant from him—a lower cringe, trembling, head of peppercorn curls turned up in a protest of innocence to the younger face, his neck extended in a gesture of sacrifice.

Balfour watched how high the policeman rose on tip-toe, his arm strained up towards the sky. Sunlight gleamed along the length of his weapon. It seemed slow, the way he struck. There was red under the brown baton.

More police sauntered forward from the van to close in. An unhurried cluster dragged the driver, limbs limp, from the crane while the van reversed nearer, tyres skidding on the gravel path. The back doors were slung open, the body heaved in, doors slammed close, the engine revved out blue exhaust and it was gone.

Strangely silent. A few loose stones in the empty mixer drum rattled a hollow tattoo. Everyone waited.

Balfour trembled at the edge of the deck. Fists clenched and shaking at the clouds, with the thunder of an Old Testament prophet he raged "All our technics, all our planning and our skills, and a single thug with a club."

He hurried down. Why? What? Nobody knew nothing.

A panicky Burger found him. "And now?" demanded the Inspector. "Now what you propose doing about it?"

"Only one thing" Balfour snapped. "If the slab stops we've got to halt the beams as well, though it's just about the worst possible place for a construction joint.

"I warned you." The Inspector shook a forefinger under the Contractor's nose. "I kept on telling you, you wouldn't listen, you've got some bad buggers in there amongst your lot. They make me sick, the way they keep on landing themselves in the shits."

All round him Balfour's men stood, just stood, staring at him as he tried to tear his arm loose from Burger's grasp.

"Man, if ever that Senior Inspector of mine gets to hear of, I don't want to be around when he's blowing his fuses. I'll be the one to catch it in the neck, not you."

In his office Balfour jerked round the dial of his phone. Engaged.

Dougie stammered with sympathy in the doorway. "I, I could try, try drive it myself" he offered. "Take five minutes each way up and down and maybe kill somebody in the process."

Balfour shook his head and dialled again. Wrong number. Through the window he saw the teams starting to drift apart and re-cluster round the fireplace for an unscheduled tea-break. "So many kilowatts of power,

118

so many men here I control, still I'm helpless" he said and waited for the Flying Squad to answer.

"No, well, yes, yes you see, actually no, there's nothing like that answering to your description anywhere in that area. It was Lansdowne or Athlone way you said hey? Better try your local station. Sorry."

Burger poked his head past the doorframe. "Listen, you just can't leave it like that."

Number after number, Balfour groped for contact with the signal points of power in the State; through the hierarchy of channels in the Department, the Charge Office, the Detective Branch, the prison, back to the Charge Office.

"I insist on speaking to the Duty Sergeant himself", and waited. Waited.

At last, a bored and aggressive "Yes." Balfour knew he was hardly being listened to. "No, you heard me, there's no prisoner been brought in but if you want you can come down make a statement if you really insist." Click.

Balfour slumped on his stool, elbows on the table, forehead on palms. His thermos was empty. He lit another cigarette. His men no longer laughed and shouted over their tea, their silence built up to a prelude that burst out in a glorious climax of electronic sound, crane motors engaging fast, confidently, expertly.

He sprang up with a reflex leap and raced to stand beside the driver but dared not speak till the bucket was at rest in front of the mixer and concrete spilling into it. There would be a fifteen-second pause.

"What was it?" he demanded.

"What was what? They grab me boss, that's all."

"But why? What had you done?"

"Me? Who, me? Nothing, it's those law boys. You must know them boss, how they are, they's only wild."

They ignored the frantic arm-waving from the placing team up on the deck to hurry, hurry. The half-hour break had made urgency more urgent.

"But they must have told you something. Did they lay a charge?"

"A charge?" The crane-driver laughed. "Charge with what? They say nothing, keep me there in room at the back behind Charge Office, then they give me a sticky plaster." He touched his forehead to indicate the spot, stroked it with the proud fingers of a veteran caressing his medal ribbons. "Then they say 'bugger off, next time we fuck you up real good and solid'." He grinned, blasted out a piercing whistle between his front teeth, yelled "Concreeeteee", engaged a contact and sent the bucket soaring up up and away.

Again, again, hour after hour, right through an afternoon of rigid discipline.

They finished twenty minutes early.

At half-past seven on Thursday night Balfour glanced up from fumbling with his shoelaces to inspect his wife inspecting her legs in the dressing-table mirror as she wriggled her pantyhose straight.

"Actually it's too warm" she told the mirror "but then when else do I get a chance to? Does this really go with it?" A held-up string of pearls looped across her bosom. "Too dressy." Rather the jade and silver. She backed towards him for a clasp to be secured under the shampoo strands on the back of her neck. He inhaled the aromas of powder and perfume and the opulence of hairdressing.

In the entrance hall while he jangled keys she called " 'bye you two. Remember homework, practice, the piano's still open. Nanny, don't forget about the polish."

In the garage she nestled into padded contours, fiddled with finishing touches to ear-ring and evening-bag and murmured "What did you say the programme is?" A bra strap claimed more attention than the answer.

"Usual" he growled, head and gear-lever in reverse as he backed down the driveway. "Mozart, Beethoven, symphony, concerto."

At seven-fifty on the parking lot, he marched round their battered seven-year-old company Mercedes. On the rear window ledge, exposed and masculine, lay a roll of plans and a white plastic helmet. He opened the passenger door for her to swing out into public a pair of Via Veneto ankle-straps and gleaming calves; that is all she allowed the drunkard to see as he lurched from car to car and slurred "I watch after your motor hey, hey, master, madam."

Balfour's shaken head did not deter the flower-seller who waltzed towards them. The lady ignored the girl. "Flowers, roses, beautiful roses, last bunch. For you, special price master. Roses for madam's poses."

On the corner, framed by Corinthian columns and municipal granite, she waited chin-up, her face hesitating between impatience and appearance while he dug into a trouser pocket for small change to drop into the upturned palm of a whining, barefoot beggarboy.

"You look so embarrassed" she said, "like you're the naughty child and he's the boss."

"Maybe that's what it is." He felt the mantle of the day's exhaustion drop from his shoulders as he watched her settle the fur into place for its evening's duty.

Now they were another of the elegant couples on the pavement, crowded between the beards of vegetarians and the stares of yogi meditators, politely pausing for hobbling old ladies with their smell of moth-balls and German accents.

The eight o'clock chimes announced their passage past the Commemorative Plaque.

In the panelled foyer of the Concert Hall, in a perfumed whisper, "You see there's quite a few others in full-lengths, minks most likely, and mine's not really a... more like a bolero sort of." The brilliance of the smile she beamed across the carpet outsparkled the crystal chandelier.

Balfour nodded a compromise half-greeting towards a face faded to an obscure likeness; that man there was all pale decay and bent into the shape of middle-age, they could not possibly have been in the same class at school, and yet. The woman next to him was thick with carbohydrates and parentage but it must be him, for he nodded back with the weariness and confidence of a coronary statistic.

Up the marble staircase, salutations to the left, suitable chatty remarks to the right, to the discerning, the appreciative of the city. She wobble-balanced on her heels, then felt the comfort of his palm under an elbow make her ankles feel safer.

They fussed themselves into their seats as members of the orchestra meandered on stage with the disarray of a random gathering of penguins. He patted her forearm elegant above bracelets on the seat-rest and remarked against the cacophony of tuning instruments "I'm a lucky man. Eighty skilled musicians plus a world-famous celebrity who's come half-way round the world specially to entertain me. And I'm the only man in the whole hall who knows you're wearing green panties."

Her expression altered from public poise to private pride, to feeling for her man, so decent, so pained as he watched the struggle of the maestro to drag himself from wings to podium. The baton would be too heavy for a hand so feeble—amazing, it defied its dotage, rose in vigour, gathered chords together and swept them to a peak of majesty. Coughs between movements.

She leaned across to brush lips against the flesh of his ear-lobe. "Not really green" she whispered, "more like lime."

There was a certain manner of strolling correctly during the interval, a tradition, an unhurried pace, in the appropriate direction. "Going to be a lady" she murmured and with a sideways twitch of her shoulders slipped between the throng.

When she re-joined her husband she found him boyishly awkward before a silver head that trembled with seniority. Palm on back he ushered her forward. "Darling, I want you to meet my former professor. My wife, meet… and Mrs… er…"

The professor's wife, a frail and dried-out little bird fit to hang plucked from a butcher's rail, managed to twitter in the background.

"May I claim some small credit for this young man's choice? Not only of career, ah-hah, but of the fairer sex", with a bow of geriatric gallantry.

Mrs Balfour fitted a mask of charm to her face; her husband, he still resembled that boy-student the professor used to see and now only half-remembered. Her, after two minutes, he already knew better; she read the compliment of lust, plain naked lust, in the inflamed lids of the old man's eyes. She felt it warm her, she glowed, he had no need of mathematics to analyse her curves.

"The Beethoven was beautiful, wasn't it?" she simpered.

"Yes yes yes, beautiful indeed" the professor croaked.

In the aisle, chin turned to snuggle on a fur shoulder, she gasped " 'D' you see that brooch thing she was wearing? Really, and she's a professor's wife."

"Ex-professor, he's retired now."

"Even then, they weren't real, I bet you."

"An academic pension, it's not much. Comparatively I mean. Here, this is our row."

When they had edged into their seats Balfour squirmed a bit, then almost apologetically he explained "That was the Mozart they played before the interval."

Her head tossed itself to a posture of dignity. "Well, I didn't look at the programme. Besides." The orchestra's leader bowed to a polite ripple of applause. "Besides, I just happen to remember it distinctly, you yourself once said there was no difference between late Mozart and early Beethoven. Don't try to deny it."

He sighed and surrendered himself to the loneliness, the anguish and the torment of a bachelor's passion from another age.

At ten-thirty the following Tuesday Balfour managed to squeeze sideways into the Inspector's site-office; cramped, air stale with the purest freshest Virginia and the Postal Super's latest version of the bishop and the chorus-girl. His five silent assistants lining the walls must have heard it before, they did not smile.

Nor did Burger, anxiously shuffling forms in a folder under the glare of his Senior Inspector. Efficiency was no laughing matter. Especially when that freshly-shaven freshly-graduated junior representing the Quantity Surveyor's office shyly offered his duplicate copy of the list that had somehow, now where the hell could it've got to, it had been right here in these very hands not a minute ago.

"Bullshit" said the Senior Inspector. "A load of pure absolute bloody bullshit, keeping me standing around like some... he knows perfectly well there's a site meeting every second Tuesday, this proof of a fancy doll'd-up architect. I'll put him in his rightful place, you mark my words. Who does he think he is? That I've got nothing better to do than..." He tested the solidity of Balfour's chest with a rapping knuckle; this Contractor here, at least he'd come in time, an exception, almost a best friend despite belonging to the wealthy, the leisurely, the privately employed.

"See it's entered in the Minutes" boomed the Postal Super, "that they pay us waiting time."

"Ach." Burger spat out his disgust. "Gives me a pain up the backside" he whispered to Balfour, the confidant who kept his secrets and shared his long hours on the site. "Always trying to be funny. Listen, you needn't raise that business about the air-conditioning duct through the beams, will you? Can sort it out just between ourselves, afterwards. I see now there's some kind of a plan lying here all the time, they don't even bother to tell a bugger nothing."

"In one month" snapped the Senior Inspector, sharp as the pepper that seemed sprinkled on his short-cropped bristles, "one month, three weeks, four days and," he glanced at his watch, "five hours ten minutes I go on pension, and you know what? I just can't wait for the bloody day." Little ripples of impatience tensed through his body and livened him to the vigour of youth.

"Lucky bugger." The Postal Super grinned enormously, first to the left, then the right. He yawned.

"You know" the Senior Inspector continued, "when I first joined the Department and that was, oh, forty-five-years ago, things were different then, very very different. We controlled our jobs, controlled them. Now", he shook his head, "nobody knows their arse from their elbow. That air-conditioning crowd, typical, can't even be bothered, and that's after, on and on to them at the very least some kind of a lay-out. Now listen..." He appealed to Balfour. "Don't think it's, it's in no ways any different on all my other jobs, plain rank bad, shoddy, slipshod. These days, as long as they can get away with it but not on your life, I've been in this game too long. In no ways, I refuse point-blank, no arguments." He glared at Balfour. "Now don't you let me down, I'm depending on you."

"Excuse me a moment" Balfour murmured and stretched to open the window. Head and shoulders in the fresh air, "Dougie" he called, "can you come here for a few seconds please. I think you had better be in on this."

The others edged away from the foreman's darker complexion. He sensed this, came no further than the top step where he could still hear and remain unseen unless any looked directly at him. None did, only a glance, the brief inspection granted to inanimate objects. Except his boss.

"Come." Balfour beckoned to his foreman and cocked his head in invitation. "Find yourself a space."

"I'm all right here." Quiet, defensive, on his dignity.

"That air-conditioning." The Senior Inspector bristled. "Bugger them. If they don't want to let us in on their ideas so we can make allowance for, then what I say is, carry on. Let them sort out their own mess. Carry on."

"Regardless?" Balfour frowned creases of inquiry across his forehead.

Now Burger, busy busy, tidied the rolls of plans on his table and glanced towards Balfour to make sure his actions were being noticed.

"While as for the rest of the job." The Senior Inspector sighed with self-pity. "I just haven't got the time to look into every little... I just hope to hell it's not like all the rest. Heaven spare me from such workmanship. No, please..."

The Postal Super endorsed him. "Yes man, what I say, what kind of a job is this? Here's the roof up already and not a word, not that much", he snapped his fingers, "not so much as a hint about a roof-wetting." He aimed at the Senior Inspector a forefinger of emphasis heavy as a battering-ram. "I know this crowd from before." It was part-joke, part accusation,. "From them you get not even peanuts, and then only if you're lucky." He stood up and led his team towards the door.

"Hang on" Balfour called. "We're planning to, in a few weeks."

"Now that's more like it." The Postal Super shouldered his way back into the room.

The Senior Inspector managed part of a smile. He sounded less sour. "So there's one advantage in not being on pension already."

"So long I can get myself properly blotto on the house." The Postal Super slapped a hammer-blow on to Balfour's shoulder.

124

The junior Quantity Surveyor blushed.

"Don't expect anything much" Balfour apologised. "Our Chairman's away overseas with the Minister himself, his Deputy's the guest-of-honour. And set me such a limited budget, nothing elaborate, even be doing the catering ourselves. You'll be getting printed cards sent out to make it official. Also a few outsiders, a couple of locals and so on." Through the open window he could see the grey shapes of Botha and his dog, the one drifting vaguely, the other sniffing and rooting amongst wind-tossed wrappings and scraps round the cooking fire, then lifting a hind leg to dribble out a comment of derision on the beast in man.

He noticed Burger follow the direction of his glance, hesitate, then search for the warmth and safety of belonging to a cheering crowd. "A good booze-up." So Burger too was using words to make himself feel worthy. "Pour me a double and go easy on the water." Words, mere puffs of air, was that all one needed to be accepted?

"Fine" said Balfour. In his own ears he sounded lukewarm. "One hell of a party. In the meantime we've got one hell of a problem. I know what it says in the specification, but it's far more practical and gives a better finish if..."

"Please yourself." The Senior Inspector flicked fingers of dismissal. "Man, if you don't know by now then nobody ever will, just use your discretion."

"Yes, but you see the detail shows..."

"I leave it to you. Burger, hey wake up man, make out any Variation Order the Contractor asks for. So, that seems that."

"Ah, the assembly all assembled in good order I observe. Good morning gentlemen." The Architect had insinuated himself into the room, all angular joints and spinal curvature.

"My watch hasn't stopped by any chance, has it?" asked the Senior Inspector, not too loudly almost respectfully.

"Well well well, let's take first things first shall we?" soothed the Architect. "Start the ball rolling so to speak with confirming the Minutes of the previous meeting." The tweed Gladstone bag he used as a brief-case failed to yield the necessary.

"Thank you, thank you indeed" to the junior Quantity Surveyor who offered a copy and shrank back into his corner.

The Architect cleared his throat, fist to lips, and put drama into the lines. "Minutes of eleventh site meeting, held on Tuesday the seventh of, etcetera. Present, the Architect in the Chair, Contractor, various Inspectors and so on." He sighed, as Hamlet surely had. "Item Number

One: The Contractor again raised the matter of Post Office cable inlets through the basement waterproofing.''

"Oh no" groaned the Postal Super, "shit no, not again, we've been over this so many times before. Listen, if there's nothing else for me I'm on my way." He led his delegation through the door.

Dougie yielded his place on the top step and made himself invisible.

"We'll continue, shall we?" The Architect smoothed back his hair.

"Can't we take those Minutes as read?" rattled the Senior Inspector. "Should've been back in the office long ago. Land up with my balls in a vice." He unclipped a pen, all jerks of irritation, authorised his dignity by the deliberately untidy scrawl of a signature and underlined it with a curl of contempt on his lower lip. "There's nothing else really urgent for me, is there? In that case."

The others followed his example. One by one they drifted off.

Balfour found Dougie sorting sanitary fittings outside the store.

"I, well, you probably heard" he hesitated. "That roof-wetting party. I don't know if you'd be, you know, interested, but certainly, most welcome."

"Me?" The foreman accused himself with a thumb pointed at his heart. "I must come to the roof-wetting party?"

"Well, yes. Why not? You're building this place as much as anyone, aren't you? You won't be the only, you know what I mean. There'll be the few nominated coloured members of the State Council as well."

Dougie flung a urinal grating on to a turd dropped by Botha's dog. "And you expect me to stand there next to, to shake hands with lumps of common dirt scraped out from the gutter? Me? I've got no self-respect, no feelings? Let them keep their free drink, I'd sooner starve", and he stalked away muttering.

Manie was guiding an electric saw along a length of shelving. He switched off to let himself be heard giving a firm "No thank you" while Balfour was still speaking. He turned a crouched back towards his boss to finish the suddenly urgent job.

In his office, Burger was staring at the air-conditioning lay-out. "I heard what you said, those invites, and then you looked out there, to old Botha. You don't mean to tell me, hell no, you're not thinking of inviting him, him, surely, there's limits."

"Why not? He's become almost one of us, hasn't he? Besides, I remember you saying you're related."

Eyebrows arched, Burger cleaned an ear-hole with a matchstick. "You really want to know about him?"

126

"No not particularly." Balfour bent over the plan. "If only we had more details."

"Well, you asked for it. You said related, well yes, sort of, you see my late mother's step-mother, that's like a half-granny hey, well, her first husband, he had like a sort of, more like a cousin in actual fact but she's hang of an old now, we all call her Auntie, she's the one really holds the whole family together, but not actually if you know what I mean. But him out there." He shook a forefinger under Balfour's nose and blurted with a saliva-spray of passion "Don't you believe it, there's not one word of the truth in it when he comes along trying make out I still owe him money. I owe him nothing, the bastard."

Balfour's cheek felt wet. "No, he's never said anything. Please. Don't involve me.

"Yes, that's the exact words I always say, to the wife and to him as well, to his face whenever he used to come along with one of those herb remedies of his. Just ordinary bloody weeds, if all the doctors there by Alexandra can't do nothing for the child then how come he'll manage? Him with those things in little bottles and brown paper packets door-to-door up the street from out some backyard room. But this one's something new he reckons, it's special. And he talks to her, talks, talks, he'll talk the hind leg off a donkey. And you know what a woman is, a mother who sees her child, that it's just simply not growing up right. Try anything. So between the two of them, in the long end they get me pledge the insurance. That's only for a start, then so much every month. There's this one cure, he makes out he's discovered, I'm telling you true as I'm standing here it's nothing else but fucking poison. Grows there next to the dams up in the wheat country, but you can pick it only when there's a full moon. Then you just mix it with a bit of python fat and some turpentine. Just so much on the end of your finger and stick it in deep. The first day exactly like he says, there'll be nothing. The the next day just prickle a bit and the third day, it's the third day that really counts. That's when the burn starts. Well, I still don't know who suffered more, the child screaming and rolling there on the floor, or the wife crying when she's got to watch all this, rubbing her hands together the whole time like this, and rubbing and rubbing, or me having to watch the wife. So then he says we must try again, the one time isn't enough, but first the money. Not a damn. So you know what the wife, what she goes and does? Stupid, real stupid. And then this second time... no, man, no. And then it appears we're not the only ones. There's a whole crowd, half-deaf, going blind, with a crutch, they're all after him. This herbal business, it's got a bit too slippery to handle, even for him, don't pay off so good any more and it comes to a sad and sorry end. But he's not finished yet working on the wife. We must pray he says, by now he's on to faith healing. So then one night when she's there as usual along with all the others he's pulled in one way or the other, him with his Bible and all, I grabs the child and off to Alexandra. In. Finished.''

Burgers's breath snorted in whistles. He gripped the table edge, chest heaving, and turned up to Balfour bulging eyes that pleaded silently.

''You tell a good story'' said Balfour. ''I still feel sorry for him. Especially these last few days, ever since I invited the old chap. You should see the difference that's come over him lately, I was glad to help a bit, some sort of interest, a new kind of confidence almost.''

''Confidence'' Burger scoffed. ''He needs confidence you say? And me? What about me? Yes, you think with the wife so stupid that time now's the first summons I've had to battle with? And his wife, you know about his wife?''

''A bit, an invalid he told me. Another reason I felt sorry.''

Burger slapped his thighs and bounded up from the stool. Hands on hips, elbows out, he doubled himself over with guffaws too loud for mirth, gasped, again the buffoon who pranced round the office in a stamping dance and mock-punched Balfour on the shoulder, before wiping his eyes with the back of his wrists. Tears trembled wet on the hairs. ''Man, that's bloodywell priceless. Invalid and how, you should see her, she's got this arthritis there in the hip so bad it's pathetic, she can't hardly drag herself so far as from here to the door. So old Botha, Botha, he does the walking for her, he walks out on her. But first, that's not before he gets himself properly organised. This other one, she's no more his adopted than, what's the matter, you think I'm making this all up?''

He looked towards Balfour, who stood arms folded, the impassive judge nodding for him to continue.

''There's this young girl, more like no more than teenager at that time really, not even properly related, just sort of, you know, edge of the family. She's only the one child, her old folks, they used to farm, actually a glorified vegetable patch away there otherside the mountains and then one night, they'd got themselves one of those clapped-out secondhand light deliveries, coming over the pass a ten-ton truck, no lights.'' He slapped his palms together. ''So she's stuck out there, no nothing, just a few clothes in a falling-to-bits old school suitcase and she pitches up here in town. And he lets out word he's going to adopt her.'' Burger sniffed. ''Adopt my foot, that's only another way of saying uh-uh-uh.

In, squirt and out. She's the one he gets play concertina for him. You want me to go on?''

Balfour nodded.

"That's when he really got going on that Gospel Crusade of his. Climbed himself way past the silver collection to defray expenses stage, now he's at it in a big way, really big. You never seen his face pasted on the cardboard tied with string every second lamp-post our part of town. No, course not, you'd never come out that way. Well, first of all he laid hands for himself on this big khaki tent, a huge blooming affair, don't ask me from where he gets hold of it. Army stores I reckon, no trouble for him, he knows the right places to slip a fiver here and there, or less knowing him. Man, you should've only seen what used to go on in there those Sunday afternoons. Even old Auntie, what he'd managed to squeeze out of her. This girl, she's the concertina and he played ukulele for the hymns. Can't you only picture him with that music case of his?''

"No, I've never noticed him with one.''

"Not any more you won't, but in those days... anyway... so here's this holy revivalist combined faith healer complete with his wide-brim hat, long raincoat, music case, just exactly one of those fucking gangsters you see there by the drive-in Saturday nights. And that's the making and the breaking of him. Raked it in, by the fistful, there's hardly a poor bugger miles around doesn't sniff his final breath pen in hand last-minute alteration to the will. And he starts building this more like a palace really for himself. So the others, the regulars in the trade, they're no longer sitting so pretty in the saddle. Competition. You think it's only the super-market chains going for each other? Those holy wars they make you learn about out the history book at school, what you think they was about? Fighting, like in those all-in wrestling bouts, they've got nothing on it, only now he's not up against only a handful invalids, it's the big guns out. And that other crowd, you know the benediction hour on the radio and just-about the whole-day Sunday telly, they've already planted their own deacons and their elders in there to reserve it for themselves. Botha, he's got no answer, it's his fart against their thunder. It's them sees to it he gets enough publicity only this time it's the thick black headline all across the week-end paper. Here's old Botha with a half-finished building, that latest luxury model of his, only they corner the lot away from him, congregation and all. There's a bit of bargaining backwards and forwards, in the long end he himself, he crawls to join up with them and he's lucky there's the option of a fine.

"It's out of town practically on hands and knees. It's them sees to it

129

for years he's stuck away there assistant secretary to the Divisional Council somewhere to hell-and-gone way up the West Coast there in between the sand-dunes and the bush country. The equal say to a junior learner clerk in the Department. Then you remember, no you wouldn't people've got so used to all the what they call ''irregular'' business going on all the time. Anyway, the usual, funds unaccounted, the auditor's finger, it points all around and finally settles in Botha's direction. But there's this clump of fishermen's cottages there in the village, the buggers been living in them since the year dot and getting themselves drowned in all kinds weather and the storms you get that part, so Botha's boss, he's like the sort of mayor or something grand, he can sit back in comfort and count the takings from the over-fishing quota he's wangled for himself. But this boss, he's become one of the big-shots since just by-the-way, he's got a sideways eye on these cottages and his fingers, they're itchy. Anyway, to cut a long story short, Botha, he's got to be shifted out of sight from the Council Offices but they can't give him the old boot-in-arse treatment, he already knows too much what's going on behind this help-yourself affair with the cottages. And that's how he really got going. It's a funny thing. You know what?''

He pressed an index finger against Balfour's heart. ''In this stinking arsehole of a world of ours, to get on really good, to make something out of yourself, you've got not only to be on the grab, people must get know you're out to grab, then they'll respect. They got need for Botha and the likes of him them in the long black shiny Cadillacs with the chauffeurs with the peak caps and the flags on the bonnet. To do their dirty work for them, they're always the clean-hands brigade remember. He talks the same language they do, he's in with them, like this.'' Burger intertwined his fingers and squeezed them to a twist of pain.

''That's it then, they both need him and they shit-scared of him. So they ease him in there behind the counter of the concession store some of that band of blood-brothers has organised for themselves there in the kaffir location. Slap on a curfew. Patrols. Caught on the street after dark, bang-bang, handcuffs, deport back to the reserve, the lot. So where else can those black-arse bastards do their shopping? Neat, hey? And also, also I forgot to tell you, they've got this liquor outlet there, he's in charge of that as well. So you know what, what he goes and does? Fingers in the till. Now this is the best part man, you won't believe it, so smart that whole bunch, they get the Council and remember that's only themselves after all, the Council votes to write off the shortfall as a dead loss and old Botha, he slips a half back to them and now he's got the whole damn lot exactly where he wants them, like this." He tensed the cupped fingers of an upturned palm. "By the short and curlies. Eat out of his hand. Course he can't stay on longer after that whole to-do, resignation accepted with deep regret. Name the new hall after him so everything looks clean and honourable from the outside. But all that's nothing, I'm still coming to, you want me to carry on? Yes, what's up now, Dougie man you look worried."

The foreman came in no further than he needed to say "that old chap with the dog, he's been on to me again. Those aluminium roofing sheets, if there just happen to be any a bit damaged, what are we planning to do with them? What must I tell him?"

The lunch-break whistle stilled the site to silence. Outside the office two labourers groaned as they straightened their backs, folded back the threads and tatters of their sleeves and with a clasp-knife, razor-sharp, shared a loaf of bread. A few, grinning at their luck, clustered round the fire to inhale the stink of burning offal.

X

"Oh no" whined Boyboy, "no not again, I'm sick of these puff-pastry caviare things. Why can't we have something decent for a change, like hamburgers?"

"You just sit up straight and stop complaining." His mother inspected some flakes on her own plate with the cold-eyed stare of a technical expert's assessment. "Think of all those starving children in the reserves or homelands or whatever they call them, they'd be only too grateful." To herself she muttered "Tiny bit soggy still on the bottom. Another five minutes at one-eighty." To her husband, silent and withdrawn at the far end of the dining-room table, she chirped "Don't worry, I'll get them perfect for the big day."

Balfour grunted. "Doesn't really matter. Long as the drinks order is delivered."

The parents watched their daughter push away her plate. "Smoked salmon makes me sick." The nose crinkled with adolescent disgust, then the nostrils flared out resentment as she bounced up from her chair. "Grown-ups also make me sick, all you can ever talk about is this unreal roof-wetting party of yours. Fabulous." Legs spindly in their encasement of faded jeans, the loose blouse only slightly lifted by her swellings, it flapped as she stalked out and Boyboy hurried after his sister.

"You'd think it tasted too much vinegar" shouted her mother, "to judge from those faces of theirs. I'm just about sick and tired, but I bet you, I bet you."

Balfour raised his eyebrows. It saved him the trouble of answering.

"Once the party really gets going, the swing of it you know, and she's there going round with a tray of these savouries and everybody fussing over her, she'll love it, she'll lap it up, I'm telling you, good for her, experience, all part of growing up."

"And Boyboy" asked Balfour, "what about him?"

"All organised." His wife inspected her cuticles. "He'll go down with Nanny and she can help with the washing-up, then if he gets you-know, tired or, she can bring him back here. You've got the kitchen part set up okay? I know I should've gone down and had a look what you've done there but time, time, I just don't know where it goes to, which reminds me." She stood up. "Now where's that mother of mine got to? She jollywell knows it's lunchtime."

"Temporary plumbing in future canteen, trestle tables, so many crates of beer, whisky, all part of the job, work is work. I'm sure even film stars have to sweat away at being glamorous. Any more coffee left?" He had to help himself and stretch across the table as his wife stretched her strides towards the kitchen door.

At the working-surface, flour dusted on her forearms, Granny hummed as she rolled and turned and slapped a lump of dough.

Nanny muttered to herself and clattered stacks of mixing bowls and baking trays on to the draining board. Her madam had swung in too sharply for peace and now there she was going at it with the old-madam.

Granny nudged back the sleeves of a floral wrap-around. Her elbows looked more inflamed than her voice sounded. Sadly, wisely,

"Anyway, I always said that oven of yours, and so expensive too, for that price it should've had side elements."

"Mommy, for heaven's sake, how many times have I told you, d'you honestly expect anybody is going to even look at things like that?" Ringed fingers flicked in contempt against the latest batch of burnt offerings.

Again Granny pushed back her sleeves, now firmly; the gesture branded her as belligerent, fists bunched and dimpled. "Well my girl, you do it your way and I'll do it mine."

Her daughter marched out, straight backed, head high, lips pressed together in an eloquent line of silence, the skirt swishing out the comment. Back in the dining-room she slumped down on a chair next to her husband, leaned across and hissed "I just wish to Christ there'd be one of those old-time film festivals like they sometimes have, I'd book them their tickets. Can you only imagine what it's going to be like? We should never ever have involved family, got caterers, I know it's my doing. Can't be right all the time."

"Ease up, ease up" said Balfour. "There are still a few days, things will sort themselves out. A roof-wetting's not all that important."

"My old man with a few pots too many in him, what he'll say about you behind your back to all those officials. And," she jerked a thumb

133

towards the kitchen door, "to everybody in the room, one after the other, what a beautiful baby I was. Heaven spare me."

"Toilets" said Balfour. "Remind me on Monday. We'd better connect up say three inside the building. Imagine our honoured guests squatting in a rusty shed over a bucket."

"Drawing pins" she answered, "for the tablecloths. And paper serviettes. Well, let's get cracking, what are we waiting for? Now where's that notebook of mine got to?"

She swirled out of the room, into a vortex of hairdresser's appointment and altering the hem of her turquoise, another three dozen teaspoons from Catering Hire and dishcloths for drying the glasses; day after day, panic after crisis, exhaustion after excitement.

On Friday morning Balfour, stiff in a suit, moving carefully to try and keep clean, edged his way over the site. Dust on the gleam of his shoes could be brushed off later. "Dougie" he said, "everyone on a general tidy-up, make it look like one of those prize-winners in the neatest site competition. Then early pay parade at twelve with a full day booked. Do they understand that? Then all off the site, unless you still want to change your mind."

Now in the early afternoon, in uncomfortable silence, in the empty volumes of the structure, he inhaled the cold and wet smell of a half-finished building. Raw walls enclosed him, bare, harsh, a protection, his natural environment polluted in a single room by paper lanterns, a sofa, a few kitchen chairs and trestle tables obscene with lace doilies under arrangements of stuffed prunes. The dusting of paprika was neater than the pile of dried mortar shovelled into a corner.

Grandpa was quietly occupied, stooped over a regiment of bottles paraded in straight lines. Beer-mugs to the left, tumblers to the right. His suit hung loosely on him, faintly musty, faintly naphthalene, the trouser seat folded over into a pleat as though bought many end-of-season sales ago for a fuller man. He nodded to his son-in-law; the ice-bucket needed shifting a bit to the side.

In the makeshift kitchen, Granny's floral wrap-around protected her crimplene. Her head trembled with energy, a spherical helmet of parallel corrugated waves. "Busy-busy-busy, busy as a bumble-bee" she hummed.

The main concourse was vaulted with the silence of a deserted cathedral. Balfour heard the echoed excitement of a party of intruding trippers, his children's chatter, his wife's yodel, "Where are you? So there you're hiding. Do I look all right? Shouldn't you be waiting outside to welcome?''

She hurled herself into an orgy of last-minute touches and re-arrangement. ''Nanny, Nanny'' she called and trotted down a corridor, ''where d'you put those trays of vol-au-vents for heaven's sake? You children, come, make yourselves useful.''

Balfour stood frowning on the rough concrete of the yet unmarbled main entrance steps. After the cool and shadows of the inside the sun glared hostility at him, a few pram-wheeling mothers barely glanced up as they strolled past. A couple of loafers were too busy lounging to notice the impatience of his foot-taps or the dust on his shoes. Five minutes to the invitation time. Not a single arrival.

At last, three youths, two languid boys heavy with cameras and a shabby girl fidgety over a notepad.

''Argus.''

''Times.''

''I'm from the Citizen.''

Balfour mumbled suitably. Were these the moulders of the shapeless opinions of thousands? The same way he placed wet concrete into forms and it set impervious to changes wrought by passing centuries?

It was Naidoo, bounding up the steps to whisper ''Mister, mister, I hear you have party. Good, good idea, celebrate, very good. Next week I also, family party for the new lines. Those video games, they bring the bad element, only bad so now, rather the potato crisp, cigarette, no stale stock. That new outsize filter, very popular.''

''Who's that?'' drawled a cub reporter.

''No, nobody'' said Balfour. ''Should we go inside?''

He led the way to the party room where Grandpa was dispensing a measured tot for the Consulting Engineer.

''Didn't see you come in'' remarked Balfour. ''Must've slipped in, side entrance.''

The Consultant nodded his thanks to Grandpa. ''Well, cheers'' he said, and sipped dutifully. ''Look, that was a crazy lay-out for this place they sent me I had to work on. Mind if I slip off a bit early?'' He glanced at his watch.

The room felt too big, the pauses between each politeness too long.

''You remember the old prof?'' So obviously small-talk. ''Well, I bumped into him a few weeks ago.''

''He's still alive is he?''

''Yes, sort-of, rather frail. Look, I'd better, you know, see how things are getting on. Excuse me.''

It was pleasantly busy in the kitchen, warm with the bustle of wife and Nanny and Granny and a couple of helpers and scrubbed children being helpful. They chased him back to his post, his centre-stage role of host who welcomed guests with an extended arm, who clutched a glass of whisky as the core of boredom round which parties cluster. Ten past already and still only half-a-dozen.

Seven, when the Senior Inspector hesitated in the doorway before inhaling a deep breath, squaring his lapels and marching a few smart paces up to the barman. "Yes" he ordered.

Grandpa, grasping his own glass like a social tool, inclined over him with rheumatic dignity. They agreed, experience, that's what really counts; the veteran of retirement handed out tips to the postulate. When Balfour joined them they ignored him for the few blissful moments when a host can be anonymous, can stare down to his glass as though a solution, a successful mixing, a warmth swirled there instead of whisky.

Back in the kitchen Granny flapped a damp cloth at her son-in-law. "You mustn't come traipsing in here motherless like a lost sheep offering to help. Look, nothing to do, all organised. You know what, you're just trying to get away from. You take my advice, you've got a job on your hands, be social, you start getting that party of yours going with a swing."

Burger had arrived. To mark the formality of the occasion, to help shake loose a tightness in the arm-pit of his suit, he offered to shake hands. He pressed close to Balfour as though clinging to some prior claim on the host; after all, the Inspector right here on the site, it was him had more closer dealings with the Contractor than any other bugger in the room. "Shit" he said, "but don't you find it hot here all dolled up like this? Man, give me a safari-jacket any day rather." He shrugged in discomfort and forced a finger between shirt-collar and the pressure-bulge of flesh that rolled on his neck.

"Any good stories for today?" asked Balfour. "Drink up, there's plenty more where that one came from."

"There's what?" Burger cupped a palm behind his ear.

"Plenty more." Balfour spoke up, realised he needed to speak up above the muted hubbub in the room. A quick glance of inspection confirmed the crowded feeling, the room had nearly filled up.

Now he understood why so many officials from the Department had kept dropping in to the site the last week or so. "Just to have a quick look round hey." They were arriving in car-loads, usually one in each batch clutched and waved his invitation with the assurance of a season-ticket holder confronting a conductor or doorman. For the others a sheepish grin sufficed, or a remark to the host like "Man, I hope you don't mind, I just happened to be together in the car with old..." A few slipped in on tiptoe, with a sideways sidle.

All were stiffly encased in a social armour of formal clothes and formal manners, all hesitated for a second of politeness before allowing a drink to be pressed on to them. And from the way they stood, weight first on the one foot, then the other, from the subdued tone of their voices, the way they held the glass, it was obvious this was a special occasion calling for a special effort—to show that wearing a suit, sipping whisky, talking softly, behaving smoothly, for them this was just everyday.

The room settled to respectability, to dullness. At the far end wife and daughter used savouries on trays to try and feed the flickering embers of jolly-good-party. Vol-au-vents were lifted with blunt finger-tips, spillings on to lapels and sleeves would keep dry-cleaners busy on the Monday. A disaster, a plop on to the concrete floor was squashed by a heel into a mess, forced into a joke.

Balfour needed a joke around him, a pill dropped into the flat soda in his glass to fizz it up. "Come Burger, where are the stories?"

"Yes, well, no but you see... okay, I'll have another. Actually, whisky man, I can't stand the taste of the fucking stuff, I'm strictly a brandy boy so drown it in the coke."

The Architect today seemed more elegant, more charming, more lanky than usual, more aware his height set him head-and-shoulders above the turmoil. "And where's the Guest-of-Honour concealing himself?", with one eyebrow raised.

"The who?" Balfour's forehead creased into frowns of concentration.

"That Deputy Minister chappie, or whatever-he-calls-himself."

"Oh, him, no, he hasn't arrived yet."

More carloads of uninvited officials disgorged themselves into the room which now was so crowded those at the rear pushed impatient palms on the backs of those in front, so noisy they could afford to shout "Gangway" or "Give a bloke a chance man" or "Where's the booze?" Few bothered to greet the host. Some of the newcomers' faces he recognised, clerical staff passed in the Department's corridors, Inspectors from remote sections he had last dealt with years before, if at all.

Clothes identified them more than the carbon copies of the forms in triplicate which marked their week-day status. "Brown suit over there" hissed Mrs Balfour into her husband's ear, "he needs a refill," and set him working, working at it like another aspect of the contract. The interlocked planning, preparation, initiative to get the operation moving, the party had acquired its own momentum.

Who were those four, there in the corner, striving to counteract the rudeness of their intrusion with a contribution of decorum? A navy blue, a powder blue, two bottle greens, they seemed to have ants crawling inside the pads of their built-up shoulders. From Head Office, Community Co-Operation.

Balfour gave up trying to make his guests feel welcome. No longer did he bother to smile weakly, shake hands and murmur "I'm so glad you managed to come along, you must have a drink what'll it be?" He slipped out into the corridor for a whispered consultation with his wife.

"I think it's going more or less as expected" he said.

"The hot trays in about five or ten minutes" she answered. "But for heaven's sake try and, you know, sort of ease up. You're so bloody humourless just when you shouldn't. D'you think I'm enjoying it any more than you?"

Duty re-called them to the room.

It was easier now, the rigid protection of the officials' demeanour melted as their suits became crumpled. A voice shouted "Fill it up man, to the brim, pour with a shaky hand," and another answered "I've lost count already." A man's level could be measured in the depth of a full whisky glass, all those fancy eats on the trays they meant nothing, nothing, that lavish lifestyle, it meant nothing to men who could hold their drink better than, better.

A group in the corner, foot-stamping, faces flushed, bellowing, their pig-eyes out of focus, too rowdy till Grandpa subdued them with a bland of friendliness, of dullness, of senior calm. He was having black coffee, wouldn't they also like a cup, nothing like black coffee.

Boyboy was careful, neat with cups and saucers.

A flat palm slapped the host's shoulder. "What's up man?" A pair of inflamed cheeks leered at him, blood-shot eyeballs wobbled. "You forget now how to knock it back no more."

Balfour the failure. Mrs Balfour the success.

She queened it on the sofa, eyes aglitter with a radiance of jewels, her cocktail glass a sceptre, and as though cupped in her palm complete and solid as an orb, the admiration of her burly courtiers.

She leaned over the proffered tray balanced on her daughter's hand, selected a dainty and nibbled at it so delicately with her front teeth, lipstick stained, all the males clustered round had to copy her.

Burger rammed one in whole. Pastry flakes on his jaw scattered on to his lapel as he chewed. He brushed them off, scrubbed fingers fumbling—a bloke needed to be smart when he with a full mouth. "You heard this one? Once there's this bugger at a party, he's more than slightly sloshed, he meets a bit she's like stepped out some calendar picture and he's got just this one thought on his mind if you'll excuse me you know what I mean." He forced himself to swallow.

Balfour heard his wife's voice register a higher note, a soprano solo shrill above the male choir, her delighted shriek of shock timed to punctuate the punch line of the daring joke.

Wrist over wrist over knee over knee, her fingers curled up to a climax of crimson manicure. A bank of hot eyes was fixed in fascination on the forbidden, the Aladdin's cave of mystery trapped in shadow under her skirt; only a glimpse of petticoat frill, a smooth gleam of calf, an instep curved in tension over a stiletto heel obscenely long. Her mask of cosmetics was set in a smile, the weightless fluttering of eyelashes made the muscles of the men feel heavy. To left, to right, she fawned on her admirers and in turn they saw a back arched kittenish for the convulsive leap, danger and love, poised to pounce with the soft cloth of her frock taut over shoulder-blades and exciting with the ripple of a bra-strap.

The Postal Super was the resident giant tame with loyalty. "Lissen hey" he boomed, "you'll more'n likely piss yourself laughing over this. Okay, just the one last one, but make it a stiff one. It's good for you, settles the stomach." He patted his bulge. "I never suffer from, but go easy on the coke even if it helps take the taste away. Now where was I... oh yes, talking about stiff ones. There's this raw kaffir straight out the bush, still blanket and all and he comes to town. He's looking for work and he bumps into one of those monk brother things togged up in his long robe affair outside the whorehouse, so... shit, I mustn't talk so loud, there's ladies present, hey girlie, girlie come here, your mommy there on the sofa..."

He lurched forward a pace and lunged vaguely. Beef fingers crushed the girl's wrist. A slight twitch of her neck set the head at a more imperious angle, green eyes froze cold between narrowed lids and the question seemed to come from raised eyebrows rather than her lips. The consonants were clipped to sharpness. "What do you want?"

She flung off his grasp, discarded him with the contempt of an orchid-lover dumping a boulder on to a rubbish-heap. One side of the room was flattened to silence. Shouts snapped off in mid-boast and they heard a stillness round them. The huge figure recoiled from her disgust, the movement of his bulk set a swell of foot-shuffles spreading to the opposite wall. Soon all listened to the quiet in the room and the memory of loudness made the previous noise seem louder.

Those round the sofa sighed as they inhaled lungfuls of perfume surely labelled 'Glamour' or 'Romance'. The aroma drugged them; to look, only look at her was the nearest they dared come to a narcotic dream where kitchens never smelled of cabbage, rooms were not cramped and there were no dents in the fenders of their second-hand cars. She was the vision of what their faded wives should be. Even an important State Official, really important, actually let's-face-it he didn't stand a hope, he had to know his place.

Not like those three over there who first stood cringing in the doorway and then came barging in as though they owned the place, the two fat men and that woman with them. Their complexions alone were enough to turn anybody's stomach, let alone someone with four doubles in him on top of all that rich food.

"Now who the hell d'they think they are?" the Senior Inspector snapped at Balfour's ear-lobe.

"Nominated Coloured Representatives, one with a wife."

"The what?"

"The State Council" Balfour explained.

"Well." The elder bristled righteously. "By me, so far as what I'm concerned, I'm telling you a hottentot is still just some kind of savage and a bushman, he'll always be a bushman."

Balfour watched all those already settled in the room recoil a half-step of distaste, of social distance. The two men's suits were too tailored, there was strain across their waistcoat buttons and their handshakes worked at acceptance with the force of a pump. The woman's grimace of respectability pressed dimples into both her chins and as she minced across the floor he sensed the constrictions of her secret elastics. The three dark faces were outshone, out-pinked by the varnish glazing her straw hat. They were the organisers, the driving-force behind their church bazaars.

They spotted a corner for themselves near the heap of mortar lumps and edged towards it, heads jerking in time to each step with the over-confidence of outcasts.

A huddle of clerks near them flicked glances over dandruff shoulders, bent the hair-oil of their blonde strands closer, and giggled. Mrs Balfour unwound herself from the sofa, smoothed pleats against thighs and remembered the poise of ballet-classes to twist across the room. She spared a full two minutes to be gracious. She knew how to smile sincerely.

140

The room flickered back to tepid warmth. A restrained behaviour, no shouting, no doubles grabbed and gulped, please-and-thank-you singles sipped, that would set the right kind of example to those there in the corner. Comments on the intruders were hissed too softly for them to overhear. The buzz of subdued conversation settled to a steady hum as Balfour watched his son dart across the room, the boy's mop bobbing between gabardine and worsted adult thighs. A treble shrilled from the sofa, "Mommy, Mommy, she tried to pat my head. What's she doing here, why isn't she there in the kitchen with Nanny?"

Balfour winced. Wife to the rescue—there she was, managing to hold up her end of it. Grandpa too, he kept bending for a few attentive moments over each of the solitaries always found in the corners of any party; like that junior from the Quantity Surveyor's office. And Burger? Where was Burger? Over there, frantically beckoning the host towards the door.

A figure, middle-aged nondescript, shouldered its way into the room with the unsure aggression of a climber overawed by the height he had managed to scale. The head was obscured by a hat one? two? sizes too big, hard down on the ears.

A familiar face; despite the clothes only another of the ageing gangers one half-pitied for their semi-uselessness, at their age still having to be out in all weathers? Or maybe one of those truck-drivers, in the sixties finding it no longer so easy to control a ten-ton tipper and endure the broken seat-springs? It could not be him, it could, it was.

So this then was the known face, the sour raisin, lips downturned to acid by the taste of newsprint that often etched his features below a headline of accusation and reprisal.

Two aides, a respectful pace behind, both with the bone and muscle and close-cropped skulls of rugby toughs, protected the Deputy Minister's flanks. And Botha modest in the rear, a grey shadow of the celebrity who had led in the last of the late-comers.

No dog, no smile to welcome him, Botha hung back at the door and when at last he slunk in on tip-toe, so delayed was his entry all present knew no more guests could possibly arrive. The cast was complete.

Impatient, with steps of ratty energy, the Guest of Honour bore in towards the host and a pressure wave seemed to force the room apart. Into the void, into a vacuum that demanded his presence, the politician dominated the centre of the floor.

An aide bent forward and whispered in the ear of his master, who whipped off his hat and with a flick of the wrist, held it horizontally. It was Burger who received it, Burger who wiped with his sleeve at a speck of dust and stood there gaping that a crown so heavy, actually it felt quite light.

Nod and handshake, nod and handshake, the public figure toured the traditional round of private greetings. Between each instant of movement, the face reverted to stone.

Burger clutched with excitement at Balfour's lapel. "Man, so he was standing there, just like the two of us we're standing here now, and he puts out his hand just, just puts out his hand to me. Shit a brick, you'd never say a big shot like that shaking hands, and that hand." Burger glanced down to his own, limp with feeling as though the wrist was sprained. "It had signed all those regulations and laws and banning orders and so on and so forth."

A Nominated Coloured Representative wheezed up to the host and demanded full attention, full. He tapped a forefinger a few times at his greying temple "Say what you like, he's got it up there, they all have, know exactly what they're, know all right. And still some people criticism us behind our backs, don't have to tell me, for working together, working to the benefit of our own people." He nodded a few times, his voice climbed to a peak of emphasis. "Man, you've got to face the practical realities."

The Architect manoeuvred the Contractor into a vacant space. "Would you prefer it for me to do the honours?" he murmured. "A few words of introduction."

"By all means." Balfour drooped with relief. "You carry on, please do, as soon as you feel the time's ripe."

It was graceful the way the Architect held up a plate above his head and rattled a knife against it to call for silence. Balfour shrank back against a side wall. The Consulting Engineer winked at him, raised a discreet forefinger of farewell and tip-toed away between the listeners. The Quantity Surveyor's junior edged towards the side door and slipped out. Burger whispered to his neighbour, held up his hand to be examined, and blushed. The Postal Super cleared his throat. A trainee slow in finishing his story was glared at by the room in general and hissed to quiet-man. Mrs Balfour was suddenly serious with a woman's understanding of her place in a man's world.

The honied phrases flowed with sweet praise, on and on, no word was sticky on the Architect's tongue. A smooth introduction.

At last. The Deputy Minister stepped forward. He waited for the silence of expectation to fill each single ear.

"Can everybody hear me? Can you hear me there at the back? Step

142

forward, step forward there from the back, there's plenty room here in front. Don't be so frightened, come on, I don't bite."

He accepted a sheaf of notes from an aide and flipped through them. "Before I begin on the speech proper there's just the one thing. Don't for a moment think I enjoy saying what I've got to but."

His glare accused each member of his audience. "There's some, maybe right here under our noses in our very midst, they think it's smart to play into, they're the tools, right into the hands of... do I need to continue? And I want to issue a little word of advice, just friendly advice at this stage but remember we can bite as well as bark. Rumour-mongering, that's a crime nowadays, a serious crime. So let's stick to the facts, plain hard facts, the truth." He sniffed and glanced down to his notes.

"Ladies and gentlemen" he began, "it gives me..." His voice rose, rose and fell in the sing-song intonation of a speech. Then he lowered his notes.

"There's just the one other thing. What's called 'pressure from outside' I say 'called' remember, because actually it's even far worse than that. From inside as well as, as from other places. And still, in spite of, of this..." A hand groped the air as though trying to pluck a word from the atmosphere. "This treason. Yes treason, I know that's a dirty word, that's a serious thing to say and still, why is it, why is it I ask you, here's still the finest, the finest country yes in the whole whole world, for investment. The safest. And I'll tell you why, I'll tell you. Because there's some real men here, determined, determined yes not to just give up what's theirs, what they've created for themselves and what they've fought for. And are prepared to fight for. Just remember that." A fist quivered with the passion of his conviction, knuckles gleamed white. It needed five, six breaths to regain his composure.

Quietly, coldly, his eyes pin pricks of ice, word by word he added, "and with men like that you don't play around, you don't go out from your way looking for. A real man, he's patient, he's patient all right, he can afford from his strength be patient, till there comes a time when."

Now he held his notes at arms-length, a little closer, a little further to focus them. "Ladies and gentlemen" he repeated, "it gives me great pleasure, no, more than pleasure, a deep satisfaction to be present here today. Because today marks the occasion..."

Balfour's eyelids drooped in boredom. Suddenly he jerked up straight, face shining. A brilliant idea. If the Bureau of Standards issued Standard Specifications for sewer pipes and toilet bowls, then why not too for speeches?

"... so you see, you see, even Sales Tax on a thing like food, it all goes to a worthy cause." A pause for the customary laughter to follow the customary joke. The Deputy Minister bared his gums; teeth too perfect to be true.

Burger obliged with a titter.

"But to continue on a more serious note. This then's a source of pride, yes real pride in our policy and the way we stick to it, come-what-may, fair weather or foul, through thick and thin." A forefinger wagged defiance. "... judged correctly had arrived at a point in time to create, yes create for those others lacking up to now opportunity gain for the future necessary commercial experience."

He lowered his notes, lowered his voice.

"Now I want to let you all into a little secret. The whole Cabinet, yes right there at the very top, felt it was a duty, a duty. My Minister, myself, the whole Department officials, and once our mind's made up, no turning back, no promise today and that's the last you hear."

He referred again to his notes. "Where else could such an example of, where else? In America? Behind the Iron Curtain? No, that I don't even have to begin tell you the answer. In China, in Europe, in say, say other parts Africa? No ladies gentlemen, not nowhere there, it's here, right here in front of you. Here's one of the most valuable and prime situated sites in the whole city. And this is where I must express my gratitude, on behalf my colleagues their gratitude as well, that Federal Investments, now that's what I call public-spirited, prepared donate this site, donate mark you for not a cent, not one single cent more than what they themselves, their own outlay." He half-turned to his aides and nodded. They led the applause.

"Let me assure you four-hundred-thousand that's indeed a most reasonable sum for such a valuable, a prime situated site in the whole city. Most reasonable." Again he lowered his notes. "By today's standards that is," and continued reading.

"Now anybody'd think the so-called public companies, other organisations, so on so forth, they'd all come rushing forward full of offer help run this beautiful complex. But did they? Did they?" His voice scaled up to a falsetto of outrage. "No ladies gentlemen, it's my sad to report not one single, none, not prepared put their money where their mouth is. With sole exception, the only and solitary offer of Federal Investments, alone comes forward to undertake for a purely nominal sum, per annum that is, undertake the dedicated task of preparing others gain commercial

144

training. All no-strings attached in a spirit of."

A sip of water.

"Also community centre and there'll be expenses, it all costs. So it's only just, and we believe in justice, believe me we believe in justice, on a one-for-one basis.

"Not the end of our troubles, far from it. Now where to find who's to run this whole beautiful complex, come on, you tell me. Decide on the spot so to speak yes this is right no that's wrong, you know what I mean. In charge of day-to-day, the details, shoulder responsibility, keep things moving. Some man absolutely..." He repeated the word and a shaking fist separated the syllables. "Ab-so-lute-ly can be trusted up to all the way, with experience of ..." He bent over fingers one-by-one. "Handling members other population groups; knows intimate finance business matters in general; dealing with official bodies; various councils so on; record of public service to his faith; of extending helping hand to his fellows in their times of suffering and need; team-leader with reputation preceding, even commemorated on public buildings named after in honour of bearing his name. All this combined in the one man? Impossible you'd say. But I'm pleased to see he's already here right here amongst us occupying his rightful place so to speak. His home ground from now on you can say. Ladies gentlemen, I have the honour to present you our Manager Designate. Mister Botha—it's congratulations. Sincere congratulation on behalf of all us."

Balfour saw the grey man stare down to the floor in modesty. He seemed to be trying to shrink himself. Then he risked looking up, a hesitant glance, lonelier than before, authority had distanced him further from his fellow-guests. He searched the gallery of flushed faces for acceptance by some one, anyone.

Through a haze of cigarette smoke and alcohol fumes Burger sensed that Botha was staring at him. The Inspector made sure the tie strangling him was exactly central, he wriggled his neck loose inside the garrotte of his collar. He saw Botha lift an index finger and slowly bend it to beckon him nearer. It wasn't, wasn't that easy find a place put down your glass without spilling more a few drops or two. Four elaborately careful steps brought him to a spot suitable for standing at attention; not too far so you had to shout, not too near neither. "Sir called me" he slurred.

The Deputy Minister flicked his notes to one aide, grabbed his hat from the other and with a pat on the crown started a hurried shuffle-shuffle down the passage, round the corner, out through the main entrance. A respectful Indian skipped out of his path; a remnant of urchins, forlorn in their last days in an estranged suburb, wiped snot from their noses as he ducked past a peak-capped chauffeur, into the limousine.

Mrs Balfour watched it glide away, a few seconds too late to play the hostess charming "a pity you've got to leave so early"; instead the puzzled wife tripping through the building asking "Has anybody seen my husband?" and "D'you know where he possibly could've got to?"

Through dimly lit chambers, out the emergency exit, down the fire-escape to blink in the glare of the parking area. Car still there, so, now what?

Back along corridors, her heels clicked a quickening staccato of anxiety, of alarm, of fear, broke into a desperate rattle of panic. Under stairs, inside cupboards, behind stacks of bricks and tiles.

She found him deep in the basement, leaning against the central column, forehead resting on its rough concrete and arms embracing it in a lover's grasp to draw out comfort from its strength.

"So there you are what on earth d'you bury yourself down here for you had me worried." Her voice rang out relief, echoed back to mock her with his silence. She came closer, hesitantly. "What's the matter? What is it? Too much to drink?"

The silence of a catacomb, low ceiling, corners invisible in shadow. "Can't you answer me?", pleading on the edge of anger.

A long pause. Her eyes were getting used to the dim light from a row of glass bricks. She saw his face, pale with the translucent pallor of a corpse. At last he whispered "Where's Boyboy?"

"Sent him back home with Nanny. Are you all right?"

He rolled round to face her. "That's good", with the sigh of a deep breath. "Better to get them out of here, out, the children shouldn't come in here again, this is no place for children."

"I've never seen you like this before. You're sure you're not... you know?"

"One weak whisky, four apple juices."

Now she came right up to him, her head cocked over to the side in puzzlement, in inspection. "You don't look well." Her aroma of luxury was incongruous in the musty damp that stifled them. A drop of condensation trickled down the column helpless as a baby's tear.

"Well? Isn't this whole set-up enough to make one sick? A training centre to teach Federal how to draw up better balance-sheets, that's all. Where do I fit into this, this swindle right under my very nose? I'm gullible, that's what really hurts."

The veneer of formal clothes and carefully applied grooming seemed to drop from her. It was the nurse, the trained sister keeping a balance between sympathy and clinical experience who asked "Where is it sore? Come, show me."

He shrugged. "Show what? Can't you see I feel trapped and the feeling's a trap in itself. I can see it all around me, so clear, I'm no longer blind. The truth tastes bitter y'know when you're forced to swallow it. It's poison, it's going to infect me."

"Don't be silly, a poison's not an infection."

"Then what did you make of it, the lease, the transfer of the site? All above board? I wonder how much that little Indian got for his ..."

"Anybody can suck poison out of words." Her laugh was too gay. "Some kind of business arrangement like any other. Goes on every day. Your contract won't be affected will it? Fairyland, that's where you'd feel at home, between the covers of some story-book, not here of all places. When it comes to business the rules are different, you should know that. What kind of a person are you anyway?"

"That's exactly what I've been trying to decide." He stroked his chin. "Do I have to live with it or should I fight it? Or bend and dodge and twist? You tell me. You see, either way leads to hell."

She blended patience with annoyance. "Well, anyway, you've got to finish the job, haven't you?"

He nodded. "I suppose so, I'm committed to myself. Say I don't, down the drain goes a whole career, a reputation, financially... as well as having to see you and the children dragged under with it. So I'll be accomplice to a corrupt gang of gutter thugs, I'd much rather be just plain myself."

Again he faced the column and stroked his fingers along a minor ridge where the shuttering had bulged a fraction. "I'd grown almost fond of all the harmless little blemishes that no one else would spot. Look, look around you, everything you see is flawed if you inspect it critically enough. Seems perfect when the light is dim like this. But after one's been shown what no longer can be overlooked, that the whole structure is rotten to its very foundation, what then? Close your eyes? Most people work like that. My job's to keep my eyes open, my job kept me going the same way this column keeps the building standing. We've seen couples coming near the end of their affair, no longer trusting, has one of them been betrayed or not? Does it really matter, once the crack has been imagined then the break's already there."

Two strangers stood and stood and stared at each other. Nothing to say.

"There's still a crowd upstairs. You're not being very mein host are you?"

No answer.

"Well, I suppose I'd better be getting back on duty. You stay down here and sulk."

She was planted firm in her upright poise, and against the column he drooped a little lower.

XI

The Monday morning following the party differed little from the Monday morning that had preceded it. A few more walls plastered, another row of window-frames set up and bricked in, the floor-tilers had made a start at last then got stuck—total progress during the week equal to say 1,5%, maybe as much as 1,6%.

Balfour's routine was unaltered, so too his appearance. The same wind-break, same suede ankle-boots. He plodded through the usual beginning-of-the-week tasks, nothing seemed particularly urgent, or really important. Not even interesting, except, except for one puzzle that made him squint harder at the front facade seen upside-down in the lens of his dumpy-level. Could others notice that the fingers fumbling the focusing adjustment were a trifle hesitant, without the snap and firmness of the week before?

When he tried to make the shape of the building stand out sharper it became a blur. The cross-hairs in the eyepiece too were somewhat hazy and he had to re-set them to bisect the target clearly. Which upset the image even more, it needed a compromise to reconcile the two. At last he got it good-enough, not perfect but good-enough to mark a fairly level datum line on both sides of the main entrance.

Anything could drift along with everything, lethargy with duty (or was it merely habit?), the end with the beginning, the end with the means, reasonable progress and hefty profit with a lack of liquid funds. The ten percent retention on each monthly payment was building up to a tidy sum. By the time the job was handed over and the fund released the same men would be starting another contract much the same.

He wandered into the Inspector's office. "Hello" he said. "I suppose I'd better remind you, this month's certificate, I presume you've sent it through in time."

149

"Sure thing" said Burger. "Hell, what happened to you Friday? Just disappear like that. You should've stuck around man, priceless, to see the buggers how afterwards they really got stuck into it." He hammered a fist on the table-top and chortled. "Know how to only knock it back. Doubles nothing, in the end going at it trebles. And the speech hey, how'd you fancy that? He knows for sure how to stick those words together. Now that was something else again, how he, just like that, with the Federal Invest bit."

"Someone has got to run the place I suppose." Balfour shrugged. "If not them then some other crowd."

Burger bounced on his stool. The recollection of excitement excited him to shout "That was one hell of a do and those Fedinvest boys, you got to hand it to them how they got everything tied up. Shit but there's no flies on that lot, shrewdies the whole bunch. Man, you can't do nothing except hats off to them and good luck." He kissed his knuckles. "What goes on behind the scenes nowadays."

"Then what's so different about this one?" Balfour frowned. "In any case towards the end of any job the Contractor gets driven up the wall by whoever's going to occupy the place. You've just got to try and work hand-in-glove with them." He lit a cigarette. His words rolled out with coils of blue smoke. "Whoever they happen to be, otherwise it'd be sheer hell, wouldn't it? All part of the game.'

The Inspector pressed both palms down on to the seat of his stool to heave himself upright. He tapped a forefinger against Balfour's breast. "You know what? The name of the game, it's money", and rubbed a thumb against an index finger.

Balfour laughed. "For them or for me? As long as this month's payment comes through in time I don't give a damn who moves in here after hand-over."

"It's a bugger hey." Burger slumped down again with a Monday-morning sigh. "The shit poor bastards the likes of you and me's prepared to swallow just for peace sake."

"You're probably right." Balfour leaned over the table and unrolled a plan to show the discussion now would be official. "I've been over the whole job with a fine comb and there's nothing really, only a few minor bits and pieces we'd better check. On Plan S13 it shows..."

The working week had started moving peacefully, it would roll on through its days, its 1.5 or 1.6 percent. The delayed delivery of floor-tiles had arrived at last, only three days late. The longer list of absentees on a Monday, that too was routine. No sign of rain, Manie and his team could start closing up the roofs of North and South wings in a day or two. The usual half-an-hour to escape from Burger's stories.

"I've set a level datum line" Balfour remarked to his foreman, "across the main entrance for those floor tilers. Missed a good party. Pity, you should've come."

Dougie sniffed. "Don't worry, I've seen this morning's paper. A bunch of racketeers, that's all they are. I don't approve of bad words, that kind of rough talk, but there's no other way of putting it."

"Aren't you jumping to conclusions? Guilty till proved innocent, without all the evidence? Exactly the kind of thing you accuse them of doing?"

The foreman did not deign to answer. Instead he jerked a chin towards the grey figure with the dog standing next to Burger behind the stack of aluminium roofing sheets. "There they are" he hissed. "I think they're waiting for you."

"Come come." Balfour laid a calming hand on the overall sleeve. He felt muscles clamp tense under the cloth. "Whatever it is, whatever is or isn't going on doesn't concern us in the slightest. We've got a contract to fulfil, it's quite apart from any... the kind of thing you're suggesting, nothing to do with us. Nothing", he repeated loudly as Dougie too suddenly remembered an urgent problem inside the building.

Botha called "Hey" across the stack of roof sheets and waved a grey arm—his usual salute, his usual invitation to a friendly little time-wasting chat. Stiff, formal, unsure of his reception, sticking to a tried routine, he still looked forlorn despite having Burger at his side.

Balfour hesitated between snub, formal greeting and congratulation. The alsatian slobbered through its fangs; instead of the expected saliva-gleaming white he saw they were a blood-streaked yellow. Not menacing him but Burger as the Inspector squirmed his safari-jacket straight. A whispered consultation, an urgency, almost desperation in the way the two men now argued with palms chopping the air in emphasis, in refusal and demand, in insistence. At last from Burger a nod, a shrug of acceptance.

He approached Balfour with a pause of hesitation between each pace. The way his toe-caps met the gravel seemed to fascinate him. He resettled the shoulders of his jacket to a more comfortable drape.

"Well actually" he said, "all this really's none of my doing but you see, man, it's those, you know." He hitched up his trousers. "These damn aluminiums of yours" he blurted and hung on to the lapel of

Balfour's windbreak as though it would support his plea. "Just a few man, you can spare them, you won't hardly notice it there a dozen or so short. Not me, no, just it's the Feds, they're... "

Formality was a shelter, a defence difficult to crack. It had always held up in the past and this job was routine. "Sorry" apologised the cold and dignified Contractor, "I'd very much like to help but I'm not allowed to. Not mine to give, government property, you know that, once it's been included in the certificate under 'Materials on Site.' "

"You talk about certificates" said Burger. "You realise from now on all's got to be approved first by the Fedinvest otherwise..." He broke off his recitation as though realising its sing-song intonation implied a lesson learnt by heart, to be repeated on demand. "Ach come on man" he whined in appeal. "Just for oldtimes's sake, we've become sort of like pals. You can help the buggers out. And also." He looked down and cleared his throat. "I wouldn't mind, actually I could use a couple for myself while you're about it, seeing as... "

"Seeing as what?"

Burger lifted his head for a direct stare of courage and of honour. "Seeing as how the Feds, there's always the outside chance they'd condemn in any case." A heaving chest pumped blood into his face. "They'd say who'd expect to use rubbish like that and still hope to get away with it. Have a heart. Tell me I must write you out a Site Instruction, just like that, 'To Be Removed From Site'. Got me by the balls, same like you."

Balfour had already sprung to the nearby stack and crouched over it. His forefinger stabbed downwards. "For one or two tiny dents in a few corners? We can work them into offcuts or under laps, even get them panel-beaten if you insist on being utterly impossible. It's exactly what's specified, it's got the Bureau of Standards stamp, what more do you want?"

Burgers's hands fluttered in protest. "Hang on, hang on a sec. Just hold your horses. Look, this isn't actually any of my doing, hang on, don't go jumping off the deep end." He scurried back to Botha and again they consulted head to head.

They approached Balfour slowly, side by side. Botha was almost smiling. Determined to be friendly. Eager to talk.

The fingers he laid on the windbreak's sleeve tightened to a vice-grip of steel. "Listen my friend" he advised, "you don't have to tell me, me, that that little thing down there, to you and me it might look like some kind of Standards Bureau stamp, it might maybe have the same letters and the same shape, it can even have the same colour for all they

152

care but so far as what anybody from outside is concerned, it's worth not that much.'' He snapped the fingers of his free hand. ''And when it comes to that so-called certificate of yours you come along claiming, look, I'm here to help, that's precisely what I'm here for. Actually it's got sweet nothing to do with me I could just as well wash my hands of it but your best bet is go speak to them there by Head Office. They know your type. Explain nicely, otherwise it looks like money, that's all you're after, that's the one thing you can think of, money. You'll find them quite reasonable, long as you're entitled to, fair enough.''

''Very well.'' Balfour's words had the cold, slow power of a glacier. ''I'll phone the Bureau. They'll send an authorised laboratory technician to come certify the mark right here on site, in front of you. If that's what you want.''

Botha's talon released its hold on the Contractor's bicep, ''Fine, it's fine by me, have it your own way if you insist. That Standards stamp, I'm quite happy long as you're satisfied, I won't even bother argue with you on that score but let's get the one thing quite straight. I don't want there to be any grounds for misunderstanding. Let's get this clear, I think you're on the wrong track altogether. I can't for the life of me make out from where you get hold of the idea anybody's out to get something for nothing. That's not the way it works. No, oh no. You can charge whatever you like, it'll all get paid for, whatever it's worth, you can charge whatever it's worth for this damaged scrap.''

''Scrap? Scrap! In exact accordance with the Specification. Go and look it up, go on, I'll tell you what section to look under, what clause.''

''Only it's from your side it's already been reported damaged, make no mistake about that.'' Botha fished deep in the pocket of his grey raincoat. ''In that condition you yourself say it's in, I can't see there's any way Fed's going to allow it be used on any job of theirs.'' Licked finger and page, licked finger and page, he busied himself over a notebook. ''Here, it was on a Thursday. If you want the exact date, here it is.'' He pointed a thumb rigid with conviction. ''Your exact words. I've got it down. Now listen nicely, this is what you, out your own mouth there with the off-loading. 'Look this corner is bent'. Wait, wait, there's more coming. 'Real damage.' '' He snapped his notebook closed and the sound self-satisfied him. ''Word for word. So it's only from yourself I'm trying to protect you.''

''Wait.'' Balfour zipped up his windbreak. ''Let's get some others involved in this.''

''Such as who? By all means, whoever you like'' Botha fiddled with the studded collar round his dog's neck. It needed his full attention.

"The Architect, the Consulting Engineer, the Quantity Surveyor" Balfour answered. "Let's hear what they've got to say shall we? Not be hasty, it can wait a day or two. I'll phone them', and strolled away with a saunter of controlled calm.

And sensed two pairs of eyes still burning on his back when he reached the young man waiting on the step outside his office.

The salesman's arm shot out with the precision of a piston controlled by a system of conditioned reflexes. It started sawing the air even before his fingers had found Balfour's and closed on them with a prescribed firmness. A digital watch heavy with optional functions and waterproof guarantees, worn on the inside of his wrist, peeped out below company-logo cufflinks. The smile was set in a fully operational curve. "Hello there. Hello-hello-hello, don't you remember me?"

"Dale Carnegie I presume" growled Balfour.

The young man jerked back from the shock. The curve of his smile stayed constant but an eyebrow twitched up in puzzlement. "I don't remember you. You weren't on the same course were you?"

He followed Balfour into the office and fussed through a ritual of unclipping a silver-branded briefcase, handing over his card, holding a presentation ballpoint poised over an order pad.

"Federal Roofing" said Balfour. "Never heard of them. Look, I'm busy now."

"No problem" the salesman chirped; those eight lectures of the confidence course would surely do the trick. "New on the market, will soon be the biggest in the country roofing-wise. Already the best ha-ha. Part of the Federal Investment Group so that's your guarantee."

Balfour flipped idly through a brochure. Topless models balanced thighs and grins on sloping aluminium roofs. "Try the Inspector of Works next door" he said, "he might be interested", and reached for the telephone directory.

"Who's that? Mister Botha or Mister Burger? Look, I'm not in your way or anything am I? I could come back later but it's the early bird catches the worm." Never offend the customer. "Books the order" he corrected. "The service we offer is coupled with…"

Balfour interrupted the recitation. "I didn't know Federal Investments went in for roofing. Since when? I didn't ask you to call here."

The salesman winked. "You'd be surprised, we've got a finger in just about every meat-pie on the counter. Lots under other names of course, but each time you buy, well, just about anything, as like as not it's Fed's hand you'll be eating out of. The service we offer..."

Balfour swept a pile of brochures back across the table. "Our order was placed months ago. Besides, as for the future, your profiles are useless, they don't comply with anything."

"Our what?"

"Profiles. The shapes." He started turning the pages of the telephone book.

"Now I get it. The girlies, their figures, they don't turn you on? Well anyway, well, yes, you see, the service we offer... no hang on, you mean the shape of the sheets? That's nothing, in every spec it always says 'equal or approved' so that's no problem."

"Please." Balfour made a polite word sound rude. "All sheets are on site already. Now are you going to leave me in peace?"

"Then I just don't know anymore." The salesman shook his head. "You mean you're not going to book the order with me? That I simply can't make out, it doesn't make sense. Look, I've got it all written down already, our own drawing-office took out the quantities from the plans and those were sent us by Federal Investment themselves, so it must be spot-on. So many of each size, hook-bolts, washers, the lot. Besides, listen, the service we offer is coupled with a back-up of technical know-how, prompt ex-stock deliveries and generous trade discounts to approved customers."

"Not if you gave them to me for nothing. Yes Dougie, what is it?"

"I'll leave these with you" said the salesman. He heaped pamphlet on to brochure on to loose-leaf catalogue and crept out.

"We'll be needing to know one of these days" said the foreman, "what final colours they'll be wanting so we can tint the undercoat."

"Right." Balfour nodded, pushed away the phone book and crossed to the Inspector's office.

"Man" said Burger. "Don't get hold the wrong end of the stick. I reckon you got the whole story wrong. He goes out his way trying to help you out and you go climb on your high horse. I know him, you must first get used to a bugger's ways. From the old days still through Auntie, you remember I was telling you what a character."

"I've thought of a way out of the problem" said Balfour. "Let's go through the stack, sheet by sheet. You can give me a Site Instruction, so many to be removed from site. Make it official, then the supplier will have to replace at no charge. A bloody nuisance, a delay, at least it won't waste anything."

"Ach no what" said Burger. "Those couple little scratches, got nothing to do with the price of cheese. Forget it man, forget it. Just forget all about it."

"And the monthly payment?"

"I checked up" said Burger. "It's there by the Fed crowd. I expect they'll post otherwise it'd be quicker you could go fetch."

"One other thing. We need to know the colours for the finishing coats."

There seemed to be a puzzle in the corner of the Inspector's ceiling. "Now you ask me something. I reckon, at this stage, stick to white. If black is beautiful then white is right. You talk about black and white, now you tell me something for a change. What happens you cross-breed a kaffir with a jewboy? You don't know? The night-watchman who owns the building."

His bellow almost blew his visitor through the door.

Back in his own office Balfour held the salesman's glossy colour-prints up to his nose and smelt them before dropping the whole bundle into the wastepaper-basket. He allowed himself the luxury of a leisurely stretch-and-yawn, a few plastic sips of coffee from the thermos, a glance at the Times. Yes, the party had been featured, mainly a summary of the speech, two half-columns at the bottom of page four, it all sounded rather admirable the way it was reported. A folded newspaper joined the Fedroof literature.

He added a few items to the list in his notebook. No major problems, it was the finicky little nuisances that nibbled away minutes and drove a sane man crazy, not the big decisions, for these there was never time or courage for reflection. Every Monday had its own annoying petty incidents, set-backs that needed to be wangled straight somehow, a bit of tact, a bit of patience; the ignorance, inexperience, stupidity in others— temporary pinpricks best forgotten before getting stuck into the solid work, the technical, the permanent. When a tooth stopped throbbing in the waiting-room, it was hard to believe the abscess had ever been there it felt so normal. A normal contract, a normal Monday morning at the start of what should be a normal week. He chewed the end of his pencil, wrote 'White U/C', and went out to start his round of inspection.

Sun, dust, wind, delivery trucks, labourers with shovels, artisans with queries, a sub-contractor with complaints, brick stacks and roof trusses, and as usual hurrying through the entrance gap in the hoarding—

Naidoo intercepted him, brown knuckles rattling in agitation against a newspaper folded on page four. "Mister, mister, what this it says? First I say to myself no don't believe anything it says in paper they always make the mistake so I go to Deeds Office I go there to Deeds Office in town pay search fee pay pay and transfer transfer. Five, six time in one year. Six.'' He held up all fingers of one hand plus a thumb. ''First to Fed Trust then Federal Estate, Fed Develop, Fed this, Fed that. Each time, each time sell price two three times buy price. What you make of it hey, what you think? The thousands, how come they say the four hundred when I get the four?''

''Please'' said Balfour, ''please, I suppose that's the way things get done, I don't know, I really don't know, that side of it, I can't tell you anything. Sorry, they're waiting for me, I must go.'' He moved towards his foreman's beckoning arm.

''What must I tell the driver?'' asked Dougie.

''Listen, I've got to dash into town, I shouldn't be long. What driver?''

''A trailer. There's a trailer there outside in the street. The driver says they're supposed to load some aluminium sheets but him there…'' The foreman jerked a chin towards Botha and his dog. ''He's sending them back again, says there's been some mix-up. Even if like it says in the paper he'll be sort of in charge after we've handed over, does that give him right to order around here on the job?''

''Cartage contractors'' said Balfour, ''I've never heard of one ever getting anything right. Or anyone else for that matter. It'll all sort itself out,'' and shouted a few words across the street while unlocking his car.

Eight minutes to town along the new free way, twelve to find parking fairly near a central block of Barclays, United, Standard, Federal and Allied. It needed Balfour's expert eye to distinguish one building from the other.

Security at Federal was strict. A voice, muffled through a brass grille, sounded reluctant to admit him, relented, and the bronze door opened a crack for him to slip in sideways. It clanged behind him.

The 'Enquiries' desk in the foyer was deserted. He studied the white plastic letters of a black ribbed notice-board next to the lift shaft. The Company Secretary on the seventh floor seemed a likely place to start but when he pressed the 'Up' button the lifts refused to move. Pressed again. Nothing. Pressed pressed pressed; numbers lit up on the display panel above the door, but not consecutively. Quicker to climb.

The Secretary's secretary, no, she knew nothing about, better try there by the Project Manager, maybe he could.

''Where can I find him?'' said Balfour.

"Now you're asking." She shrugged.

When at last Balfour discovered the Projects office there was no one in it. Along corridors, past fire-hose reels, around corners, up and down emergency stairs. Through open doors he could see computers spewing sheets of print-out, fold upon fold.

On the thirteenth floor the Chief Clerk went on copying from one sheet to the other without looking up while Balfour explained "There's a Progress Certificate somewhere in this building to be countersigned before it can be presented to Community Co-Operation for payment."

He went on copying. "A what?"

Balfour repeated his speech, adding "Please. I've got accounts to meet. It's a sheer waste, to lose the cash discounts."

The Chief clerk laid down his pen and confronted the intruder with a full-face stare. "And so?"

For the third time Balfour... "I heard you the first time" interrupted the Chief Clerk. "Listen, this here's Federal not Community Co-Op even though we've got plenty dealings with them. But anyway, you can go chance your luck there with the girls in twelve thirty-four. That's on the twelfth floor y'know, one down," and he went on copying.

There was a counter-shelf across the door of 1234. Behind it a girl and a girl and a woman; an eighteen, a nineteen, a not-so-young; a blonde, an auburn, a vague mix of leftover colour-rinses streaked with grey, name-tag and badge pinned to the lapel of a tailored costume.

"Hang of a gorgeous." Balfour overheard the breathless blonde. "Genuine marked-down half-price with see-through lace from here right down to, you know." She tossed her hair. "Exclusive, really, naughty enough for my wedding night," she giggled.

"Excuse me" smiled Balfour, faintly interested, faintly amused. They ignored him.

"For your own good" warned the not-so-young, "keep that kind of talk for strictly between ourselves."

"Ourselves." The auburn head bent respectfully low; she made it sound like a magic incantation. "How did he put it, the Minister, there by the farewell for his overseas trip? Yes, 'we are different because we are ourselves, and we're ourselves because we're different.' Brilliant, all our directors are absolutely."

"There's a certificate" called Balfour.

The older woman stared across a ventilation shaft to the adjoining building, to its narrow windows and drainpipes on a grimy wall. "Yes,

158

different, you two girls don't realise just how lucky, it's a privilege to be in here and not say over there." She shuddered. "Look at it, how ugly, those drains of theirs, the filth that must be flowing in them. There they are, the others, you can see them there, not really talking together like we are here. Besides, they even speak in another way, a decent person can't make out at all what's it they're trying to say, but the Good Lord will forgive them for being what they are because in His wisdom He's put this space between us and them and we should be grateful."

The phone rang. They let it ring. And ring-ring, ring-ring, silence. Balfour rapped his knuckles on the counter till they hurt.

"God is love" the woman hissed. "How like I used to squeeze that concertina with a love no mother can feel when she squeezes a child. Yes, I still love to watch, Sunday mornings at the corner from behind a hedge where nobody can see me, how proud a man can carry himself in that charcoal suit of his and the sun, the way it shines, it shines in glory on the gold page-edges of his Bible. In my room I pray may goodness always be rewarded. They had to beg him on their bended knees to be an Elder, and now take on some enormous scheme to uplift those... the others. And all you girls can ever think about, what you call 'having fun'. You'll still find out, it's more fun not to go wasting your time on fun."

"I couldn't help overhearing" said Balflour in a loud voice. "That may be the contract I've come about. There's a certificate. Please."

A teenager flicked a mascara glance towards the door. "Can't you see we're busy?" In a corner the two girls whispered excitements. "... just listen who's talking she's a fine one to speak... as though it's really her uncle or guardian or something." They pressed crossed palms to lipstick, doubled over and sniggered.

When the phone rang again the senior answered it, "Yes', and listened with the frown of a deaf-mute before banging down the receiver. "Papers" she exploded, "the Department keeps on pestering about papers. What do they expect me to...', and used a stiff arm to sweep a litter of folders from her table to the floor.

"I'm coming" a junior sang over her shoulder towards the door. "Just hang on a sec, keep your hair on." She tidied her own before a hand-held little mirror. "You others fancy me with a fringe?"

Balfour leant right over the counter. The edge pressed sharply against his diaphragm. "Listen" he shouted, "I can't wait the whole day for one rubber stamp on one sheet of paper." He saw the older woman march up to the younger pair.

"I'll tell you what'll suit you." She clenched her teeth, a series of tremors kept her arms pressed tight against her sides. "Your every minute, it all belongs to Federal, your place is here, right here, not anywhere else, not in some fancy hair-do parlour. Pay respect" she screamed and jerked her right hand up to point in triumph to the minister's framed portrait on the wall. "After all that gets done for you, our own canteen, office prayer-meetings, even our very own cultural outings, all to try keep you decent. Other firms, d'you think they have anything like that, do you, do you? Answer me."

The girls' heads hung heavy with guilt and hair-style. They brushed stray strands from before their eyes, blushed and shuffled their sensible low-heels.

"Damn you" Balfour exploded. "For bloody Christ sake. Are you supposed to be in charge here?"

She noticed that rather presentable gentleman waiting at the counter, actually quite not bad looking for an outsider, and minced with dainty little steps across the room, head cocked to the side, smiling so nicely. "Can't I help you perhaps?", and tucked a lock of grey out of sight behind an ear.

She listened to his request with nods of patience and understanding. The smile tensed to a grimace. "Yes, long as he's sent you then yes certainly, just leave it to me. Come back say sometime next week can you? Ask for me by name."

Back into the maze of corridors and dead-end passages, minutes and minutes later Balfour was still searching to find his way out.

"What? What's that?" Burger hesitated at the open front door of his flat, car keys in hand. "Speak up, or you too fucking pissed even to stand? For the hundredth bloody time no, we're not going to Alex, I've got to go see Auntie it's for your sake also, I must go visit. What?" He banged the door closed, leant his forehead against the glazing beads as though in prayer, peered at his wife's vague shape blurred by obscure glass and uttered "Shit shit shit, you bitch, you criminal, you think I don't know you suffer."

Next weekend clean plugs and points, not pulling so good along the Main Road past Funeralparlour Mobil Ultramarket Pentecostals Bank Trafficlight Red Green Insurance Launderette Fatherchurch with Hall and Rectory Autolot Adventists Fastfood Apostolics Bar School Boutique right turn to station parking.

160

It was hot on the footbridge over the tracks, sun glaring on the rails like it always used to. Nothing ever changes; a bronze plaque honours the service of a somebody, paint flakes off domed rivet-heads, arrow pierces heart, prick luvs pus. Down on the platform schoolboys in striped blazers still squatted on fibre cases, staring pimply at folded-over comics and ignoring the black stockings and solid buttocks of the girls. Twenty thirty years ago could be today.

The street was still the same, the single-storey houses all in line, all with alternate red and white sheets of curved corrugated iron over the verandah, cement block pillars of imitation rock coloured glossy yellow, every steel window orange-brown.

Auntie's blue-and-white enamel number-plate was chipped, her wire gate needed a new hinge. The path across the strip of front garden had borders of bricks laid in a drunken zig-zag. Tired daisies, weeds, dust on maize-stalk leaves. Burger peeped through the lace curtain across a circular window next to the front door; the knocker he banged had the shape of a wagon-wheel.

Ferns drooped over the edge of a silver painted tyre cut away to form a basket, hanging above a mounted buck's head that stared at kapok springing from burst seams in a settee.

He waited. The suspected sound of a shuffle from the back of the house. A clock chimed on a church tower.

Another shuffle, so slow and laboured he could sense the effort and the strain, heavy weight, feet that refused to hurry and joints stiff with decades of dusting and polishing.

Slippers scraped across floorboards. sighs and hoarse breathing—now the rattle of a chain and the turning of a key. The door opened a crack.

"Yes, who is it? What you want?"

"It's only me Auntie."

The door opened and a shapeless area, all loose folds enveloped him in a tent of black cloth as she embraced him. He could feel the slack muscles in her arms sag against his shoulders, see soft flesh hanging in bleached bags of wrinkles with blue veins. Before his eyes the deep valleys of her neck lay in crevasses, magnified and geographically complex. He held his breath against the musty smell of an old woman and gently eased himself away.

With the knuckle of a bent forefinger she wiped the corner of a red eye, and sighed again.

Sparse wisps of silver, fine-spun, spread thin across a shiny scalp, were framed by the gilded border of an oval mirror behind her. One eye was

161

half-closed by the pouches of its lids, the other bright in the socket sunk into her skull, above a parrot's-beak of nose that arched down to the moisture of gums and the arid watercourses of her jowls.

She clawed the lapel of Burgers's jacket. "I knew it in here." A fist knocked weakly at her breast. "That you'd come back. The blood, it's the blood would call you in the end."

"I've come see Auntie about something."

He looked down at the coir mat while she wept on the doorstep. Across the road a housewife opened the front door and dusted a rug on the steps, slap-thud, slap-thud, head twisted round to keep eyes steady on them as her body jerked.

"Come." Auntie turned away. Each step needed another handhold further into the gloom of her passage, into the smell of an old person's retreat, cooking and disinfectant. She stopped, exhausted, and leaned against a glass-fronted display cabinet while Burger closed the door.

"Yes" she panted, staring at the ball-and-claw legs, the pink glaze of china, sea-shells, an ostrich egg. "You must keep the door closed on them. They're not our kind, they've put out some fancy electric bell. It's disgusting."

Through a curtain across an arch, another step, wrinkles on her knuckles, she gripped the edge of a french-polished dining table. "Anyone can press it, even hawkers" she hissed over a shoulder and Burger felt a spray of droplets moisten his face as he threaded his way in, bumping against the closely-packed furniture.

"Sit" she ordered and pointed towards a settee upholstered in shiny plastic and cushioned to discomfort, while she eased herself with moans and grunts on to a wooden kitchen stool.

"No no" Burger protested, "Auntie must come sit here."

She flapped a hand to silence him. "You'll never see me sitting on a thing like that. It was you gave it, yes you yourself remember when the whole family, they decided for me I must move in here. Your so-called present. He knew what it was I wanted."

She patted the leg of her stool. "Went to all the trouble to get me this, just told me how much, that's all I had to do, some people are too good for this wicked earth of ours and him so busy with importants." She pointed to the wall-mounted photograph above her; an earnest Botha and a grim-faced Minister stared full-face and shook hands at a flag-draped Festival. "This is what I'm used to, a hard stool is good enough for me. You wouldn't remember those days, at first we didn't even have that much, we were the worst-off of all. I don't mean the locations or reserves,

162

that doesn't count, I mean amongst the civilised." She nestled a heap of chins against her breast-bone and sighed. A clock shaped solid as a monument piled with hammer-blows more seconds on to her years.

"Whatever belongs to Auntie" said Burger, "she deserves it. House, furniture, everything."

She spat into a handkerchief, examined it critically, then crumpled and hid it in her sleeve. "All houses in this street, the whole suburb, the last one of them belongs to, all solid Federal. Our houses, our savings, except for that crowd across the road. That's how it should be, keep everything amongst ourselves, once we start taking in from outside, we'll rot, forget. In towns people forget who they are and rot from sitting on soft chairs." She chewed her gums. "They get dirty from looking at pictures of colour bathrooms in fancy magazines. When there was red dust on our faces and stinking sheep manure on our hands, then we were clean." She banged a clenched fist against her breast. "We knew who we were and we were clean inside, inside here." Again the thud of flesh and bone.

She bent still further forward with head just above her black lap, and rocked herself. Below the threads dangling from the hem of her dress, crumpled opaque stockings sagged round her ankles in a series of flabby loops and her slippers were worn threadbare on the outer edges. "I'll tell you, I haven't got much longer on this earth but one thing I've learned over the years, why things get done properly there at Federal. Because the people working there, they're still pure. Not like other places, with young men all drugs and anything that's foreign, and the girls, all they can ever think of is doing up their hair and ribbons on their private clothes."

"Auntie" said Burger, twisting against a cushion embroidered with the Coat-of-Arms, "I've got some trouble I think maybe Auntie can help me with."

"Now he's with them again, praise be the Lord, for they need him, they realise at last. And they take only the finest y'know, pick and choose, the very finest. Yes, look after their houses and us people in them. How he's always ready to take in and shelter and adopt the homeless in our family. Like this old roof of mine, the way it leaks. Even promised me a new one, pure pure silver not corrugate iron like for a shanty-town, whatever they call it, going wasting good money on still more sheds in the locations when those savages, they actually prefer it under the branches of some thorn-bush. And for nothing too, only what it costs him, not so much as that much for himself, that's the quality of man he is.

163

I was keeping the money, had it safe there, my savings with our people there by the Federal.''

"Auntie must listen to me please.''

"When you get service like that, you must be prepared to pay. What's fair is fair.''

"Yes Auntie, I'm working with him every day now.''

"Then count yourself lucky to be under such a... can learn from him about building. Every time, whenever he used to come and stay here with me between each appointment, you've seen all the things he did himself? Bricks both sides, yes both sides the front path and that fireplace in the back yard. You should go and see it. And you know what? Y'know it worked perfect from the very first time we tried it. All with his own hands, his own. The builder, does he appreciate, all that knowledge, that experience.''

"Well, actually Auntie, the builder, he doesn't really do any of the work himself. Leaves it to others, that type, he, sort of you know.''

"Not one of us.'' She spat out the words.

"No'' said Burger. "Yes, he's I suppose, not altogether on his ease yet with us, still got to get used to our ways.''

"Then he must learn. Your job is to teach him. must be made to learn, so long you don't go picking up any of his ways. Keep the cattle in their place and the jackals other side the fence.'' She paused and panted, squirmed into a position where she could begin to prise herself upright. "We in the family, we must stick together otherwise we're finished. How else d'you think you're going to keep your job? I'll make us some coffee, real coffee, with chicory, not that rubbish powder out of tins people buy in filthy coolie shops.''

It took time, time, tiring effort to rise while Burger shifted forward to the edge of his seat. "Auntie, there's a, a... '' he stammered.

"You've always fancied the sound of your own voice. I know what's coming. The drinking. And when you first introduced her to us you said 'sport'.'' She lumbered out to the kitchen.

Forehead heavy on his palms, elbows propped on knees, Burger waited. And waited. A narrow shaft of light thrust itself between overlapping plush curtains to illuminate the uneven stitches of 'MY LAND IS MY TRUST' on the stipple-plastered wall. Dust-sheets draped in folds shrouded items of furniture more crowded than a display window stacked for a final liquidation sale.

Auntie's voice from the kitchen doorway startled him. "While the water's cooking.'' Phlegm boiled in her chest as she steadied herself against the frame. "You know where you made your biggest mistake, the biggest of all? You thought you were being smart, trying something new, you knew better than what everyone else knew all along. I remember it now like yesterday when you were just born, there you were, a baby safe in a cot, not a dirty thought yet come into that little head of yours, all of us around you. And now? Now? You could've made some decent girl happy, a family. That child of yours, that drunkard woman I'm not even going to call a wife, it's the curse of God been put upon you for defying."

"But Auntie, Auntie must listen nicely now."

"Look at him." She pointed to the photograph. "Go on, look, that wife of his, the cripple, how he bears his burden with a dignity. There's real tragedy for you, yet never the one word of complaint has ever passed his lips and still he finds the time to give praise to our good Lord every Sabbath. When last did you? Answer me, when last? I took only the one look at that servant girl of yours and I knew for sure."

"But Auntie, it's not actually what you think, I promise you, she's only a quarter Portuguese on her great-grandfather's side, that's why she looks like sort-of, a bit, y'know, they call it an olive complexion. And the hair, you ask about the hair? But Auntie that's the fashion now, it's all the latest."

"Wait" she answered. "I think it's boiling."

She shuffled from the kitchen back into the room with a tray held high in pride and triumph. Burger jumped up to clear away a miniature rock-garden of painted shells, to free a corner of the dining-table. He took the tray from her and laid it down.

Auntie pointed to the nearest chair. "Sit."

He managed to slip in sideways but could not move the chair back far enough to sit squarely at the table, and had to twist around to say "Not too strong for me please."

Auntie ignored him. She guided a pink-gold cup full of dark liquid across the table. Some slopped over into the saucer. Burger lifted the cup carefully, scraped its bottom against the rim of the saucer before emptying it back into the cup.

She eyed him distrustfully. "There wasn't a drop perhaps?" It was a reprimand. "I'd hate it for a mark. That's where he likes to sit so I'll go on looking after till the day."

Auntie lowered herself on to the stool and slurped from a chipped enamel mug. "For him" she gasped. Each breath cleared away the steam clouds before her face. "For him you can't make it strong enough." She

165

cupped her mug between bleached hands and leaned forward with elbows balanced on spread knees, intently interested.

Burger brought out a small brown bottle, hooked out a strip of cotton-wool and shook two little pills into a palm. He clapped a hand over his mouth, threw back his head to swallow hard, gulped down a mouthful of coffee and explained, with the faint smile, the bravery of an invalid, "The doctor, he says it's from nerves in the stomach."

"Doctors" she sniffed. "All they're after is your money. If I'd listened to them at the hospital that time, how they said, the pains, they'd only keep on coming back again. How many times is it already he's cured me of them? He's left me the most wonderful remedies you'll find anywhere. Garlic, that's good for you, also cloves, also coriander." Her nods implied the dried leaves, seeds, shrivelled lumps in screw-top bottles or brown paper packets on her kitchen shelf. "Eat" she ordered, and watched Burger lick his lips while she fumble-fingered the single black hair of a wart on her cheek.

He lifted another sticky confection and bit it. "Nobody can make like Auntie does."

The lace doily on the plate, her hand wavered out to tidy it. "The secret is to twist them. Others, they make theirs round with a hole in the middle, then they go calling them doughnuts or something. Round, I ask you, with a shape like that you can choke on them, they'll stick in your throat."

Burger held the curly cup-handle between his thumb and forefinger, stroked it, pinched it as though its gold-leaf decorations were the rings on a fleshy lobe.

"It's not the drinking" he blurted, "it's the track-suits again." He fished a summons out of his back trouser pocket and smoothed it on the table. "Auntie can talk nicely to him, he'll listen to Auntie. He knows how to, the right kind of, there's a way of going round things."

"It's the Almighty punishing you for your sins." Her voice broke and Burger watched her weep. Backwards, forwards, she rocked herself till he edged around the table to embrace her and they mixed their tears. She pushed him away.

"Well Auntie, I suppose I must love you and leave you now."

"Go" she mumbled. Her jaw trembled to set shaking the loose red folds of her multiple chins. Then she clamped her mouth so tightly shut Burger wondered how she still could speak with gums pressed hard against each other. "We must keep this disgrace amongst ourselves. Even from ourselves. There has been no disgrace."

Helping her to stand helped Burger to keep upright. At the door he turned, watched her hobble across the room and brush a palm across an ornamental musket to remove a suspected fleck of dust.

XII

"I still remember from myself" said Mrs Balfour, "it's a difficult age for girls. Even then, there are limits, I wish you'd speak to her." She bent over the pages of a knitting pattern and concentrated too intently. The needles clicked and jerked. "Bangs the door and locks herself up in her room for hours on end. It's not natural. And please stop pacing up and down like that, tiger in a cage. Put on a record, anything."

He paused and fingered a tasselled curtain cord. "These are new aren't they? When did you change them?" Between the overlapping folds a strip of night showed black as the interlining. Garden, suburb, stars— did these still exist? Had they ever? "Tiger? You mean a rat in a trap. What's that you're making?"

Bitten nail-varnish pointed to an illustration. "Only orlon but you can hardly tell the difference. Going cheap, something wrong with the dye lot and doing it myself, it'll come to not even half what they'd ask in a shop." She twitched loose a loop from the skein. "You said things were starting to get tight for a while."

"A ski-cap is it? Complete with pom-pom, how charming. For when you decide to grace some exclusive Swiss resort?"

The way she laid down the needles made her words seem pointed. "Can I help it if he keeps on sending postcards? I see that pal of his the Minister has returned in triumph while he goes flitting from one glamour-spot to the other. At least, damn it, he knows how to live." She grabbed her knitting and again he paced across the crimson desert of an Afghan in time to clicks. "What do they say at Head Office, in other branches? About when he's coming back I mean."

The leather chair he slumped into creaked as it deflected under his weight. "Nobody knows anything. Usual chaos. I'm stiff. Been climbing scaffolds the whole day, up, down, over and over. The condemned repeating his last journey, not even some prisoner locked in his cell. I've had a thought."

"What?"

"It's not the animal or criminal that's dangerous, it's the cage itself, that's the real menace. It's all around me and I can't find from what angle to view those bars."

She purled, she plained. "Just try to relax." Knitted two together and dropped a stitch.

"The job stinks. Every now and then one comes across a bad one, in any career, that's in the order of things, at least these days it is. So what does one do? Pretend that shit smells of roses? Say that it stinks everywhere the same and so what? Say that it's none of my business, at least the major part that doesn't affect me directly? Or shrug shoulders and accept and try to manage somehow?" He lit a cigarette, inhaled deeply with a sigh and frowned at the smoke. "I've tried, I've tried this way, that way, nothing seems to work."

He got up and started drifting round the room, fingering the ornaments, setting a picture exactly level; a thumb-print marred the patina on a silver Georgian candlestick; passed behind her, to the side, in front, stopped and looked down at the knitting on her lap. "That's a hideous colour. Revolting. No wonder they rejected it.
You remember that thing you got just before the job started, to celebrate? I can't remember ever seeing you actually wearing it."

"We haven't been going out much lately. Especially not to the kind of place where."

"Well, I dare say it'll look good under candlelight on a deck in the yacht-harbour at St. Tropez."

She picked at a tangle in the skein, it seemed to become so heavy she had to lay it down on the low inlay table next to her. The hands of a weary housewife clasped a knee. The glamour-gloss of fashion and mistresses stayed on the inside pages of the magazine with knitting-patterns in its supplement. "Listen my boy, just don't try provoke me, don't try tempt me, you're not the most easy of partners these days. I can't decide whether to sob like a schoolgirl over her first romance, or slap your face, or what. You make up your own mind, that's all, I'll do whatever it is you want me to do. But I'm getting just a wee bit sick and tired of these sulks, the moods of yours. You're bloody impossible lately you know."

He dumped himself back into his chair, gripped his thighs and leaned forward. "Who? Me? I'm impossible? I'll tell you what's impossible, to get in even five minutes a day of real work on the site. If that much. The whole time the two of them hanging on my neck, every single little thing, it's all got to be explained twice, fought for double, argued about in three directions. Can't seem to get the job properly organised. It's not only the usual snags, where must I find the time to impose my will on it?''

"Then do what you can. There's a limit, you push yourself past the point and then manage even less."

"I suppose there are some who'd manage to get on with them but I don't understand those people. This Botha, this greyness, this through the proper channels according to his regulations, I can't bring myself to see him as fully human. I try to guess what lies behind that formal frozen mask of his and the worst sins are the ones we imagine. Is that all there is to him or he fits some theory about the nature of pure evil incarnate? To hell with him, I've enough on my fork to see nothing goes seriously wrong on the job."

"That's doing at least a bit of what you think is right." She picked up her knitting and hunted for the lost stitch. "Better than nothing."

Again he patrolled the room, now in a rectangle close to the walls.

"I've often heard you" she said, "when friends ask for advice about cracks or sagging roofs. The cost will be too great so learn to live with your problem. I've learned to live with you and heavens you are behaving like a problem child you know." Her needles clicked, clicked, steady as a healthy pulse. "At least I'm trying not to be a problem to you. You'll never know how hard I try. When you're twisting and turning and think that I'm asleep, so peaceful. Sometimes I wonder at two, three in the morning, if you haven't got another woman."

"And I've got a feeling, just a feeling but it's getting stronger all the time. It's not a question of, of when he's going to be coming back, but if."

"What makes you say that?"

He switched direction from clockwise to anti-clockwise. "I said, a feeling."

"Another postcard did come, just like you said it would, addressed to me but not from Zurich. I mean it showed a view of the Alps and things yet the postmark was Paraguay. Where's that?"

"When did it come? Why didn't you tell me?"

"Yesterday. I didn't want to upset you."

He stopped and scowled. "That was very wrong of you."

Still she kept on working at the pattern. The sheer monotony of it was therapeutic. It helped her to murmur "Sorry. What else can I say? So what if I was wrong, what should I've done? Look at yourself, how you can't decide what's the right or the wrong way to handle things. Once you ask, it's wrong. When you know you're right you don't need to ask."

"What do you mean?"

"Well say you can't decide on a... way of what to do. Fine, once you've decided, that's fine. Maybe whatever you do is wrong because something else would've been better. How'll you ever know for sure, things keep on changing. So everything you do could also be right. Only stop worrying, I won't criticise, that's the one thing you can depend on."

He stopped his pacing long enough to crush his cigarette into a Wedgewood ashtray. The stump lay amongst its fellow victims bent to the angle of a snapped neck. "Depend" he repeated. "We used to be the most dependable firm in town, work tip-top, accounts always paid on the dot, extra discounts to tempt our orders. Now every certificate is so delayed, there seems to be, almost a reluctance to deal with us. Rumours. Behind the back talk. And I put so much into building up a reputation, so much. That's still another waste of time and money. Discounts down the drain, begging for and paying overdrafts and loans. It's sick."

"How do all the others manage? Surely it's more or less the same for all the firms."

"They wangle, they tell the 'tomorrow for sure' story. So now I've got to do the same. Fibs, evasions. That's what really hurts, what those bastards are doing to me, making me less of myself, or at least the kind of person I wanted to be, making me more like themselves. Cagey, suspicious. When someone says 'Good morning' to me I start wondering why they said it. What's in it for them? I feel, feel degraded."

He lit another cigarette and again prowled from grandfather clock to standing lamp to tallboy. Suddenly he stopped and squatted down before her. She leant forward as though expecting him to embrace her knees but saw him pick at a loose sliver in the inlay table.

"You should get this seen to. Before it goes any further. It's quite a valuable piece."

"I know." She nodded. "I've been meaning to send it through to those Medici people, they did quite a nice job on that ormolu last time but I didn't want to bother you, with the expense I mean, not now. They're quite pricey."

He stood up to tip ash into the Wedgewood. "There's a cabinet-maker more or less across the road from the site. About the last left of the originals. Workshop shed in the back yard with a tiny sign over the door. One of those painstaking craftsmen. Medici send all their jobs to him."

"How do you know?"

"They've got a little boy who insists on playing on the site because that's where he always has. His mother keeps on coming to look for him. You know when a family is almost too conscious of being respectable."

"Anyway I'd better still send it to Medici and pay the bit extra. They've got a reputation to keep up."

He laughed. "You said 'keep up'. What's just occurred to me. Imagine our beloved chairman and that Minister in a five-star restaurant not knowing what all the fancy items on the menu mean and unsure which knife and fork. I should be grateful to them, they make me feel so damn superior."

He stubbed out his cigarette. "Really grateful because here I am practically middle-aged, I should be accepting, complacent. Instead I've got something to rage against, I'm burning with resentment. They're keeping me an adolescent."

"If you really are that young and so much on fire" she asked, "do you realise when last we did it? It seems like ages, I feel quite virginal." She blushed. "I wonder if I remember any more what to do."

"When you're in that mood I suppose even work is no excuse." He grinned. "Or are you only being dutiful to get my mind off problems?"

She dropped her knitting, reached out and felt him. "Come" she pleaded.

"Don't risk using a double-meaning word like that" he teased. "It could lead to what the experts call an 'embarrassing incident'."

Hand-in-hand they hurried up the stairs.

Monday and still no payment.

On Tuesday morning Balfour broke off his early-morning tour of the site and rushed to town, to a long fidget outside the bank manager's office. The financial magazines on the low table were all limp, the tea and welcome tepid. To a trust company, to the auditor who suggested trying an attorney rumoured to have funds available on short-term high-interest loan. Two hours wasted for a two-month respite.

He parked in the shadow of the tower crane. Over his head dangled the hook hanging from the end of the boom, menacing as the noose of a gibbet. At his feet lay an urgent problem—this latest load of face-bricks begged and paid for in advance, they seemed a shade darker than the panels already built.

Botha's dog lifted a hind leg to the stack as Dougie bristled towards him. The foreman's hands were eloquent. "I don't care if he's manager or even owns the place, just tell him to get off my back. I'm not that kind of a... I just don't do things like that."

"Like what?"

"He must stop his interfering. I've got work to do. Look, why don't we just pack up the plant, break down the sheds and clear off the site?"

"Dougie, there are things it'll take a long time to explain. If I can at all. What happens here, the building itself, it's only one part of something bigger and more complicated. Now what the hell's going on?"

A commotion, a shouting, a running, a Burger re-living his days of athletics to chase a little boy from the sand-heap across the future parking area; a darting, a dodging, a pair of heavy legs pounding and small ones stumbling, a catching, ear-twisting, yells, figures converging to weave in turmoil, caps and helmets rolling in the dust.

When Balfour reached the spot it was quiet and deserted except for a Burger hands-on-hips panting in triumph. "Little bastard, he was asking for it. Now he'll get what's coming to him, serves him bloodywell right. They'll fix him, they know how to deal with ."

"What do you mean? What happened?"

"He thinks just because he's still living here across the road. I warned him. I've had plenty repair and renovation jobs in police stations, juvenile courts and so on and so forth. I just happen to know what I'm talking about, what goes on in those places, how they hold them down there on a bench one sitting on their head, another at the feet and the cane they use, true as God it's so long and so thick, and wah-wah-wah. Scream, you can get deaf from ten blocks away and the room itself, just all piss and blood and shit. You should only see their little arses afterwards, like practically ripped open with a knife right across from here to here, across, across, across." He clutched his buttocks and pretended to cry, pranced round in small circles a few times and laughed, then fished a finger of dried sausage out of the pocket of his safari-jacket, broke off a piece, popped in into his mouth, chewed and held out the rest in offering past his listener's shoulder.

Balfour turned to see who had been standing behind him.

Botha shook his head in refusal, in formality, in upright dignity. "That kind of talk" he warned, "words like that get used to give us a bad name. All those against us, their ammunition. They try make out we find it safer to punish a dozen we're not sure of rather than let the one guilty get away

173

with it. But in actual fact it's precisely the other way round and you of all people should know exactly what I mean." He stalked away.

"What did the youngster do? You must tell what happened to him" Balfour insisted.

Burger shrugged his shoulders. "Nuisance. He's got no right to come play here on site." He chewed and swallowed. "How must I know what'll happen to him? The law's one hell of a bugger."

"I suppose so. You should know" Balfour sighed.

The Inspector jerked as though stung with the sudden agony of stab or slash. White-hot, seared by a flame of resentment, he trembled with self-control, grabbed a windbreak lapel and tried to shake it. "Watch it, I'm warning you, just watch it, be careful what you say."

Balfour managed to detach himself. "Sorry, sorry, only I remembered you mentioning a few months ago, that case, your wife, isn't it coming off about now?" He watched the line of Burger's moustache twist and curl and writhe, the black side-burns seemed lopsided on either side of heated cheeks. A forefinger wagged under his nose.

"What case you're talking about? For your own good, don't come along accusing, trying to make out that wife of mine's some kind of shoplifter or alcoholic or something. There's nothing I've got to be ashamed of, nothing, no case, no charges, nothing, all withdrawn. For the future, you must keep that big trap of yours shut tight', and he stumped away.

An hysterical and weeping mother came shuffling in slippers across the loose stones of the parking area. She flapped her apron at Balfour, then used a corner of it to cover her face and bowed with sobs, shoulders in a hump. "You must help a mother, maybe a little naughty but not a bad boy, not bad."

Balfour tapped her shoulder. "Come with me to the office, we'll try and phone. I won't lay a charge, I promise you but I can't say about the others, or what'll happen even without a formal complaint. Come along now. Panic won't help any."

The father came across the road to join them, a craftsman slow and heavy with confusion, fist clamped on a chisel as though to keep some hold on the sane and normal, not as a tool or weapon.

The parents stood mute and respectful in a corner of the office, watching that man who was in charge, how he phoned and phoned. A few times they muttered to each other, then hushed themselves not to interrupt and leaned forward striving to catch from Balfour's intonation and the way he listened, what was being said at the other end.

174

"Here, I've done what I can." Balfour glanced at his watch. "I'm already late for a meeting. Try this number and this one, you can use the phone here, then go to this address I've written down."

He hurried out and took a short-cut across the sand heap. On the crest of it the bricks of a toy castle lay scattered. Wind-blown sand was already filling in the footprints of a tussle, a last stand without a hero, without recorded history or fabricated myth. A carefully groomed youngish gentleman called up to him; the drooping Edwardian moustache emphasised the tear-drop shape of oversize dark glasses.

"Say, you're just the fellow I was hunting for. Hell, but you are elusive, I've wasted hours already looking for you. Don't you usually keep appointments?" His shirt glared an uncreased white, and even though the jacket of his suit was folded over a forearm, the cut and cost of its tailoring was obvious.

Balfour slithered down the slope of sand and confronted him. "Yes?" Grains had spilled over the upturn of his boots; it felt uncomfortable. "What's this appointment you're talking about? There was no..."

"Look, I've been appointed by Federal Publicity to do a feature on." It was a serious matter, a responsibility. "So you've got to supply all the necessary facts and figures, clue me up on... you know." Interviewer's time and full attention was a right he seemed accustomed to.

"I can't help you."

The smile would suit the man-to-man confession; charm was a marketable commodity. "Look, they're paying me one hell of a big fat fee so I've got to produce. It'll be the usual kind of, they're all the same really. So you'll have to cook up something for me. Like, er, say how many bags of concrete in the whole to-do, if you know the kind of thing I mean."

"You probably mean cement."

"What's the diff? It's only for the public, what they'll be told. And bricks, how many bricks would you say?"

Balfour began to edge around him "Facings or red hards or..."

"Makes no odds. Whatever's the more. Should I say a million?"

"You can say whatever you like."

"All right. What should we make it? We'll say two million then. And, anything else of interest? Features?"

Balfour looked back to watch him stroke his hair-cream. Ten minutes late.

The Site Meeting was well under way in Burger's crowded office. As he squeezed his way in the Senior Inspector clapped hands in applause, in derision.

"Sorry I'm a bit late. Surprise, you've still not left us to go on pension."

"Not a damn, not till I'm carried out feet first. Staying on long as they'll have me. Listen, this concerns you." He pointed to Botha.

Who shuffled some papers and turned to Balfour in a fidgety appeal. "Look, must try to work together on this. We... " His voice faltered and died away under Balfour's stare at the same grey figure that had drifted across the site, still lost, still aimless. Botha forced himself to face his audience, squarely. "What you think, the best way? It's concerning those announcements I was talking about. Item number, er, on today's agenda"; more confident as the committee-member. "Week's bargains, special offers and suchlike, hook attention, make sort of lively. That's between the kind of music they play heavy. Whole ring of loudspeakers, here and here, might as well stick up another couple over here as well." He pointed to a plan, jerked up his head, waited for comments. "So, nobody got anything to say?" Botha in command. "Just to make them pick up their ears. What actually counts is the news, what's going on in the world. If the government's putting up the money, only fair, we're obliged put forward the facts so everybody can judge for themselves. Then if people don't want to listen we'll just make sure they can hear." All could see he had a sense of humour, he could quip "So what d'you say mister contractor, you're the expert."

"Not particularly partial to the idea of drilling those beams." Balfour frowned. "Dare say a few small expansion bolts providing the load's not excessive."

Botha pushed across a Fedasonic catalogue. The largest of the 'Mammoth' range was ringed in red. "Now suppose you'll come along claiming extras here there and everywhere for hanging them up." Half joke, half challenge.

"Certainly not" Balfour protested. "These things must weigh a ton. Everyone made use of those beams, electrical, fire, storm-water, with hardly space left for concrete. Even the dead load of their own mass is damn near critical. Then air-conditioning roll up out of the blue and practically smack the poor things to pieces. Sorry, don't want to be responsible, or even associated. No."

"Hell" growled Burger. "Making an issue at this stage. All finished and done with, that's what you gave me understand."

"First you promised we'll work together." Botha sounded offended. "Work nicely, now you come make out, fall on top all the crowd there in the main concourse." He looked down humbly. "Look, I don't claim

176

to be... you use your workings-out, I'll use common sense. Just like that, bloomps, finished? That'll be the day."

"If we hit snags" suggested the Senior Inspector, "one reason and one reason only. You'll agree not constructed according to..." he included the Architect who had coiled his way into the room.

"The informal social gathering's more or less run its course I take it" he observed. "In that case should we commence with confirming the Minutes... ?"

Botha's waved hand demanded silence; he turned to Balfour. "Listen, now just listen, I'll do my job and you'll do yours, all right? That way we're not going to tramp on each other's toes. But please, I'm asking you nicely now, like from one man to another, I'm not for one moment suggesting you're... but that Mammoth 17K, you said, no no wait, just wait, you said one ton. Well, not really for me to, more in your line only I've taken the trouble to check already. Way under what you claim, so please."

Balfour shook his head, "I certainly never claimed it can't be done, but from those radial beams as they are now, never, they'd have to be strengthened one way or another. And that costs money."

For a moment there was semi-silence in the room. The Postal Super, mighty on his stool, rubbed his thighs and sucked a hippo-yawn of boredom. His assistants stared ahead. Burger chewed his last piece of sausage as quietly as he could. The Architect bent down an ear to the Senior Inspector's whispering lips and nodded. The Junior Quantity Surveyor in the corner coughed politely behind a fist.

"Most contractors" said Botha, "once they reckon they've got the other side over a barrel, feel here's their chance to make some easy money. Those rich people, the more they've got the more they want. But if you're still unhappy, well let's hear, you must have some idea tucked away up that sleeve of yours. About how to fix those beams I mean."

Balfour paused long enough for all to see that he was thinking deeply. "Sorry, I can't provide an instant answer. It needs a lot of, of going into, into all alternatives. Possibly rolled steel angles bolted either side, I can't say offhand. It'll look terrible. Maybe the Consulting Engineer could come up with some detail."

"You leave him out of this" snapped the Senior Inspector. "He'll only put in some report blaming all and sundry for not being kept informed. No ways. You're supposed to be an engineer yourself, you take a pencil, you take a piece of paper, you work it out, you say so much. Simple."

177

"The cost would be, well, staggering" said Balfour. "At this stage, very difficult to assess. Very very difficult. I wouldn't even like to hazard a guess."

Heads nodded approval. His whole approach had been so reasonable, professional, cautious.

"You could put me in a hell of a spot" said Botha, "only I'm trusting you."

"Shouldn't be a problem" said the junior Quantity Surveyor from his corner. "Keep a note on the labour you put on it and photostats of invoices for material.. Once it's signed and confirmed, details go into Final Account and that's that. As long as you don't lose out on the deal. Fair's fair."

"Bullshit" said the Senior Inspector. "Excuse me" he apologised. "No, we're not going to put up with them there in Accounts poking their nose into and picking on all sorts of queries. Not a damn. Lump sum as agreed, finished. Burger, start writing, just leave a blank for the amount, Mister, Mister... the contractor, he'll give you the figure, you can fill it in later."

"I can visualise it" murmured the Architect with his eyes closed. "After all, what is architecture all about except turning a challenge to advantage? Not try to hide anything, a feature, a point of interest with suitable colour contrasts in some of the brighter shades of orange say, even an off-purple. Please, a selection of colour samples for me to approve. Thank you."

Balfour overheard the Senior Inspector whisper "What a load of crap."

"Repeat the theme" the Architect continued, "at floor level, I presume not much progress been made yet with tiling. Time to amend the original. Frankly, never very happy with the Department's requirement, quite lifeless. Seize the opportunity."

"Settled" said the Senior Inspector. "Next item. Now those taps and stopcocks. I don't give two hoots if they're on site already, we can effect quite a saving if we switch from chrome to brass."

"The what?" queried Botha. "Just show me exactly what they look like and where you intend putting. I'm not being unreasonable am I?"

"Start messing around with plumbing fittings at this stage?" asked Balfour. "It'll mean sending every single one back to the supplier."

"Well" agreed the Architect. "That'll hardly affect the functioning of the replacements."

"So" said the Senior Inspector, "then it seems like we've got through it in record time today. That's about the lot I take it."

178

The meeting fragmented from a unity, from construction to rugby and caravans and limericks. The doorway became crowded with impatience.

The Architect drew Balfour aside. "I say, not for one moment do I suggest your various objections weren't valid but I'm only one in a firm with seven partners and this isn't the last project the Department's going to put out. We could all do with their goodwill, couldn't we?"

Only the Postal Super remained seated. He half-turned and nodded to one of his silent assistants, who extracted a sheet from the folder tucked into his armpit. Wordless, he laid it on the table.

"What's up?" the Super roared and doubled over at his joke. "Nag, first you nag me for a detail of those cable ducts, then when you get... still not satisfied?"

"But we worked to a slightly different lay-out" Balfour protested, "and that was months ago. Nobody said, there was nothing definite one way or the other. What we've done, it's every bit as..." The others crowded back around the table.

"Here, let's have a look." The Senior Inspector turned the sheet towards him. "What's wrong with this? Quite right, Postals use these and these, electricity supply through here and here. There's been a circular, it's got its own serial number, makes perfect sense to me. That's precisely how it's got to be, no arguments."

"But" said Balfour.

"But what?" demanded the Senior Inspector. "But you show where you had authority to do what you did, where it says on the lay-out. Okay, there's an arrow there I grant you, it points 'cable inlet'. So what? Doesn't say what type, not on your life it doesn't." His head trembled as though to emphasize how steady the draughtsman's hand had been. "Nor exactly where, no dimensions, no serial, nothing."

"He must have stuck to some plan or other" said Botha, "so what's the problem?" and began moving towards the door to show that he stood clear above any dispute. He beckoned to the other officials to join him in a conspiracy of innocence.

"Hang on, hang on." Balfour barred their exit with an arm extended across the doorway. "This is, it's absurd, it's..." He stammered towards some stronger word that eluded him. "Absurd" he repeated. "Explain how were we expected to proceed on schedule without, without this?" He pointed to the detail sheet lying so inconspicuously, a mere slip of paper on the table. "And why wait all those months to find objections if you weren't satisfied? You know, I'm going to write in officially for inclusion in the minutes."

"As chairman" noted the Architect, "may I remind the contractor the meeting has already been adjourned."

Botha spun round to measure the lanky figure of elegance up and down. "Chairman." It was an insult. "You the chairman? I'm supposed to be in charge here, from the day I set foot in this place I'm the one to say what's what." He stared in turn from face to face and spared a word for each. "Don't any of you forget it. And the contractor here, he must be allowed to get on with his side of it." To Balfour he added, it was almost brotherly advice, "See you get going on it straightaway, exactly like it says."

"Time and materials" said the junior Quantity Surveyor. "Simple, no problem."

"I'm quite willing to stand there with a stop-watch in my hand" Burger offered, "if need be. The whole day."

"Not one of those fixed-quote variations like the other one" said the Senior Inspector. "Too much of a temptation for a contractor, not that any's ever dared take me for a ride, oh no. Here we've got an official detail so it's a case of clause four, I can't remember now, para one section six, I'll look it up." He turned to the Quantity Surveyor. "You'll let us have a breakdown of their claim with no mention anywhere in the file of fruitless expenditure."

"Let's get one thing quite straight" Balfour insisted. "Right, so we'll block up the old ducts, we'll form new that to anyone'll look pretty much the same. Fine. But please, I ask you." His arms rose in appeal. "To puncture the waterproofing, then try patch it no matter how carefully, at this time of year with the pressure of outside groundwater rising day by day, it's too late, it's too late I'm telling you. And we took such care to make it safe for you." His arms collapsed in surrender. "All right, but with a written guarantee."

Botha nodded. "As a mater of course we'll be needing that."

"That it's going to give trouble." Balfour's voice was solemn as an oracle's predicting flames and thunder at the damning of the gods. "No matter what or how, trouble. You can't risk changes to the structure at this stage and expect that its stability will stay unchanged."

Now the Chief Superintendent, Postals, (Building Section) heaved himself up from his stool. The mass and height and girth of his body dominated the room; it seemed to become more crowded, the other figures slighter, mere insects cringing back from a crouching mammal that reared up to reveal itself.

"Bullshit." He roared defiance. "It's your business to make a proper

180

job of it, that's what you're here for, to fix things up the way it's supposed to be. D'you realise', he pointed to the detail, "that's the most importantest part of this whole place, what joins it to the rest of, of the outside. Two-twenty volt supply linked into the national grid, telex, cable TV, telephone, direct dialling, we Postals, we're on the ball these days. Just pick up, dial and you're through to Wall Street, Downing Street, you name it, to anybody you like has some interest in what goes on here. How d'you think this place, it'd run for even one day on its own?"

"An umbilical cord" said Balfour.

"Cord's arse" replied the Postal Super. "Not cord, cable, hang of a thick bloody cable. Thick like this." He pulled back a sleeve to reveal the forearm of a Victorian boxer's stance, a forearm thick as, thick as a cable.

"Then what happens" Balfour asked, "what happens when this half-baked patch we're expected to do, when it starts to leak? If the basement floods, if that central column, if it settles so much as a hairsbreadth and brings the whole level down with it and so ruptures the waterproofing sheet? I'm warning you it's dangerous."

The Postal Super sighed and slung a heavy arm across Balfour's much lower shoulder. "What's that to you? Hey? What's your maintenance period? Three months? Six months? Man, listen, you work yourself up for nothing. It'll last all right, for so long as you and me's alive. Who follows us, let them worry, let them bloody-well sort things out, we've done all right. I'll tell you something." He addressed the room in general. "Anybody guess what my bill for water came to last quarter? No, hang on, I lie, not last quarter, it was the one before. Well anyway, that well-point pump, it's no bigger than this, honestly. You just press a button and pssss… it pisses out a solid stream thick as my finger here. So what if you do get the odd drop from a little leak now and then? You stick in one of them. They're not all that expensive."

The story how he had got his cheap dragged beyond complication.

"In view of the fact that all this will be out of public view, I'm hardly…." The Architect excused himself from the meeting.

"That's settled then." Botha ticked off an item in his notebook. "Anything else?"

"One final word." Again Balfour pointed to the detail "I'll need a Site Instruction."

All ignored him, all jostled one another in their hurry to get through the door. Outside in the sun they stood in knots tight-knit to exclude the contractor as he brushed aside Burger and moved from one turned back to the other; from Botha, who beckoned to the Senior Inspector and the Postal Super and stood tapping his foot till they had come closer. Three heads nodded, then turned to stare at Balfour's back before they joined the others already strolling to their cars.

He entered the building shouting "Dougie, Dougie, a couple of urgents. There you are, listen", and left saying "I'll be working on our side of it at home."

Balfour bounced from his car to the rose-bed where his wife was picking at faded petals with rubber gloves and secateurs.

"Garages do it" he bubbled, "and lawyers. Provided the list of items is long enough any total at the bottom can be justified. There's a whopper of an extra coming up and from now on I'm going to screw the bastards. Why not make use of them? Everybody else seems to."

As she straightened her back her lips twisted with a twinge of pain.

"Rheumatism" he said. It was a joke. "Come on, cheer up, we'll be able to afford plenty of pills and injections."

"It's not the idea of getting old" she answered, "that upsets me. It's you, this sudden streak of the little boy in you. Either it's all too heavy, worry, or you try too hard to make a sport of things. Like Boyboy with his bat and ball, one shot more or less is so important."

He started edging towards the house, his study, his desk, his calculator.

"This is something new" she said. "If that's the way it's going to be" and stooped to pluck out a weed, "I suppose I'll get used to it in time." Her fingers dug into the earth and seemed to join her to it.

From the study Balfour phoned the Consulting Engineer. He enjoyed being brief, precise, understood. "Sorry old chap" he heard, "if I'm not officially informed leave me out of it, I designed according to the information given. I'm sure you stuck to my detailing and that's that as far as I'm concerned."

At lunch he said "I've more or less hit on a preliminary sort of figure."

When she brought him tea and puff-pastry at four he crouched lower over sheets and sheets of scribblings and announced "I've managed to double it."

Over coffee after dinner he whispered to her so softly neither the children nor Nanny clearing the dishes could overhear "Give me another couple of hours and I'll double it again."

At a quarter-to-nine she peered into the smoke-fug in the study and told him "There's a Mister Botha on the phone. He says it's important."

"Damn." Balfour frowned. "Now that specimen has invaded even the privacy of my own home. I'm coming, I'm coming."

He returned smiling. "Hang up on special brackets sixty-six jumbo television screens with fancy surrounds, like those Arrivals and Departures you see in airports. This is going to cost them till it hurts, I'll suck blood till they're dry."

"At least it's a pleasant change to see you so chirpy" she said. "More than slightly impossible lately and I'm the one's had to put up with it."

"Not that it's their money they'll be putting up', he tapped the litter of paper on his desk, "not out their own pockets. More like ours, pulling bread out of the public's mouth, but if not them then someone else would. And if not us, why wait for others to ride them? One last late-night cuppa please."

Each type of bolt, each different length of rolled steel section was listed separately. Then he remembered about the prevention of corrosion, not really necessary indoors but why not? The most expensive method. With figures, with imagination, he stretched the elasticity of steel to deflect the profit up and up. A smile—it looked a bit ramshackle, but they lacked the tools to probe how it had been stuck together.

When he crept up to bed she was already hugging her pillow as though to squeeze from it a warmth and comfort not found elsewhere. In an instant he was asleep.

He woke at two and knew she too was awake. "I've been lights-out. What's the matter?" and reached over to stroke her shoulder.

She shuddered at his touch and brushed his hand away.

"Now what have I done?" The whisper of an offended toddler.

She made him wait, intensified the insult by confiding to her more understanding pillow. "How long before you get tired of this new game of yours? But if you feel you can keep it up... you should know me by now, I could change myself, could if I had to, if you really really wanted me to."

"Change into what? What are you talking about."

She sat up, bent-backed, head forward, hair hanging, in the floppy posture of an invalid. "If you're going to be all that not so absolutely straight, carry on the way you say they are doing things, might as well go join them. It pays, if that's what's going to make you happy. Look at that boss of yours. Isn't he making a good thing of it? Why not go whole-hog if you think you can pull it off?"

He too sat up and hugged his knees through the blankets. The fact that he had copied her was an annoyance; she let herself drop back again and sighed to her pillow, "I'm willing, perfectly willing to learn a few of the right sentences to say, behave like they do, find excuses, even praise any kind of goings-on. It wouldn't worry me, not in the slightest, to know we'll never really be accepted, maybe sort of at best tolerated, joked at behind our backs, put on display like to show here's the one couple from the outside sort of won over, been properly tamed. But in with them enough so you'd never have to worry which side your bread's buttered if that's what you want."

"So?"

"I wonder how if actually you're a good man right through and through, or only feel you ought to try be one. Not that it matters if there's any difference between the two because there'll always be this difference between the two of us, you absolutely revel in being miserable. It's practically infectious. Why can't you be like everybody else? Just, just ordinary. I'm not asking for the impossible. Don't even touch me, leave me alone."

Later, much later she blurted "Well, say something. Don't just sit there like a, a, say something."

"I know the kind of hanger-on you mean" he said, "the cheap opportunists, the pretending they're not some kind of mongrels scrambling for crumbs the lions let drop from their table. Leftovers. Scraps. That kind, they're despicable, the way they creep around self-consciously on the outskirts. It's unthinkable, practically a religious taboo for me, for anyone with a grain of dignity in their toenail. Not that I've got much left of dignity."

Her silence was so intense he knew she was listening.

"Disappointed with myself I suppose, for what I'm going to do. Not even one percent of the total, a minor help, that's all, it's still heading for a God-almighty cock-up. All I wanted, now the way you've put it you've spoilt even that for me, the one second of relief when a man who knows he's drowning, as he clutches the straw, before he realises again for sure. Look, if you're not prepared to help me then at least keep out of the way."

She took, it seemed an hour to reply. "Imagine what terrific kind of terms they'd offer you. As it is you're working for a lousy firm, the others, the Feds, at least they're making a go of things. And besides, there's a good chance there might well be decent ones amongst them, just finding themselves there same as you're where you are now. Has it ever occurred to you, this?" She rolled over to her side, propped herself on

184

an elbow to breathe into his face. "This trying out a new kind of being smart, it's just to prove to yourself. And as usual making a torture over nothing very special. I was right all along, somebody like you, they couldn't do it, not even if they tried. If, if say, took the step, you'd be even more, more itchy. Just think, nobody can ever see themselves, not clearly, what you'd be like to yourself and me, say they offered you the moon for nothing. Difficult enough to live with as it is, the heaviest man I've ever come across and that's the one I've had to land up with." She lay back palms crossed, a statue on the tomb of a mediaeval martyr.

Dark in the room, in the enclosing claustrophobic walls, even though outside in the garden birds had began to twitter.

Still he sat, still clutching his knees. "You never know what they're going to do, that lot. You'd think, there must be some limit, surely, but it's like the horizon, always something further you can't see, can't imagine. What's still coming? I never dreamed I'd come to play the game according to their rules, go about things the way they do. It's their victory. Not mine, theirs."

He too lay down, twisted, waited for the dawn, turned, tried the other side, always maintaining a careful space between their bodies.

When the alarm trilled a glimmer of light showed at the edges of the floor-length curtains. He muttered "We might still manage to break even.'

"Feel up to shit."

"Me too, that makes two of us. No man, cut it out." Burger sounded impatient. "Cut out all those fancy explainings of yours, just give me a figure for that beam and TV alter." He copied on to a Site Instruction form in quadruplicate the total under Balfour's index finger. "Here, pink one's yours. It'll take them till the cows come home to type out the official Variation Order but this here I've signed already, so in the meantime you carry on."

Burger breathed a weary sigh. "That's them dealt with. That duct waterproof affair, somebody should've spoken up and told those Postals where to get off." He slumped down on to his stool. "Tired. Suppose I could write out a instruct for that as well, hell, I don't know what's come over me lately, I hardly know what I'm doing any more. D'you mind me talking to you like this? Somehow, you sort of, well, you can say you kind of, all what I've got to put up with. I reckon my troubles, they're by no manner of means over. Only starting. It's the next time, the not knowing what, what get up to next… no, I can see you're not really interested

in what doesn't concern you. Okay, fair enough, I'll remember that."
He managed to grin. "Only we're in the same boat really, the two of
us, we're both heading for deep in the shits."

Balfour shrugged and hurried away to hunt for his foreman all over
a project suddenly transforming itself from stark engineering structure
to a building suitable for human use. At last he spotted him, too high,
too far away to reach, a diminished figure remote at the topmost point.
Instead he dashed to Manie, busy with his team covering the north wing
roof. The syncopated banging of half-a-dozen hammers thundered a sweet
music that set his temples throbbing. Manie stilled it with a conductor's
gesture, cupped a palm behind an ear, bent down and yelled "What?"

"When you see Dougie, tell him, will be in my office."

Half-way across the site Balfour changed his mind, changed direction
to cross the street and find out what had happened to the cabinet-maker's
son. The house stood deserted, locked. Through the windows only a few
empty rooms, still littered with the discards of a hasty retreat. In the yard
at the back the workshop shed was open, the door askew and half-torn
off its hinges; all the years of skill and effort—to leave a few patches
of glue and shellac on the floor. Nothing else. A row of dahlias in the
garden needed watering or they would die.

In the office he phoned a likely number, and another and another, and
found out nothing. No, certainly not, Medici had never heard of, they
did all repairs themselves, they could accept an inlay for restoration but
it would take at least six weeks they were so snowed-under. Through
the dust of a cracked window-pane a pyramid of sand glared whitely,
enough to patch the beams where they would be damaged. No bricks
atop the heap, the toy castle had been absorbed into the structure, a little-
boy's passing make-believe now part of something permanent and real.

Real, pressing, to order expansion bolts, the fixed-head type and car-
bide tungsten bits to drill the concrete beams and find some galvanising
firm with a tank long enough to take the full-length rolled-steel angles.

When Balfour trod on the broken piece of precast kerb-block that served
as step to his office, he nearly tripped over Naidoo's blue-suit trouser-leg.

"Mister, I get the wonderful idea, wonderful. What you think? All
people come here for community and get the training when you finish,
they'll need it, the fruit juice, the cigarette, potato crisp, newspaper,
chocolate, boilings in ready-pack. A counter, that's all, very small take-
away, no space at all. You got it, the space somewhere? Like so, that's
all, give me broom-cupboard say."

"Not for me to give, sorry, you'd better write in to the Department, excuse me.''

He found his foreman snapping at the stooped figures of a team of labourers in the main concourse. Hammers rang against chisels as they crouched under scaffolding-stays to hack loose the floor-tiles. The blows dazed him.

Balfour steadied himself against a freshly plastered wall. ''As soon as they're through with this... ''

''Tomorrow we'll make a start with changing those cable ducts'' said Dougie. ''I don't fancy it, the waterproofing, they'll still start hunting round for someone to lay the blame on and they're bound to pick on us. Whoever set up a mess like this, they're useless, the whole rotten bunch of them.''

''Not all'' said Balfour, ''not every one, not all the time, it's not an individual who said 'that's it'.''

''I still say it's a mess, it shouldn't be allowed.''

''Don't blame the other man, we've all of us allowed it. With thing's the way they stand we're all in for headaches. I can feel one coming on already.'

XIII

"Come, come, you can do better than that." She knelt on the side terrace next to the chaise-longue and her coaxing made an invalid of the convalescent, a helpless infant from the father of the children she had mothered. "It's chocolate flavoured. And you the one used to love chocolate so, a whole slab of Cadbury's was nothing. Come." The last word less patient, more firm, almost an echo of the crackle in a starched and ironed uniform. She held the cup up to his lips.

On the yellow cushion, on a loose-jointed neck, Balfour rolled his head away. The faint and isolated smile of a deaf-mute, unreachable, nirvana, fascinated by the slow pile-up and darkening of cumulus. He looked down, past her, rather to the random drifting pattern of leaf-shadow on a whitewashed wall.

"All right then" she insisted, "we'll strike a bargain. A half, only so much, down to here. And you know what?" She laid the cup on the low glass-topped table and perched at his feet. "By the time you've finished even half, it'll give you such an appetite, you'll down the rest and yell for more. It's terrific stuff this."

Leaves and clouds and silence. A three-day growth tinged with silver. Buttons mis-matched to their holes in a flannel pyjama jacket. She tidied the cashmere across his knees and gave them a little hug. "A big tough boy like you"—another line drawn from a stock of professional banter. "There's nothing to worry about, really, between Dougie and me we've got it." She gave a thumbs-up and a wink. "Should leave everything to the two of us from now on." Then realised her mistake. "At least till you're up and about and longing to get back into harness again."

One minute. Two minutes. "Thanks". It was a murmur.

"The last thing on earth you should worry about is yourself. Look at all the specialists who've examined you, and the tests, even I didn't know there were that many of them. And every single one of them all clear. Listen." With little pats of comfort and a sing-song lilt, she made a fairy-story of it. "All these, these viral type of infections, they're all more or less the same, follow the same kind of course. Headache, temperature, debility." Through the rug she made one-piggy of his toes. "Aren't you relieved to hear you're normal?" A giggle. "Not some kind of perv. So hurry up and get... you know." She used his ankle as a pivot to rock his foot.

Time to do nothing in the middle of the week. The pages of Punch were curled. A bee hovered for a major portion of its life-span at the cupped petals of a flower. What were they called? Daisies? Or marigolds? Did it matter?

"What was that?" It needed a grimace and a groan to lift his head a fraction from the cushion. It gave her a chance to plump it up before he flopped back again. Tyre-crunch from the driveway followed by the quiet of a switched-off engine. Footsteps. He knew it would be Dougie, knew why she called so cheerfully "Be good" as she left.

Knew there would be whispering across the table, over the carefully handled cups of tea, a passing of papers, signing and comparing. No wind, no movement of the clouds, the leaf pattern static.

Dougie approached him with the respect accorded to an invalid, hat removed, steps hesitant. Suddenly Balfour realised that never before had he seen his foreman's uncovered head. The hairs spread across the patch of baldness made him seem more bald, older, tired. He was the one who looked ill.

"No, well, you don't look too bad" Dougie stammered. It was the recitation of a hurried lesson she had taught him inside the house. "And everything's okay on the job, so there's nothing to worry about."

She came swishing through the french doors, eyes narrow with decision, lips wide in a smile. "We make a tip-top team, don't we Dougie?" she chirped.

"Fine, fine" said Balfour, and played with the cashmere's fringe to hint that they should go, not strive so desperately at being cheerful, just go.

"Well" said Dougie, and looked down to his feet, and altered their positions slightly, "I suppose I'd better be getting along. See you tomorrow." He seemed to find relief in hurry, then stopped and turned. "Provided I can get away."

She leant over her husband to confide in him. "I'll just see Dougie off."

Clouds and leaf-shadow. Still the bee.

It couldn't have been far off that they stood whispering, near enough to overhear the hiss and tone of urgency in their exchanges.

When Dougie returned it was with a different gait; Balfour was aware of the stretch and resolution in the tendons of his foreman's legs. He marched to an abrupt halt. "Look, there's something I forgot to mention. You must tell me what to do. That Burger, he's an idiot, all of them."

Another bee, another flower. So nothing had changed, except her tactics. Trying to rouse response, use Dougie as agent, Burger as goad. On Sunday mornings—was it months or weeks or years ago?—there were often bees on the strawberry jam, her home-made preserves. Could always sell the silver tea-service, great-grandparents known only as its owners, no longer even as remote ancestors, so who would mind? No one was still alive today who remembered them.

"Not all" Balfour murmured, "not all idiots. Remember, only a few years ago?" He propped himself up on an elbow. "The kind of man they used to have, not all, but some, the old kind who knew their stuff. Practical. I learned so much from them, so helpful. A few left in the background, it's they who keep the Department from collapsing."

He sank back again while Dougie nodded and reminded him of names and incidents, two veterans reminiscing, and then asked "That patch in the basement waterproofing, you'd rather we used a pressure-sensitive tape or tried one of the contact adhesives?"

It was to the clouds that Balfour whispered "Anything, use anything. They get retired early, or shunted, no promotion, nothing unless they're part of the set-up. A dying breed."

"Then the two of them... " The foreman's shoulders seemed itchy. "That Burger and that manager, they're like this." He entwined a middle and an index finger. "They said, they came up to me together just like that, they said, those dozen or so aluminium sheets left over, the time spent on changing those cable inlets, they'd let us book some extra hours."

"Anything" Balfour repeated, and stroked the stubble on his jaw. "You remember on that bridge across the freeway, that old inspector there, when the crane blew all its fuses in mid-cast? Was it half-past two or three in the morning? Dedicated men. Now what was his name? Even their names fade."

Only the infirm, the toddlers and the seniles, were tolerated with patient and indulgent smiles, allowed to ramble, to doze in mid-morning on a working day.

When he opened lazy eyes Dougie left, a wife still sat at his feet leaning slightly forward to stare at his pupils, grope for a hand, cradle in her palm fingers limp as the pages of a dog-eared magazine.

He drew away his hand, it seemed too heavy to keep against his side, and let it droop over the edge, fingers curled, knuckles brushing against weeds in the cracks between the paving slabs. ''Must remember to tell the gardener'' he said. ''And I always used to do the weeding myself.''

''Next week'' she assured him.. ''Another few days and a cup or two of this chocolate-flavoured and you will. I promise you.''

Her forced smile was acknowledged by his nostalgic one. ''It feels like a Sunday'' he said, ''that flat, dead... you remember, the teas out here on the terrace? It was different then, wasn't it?''

He noticed her glance towards the french doors where Boyboy stood hesitating with bat and ball clutched in either hand. She got up to usher away their son, the understanding mother stooping arm-across-shoulders to explain, in the gentle whisper of respect for illness, ''Daddy must rest dear. You go along and play rather with your building set. Made a big-big place just like Daddy does.''

She returned to lift the cup up to her husband's lips. One sip, then he shook his head with a slow sideways roll of refusal. ''Tired, so terribly tired of it all. I think it's the first time in my whole life, the very first time I accept being sick. The advantages. Can just lie here, or anywhere, just lie. I wouldn't mind dying, it's tempting, the peace and the rest, if it wasn't for you and the pair of them. Why aren't they at school?''

''Holidays.''

''Think, not ever having to do anything, no struggle, just idle away the days. Why don't you take them to the Marina, like last year?''

''Boyboy got a gold star on his report. He's terribly proud.''

A tepid almost-smile. ''That's nice.''

''And there's that Chopin piece, she's getting the hang of it at last, she'd love you to hear... '' She watched him drift afar from her on the ebb and flow of doze and dream, tip-toed away and leant her forehead against the teak frame of the french door. It felt solid.

''Where the hell are you?'' he called.

She rushed towards him, to a body tense with agitation, struggling to sit up, restless. ''What's the matter?''

''I'm fed up with myself. It's bloody disgusting, solves nothing, only makes it worse, this not reacting. I would've been content to, to let things go, they went too far, there has to be some limit. How when Dougie, about those sheets, only left-overs, still... I should've sent a message, now they can really put the screws on me, should've told them to go and get fucked.''

She ruffled his hair. ''I never thought I'd feel my eyes get wet like this to see you in a mood. D'you know what it means? It means you're getting better. And tomorrow, at last I can look forward even to the idea of tomorrow, tomorrow please be full of nonsense. Utterly impossible.''

He groped towards the cup, drained it with a few gulps and grimaces, wiped the back of his hand across his mouth. ''Tastes like shit. I suppose I'd better eat something. What else have you got in the house? Something plain. A grilled sole?'

''Just like you'' she stormed, hands on hips, elbows out, glaring down the path towards the sundial. ''Typical. Overdoing things, can't you look after yourself? One extreme or the other. Up no more than a couple of days or so and next thing you'll start mowing the lawn.''

''Fed-up'' he confessed. ''Just wandering around. Should go and see how things are getting on... funny, how I've lost all interest. Bugger work.''

''You've taken that tonic?''

''If you say I must. One of these days I'll have to think about getting back on the treadmill.'' He snapped off an infested pear, watched the white worms wriggle, and tossed it away. ''You know what I wouldn't mind?''

''What?''

''Going for a little drive. Park. Stroll along somewhere, some place I haven't been for ages, or ever before, neither home nor storage yard, no, not site. D'you understand? Look at something new, at myself, collect the bits of me together, I'm in pieces. Find direction, decide who and what I am, or have been, or will be. All very confused.''

''But Mommy and Daddy said they'd be coming over after... ''

''On my own. I need to be.''

''You sure you'll be all right? You haven't driven for ages.''

A cautious reverse, a grinding first, the shift into second was easy, easier into third, the gear lever slipped into its slot and away, away. There was power, smooth power in the motor and joy in the control of it.

He parked on a gravel strip behind the railings where some sea-gulls strutted. Waves and sand, a smell of salt and decay from the rotting seaweed trapped in rock-pools. This the fate of all the kelp, a bank of it bobbing and heaving in the swell beyond the furthest line of breakers?

Through a windscreen blurred by spray Balfour watched the succession of the waves. The end of each, a slow spread of foam and water across crushed shells and sand, was absorbed back into the beginning of the next. Every one distinct, yet all identical. Perpetual, churning without effect, the turmoil of each so temporary.

He selected at random and concentrated on a particular wave, through all the complex geometrics of its cycle, its changing curves and colours; a solid grey, translucent blue-green and broken white, watched it being born from the swell, rear impatient, roll up to a climax and collapse in an orgasm of spume and splash, bounce a few times, weaker and weaker, spend itself upon the shore with a hiss, a tiredness, a sigh. That's all. The next was already in its place.

Only when repeated, repeated over centuries against the granite outcrops, the fabric and structure of the earth itself, did one wave matter. Theirs was the power regal, innocence impartial, they eroded rock only where decomposed, destroyed, to build up the continents. Without bricks. Without a signed and witnessed legal contract.

And that was how the world was formed. Each wave by itself impotent... one building more or less... reinforcement in the concrete promenade had rusted and spelled away its concrete cover. Now exposed, it would corrode even quicker.

He locked his car, leant over the railing and stared down at the beach. A mere scattering of bodies, three distinct generations; spade-and-bucket toddlers, sun-tanned couples, and on slatted benches in a shelter, the retired ones, the shrivelled and the bloated with blue veins of high blood-pressure in their purple faces, in hand-knitted cardigans, pushing away cigarette butts with rubber tips on their walking-sticks. "He's still alive is he, old..." Dodderers with nothing-to-do except regret their past; "D'you know I could've bought when it cost no more than..."—this the only future for all active men?

Balfour went down the steps on to the sand, drifted from changing-cubicles to tidal pool. Still the same, except more litter, cartons and plastic packets even where the limpets clung. A crab shell stared as though it could read at 'preserved with sulphur dioxide & benzoic acid, artificial colouring & flavour added.' The notice-board was new—'Reserved for—'; sea-gull droppings obscured the other letters.

It was difficult to walk across the sand, its powder looseness made his feet feel heavy; even more difficult to decide to where? The tidal pool? Where waves kicked and exploded against the wall, and part slopped over. The tide was coming in.

Here, what about here, at this terrific mound of mussel-shells? He squatted down and sorted through them all, found the very very biggest of the lot, a giant, held it in triumph to the sun mast-high above a tanker on the horizon. A mother-of-pearl galaxy of colours gleamed on the inside curve. Balfour used it to scoop up heaps of sand into an abstract pattern. Temple? Fortification? Play-play house that had been safe and dry when he started, now crumbly at the water's limit? The next wave claimed it back to the ocean.

He got up and strolled further. It was here, exactly here, in the shadow of this rock, was it fifteen years ago already? A black one-piece, the faded blue of her floppy linen hat and sun-tan aglisten on her shoulders. All the springy surfers who bounded past, their sun-hot eyes had feasted on the places where she rounded.

He lay down full-length on the beach, forehead cradled on forearms, the sun was barely warm, it was getting late. Wind-driven sand now filled the hollows where their bodies used to lie; instead of teasing banter the repeated crash and thunder of the tide; the tentative half-gropings, fumbling finger-tips;—grains spilled off the back when he dug in his hand and lifted it. The sonnet she had listened to with patience, with unlocking arms from knees to brush away stray strands of silk the breeze had teased across her eyes; so certain then, so easy to record the whole of wisdom in its verses. With words like 'ultimate' and 'fate' and 'destiny'.

Strangely quiet except for the ocean and the birds, their sounds did not intrude; the last shout of a couple plodding off, dragging their sodden towels; all others must have left the beach already. She would be getting worried.

Still he lay, half-dozing towards an evening of pearl-grey, oyster-grey, an hour when all would have faded, calm.

No. Each succeeding wave was lapping closer to his feet. He felt a rising damp permeate the sand on which he sprawled; levered himself upright and brushed down his clothes.

Home through evening traffic like those other men at the back and the front bumpers, who had slaved away that day. It was work-problems that made them frown, not trying to remember where could be that sheet of paper with its fourteen lines of truth.

He spent the minutes before dinner scrambling the drawers of his desk, then clawing and scratching rubbish, rubbish at the back of the built-in unit in their bedroom. Discarded junk waiting for a rummage sale, each item once a luxury, almost a necessity—tennis rackets, lambswool knits, a punctured inflatable canoe.

And could not find what he was looking for.

"Crap. You mustn't come try offload a whole heap of shit on me, not a damn" snapped Burger. "It says so, there in the contract clear as daylight, it says 'Afford facilities to outside contractors'. These shop-fitter teams, they've got sweet buggerall to do with you my friend." His arm swung in a wide sweep of confidence to point down the main mall leading off the central concourse. "Here, follow me. You don't know your way round here any more, do you?" He marched with stamping feet over trailing cables, bundles of multi-coloured decorative beading, scattered chrome cover-strips, stacked plastic signs loud with slogans.

Balfour picked his way round an obstacle of aluminium display stands anodised to outshine the brightest rainbow, past rays of colour bursting from enamel suns, reflections, gleams, curled wood shavings, offcuts of imitation veneers—a tourist hesitantly trying to hurry after the guide familiar with local history.

Burger halted to point out an item of oustanding interest, a sheet of plate glass spotted at the centre with a circle of whiteing. He bent down towards a corner, and above the hammer-thuds and whines and clatters of drilling, nailing, shouted "Look, look at it, this scratch here. It's one of your loafers did it. Fed's never going to accept. Replace and don't blame me." In the sudden quiet of the tea-break he added "There's another thing. The alter of those cable-ducts, claim's refused... no ways, what you did there that first time on your own, unauthorised. Not that you made such a marvellous patch-up job in any case. Specially considering the time you people claim you took over it."

"What? What!" A question, an exclamation. "Refuse? How can they refuse? How? I don't understand, it doesn't make sense. What does it mean? And what does this mean, this?" Balfour asked with the puzzlement of a confused visitor in a foreign territory. He pointed to some neon-tube and plastic man-sized letters lying jumbled on the floor; they could be used to spell "live" or "vile" or maybe even "evil".

"Right across the street-side elevation" answered Burger. "There's more of them to come. Now here's something else again, it's enough to drive anybody tear their hair out. How many times I must repeat myself, forget about that cable business. Finished. Look rather what you're allowing to go on right here under your nose." He continued his conducted tour of blemishes, paint smears and hair-cracks.

Tea-break over, men started coming back towards their posts; shop-fitting teams driven by an urgency, Balfour's own labourers cringing, hesitant, overawed by the glitter of their reflections in the mirrors and the sheen of luxury around them.

They were the intruders, ashamed of the sweat that once had dripped into the structure's frame when it still was raw, now not quite believing what they saw, what they themselves had built; silent men, who used to ululate in triumph for the energy that had hurled another barrowful of concrete into this column here, more bricks for this wall; the rejects of the site, unwanted because of dust on hands, tar on boots; grimy clothes leave marks. The last to enter reclaimed his manhood with a blob of phlegm.

"You better keep them out, the dirty buggers" said Burger. "The bloody mess they make each time one of them so much as sets a foot in here."

"Then how do you expect us to get the job finished?"

Burger shrugged. "That's your problem', and barged his way down the mall towards the figures of Botha and his dog silhouetted against the armourplate and anodising of the main entrance.

Balfour explored towards them past rows of half-finished shop fronts, skirting around swarms of specialist workmen who now possessed the site, who couldn't be bothered to so much as glance at who's-that-getting-in-the-way.

"This thieving" instructed Botha, "must be put a stop to." No words wasted on greeting or inquiry of health or remark about absence and return. "A complete stop."

"Same on every job" sighed Balfour. "Especially towards the end when there's so much expensive stuff lying around. It's there for the taking like fish in the ocean. Help yourself if you can, common property, precision brass knocked flat to flog as scrap, it's an attitude."

"Next week" Botha interrupted, "by the time the security system's been installed." He pointed to recesses in the wall.

"I thought they were purely decorative, not really necessary."

"What is really necessary to help me run this place, TV cameras, mikes, to pick up any whisperings. We must control those unruly elements, yes control."

Balfour's eyebrows asked silent questions.

"It's all very simple, everything's about the Fed is simple. We're only protecting what's ours, so we've got to use high-tech contraptions to go

196

on keeping ourselves simple." Botha's fingers played with the brass studs on his Alsatian's collar. "Down-to-earth, not like others smart with their fancy ways and desecration of the Sabbath."

Dougie burst apart a pair of doors in the main entrance screen. Behind him the transparent leaves swung, swung, swung slower, swung weaker, shuddered, stopped. "There's a message" he blurted to Balfour, "from the bank. They say it's urgent." He leant a shoulder against a door, against the pressure of its hydraulic trap, forced it open and held it here for his employer to hurry through.

It seemed a long trek to the pre-fab office, longer than a month ago, right across a parking area now black with premix and heavy with the smell of it. A roller was traversing across its graded falls, up to the lip of a stormwater channel and back again, monotonously, levelling the bumps, making the passing of time itself seem smooth and easy. An hour gone already and it was a promise she'd demanded, this first day no more than a pop-in visit. Those levels, somehow, looked a bit... not quite like remembered from the plan—tomorrow there'd be time to check.

"Yes" he reported to the telephone receiver, "I know, I know. Definitely. Definitely at the end of this month. Well, thank you, I do appreciate it, I realise you can't keep it up for ever but if you can give me only till the end of this month."

Balfour stood in the doorway of his office. "Dougie" he called. "Dougie, tell me, what on earth's going on here?"

"Don't ask me." The foreman shook his head. "You know that space, it's marked 'Activity Area Dressmaking' on the plan. How Manie and them, how they battled with that ceiling, to get it just-so? Now they've gone stuck some egg-crate affair only so high, just above your head. What for? And the mess everywhere, we've got to keep on cleaning up after them."

"Maybe tomorrow" said Balfour, "maybe then I'll start to try and sort things out. One keeps on saying that, doesn't one?"

"I couldn't get anywhere with that lot. From me they keep their distance. As far as they're concerned I'm only another man of colour, I've got my place here on the site and that's the end of me, only they're allowed to have a private life. Y'know my younger daughter, she's got her book-keeping now and looking round. That time, before her exams, I still thought, here's a commercial training centre."

"Give me a day or two, I'll find out more. I'm still a bit, bit dazed."

Balfour rattled a bunch of keys and started trailing back towards his car, making a slight detour for another look into the building.

197

Another look into another way of looking at the building. Another building? The same as defined on plan and elevation with lines and lengths, but with a hidden dimension, an unexpected atmosphere. When persons changed identity, were they still the same, still entitled to the hand-in-hand offered to the first? And the contract entered into, solemn with its formal phrases, did that still apply? Morally?—possibly. Legally?—binding.

He frowned up to the false ceiling Dougie had described. A sign-writer was setting out the letters of BOUTIQUE, a curved clothes-rack was being manhandled through the door and Burger was grabbing his elbow.

"Listen man, there's a couple other things I've spotted. You've got a big think book there to take some notes? And you're going to need one hell of a long pencil."

When Balfour dragged heavy feet across the entrance-hall he knew exactly what his wife would say. "I knew exactly what time you'd be back. A full day's work. And exactly what colour you'd be, a sort of grey-green. Now off with you, I'll bring your supper up to bed."

At breakfast the inevitable warning. "Now for heaven's sake don't go overdoing things like yesterday. Come back into the swing of it gradually. The tonic, don't forget. Anything I can do here to help?"

He found Burger trading mock-punches with a safari-suited figure outside 'Activity Area Electronics'. Back-slapping, a bout of friendly wrestling, loud cheerios. "See you hey." 'Keep smiling."

Still grinning, panting, the Inspector explained "He's from the number three shop over there. Hang of a nice guy though you wouldn't say so from the look of him."

"Shop? I thought it was for, for hobbies, radio hams, evening classes, that kind of thing."

"Yes that's right" said Burger. "You see, his cousin on my mother's side and Mister Botha's like our sort of godfather you could say. Promised get me one of those video gadget affairs on the cheap. Portables, cassettes, tape-decks, TV's all that hi-fi kind of, the lot. And he's gone got hold of a, from the Tech or somewhere, must be a sort of a half a chink or a jap somewhere along the line he squints so, but smart. Man, I'm telling you, true as I'm standing here, he'll fix anything that little short-arse. Of course training, that's what this whole place is for, where else would a, he's not all that dark but still, where else he'd get to run the whole bang-shoot all on his ace? Chance to really learn, get a kick out of it, chucking his weight around so all's thinking he's the number one. Just my old pally over there, he'll be looking after the books and the cashing-up and so on. After hours that is.''

''Your friend, what does he do during the day? His job?''

''Something or other on the Railways. I can't say for sure exactly but sort of like in the ticket office so he'll have plenty know-how for entering, balancing cash takings, that kind of thing. They got the right bloke there okay. Mister Botha by the way, he's on the look-out for you.''

Balfour found the main mall blocked by a furniture-removal team grunting and heaving a bedroom suite into 'Activity Area Woodwork'. He took a long way round through the central concourse where the inquiry kiosk was being assembled. Posters issued by the Central Information Service were already on display. 'Back The Boys On The Border.' 'Your Country—Love It Or Leave It.' 'Don't Ask—Your Leaders Know The Answers.'

He nearly bumped into the Senior Inspector outside the boutique instructing the sign-writer ''No man, she's what you'd call fashion-conscious, she'll never accept it the way it is. Rather put some gold and a bit of that other shiny stuff.''

''Dressmaking?'' asked Balfour.

''Yes of course dresses, ready-mades, what else you'd expect to find here, do-it-yourself? What place they're going to learn about high-class clothes? I suppose in some squatter-camp. There's space there at the back for alteration-hands behind that partition you stuck up, for at least two of them provided they sit sideways.''

He found Botha inside 'Household Management', supervising the fixing of a bronze plaque splendid with the crest of The Federal Commercial Bank.

''Another Bank?''

''For sure'' answered Botha. ''Fair's fair. I mean after all, if Fed's going to have all the hassles running the place for them, it only stands to reason. How we're going to finance new developments except they deposit their wages comes pay-day when they shop here? We pay on savings, same as the others.''

''Once the houses around here started getting dolled-up,'' said Balfour ''Barclays have opened a branch practically across the road and the Standard around the corner.''

''Then all the more reason. In a free enterprise economy there should be competition, so long as it's not competitive. People don't appreciate, only one point seven percent on turnover in a supermarket, it's hardly worth the trouble, we're actually putting ourselves out. What helps, it's the interest we get on the takings and the bank here pays that, so it costs the customer nothing. Listen, this place isn't half big enough considering the volume we'll be getting. This wall here, it's got to come down."

"It's a load-bearing wall." Balfour sighed himself into the launch of yet another argument. "Impossible."

"Well, if you insist" Botha conceded at last. "All we had in mind was to offer service to them as part of the commercial training; seven days a week come rain or shine, I'll even have to cut short my ministrations to see to the cashing-up. A real community centre, part of the scene, we aim to involve ourselves. Every year, I promise you, I'll see to it myself, strings of sausages, choice grade selected, to the local police station for their annual do. Get to really know our customers. We've got a congratulation card for births, each baby gets, with our logo in either pink or blue. Floral tributes for the bereaved, there's always a bunch or two starting to go off a bit in the gardening aisle. Even charity, we make donations, oh yes we do, and not expect so much as a thank-you in return. 'Cast thy bread upon the waters'. That's Ecclesiastes, chapter Eleven, Verse One. But somehow the word gets round, we make it our business, we make pretty well sure that it does."

He beckoned Balfour to follow him down the mall, past the Activity Areas marked on the plan as 'Rug Making' and 'Photography' and 'Art'—past counters of plastic laminate and computerised cash-registers, floors fitted with foam-backed carpet squares.

In the Library the Gospel Mission's board gave the times of Bible readings in the vernacular for various ethnic groups. Conscripts from the Adjutant-General's Headquarters were testing an overhead projector advertising a Recruitment Drive in the Assembly Hall.

"From now on we count in weeks, then days" Botha hissed, his neck and shoulders racked with tension. "And if this whole mess hasn't been cleared up ready for the opening then somebody's going to find out what trouble really means. And I for one wouldn't care to be in their shoes. And that applies to both you and me."

There was an extra edge of sharpness to his movements as he strode away, a forced-march of authority that brought him past some boundary that Balfour sensed, into a threatened realm where bluster passed for language and arrogance for confidence, where barks and bites were reflex instincts of defence. Botha whistled to his dog and led it by its leash toward Burger, who stood blowing steam and slurping coffee from an enamel

200

mug.

As the dog nuzzled him the Inspector spilt some on to his leg, slapped his thigh, wiped it with a clumsy palm and exclaimed "Fuck it, there goes a clean pair of pants."

Balfour found his foreman with a roll of plans under one arm, a Bill of Quantities under the other, explaining to a joiner "If it shows a mortice on the detail section, make a proper job of it."

"Dougie, look at him." Balfour pointed to the Inspector, still dabbing at the stain. "How long d'you think he'd keep his job if the whole Burger family didn't go on banking with the Fed? And the Federal themselves, what hope they'd stand against the other chains and multinationals? Protection and pay-back."

"Those gangsters go too far." Dougie slapped the roll of plans against his leg. "Gone to their heads, it's only the use they can get out of us, except they're also making it more or less impossible. How can anybody be expected to work like this? We'll never be ready on the handing-over date. Never."

"Then the usual argument about penalties for delay. I don't know where to start there's so much left to do."

So much to do that again Balfour got home barely in time for the evening meal.

The following day the same, always Burger and Botha, Botha and Burger. Even the Architect began dropping into the site more often. Time before his next visit shrank and vanished.

"Really" beamed the Architect, squinting into the sun, "really beautiful. Wish I was given facework like that on all my contracts." He turned to Balfour. "I propose we enter in the next Minutes an item congratulating the contractor. If ever you do venture into an investment programme the designs could be composed from facebrick planes of intersection."

"Not to me it doesn't" complained Botha. "How you can come along claim a thing like that, there's at least two three bricks in that screen wall so much lighter than the rest you can almost notice it. Sticks out like a sore thumb."

"Like a sore hand" Burger agreed.

"Lighter?" Balfour's eyebrows twitched. "If anything that last load of facings was a shade darker than the rest that we selected. You mark with a piece of chalk which few you said are bothering you and we'll replace them."

"I said nothing of the kind" Botha protested. "Have it your own way,

I won't argue, all right darker then if you insist but either way I'm in two minds to make you pull the whole lot down. Only the one thing saving you. You're in luck's way."

"Hell of a lucky." Burger nodded. "Really should come down except for just the one thing."

"And that is?"

"I've arranged next month for Fed Fast Foods to come erect their sign. It's there on their workshop floor all laid out already, you should only see it, it's the biggest chicken in the whole of town, a landmark. The way the head moves like this and then like this, that's besides the tail feathers. So with quite a wide border of arrows moving round jerk-jerk it'll just about cover all those facebricks of yours. What's left over from the lettering that is."

"Who?" asked Balfour. "Who did you say? What's a fast-food outlet doing here? In a Commercial Training and Community Centre? It'll help uplift some underdeveloped ethnic group?"

"Well, they eat and they drink and they pay exactly the same as you and me, even so they're different. That sign, don't for one moment think" added Botha, "you're going to squeeze us for hanging it up like you got away with that other time for the speakers. Or the way you hoped to work a nice little point for putting right your own mistake there with the cable ducts. For all the fine talk, once it comes to anybody's pocket, they're all the same. Oh no, Fedsigns do their own, only you must leave the scaffold there for them to work on and pick up the sign itself with that crane affair of yours."

"I take it" murmured the Architect, "they'll be operating in the section designated 'cookery' on my master lay-out."

"Correct" said Botha. "You should know, they themselves supplied you all the cupboard details, fridge and cooker spaces; so on."

"And I suppose" said Balfour, "another of Federal's subsidiaries will occupy…"

"Hang" exclaimed Burger, "how d'you come to find out about that?"

They began wandering across the parking area towards the structure. Naidoo bore in and cut out Balfour from the herd.

"Mister, I write in to Department like you say, for take-away. And I get answer, I get." He waved a brown postcard and read " "matter is receiving attention'. So will be nice hey, what you think, I come back to my first place again and carry on the business. Very nice."

Balfour turned back at the entrance and saw him smiling and waving his card and smiling.

"So what else could I do?" Balfour appealed to his wife, "What could I? Except gape and stagger around with my mouth hanging open. Quite blatant, using the public's money for lining their own pockets, so blatant they'll get away with it. No cover-up, well hardly, that'd look suspicious. Wait, they'll still make it a crime to even accuse them... I feel concussed."

"Don't shout, you'll wake up the children. D'you bump your head again?" She laid down her sixhundred-page historical romance. "Here, let me have a look. Without a helmet as usual."

"Not that way. It's ... you know when something in the background comes forward, only then do you realise it's been there all the time, you've been staring at it all along without recognising shape or colour. Which reminds me, where d'you put the chocolate?"

"Usual place, top left-hand. There's your favourite Cadbury's and a new kind of Suchard I thought you might fancy. Honey-almond. On specials. It's nerves, that's why you crave."

Tearing silver foil distracted him. One block. Another. Another.

"Last row" he said, "or d'you want to share? A half? My mind keeps on jumping—shares. I should really go up to Head Office but how on earth can I get away? Now? At this stage? Besides, I don't even know the difference between a stock and a share, they've got accountants there, let them sort it out. Definitely the last, then I'll put it away. It's crazy, d'you see on the financial page, we're quoted at an all time record high. Must be those insurance pension funds still buying, investment consultants putting clients on to a sound thing, why shouldn't they? Last year's figures still looked good and they haven't the vaguest idea what's happened in the meantime. Up it goes, so the small man follows with his savings and up some more. I'm sick of it. I'm going to bed."

She slipped a school-fete bookmark between the pages and closed the covers on crinolines and braided uniforms and waltzes in the moonlight. "How bad? The loss on this one I mean?"

"Sick, but not quite fatal. Not that the other branches are looking all that healthy either. I'd say at worst, at the very outside it's back to where we started in the dim and distant past. There's even a report his royal highness will return in state to remount the throne in a month or so, and d'you know what that means? Shouting and screaming over this year's losses and profits for ever after. But of course a lot depends, like providing retentions are released on time, I don't know."

"Well, I certainly don't know" she said. "But this I do, I know it for sure, your health is more important to me than any share. At least to me it is, so I got rid of those in my name. Me, dealing in shares, me of all people. It's easy. I simply opened the Yellow Pages, picked just any broker and they did everything. I didn't want to tell you, I thought it might upset... yes, you need to rest.''

While she was brushing her hair at the dressing-table he told her reflection "Did the right thing. Sometimes you're almost sensible. I can't of course, mine are pledged, so's the house. In any case...''

"I knew he was coming back''. Varnished nails plucked strands from bristles with the care of a harpist. "I answered some of those pretty-pretty pictures. One of us had to keep on the right side of.. just in case, in case you decide to stick where you are.''

"Yes I'm going to'' he said, "I'm going to finish off this job at least, I've decided. For myself mainly I suppose, I'm committed to myself. There's a legal obligation but that's a minor matter, law's no longer a frame to give society a shape to move around in freely, law's only another one of Fed's enforcement agencies, Fed and others like them. Say I'm selfish, my own sweat and satisfaction, a weekend round-the-block jogger forcing himself to run the marathon.''

She laid down a brush and comb that seemed to weigh a ton, smeared away her mask with tissues, cold-cream, dabs of cotton-wool, stared back at the face of an ageing woman who bore the lines of suffering, who was too weary to suffer more, who pleaded "Surely it can't carry on like this, it can't, it must come to something definite.''

Balfour tussled with his boot-lace knots. "Why? Why can't it stagger on from crisis to crisis till that becomes the norm?'' The left yielded to his nails. "Till you start to feel uneasy without a crisis and set out to create one.'' The right slipped loose. He kicked off his boots and wriggled his toes. "That's it. Feels better.''

He watched her unclip her necklace and hold the ends between finger-tips for it to loop in a curve of flash and colour, the catenary cable of a suspension bridge spanning the distance between hand and hand, between hand-to-mouth and opulence. One end dropped and she dangled it above her jewel-box with the mixed pride and revulsion of a snapshot poser displaying the segments of a killed reptile. "We could always sell these, they're useless anyway, and the silver too. I know you've thought of it, I know every thought that comes into that head of yours I've only got to look at your face, or you don't even have to be in the room.'' The necklace dropped with a click-click-click. "Does it really matter what we drink out of? It's not the grade of tea that counts, it's the idea of it, the fact we're drinking out the same pot. Except of course if you'd resent, depends the way you look at it and I wouldn't mind a bit, not that much." The laugh she forced out burst from her lips to ring hollow, hollow in his inner ear. "They say those brown supermarket chinas, they're the ones that draw the best." The buttons of her blouse, one by one; she peeled it off like a sunburnt skin. There were freckles on her shoulders and a line of bite-bruises on the ridge. Head back to unhook her bra, she shrugged her breasts loose. "The one thing I'm glad to see, you've found out for yourself, you can't just let things drift. That sort of apathy of yours, it really had me worried."

He stood up and sucked in his tummy to unclip his belt. "Don't panic, comes to the worst, the absolute worst, we'll still be better off than most. All firms have their ups and downs. I can afford to decide in a cold deliberate way, not with the blind reflex of some trapped and desperate..." He stepped out of his trousers. "And whatever I do decide, the one thing I must still be able to afford, it's not a luxury, it's a necessity..." He slipped off his underpants. "Is being able to stand straight and look in the mirror with nothing on, nothing hidden, and not feel ashamed." He slumped down on the edge of the bed and watched her twist her skirt around to fumble with its eye-hooks. "Except I wonder if they haven't cut my backbone out of me, permanently. I'm still too limp, washed-out, a sort of damp rag."

"That time" he said, "the rain, how it caught us in the pines. Remember? What rattled us, it was not the wet, it was the trying to keep dry. A couple of drops inside the collar and we started squirming. Then when we got soaked through and every step went squelch, to hell with shelter, then we couldn't give a damn any longer. It's more or less the same."

She dropped her skirt and folded it. "So the moral of the story is not to worry. Is that what you're trying to say? I'm glad to hear it."

"Why we found it so easy to put up with, you know why? Because we knew there was a comfortable house waiting for us and clean dry clothes. For a hobo, somebody like that, under the same trees with us, the same rain, for him it's different, he's got no choice. Even if we have to move from here, or decide we want to, there'll still be a roof over us, we'll have a choice. Only what to choose? And for us there's no such thing as a ready-made system to lean on."

At her feet lay a puddle of sheen on the carpet, translucent folds and films, a froth of lace. She walked differently when naked, exposure of the covered secrets altered the feel of skin on skin, a hand displayed in public became intimate under an elbow roughened by cement. "It's only really bad cases need depend on crutches, the rest, once they come to rely on support, they never learn to so much as hobble.'' The upward pressure of her palm felt strong. ''Come on'' she said, ''come on, stand up.''

''Yes, I must see what I'll look like on my own two feet.''

He stared into the mirror with the quiet satisfaction of an artist admiring the masterpiece he had himself created.

Wednesday after Wednesday Balfour stumped back into the house from tender openings with his forehead creased to a frown and his lips set in a reminder of the taste of vinegar.

Week after week she said ''Don't worry so, for heaven's sake don't take it so hard. You don't even know if you're going to stay on with the firm.''

And always he answered ''Doesn't make much difference, I've signed personal security in any case, stay or leave.''

It became a ritual.

At half-past eleven on a Tuesday night she brought him tea to the study and crinkled her nose at the stink of stale smoke. ''It's funny, how it feels quite different if you're working late on a final account or a schedule say, or on a tender. All of us, we can feel like fingers probing what you'd call guts.''

He rapped knuckles on a litter of scrap paper scrawled over with the numbers and signs of a cryptic code. ''This is it, I've got that feeling, I somehow know. Maybe from all those near misses, I can judge exactly, I'm going to make sure. At least now I can decide for myself, the final figure I mean, without interference. And even if I do resign it's the, sort of continuity, leave the place tidy, not simply walk out.''

When he came in on Wednesday she remarked ''You look a bit better but still not quite.''

''Too big a difference'' he said. ''Eight-an-a-half percent below number two, that's a lot. I made a bit too sure. Anyway.'' He sighed. ''There'll be at least something to show at the end of it and besides, the timing's perfect. Switch straight from one to the other. What about a drink?''

They sat on the terrace with their gin and tonics while the sky blushed.

''One thing, the money's safe working for the Department. And a telephone exchange, always interesting, this one's especially technically complex but we've got the experience. Without that any firm'd be heading for trouble. We're practically specialists. I should've realised, that aspect, how it'd tend to scare off the others."

"A red sky at night is a shepherd's delight" she said, "only you're still not really happy. How long? I mean before the handing over on this present one."

"Another few weeks, not that any job ever gets really finished." He topped up his glass with tonic and rattled the ice-cubes. "Just usually a certain stage is reached, everybody's so sick of it by then, it's a case of "Ugh leave it, nobody will ever notice if this and this is still not absolutely perfect'. Or else there's a deadline like a formal opening. Not that we're likely to meet ours with all those last-minute changes. At least one thing we made damn sure of, our work's of a pretty high standard. Pass me the lemon."

A long silence. The sky faded. A cigarette. Another cigarette.

"And so it goes on" she murmured. "Funny, those weekend afternoons on the beach and then afterwards you twanging my elastics there on the Marine Drive in some parking spot, from those days, did you ever imagine we'd land up here like we are, with our what they call a way of life."

"Yes, as you say, so it goes on. Only a way of life never reaches anywhere except the grave and I still can't make up my mind which path to take there. From the grave you can't go on, not on to a bit of peace for a change. You'll find nothing there. Nothing. It's here, here you can still find it, or make it, try to make something from each minute of the few days left to us."

XIV

"Only a few days left" stormed Burger, "and don't say I didn't warn you, right from the beginning there with the handing over site, I warned you at the time. Penalties for delayed completion, so much per day, no arguments. And this opening date now, we'll have to put it off again, that's for the third time already."

"Nonsense." Balfour sidestepped to prevent him stumping away down the main mall. "This morning a fresh batch of Site Instructions this thick, a whole mass of changes and by this afternoon I'm supposed to have it all finished off. I'll say it again, it's nonsense."

"Hang on, hang on a sec" protested Burger. "Applications for to condone delay, they've got to be in writing and there's nothing on the file for this today's lot, so don't come along try blame me, that's all."

"Excuse me" requested the Architect, pinching his chin and nestling an ear on a shoulder, "the colour tone-value of that feature there, it's not yet quite... a half-shade påler still I'd suggest."

"But it's plain white" explained Balfour, "straight out the tin. It's picking up pink from that Coca-Cola sign across the way."

Manie barged his bulk between them. "You know all those solid brass fittings on that type C3 door, locks, handles, flush-bolts, kicking plates, the lot, gone. I find this on the rubbish-dump just inside the fence, they must've dropped it getting over." He held up in display half a pair of lock plates.

"Just come here a sec." The Senior Inspector crooked a finger to beckon the contractor nearer. "Not my idea but it's been decided, more space needed in Activity Area Dressmaking, so..."

"You mean in the boutique" interrupted Balfour. "Too late. Sorry."

"All right then." The Senior Inspector twitched his shoulders. "Here, here, come have a look here, this paintwork there at the back, you can see it if you lie down flat and shine a light up, man, the kennel in my back yard for the dog, it's painted better."

"Not specified to be painted. We primed it as good practice."

"Not specified? All right, I'll take your word for it, I'll take it, if you say so. Not anywhere? Then I could just as easy say it's got to come off. Off. Don't for the life of me know how you'd ever reach up there short of breaking out the whole lot and supplying new but that would be your problem brother, not mine."

"There's a message" panted Dougie, "they say it's urgent. Will you please phone the Chairman at Head Office soon as you can."

"So you got to phone have you?" boomed the Postal Super. "Gee, I wonder how anybody'd ever manage nowadays without us Postals. That's why you surprise me so, you, of all people."

"What is it now?"

"You should know, you fitted so many for me before. Man, how's the phone connections going to? Just lie loose across the floors for all and sundry to come trip over? There should've been whole rows of those hollow skirting whatyoumaycallits. How come you slipped up on your banana over that one?"

"It's not shown anyway and besides I queried..."

"No ways. No need for queries, it's all there in the standard Postal Code of Practice clear as daylight."

"But my contract's not with Postals. I can't take instructions..."

A terrazzo polishing machine scraped away their words, two floor sanders whined a dirge of dust and abrasion. Angle-grinders, buffers, disc-pads spinning, belt-sanders humming, a battery of power tools. An industrial vacuum-cleaner sucked pressure on to eardrums and a stranger in a dustcoat with 'Federal Shopfitters' stencilled across the back was shouting angry, unheard accusations. Balfour cupped a palm behind an ear and leant towards him.

"... never been buggered around like this on any job before. Never ever."

"Then better go sort it out with your Federal's own manager."

Balfour burst apart the side entrance doors and strode out into the glare of the parking area. In the centre of it, astride a motor-cycle, a dove-grey figure against a matt black background, a sergeant of traffic police was easing off his helmet. He strolled over with a creak of leather leggings.

Balfour halted. "Yes? What is it."

"Man, the marking out of those other parking bays and the throughway route."

"I don't know what you're talking about. This whole premix paved area, it provides parking for the complex. That's all, no through traffic."

"Well, not according to." The sergeant pointed towards the main street running through the suburb, to a gang of labourers lounging there cross-legged against the side of a truck marked 'City Engineers Dept Roads & Drainage.' They watched a grader deploy into position, lower its blade and start ripping up the carriageway. "So up there at Planning, the diversion, about where exactly to stick up the signs, No Parking, No Stopping, No Access, that kind of thing. Temporary for the meantime till Roads Drainage got the main street blocked off, then permanent for later. It makes more sense to you now? I reckoned you'd have known what's cooking."

"No, not a clue. The original levels were amended, yes, for no apparent reason."

"Well, now you know." The sergeant tugged a notebook from the back pocket of his baggy breeches and unfolded a plan. "Main street up and down streams, re-routed to pass through, it's more or less exactly where we're standing now."

"Sounds like a recipe for chaos" said Balfour. "The traffic jams, it'll be dangerous with pedestrians and children... You're sure you've got the story straight?"

"Couldn't agree more." The sergeant shrugged. "Accidents but plenty, I'm telling you, by the ambulance-load and half-hour snarl-ups but what can the likes of you and me do about it? It's what they asked for, so they'll get it." He unhooked a tape from his belt and started unwinding it.

"Spineless" remarked Balfour, "this city allows Federal dictate to them," and he raced to his office before Naidoo could intercept him. He spun round the numbers on the phone, direct dialling to Head Office.

"And what brought you back?" he asked the Chairman, who supplied no answer, only demanded explanations why payments were overdue, why the wait till the last moment before landing another tender but anyway better late than never, at least the new job would set the firm back on the road to profit but in the meantime why the delay in handing over and with it the delay in release of retention because that's exactly what the bank was screaming for to see the firm through this rough patch and how was the wife keeping, the lovely lady, you're a lucky man, and again back to pushing through an urgent payment certificate and getting the Department to take First Delivery and release at least part of the retention.

As Balfour stepped out of his office-shed Naidoo trapped him. "Mister, any day now I think they answer. Receive their attention, won't be long. Already I'm making the arrangement, Pepsi, Seven-Up, Schweppes, Nestle, they've put out new small-pack lines now, good these small-pack lines, very good. Suppliers, they all know me, for years now they know me. Thirty day, sixty day, Mister Naidoo maybe you like ninety day but even better you make cash. COD.''

Botha was petting his Alsatian in the central concourse, indulging in leisurely strokes and pats that kept him remote from the surrounding frenzy. There was nothing urgent in the way he halted Balfour's approach with an almost teasing "So they're giving you a hard time are they?"

"This amuses you does it, this deliberate refusal to take First Delivery till your shops are ready? Our part of the original contract's in a state of virtual completion and this mess, take a good look all around you, it's not our doing. Give me another day at most for the odd paint spot and fittings for that one door, that's all. And tomorrow it'll be changing the gauge of half-a-dozen screws back to what was specified in the first place. It's gone beyond the limit, it's... "

Botha's interruption was predictable as the cold of winter. "Nothing I can do about it, I'm only the manager here, better go speak to the Senior Inspector."

Whose reply was predictable as the heat of summer. "Nothing I can do about it, I'm only the Senior Inspector here, better go speak to the Manager."

Botha had not moved from his place near the central column. He turned away from Balfour's scowl towards his dog to show that he would listen with only half an ear.

"Another thing, the parking area, the bays are all marked out already with two coats of traffic white as specified, on a lay-out according to plan. Now it's got to be set out all over again, and that's besides the peak-hour delays."

"Well, what about them? That's no concern of yours."

"What must all the drivers do? Just sit there behind the steering-wheel and wait for it to clear and waste half-an-hour twice a day?"

"Not in the least." Botha straightened himself up from his dog's side. "By no manner of means waste. All right, so what if it takes a few minutes to come clear. So they might as well park and pop in here. Look, they've got to in any case, sooner or later everybody's got to do their shopping. What's wrong with it? And there's refreshments ready waiting if any's that way inclined, those plastic tubular chairs, they're quite comfortable. Music, kiddies playthings, it's a convenience for the public in general that we offer. This here is a community centre you know."

An hour later Balfour again thrust words at Botha's face with the cold and sharp quiet of a bayonet. "Listen, get one thing quite clear, get it right into those ears of yours, on Friday at four the men have got to be paid. What do you want, we should file insolvency? At this stage, that would suit you? You want the bank to call up surety and us to leave the site? Think about it, I'm giving till lunch, no more."

He marched away from Botha's open mouth, away from teams of sign-writers, window-dressers, display artists, marketing experts, cash-register and scale fitters, neon-sign electricians, over coils of loose flex-wire and plastic trade-marks, through a maze of impulse-buying stands and turn-stiles, calling "Manie, Dougie, I'm dashing into town to the bank and for replacements, those brass fittings, I won't be long."

When he returned he found Botha, the Senior Inspector and Burger whispering together near an empty deep-freeze counter. They jumped apart when they spotted him. It was the Senior Inspector who advanced the few hesitant steps that set him apart as spokesman. "No, yes, well actually, what I was going to say."

"Yes?"

"It's like purely to help you out, it commits us nothing but man, you don't know even half the fuss and trouble it'll involve, to push through an interim. Take it or leave it but there's no question about taking delivery of the service as a whole so no releasing the retention, anything like that. Forget it. Okay? You satisfied now?"

As Balfour left Burger hurried after him. "Man, those paint spots, shit man, hell no, simply everywhere. And that's besides the windows. Dirt, you can't call that dirt anymore, not by a long chalk, that's filth, pure bloody filth, a fucking pig-sty." He endured his listener's pressed-lip silence and up-and-down inspection. "And besides, what about all those things missing on that door, you know the one I mean."

Balfour opened the packet of brass fittings in his hand. "By knock-off time today."

Late in the afternoon Burger approached him in a dim service alleyway, tentatively offering a hand-written Site Instruction with a grin that wavered between embarrassment and a 'you-poor-bugger'smirk. "Don't blame me." He shrugged. "Not really my idea but anybody with half a, they can see the sense behind it. It's to break out those side entrance doors and side-light screen affairs and brick up, make good with finishings to match existing. All clear?" He declined to let Balfour outstare him eye-for-eye; to the toe-caps of his brogues he mumbled "So coming from

212

the main street down to the station, bus-stop, it'll be safer they've got to go all the way along the main mall, concourse, so on and so forth. Not really that much longer through the building, away from all the traffic there in the parking. Otherwise can be hang of a risky you happen to be on foot.''

''And the whole feature, after breaking it out, what'll happen to it? The Department's paid for it already, at least in part. I daresay your Mister Botha, he'll find some use for it. Very suitable for enclosing a porch. Expensive for the tax-payer, but so what?''

''Well, sort of, only you'll have to take it up with him direct. Wait, wait man, hang on a sec.'' He hurried after Balfour and grasped his sleeve as though trying to clutch back a moment of the days when jokes had brought them close together. ''Talk about taking it up. I got a hang of a good one. Once there's this old bugger of ninety, he's so randy...''

When Balfour confronted him the manager shrugged with an air of indifference. ''Don't for one moment think you can come cry on my shoulder. You say it's near impossible to match up the existing. That's easy, what's stopping you doing the whole wall all over again? Listen, think back, the very first dealings we had together here after my appointment, remember? You didn't offer much by way of working hand-in-hand, now did you? So what do you expect from me? I should go out my way for your benefit?''

''It wasn't only the roofing sheets I kept.'' Balfour held each word under separate control. ''It was my honour.''

''Honour'' Botha scoffed. ''You talk about honour, and then try book extra hours on a repair you're not even entitled to in the first place. For you it's another word you've once seen in some dictionary, a thing you've read about. When people've got nothing else to fall back on, then their mouths fill up with words like honour.''

Botha waited—no reply. His eyes narrowed to the width of razors. ''Those side doors and screens, I want them, I want them out by tomorrow, undamaged'' he snapped.

''I'm not accustomed'' said Balfour, ''to be addressed in that tone of voice.''

''Tone, and what tone do you use to me? Superior. It wasn't in the words, oh no, you're far too much the gentleman for that, it showed in your eyes. Seeing me as one of those others, keep them at arm's length, hardly human, no feelings. Right from the beginning I was fair to you the way I see things you yourself brought your own troubles on your own head.''

The Senior Inspector sauntered up to join them. "Quiet. Calm down everybody. What's all this about? What's going on?" He turned to Balfour; it quite amused him to say "If there's anything that's bothering you, I can see from a mile off you're all hot under the collar, you should know by now what you've got to do. Submit in duplicate, write in about it." His wink confirmed Botha as accomplice.

Holding himself rigid, with a forced calm, Balfour announced past the other's shoulders "Dougie, I'll be working at home if you need me. It's important, I don't want to be disturbed, there's nothing left for me to do here on site"; spun into a sharp about-turn and strode away.

When his wife brought him a late-night cup of tea to the study she remarked "Funny, I know it can't be a tender you're working on, yet somehow it feels the same."

"Nothing much" he growled, "just something I want to have ready for the next site meeting."

"Stop pestering the life out of me" snapped Balfour across the breakfast table. "You know I can't stand cereals. That rubbish sales-talk on the carton, pure poison. Vitamins, energy, eternal health, start the day with two heaped tablespoons of a happy-ever-after. Not if it's the last meal I have to eat on earth."

"Lucky the children aren't here to hear you. You sound like on a tender-opening day."

"Not for another year or so, this new one's big enough. Confirmation's still not come through yet." He pushed across his cup for a refill of black coffee.

"Can't make it out, they're becoming even more inefficient. Should've been here by now, maybe in today's post. Don't wait for me, don't, I might be gone for quite a while, I don't know when I'll be coming back. Now where the hell did I put the car-keys?" He patted his pockets.

Wife and Nanny helped him ransack the house. He found the keys hidden in an old pair of gardening shorts in the dirty-washing box.

To the storage-yard, to the city centre, back to the yard, where plant no longer needed on the building was piling up in the abstract pattern of debris on a bomb-site. He pulled clear a vibrator that normally two men grunted over. "This bloody mess" he stormed, "sort it, clean it, paint it, get a move on, you're not on holiday. I want everything left tidy." The gang of surplus labourers who had been transferred from the complex dragged their limbs with lethargy—there was no point in just hanging around waiting for a new job to start.

At the site he parked in the shadow of the structure, in a place where now he felt estranged. The only feature that marked this bulk as different from a dozen others in the city was the scaffold still enclosing it.

Even that was coming down. Monkey-figures crawled along the grids of frames and pipes; working platforms already reduced to a single gang-plank, safety-rails gone. Too dangerous, too late to creep along the narrow boards without hand-holds, swaying in the wind, to try and etch indelibly on some plate of memory the view which he had changed, which had changed him; an achievement he could claim, one that claimed a solid portion of his life. No more than an outside hope of staring in a last look that would have to last forever, at all the streets and roofs and tidy gardens.

Abandon the idea, abandon the hope, rather accept the verdict of a self-conviction and drag feet through dust towards the final site-meeting of the contract.

At the bottom of the steps outside the shed he stopped for a moment, with eyes closed, breathing deeply, then mounted them slowly, one by one.

The pre-fab office would soon have served its function, it was almost ready to be dismantled; walls stripped of calendars and pin-ups, ceiling panels sagging from their nails, plans lay rolled up into scattered bundles, stationery half-packed in cardboard boxes.

They were laughing inside, laughing; slapping one another's shoulders and poking ribs, wiping the corners of their eyes. Then the gales of mirth subsided to gusts of titters and gasping short-of breaths. When he appeared in the doorway and stood framed against the light they all pointed at him, and pointed, and burst out laughing again.

It was an occasion, a festival. An end-of-term excitement kept them bubbling.

Only Balfour was still, pale, waiting without movement for the beginning of silence.

"So here at last's the one we all been waiting for" mocked Botha.

"We're all after your blood" jeered the Senior Inspector.

Not yet, not yet the silence he was waiting for.

"There won't be much of him left" said Burger, "by the time we're finished with…"

"This" interrupted Balfour quietly, "is for inclusion in the minutes", and without fuss, without hurry , he laid a few typewritten sheets on the table. "Officially" he added,and stepped back.

Botha snatched up the papers. Now was the silence, now. All eyes watched the manager's face to decode from it the meaning of the words he glared at. His fingers scrabbled at the top sheet and as he fumbled it over the rustle of paper deafened the room. He contained the pressure the others could sense rising within him by squeezing lips together and half-closing his eyes. "Rubbish" burst out of him. Then he rapped knuckles against the pages and trembling, flung them down to the floor.

"Rubbish" he repeated, louder, but seemed to find no relief in the explosion of the word. "Nonsense talk this, nonsense, fancy words like 'corruption' and 'unjustified' and what else, what else? 'Misuse of public funds', 'taxpayers' money to entrench private privileges'... who, who do you think you are? You, you're nothing." His voice shrilled with the conviction of injured innocence. "To come along accuse us, accuse..."

"I've written there against all manners of deceit" said Balfour. "Show me where you are mentioned by name, show me. But if you feel the accusations do apply to you, then you've pleaded guilty to yourself at least."

A longer silence.

It was Burger who charged to the rescue with a gallop of words. "You talk about pleading guilty. Once there's this bugger, he's up on a charge of public indecency..." His voice trailed away.

"None of your business" muttered Botha, now in a lower key. "This wild talk, wild, 'irregular' my foot. Once you go out your way looking for trouble..."

"Of course it is my business" insisted Balfour. "While as for trouble, well yes, in a way it is my fault, for standing back and allowing you to get away with it, for not trying hard and long enough."

"Hard and long" said Burger, "that reminds me..."

"Shut up, keep that big trap of yours shut, but tight" snapped the Senior Inspector. "He comes along stirring up all kind of shit and you make a joke of it."

"Quiet, I'm in charge here." Botha turned to Balfour and with a forefinger wagging hissed "Get the one thing altogether straight. The fact this whole complex gets opened to the public on a certain date, it doesn't for one moment mean we're accepting First Delivery. Is my meaning clear, quite clear?"

"Who are you?" asked Balfour. "Are you the Federal, merely a tenant, or are you the Department, or has government become a branch-office of the Fed? What right have you to be here in the first place?"

"Right" snorted Botha. "I'll show you what right I've got." Tremors in his neck spread down and twitched out an arm in tension. He reached, quivering, towards a bundle of plans and unrolled them with a series of jerks, then flung apart the lapels of his jacket and squinted down to the pens and pencils clipped to the inside breast pocket. At the second attempt he managed to pluck out a propelling pencil, held it up against the sun-lit window to adjust its point, leant far over the top plan of the stack and slashed across it three huge letters, an F, an E, a D. "There." He pointed in triumph. "There you can see for yourself, you can see with your own two eyes. It's plain enough for you? It says there clear as daylight, it's down in black and white. What more do you want, I should sign and date it? All right, all right, if that's what you want." He traced a few preliminary strokes in the air as though to loosen his wrist, scrawled his initials on the plan, looked up with a smirk of satisfaction, bent down again and added some illegible numbers under them. "Well, if that isn't proof enough for you, then I don't know any more. Now are you satisfied?" Replacing the pencil was a precision act, it needed calm and frowning concentration. He buttoned and settled the drape of his jacket. "Just remember why I've been put here, it's especially in order to be impartial and that's exactly what I'm being. It's as simple as that."

"Yes it is simple" agreed Balfour. "I simply refuse to accept your authority any longer. And when others hear about this and follow the example, even if it harms them for a while, that's the end of Federal Investments."

"Harm" warned Botha, "We've got the power to really hurt."

"Possibly, quite possibly, I don't deny it, my eyes are open. Bruise me on the surface yes, you'll never break me inside, or ever bend the core of me with guilt for not belonging to your Fed, or supporting them or others like them. Contempt has brought me clear of you, I've passed beyond you. So go on talking, your hollow words bounce back, that's all."

"What about your future? You'll manage to get far with the whole of Federal against you? I'll see to it, I swear on all that's holy to me your retentions get held back from now till kingdom come."

"Look look" stammered the Senior Inspector, "There is some kind of a sort of a contract. I've known, there's some firms, they raise all hell to play... I for one don't want to get mixed up in..."

"The tiniest crack" said Botha, 'So much as one drop of a leak. Then it's the rubbish dump for you, that's where you belong."

"I don't know where I'll ever belong" answered Balfour. "Accepting that uncertainty, it gives some sort of freedom, but of course that's a word you don't appreciate."

He packed his papers together with a stiff formality; the others gaped at, did not excuse himself but quietly left the shed in silence.

On the top step he turned and looked back to see them thrusting their flushed faces forward, waving their arms, as they bickered amongst themselves.

"After all those years of study at a university I land up doing this" said Balfour, "not that it's proper work for the two of you either." He handed to Dougie and to Manie a couple of soft brooms, packets of steel-wool and cotton-waste, Brasso, Windowlene and a few yellow dusters.

"Playing charlady for must be the tenth time" muttered Manie.

"Why can't he, that Burger over there" asked Dougie, "why can't he take the job over?"

"Too junior" explained Balfour. "Senior Inspector's on leave at present, only he can, the rest in their Local Office, no one's prepared to take it on their shoulders."

"Then that, who calls himself the Manager." Dougie pointed his chin towards the spot where Botha was supervising the hanging of placards proclaiming the GRAND OPENING.

"Nothing to do with him" said Balfour. "Not officially, only the Department can issue the Certificate of First Delivery Completion." He stepped aside to allow a consignment of Hong Kong lampshades to be carried into place. From Paris, from Taiwan—the goods of the earth flowed in past a row of extra-terrestrial video games.

"For the last time, an absolutely final polish-up, then you'd both better move on to the yard and keep an eye on things there. There's nothing really left for you to do here. Pity, we can't even start preparing for the new job, not till the confirmation's come."

They watched trucks and panel-vans queue up at the delivery ramps and spew out a litter of containers.

"Hang on" called Balfour, "it's today the option period expires at noon. I think I'd better give the Tenders Office a ring and find out what's the hold-up. Come with me."

The three men risked dashing across the traffic streams through the parking area and while the others smoked and paced up and down outside, Balfour crouched over the phone in the shed.

He dialled across rivers and mountain ranges, past orchards and deserts

218

to another city, another climate, and marvelled how the rituals were everywhere the same—he held on, was put through, cut off, back to the switchboard, spoke to the wrong official, held on again—at last.

"That's the State Purchases Office? The Tender Board? I'm phoning in connection with the confirmation of an award of tender, it's number... What date was it due? On Wednesday the first, exactly a month ago. Yes, I'll wait."

The faceless voice of the Machinery of State.

"But that's impossible. It's impossible." Balfour found he had risen from his stool and his voice too had climbed an octave. "Then who? Who was it awarded to? Who did you say? And what was the figure? What! But that can't be, there was no such tender called out at the opening, I was there. And what's the reason, why wasn't it awarded to us? I know you aren't obliged to disclose, I can't force you, but why?"

True. That official without a name, he had said it, his voice had come through this receiver, this same one, it's weight too heavy for a single hand to hold, there had been a phone-call, really had.

He stumbled out towards Manie and Dougie where they stood waiting. The way they looked at him, dumb, stunned already by the words still to be found and spoken...

"Bad I'm afraid. The job's off. You know the reason given? Delayed completion of this contract, officially we're over the time with penalties."

"But we've been finished here for ages already." Manie tried to shake confusion from his head.

"It stinks." Dougie's words were venom that he spat out. "And now?"

"Don't panic." Balfour lit another cigarette and inhaled deeply. "They're not the only people one can work for but it'll take time to line up another job. Time. It's a set-back, it's serious, we'll manage, somehow we'll manage, there can't be any more delays about handing-over if the opening's next week. Don't you worry, at the very worst I could speak to other firms about you, ours is not the only one around."

He knew they were hardly listening to what he said, were trying to balance Unemployment Benefits and savings booklets with rent and HP instalments and the price of school-clothes. "I'll do whatever's possible for me to do, you know that, don't you?" and drew a small comfort from their nods. "Maybe once we're altogether clear of this place, maintenance, retentions, everything, start a new, a better firm of our own, we'll have to learn to grit our teeth and pull together even more. Who knows what the future holds? Who knows?"

219

When Balfour stumped into the lounge he knew from her "you-poor-boy" smile she was only pretending to read.

"So you know do you, and you find it amusing?" He slumped down into his favourite chair and gripped the arms. "How d'you find out?"

"From that boss of yours, he phoned, quite breathless." She closed the book on her lap without marking the page and while laying it down remarked casually, as though the low inlay table might possibly be interested in a tit-bit of gossip, "or ex-boss rather. I imagine by now he'll be on his way to the airport." She straightened up and turned full-face towards her husband. "Alone" she emphasised.

"That joke's wearing thin. I'm hardly in the mood."

"No joke this time." She crossed her legs and clasped a knee. "He could be really disgusting, sometimes, depends mainly on my mood I suppose, those hint-hints of his. Usually, well, just a, sort of teasing, bad taste. At first, I'll be quite honest, even a tiny bit flattered, I'm not expecting you to understand. Besides, to help, keep you on the right side of him. Only now he was serious, really. My guess is you won't be seeing him again, not him."

"No more or less than I expected."

"How I wasn't getting any younger and what a, having to start again from scratch with nothing and if ever I changed my mind to get in touch care of his bank in Zurich. Laze in luxury, pearls and caviare. So unoriginal."

"That rat, he told you the name of the firm that got it?"

She shook her head. "Only 'how could the Minister do this to me. How could he, to me, calling himself a friend, after all I've done for him, the dinners and nightclubs and arranging of investments overseas'. What needled him particularly, when the Minister, with a dead-pan face claimed it was all outside his…"

"A new firm, their first job, one that size, that tricky. You'll never guess who." Balfour bounced up and stood over her. "Federal Construction, can you believe it? And their figure, it's incredible, the sheer crudity of it. Sky-sky high above ours. A telegraphic tender, received in good time, all as per regulation. Telegraphics needn't be placed in the box or called out at the opening. Since when? Tell me if you swallow that" he demanded and stared down at the top of her head, at the darker tinge against her scalp.

She examined the nails of the crossed hands on her skirt. "You can tell me anything, anything you like about them and I'll believe you."

"Ruthless, and I'm too vulnerable. Polite backgrounds like mine haven't prepared me for dealing with the Botha's of this world. With two cars in the garage would anyone be desperate enough to risk it?''

Boyboy burst into the room. Past the grandfather clock, round the statue, all along the Afghan, chased by his sister. "It's rude" he gasped, "terribly rude. You know what she said?''

"Shut up" she yelled, "shut up. I'll murder you if you go telling stories.''

"Quiet. For heavens' sake. Behave yourselves." Balfour's annoyance was sharper than a father's discipline, with an edge of sincerity.

"Off with the pair of you" snapped his wife, "And you haven't even started your practising yet.''

Her daughter sniffed and tossed defiance at her mother with a shake of the head. "Bach gives me a pain up my backside. So do the two of you with your sour faces.'' She stalked out of the room.

Boyboy lingered behind. "I've got nothing to do" he whined.

His parents hustled him away; his very own vegetable patch needed weeding, urgently.

"Let's go out on to the terrace" suggested Balfour, "there's less chance of our being disturbed.''

He kicked aside the chaise-longue and they sat at the edge of the yellow cushions on their chairs, elbows on the table.

"Drink?'' Her eyebrows arched up in query.

He shook his head. "Sitting out here, ice and lemon, once it was a luxury, we revelled in the almost decadence of it, now it's to keep out of earshot.''

The view, garden, gables and shutters no longer held interest. They stared down to their reflections in the glass-topped table, reconciling themselves with blurred and wavy images, with...

"A four-roomed" she said. "Either Gardens or Green Point, depends which hospital will want me. Then each child can have their own room, it's important, she'll soon start, you know, growing up.''

"Don't sound so... the way your mind is running, we could've moved already. It might not be necessary.''

"If it's got a fair-sized balcony, some have, depends, then we could still find use for...'' A ring-and-bracelet hand swept over the set of garden furniture. "At least some of it.''

Behind their backs a squirrel hop-hopped across the lawn towards its hollow in the oak. Birds cheeped the "come-back-to-nest come-back-to-nest" evening song. Nanny switched on the light in the dining-room and started laying the table with a clatter of crockery and cutlery.

221

"I've spent most of the afternoon juggling figures" he said. "We should be able to hang on here once we've cashed in the bits and pieces. We'd forgotten the pictures, there must be at least twenty of them, including the stuck-aways."

"And find it such a weight around the neck we'll resent each brick of it?" she asked. "So the house'll own us, not the other way round? I don't give two hoots what people say behind our backs. Maybe have to alter the curtains, take some of the furniture, most of it perhaps, not too much so we'll be cramped, get rid of the piano, she's starting to lose interest anyway. Besides, the house is pledged to the bank remember" she reminded him—an afterthought.

"Can always make some kind of plan. Well, nearly always. Or try to." He rested his forehead on a palm and scratched his scalp with a little finger. "Providing one really wants to."

"I'm actually looking forward to going back to nursing. The children don't need so much looking-after any more and besides, it's a bit of a waste, isn't it, if you've got the know-how and experience, not to use it. I've always loved it, the being independent, earning. At least part-time."

"Stop that" Balfour barked at her. "Stop it. If we're going to enter a new, a sort of, a new phase, why make it a, why humiliate me?"

He clenched a fist, white knuckles and distended blue veins on the criss-cross wired glass while she swept back her hair with the indulgence of a bathing-beauty preening herself. The gesture lifted her breasts, raised her awareness of the shape presented to his eyes, and she spoke with the lilt and eagerness of younger days. "Don't be so half-hearted over starting something new. Getting married, that too was a new career for me, and I admit it, I was scared."

"I wasn't, strange to say, it simply had to be, it seemed obvious."

"You remember the first time, the very first time you took me home to meet your parents? So I knew then it wasn't just all talk on your part to try and get me to. How you fetched me straight from the hospital and I kept you waiting, we'd had one of those last-minute emergencies. Remember? There wasn't even time to go past my place for me to change quickly. How tired I was, all strained and grey. Like you are now.

"And then your parents, your father, making out to be so concerned, so kind, all those gentle little lawyer's questions of his with the leaning forward with the eyebrows. And your mother, nothing but smiles and friendly, the one-girl-to-another. I could practically see, all the time I pictured it like in some cartoon drawing, the balloons popping out of their heads with the letters on them. 'Well, she's not bad looking and seems healthy, fairly respectable, decent enough I suppose, responsible, must be reasonably intelligent and all that but, but not quite, not much by way of poise, lacking in culture.' Sizing me up as a potential breeder of their grandchildren. A slave-market or a cattle-show. Them thinking I was so, so sort of quiet and on edge because I wasn't sure which knife and fork. When all the time it wasn't anything like that at all, I was proud of myself, proud, not only for what kind of work I was doing, and doing it damn well too. But how I'd worked myself up to where I was. Even for how I was saving, I wasn't quite sure for what, I didn't need their money, I had enough then and I'll have enough now. That's what you're worrying about now, isn't it? Or it's pride? That's a different kettle of fish, not so easy to handle.

"Some for my old folks for their nest-egg, then either a small run-about car for myself or even a bachelor flat, or I had some leave saved up, a trip overseas, I'd never been. Your parents telling me about those places, something safe to talk about, with me having to sit quiet because I'd never been further than... well, just nowhere. Don't just sit there smoking and frowning and saying nothing. Well? If we're both going to be holding decent jobs on a salary, that's a situation we've as a couple never been in before. And you sit dumb, like I was that night.

"Don't you understand? I wasn't up for sale, not then, nor to that boss of yours today. I knew I could've had expensive holidays and things from you but I wanted the getting of them for myself. Not even from you if it'd mean giving up myself. I told you, pride, it takes it out of you even worse than money and I wonder if I've ever been so tired as that night. It'd been one of those really heavy days, you should know after all what that's like."

"I know, I know." Balfour lit another cigarette. "Things, technical gone-wrongs one can't talk about without drawn-out explanations you're too tired and sick of to give."

"Exactly. You couldn't make it out why I was so, almost sort of pulled-away. When you took me home I wouldn't even let you kiss me good-night and for weeks afterwards, you had such a hurt disappointed look on that face of yours. Because I wasn't living up to the picture you'd built up of me as a kind of a bitch on permanent heat. Then when you started talking about a date and announcement in the paper and a ring, all that, I was the one... did you think I was playing hard-to-get? I'm more straight than that, I really didn't want to, I wanted to keep on just as I was. I was managing okay, anyone who expects more than that nowadays, they're in for disappointment.''

"Then is it wrong of me to want to keep the firm going?''

"Your taking me home like that, I knew what it meant, I'm not such a fool you know. Getting married, a home, children. I couldn't face it, the responsibility of it; that life-and-death minute-by-minute in the theatre, it's nothing by comparison, that's work, you've been trained for it. Nobody teaches you how to be a wife or mother.''

"Be fair, I also wasn't trained to be a husband or a parent. I haven't been too bad, have I? It's only as provider that I'm slipping.''

"There you go again. Your parents, what I could never tell them and it's too late now, and I've never told even you before either, why I was so shrunk into myself that night. Plain drained-out exhausted yes, also something else. They kept on talking about, of all things, now isn't that co-incidence, about the lakes in Switzerland and that other place. Matterhorn is it? Yes Matterhorn. You see, my today's little conversation, more or less the same thing all over again.''

"Now you've seen it for yourself in the meantime, it was the trip before last wasn't it? And somehow, I got the impression, you weren't all that impressed.''

"Pretty all right but you can keep it.''

He reached over and patted her knee. "Don't worry, we'll see it again, if you want to. Or any other place you fancy. Another few years, a couple of good contracts.''

"I can still give you every single word your old folks used that night, and they were the ones felt so awkward because their future daughter-in-law, she had nothing to say for herself, she just sat there in her issue tunic with the epaulets staring at all the silver she'd come to own one day. What did they think, that I was overawed or that I was pricing it? It wasn't that, not at all. No.''

"Then you wouldn't mind if we sold all of it to help keep the house and the firm going?''

She shook her head. "Not at all. No. You still don't know what I was doing a few minutes before I climbed into your car that night outside surgical. You don't. All right, I'll tell you.''

Both fore-arms on the table-top, she leant towards him. No louder than a whisper. "Y'know, from when I must've been only three or so, from then on, whenever one of my dolls got hurt or I'd pretend they were sick, I always knew what I wanted to do when I grew up. The one I've still kept, still there at the back of that cupboard unit with the other of the children's old toys, you ever noticed the hands? Well, that emergency that made me keep you waiting, it was a girl of three, maybe three-and-a-half, an amputation. And there I was standing holding it in my own strong hand inside the rubber glove, exactly like a doll's hand, a bit puffy, the fingers curled, a row of dimples across the back. Now d'you understand?''

Balfour shifted on his seat and sat up straight, with sucked-in breaths. ''I suppose the power and the dirt, the violence of a construction site, most people couldn't stomach that. It's a job, someone's got to do it.''

She smiled at his pale face. ''I've upset you? I've seen worse things than that in the theatre, plenty worse, somehow none of the others, must be hundreds... You're so busy in there, you haven't got time to think what it all means; in any case bad for the patient so just be technical, be quick, efficient. I imagine much the same with your work. You do it, finished. Once you start thinking what you're doing, then you don't find it so easy any more. That's you to a tee.''

She leaned back and relaxed. ''Still, I helped that child survive. It had to come away and maybe the whole arm or she mightn't have lived at all, I don't know. Often I think, all right so she is handicapped, there's plenty useful left she can still do, plenty she can enjoy. Must be eighteen or so by now, going on nineteen, her head full of boys and I can't help wondering if a thing like that, if it'd put them off. Maybe limit her choice and she'll be too grateful to the first one comes along wants to use her. Men are fools. Who knows? Maybe perhaps the very handicap'll be the making of her, not just all boys and discos and pop records. Or help sort out the riff-raff from one who really cares. So you see.''

''No, to be honest I don't. What's all that got to do with...''

''Isn't it the same with us? Something rotten that's part of us, that firm of yours, before it poisons everything, just cut it off and that's that. Before we lose the lot. There'll be plenty left we can share.''

''But I told you I can still keep it going. Must, must finish breaking down our scaffold, have everything ready for the opening, then they've got to, simply got to accept the handing over. A couple of minor works for Manie, Dougie, key staff, till we pick up something decent, and the few months maintenance, hell, d'you really expect major cracks or leaks? Not easy. Yes, it can be done.''

She leaned well forward and squeezed his thigh. ''Listen my boy, that night it wasn't only a right hand I helped cut off, it was worse than useless anyway, I had to cut off my career as well, my own skill, the all of me up to then.''

Balfour fumbled the carton and shook out the last cigarette. It trembled on his lower lip as he said "That's surgery, controlled cutting, not construction."

He watched her clasp hands around a knee and make the stocking wrinkle. "I'm sure it's much the same thing with a building. You see there's something gone fundamentally wrong so what else can you do except demolish, careful, quick, put it right before the whole lot collapses on everybody's head. Otherwise…"

"Yes." He crumpled the empty carton in his fist. The flame of the lighter lit up his face. "Of course, as obvious as getting married. Yes, that's clear now, clear. Yes."

She slapped his knee. "It'll be grand. Cheer up, who gets a chance to set up home twice and without even all the drama of divorce? Don't scowl like that, you're meant to laugh. And then our first leaves, we can wangle for the same times, a second honeymoon, how'd you fancy that? It's got no appeal for you? Make the most of it, grab any chance that comes along to… you know, be a bit lively. Leave it to me."

She pulled him to his feet. "That's why I'm going to that opening of yours. What should I wear, smart or casual? All of us, children, old folks, Nanny, everybody, you too. Oh yes you are, I'm saying so. Just because you've got hurt there you're going to sulk? Too scared to look the place in the face? Grow up my boy, grow up. Do what you know you should."

XV

On the morning of the Grand Opening they left the house in separate cars. Balfour waited alone in the company's Mercedes while children and Nanny crammed excitedly with his wife into her compact, waved their arms through the windows, called "See you there" and "D'you still remember the way?"

A dozen blocks from the site the congealing streams of traffic gummed up to a crawl; at an intersection a policeman waved him into a side-street where he was lucky to find a vacant spot.

He parked behind the automatic coupé of a trimly slack-suited lady with tinge-rinsed curls and a snake-skin handbag. As she locked and tested her door she smiled; at festivals one greeted passers-by. "So you must also be after opening-day specials."

A tripple of high-heeled steps and she disappeared behind a shuffle of old-age pensioners, their faces pinched to anxiety under the brims of panama hats—if that Lions bus over there could bring the others in good time then no excuse, why did Rotary have to leave it to the very last minute. The impatience of mothers overcame the tantrums of children whose arms they pulled. Prams, push-carts, wheel-chairs... male, female, young, middle-aged and old... the long and the short and the tall... the butcher, the baker, the candlestick-maker.... more and more people, people, people rushed past him in a bigger and bigger hurry. All strangers, all curious to see his creation, all ignorant of his preceding year of effort and the weariness of those he had commanded. No one even glanced at him. Only Burger.

He stumbled towards Balfour with the relief of a desert castaway discovering an oasis. "Shit man, nearly didn't make it. First the dry-cleaners." He patted the pants and jacket of his safari-suit. "Then the barber." He smoothed down his sideburns. "You on you own?" in an

227

anxious voice. "Me too."

"Wife and children somewhere about. Lost in the crowd."

"No, I'm alone here." Burger shrugged. "The child, no, it wouldn't really, you know, and the wife, well. And the rest of your crowd? That foreman of yours, he's here?"

"Dougie? Never, not him, not in a place like this has become. The others, I don't know, maybe, haven't spotted any."

Burger matched his paces to those of his companion. He smelt of after-shave. "Same on my side. You know that old Auntie I was telling you about? Remember? Like the kind of a sort of a you can say really boss of the family, well her, once she hears there's going to be some of the others allowed here, you know what I mean, the coffee-and-milks, straight out the trees, even a few, except the one's got to be working here of course, or want to part with their money, well... no fear, she's not going to so much as put a foot in the place. Not never."

Balfour quickened his pace and threaded a way through the throng. Burger hurried after him and panted "It's one hell of a show they're lay-ing on. Those school-kids, the fancy-dress girls, they come first. Special bus to bring them from way to hell-and-gone there right the other side those South-West Townships. March-past, the lot, that cross-breed so-called regiment of theirs. As though you can stick a half-caste into uniform and that'll make a soldier of him. They'll never make a toy soldier's backside. Come." He plucked at Balfour's sleeve. "I'll show you the real ones, the killer boys, just how good it's organised in case there's any trouble-makers decide come along to stir up."

Balfour glanced in the direction of the Inspector's pointing finger, to the entrance of an alleyway blocked by a barricade of white-painted bar-rels, rolls of barbed wire and a temporary 'No Access' sign. Parked fur-ther back, discreetly in the shadows, was an armoured troop-carrier with 'Police Riot Squad' stencilled on its khaki flank. Knots of young men in spotted camouflage overalls lounged in the gutter and against the lamp-posts. All nestled machine-pistols in the cradle of their hands, with the black and oily barrel resting across a forearm; all had high cheek-bones and green slit eyes, ginger hair cropped so close the sun gleamed on the bumps of skull-bone behind their ears. A few sucked hollow-cheeked on cigarettes squeezed between thumb and index finger, spat out tobacco grains, dropped the stumps on to the roadway and stamped them dead with combat boots. They seemed bored. They seemed impatient.

Burger stayed behind gaping at them and Balfour pressed himself sideways, with pointing shoulder, through the thickening crowd. He

228

spotted the Postal Super subdued by the nagging of a shapeless woman and the chatter of children who surrounded him in weekend substitution for his usual weekday entourage of silent assistants. At the entrance to the parking area, just inside the automatic ticket barrier, the Architect was condescending to be interviewed by a scribble of reporters. As Balfour skirted past them a couple at the back turned to compare note-pads.

"I'm buggering off, I had my copy ready last night" said one. "Listen to this—'The parade was led by a troupe of drum-majorettes drawn from the schools of outlying townships, specially selected and trained by the Ethnic Education Council of the Peri-Urban Resettlement and Admin Board, and very smartly too did these dusky young ladies step it out. They were followed by the band and troops of the Seventh Advanced Motorised Reconnaissance Assault, coloured in brackets, Battalion, Third Volunteer Brigade, affectionately known to the various population groups of our city by their fond nickname of 'Woodheads', here proudly exercising for the first time their newly-granted right to march through the streets with fixed bayonets. Loudly cheered by all who were fortunate enough to be present at this impressive occasion, blah blah blah...' You think that's more or less okay?"

The highway through the parking area had been roped off on either side. Down this strip of privilege puttered a double V of motorcycle outriders in escort to a cavalcade of long black limousines, pennants on the fenders, expressionless chauffeurs in front, waves of acknowledgement from the back seats.

Balfour found himself compressed into a concentration of bodies that squeezed with excitement all around him. There was pressure on his back and elbows in his sides and stomach. Someone breathed the fumes of popcorn on to his neck.

Past the dozen heads before him, along the clearing through the crush pranced a score of girls—kickety kickety kick, they stopped to twist and turn, silver skirts of satin, cardboard hats of blue, twirly-whirly batons, chewing jaws on gum, losing step as they waved to jealous friends, to proud relations looking on, to a ripple of applause—while Balfour wondered what busfare the Transport Authority charged for a journey from beyond the borders of the city. How could their parents afford it? As well as the cost of the costume? Special days to be remembered bore a price to pay. It was heavy.

Heavy as vibrations in the ground that pulsed up through the soles of shoes. Approaching bugles blared a bray of brass of brass still louder brass. The crush intensified, a pushing, a surging forward against the barrier.

A billy-goat mascot minced delicately at the end of a rope, dropping turds on the highway.

Ahead in strutting dignity, buffoon in gaudy braid, Drum-Major wheeled the gold-tipped mace entwined in cord and tassels; then a rattle-tattle-tattle from the dappled leopard-skins, kettledrums set throbbing the polish on their sides; buglers' lips all puckered up, buglers' cheeks distended; bass-drummer marched with backwards tilt to balance his protrusion, he hurled his padded sticks in thumps against the hide.

'...kurra-doemf kurra-doemf kurra-doemf-doemf-doemf...'

A veteran, gnarled and knobbly, ranked tenth deep at the back of the crush, raised his hat and waved it high in greeting—'Up the Woodheads'' he cried; and the Commandant, the officer and gentleman, pacing modestly behind the band, swagger-stick and gloves, flanked by trusty Adjutant and callow Aide-de-camp, allowed into the ice-blue of his eyes the glimmer of a twinkle.

Behind him tramped and tramped and tramped, by left and right and left, the ranks the ranks the ranks, the swing of arms the swing.

'...kurra-doemf...doemf...doemf, doemf, doemf...'

In hypnotic repetition they jerked past Balfour's face. And despite the glint of bayonets, the peaks of flat-topped caps, despite the burnished bandoleers and blanco on their belts, despite the drill that forced stiff necks to the shape of pride, the held-back heads, the rigid spines—still merely rank-and-file, still the disinherited descendants of the slaves, in bondage under service discipline, serfs indentured to their masters' sons.

"Eye-eyes right." Palms quivered up to the salute, to the dais gay with bunting and the bravery of flags, its civic dignitaries stiff in robes aflutter, their wives pastel under hat-brims set exactly level and Botha—the eminence in grey, the formal figure, Guest-of-Honour, chin tucked in and features firm with resolution.

"Eye-eyes front." Platoon platoon and company, platoon platoon and company, the Regimental Sergeant-Major swaggered at the rear.

Next... a toddle of golly-wog infants, in stumble and confusion, each clutching a pamphlet and a commemorative mug; behind them tripped two older children grinning a mixture of glory and shyness through gaps in teeth, struggling to hold almost upright the poles of an embroidered banner—'We Thank The Dept.'

'Too cute.' 'Adorable.' On the dais, Botha and the Councillors smiled suitably.

230

Burger forced his way through to squeeze Balfour's elbow. "Brought enough busloads to fill a TV screen but not too many so's to spoil things for the rest of us."

A gap in the procession set ripples of impatience swelling through the crowd; foot-shuffles, tip-toe standings, neck crannings. A brood of urchins whose early years in the area lent them daring for the one day of their return now slipped under the ropes and dashed across the strip of tarmac sanctified by the march-past and the spectators' sense of ceremony. 'They're coming.' 'Here they are.'

A convoy of floral barges mounted on platform-body trucks, 'Kindly Donated By Federal Investments.' Hair straightened, brow cream-bleached, the queen reclined in teenage majesty, in translucent muslin, on a throne of chrome and cushions that wobbled only slightly. She rewarded her adoring populace with a dental grimace and a glitter of tinsel crown. Her princesses on the floats that followed deigned to lean out far over the edge and toss their largesse to the hoi-polloi—a rose of crepe paper landed at Balfour's feet.

The flotilla rumbled past, the procession had ended. For a moment the spectators hesitated, perhaps there would be a tit-bit at the tail. No, nothing more. With the focal point of interest now removed the assembly lost its almost crystalline form and dissolved into a chaos of disappointment. Beggar-boys dared to duck under the barriers and dart between adult knees.

Burger aimed a clout at a peppercorn head. "Shouldn't be allowed" he spluttered, "They make me sick, they all make me sick, the whole fucking happy-happy, it's enough to make anybody want to hurl. Look, look around you, all those lit-up faces, here's celebration. They're the ones are sickest of all." He jabbed a thumb against his heart. "As God is my witness, how's a bugger expected to grin and bear it? If you've got a way to view the whole show and still not see the one great big hell of a mess in all directions, outside and inside you as well, then tell me." He slapped Balfour on the shoulder. "Keep smiling hey."

Balfour managed to lose him in the vague herd migration towards the building. Crowd-pressure extruded bodies through the main entrance, compression forced them to gasp and giggle and then exclaim with wonder at their sudden release into the spacious enclosure of a volume, another ambience, into a vision become real of what had been done on earth as it should be done in the adverts.

'It's heavenly.' He listened to the hushed chorus of response from the visitors drifting in awe around him, watched heads lift up towards the dome that arched above them in a reinforced concrete substitution for the sky, that blocked out the sun and blessed them with a glow of neon light—no glare, no shade or shadow; air-conditioning for weather—no heat, no cold, no mist driven by the breeze; colours brighter than a garden of a million blooms; no sound of birds or wind, only the blare of a two-for-the-price-of-one promotion on the public address; no smell of crushed leaves, dust or rain—hot oil and the reek of charring mince. It was here, on this same spot where the only tree had stood, a stall now served synthetic flavoured drinks to stain lips deeper than its fruit had ever done.

He watched ladies, real ladies from the tips of their manicures to the open toes of their Ballys, lift chins of face-powder and disdain above the palms and whines of barefoot pesterers. The flick of a policeman's hand cleared the nuisance from a press-photographer's lens and the ladies smiled their gratitude to the uniform, to the feature on tomorrow's leader page.

Outside the boutique two young girls from the Federal Head Office were chattering their excitement to the Senior Inspector. The third older one had stationed herself outside the Bible Booth, where she kept thrusting tracts from a stack on her arm under the noses of passers-by.

Yes, it was the crane-driver, who seemed to have peeled off his dignity together with his overalls, had smeared grease on his hair instead of hands and clothes, who was trying to force his way into the Disco Record Bar. While Balfour wondered which role was more true; was work only a minor overlapping segment in the full circle of their lives? Nothing else in common? Except the same announcements booming from the loudspeakers against their ear-drums.

'...a statement issued by???' 'By whom?' 'It gave great pleasure, in view of the centre's outstanding success...' The crowd-noise rose to match computing decibels. '...plans for the construction of a whole series of similar... proud to... national obligation... a free economy to counter the threat of... a lively march... the latest 7-single of the Purple Disasters and a lost little girl in a pink jersey... will the Chief Security Officer please come at once to...'

A vortex of sound, a vortex of bodies, a wife on tip-toes of enjoyment signalling a flutter-fingered wave across the main mall, over the heads of a posse of bargain-hunters. "It's terrific" she mouthed. Balfour frowned creases across his forehead and cupped a palm behind an ear. "The kiddies are loving it" she screamed.

Now tramped towards him a scaled-down model of the men he had noticed beside the Riot Squad vehicle, the same camouflage spotted tunic,

232

the same machine-gun, except that this miniature wore his shrapnel-helmet clamped well down on his head. He sprayed the mob around him with his toy weapon; as people jumped away from the clatter and sparks he chortled with glee, let them have it from the hip with another burst or two and blazed the last few rounds into Balfour's face. "Daddy, lie down, lie down Daddy, you're dead" he yelled and stopped for a busy-busy rewind of the clockwork magazine. "Look what I got." With pride, his little face ashine, he held up the gun for inspection. "It's all for nothing if you join the Junior Commando. This is how it works, you pull here, then..."

Further down the mall Balfour was accosted by a juvenile whore who leered at him, enticed him into a vapour of cheap perfume and blocked his path by gyrating her hips in time to the wump-wump-wump of a top-selling disc. A pair of skinny arms pointed in mockery at the surprise he knew showed on his face; her fingers snapped in derision at each thump of the bongo drums. Mascara had wearied her eyes to the age of shadows;" dissolute, with a slash of lipstick and an inflammation of rouge. "Elizabeth Arden" she screeched, "Helena Rubenstein, Clinique, free samples, isn't it too-too-too? I couldn't believe it when they held up the mirror. Daddy isn't it fabulous?" she thrilled, and twisted away towards the gang of denim louts who gangled their pimples and Adam's-apples at the corner.

Balfour drifted. He allowed the current of shoppers to swirl him towards the supermarket area, to become another statistic through the turnstiles, anonymous, unrecognised by the eyes of his own workmen behind reflecting dark glasses as they sauntered in slogan T-shirts. Up and down the aisles; Home'n Garden, Deepfreeze and Packaging. A hostess with a 'Fed Feeds You Yes You' sash guided past the delicatessen a disabled child whose matchstick limbs were twisted with rickets. "Not only a community centre" she explained, "also commercial training, where you can learn where the different things come from. Look, smoked salmon for example, now that comes all the way from Scotland."

Granny and Grandpa stopped him next to a stack of Pensioners Packs, their dentures gaping with surprise at the scale of everything, so much bigger than expected, it's enormous, it's beautiful, it's so modern, it seemed to have just sprung up overnight all on its own, hard to believe it had ever been real till they'd seen it for themselves. Grandpa lowered down to the heavy-duty silicone-guarded polyvinyl floor the plastic carry-bags in either hand that had been buckling him through a further stoop of years, while Granny tucked all her chins against her brooch. The corners of her lips went in and up. "This must be a proud day for you."

And this shabby old Indian sniffing at Herbs & Spices... Naidoo? Surely, no, yes, had he really aged all that in not much longer than a year or so? He crumpled Balfours's lapel. "Fine place this, yes? It'll do very good business. It's the positioning, that's it, that's what counts, and the goods. The right goods, I know, I know what items, some items go quick-quick, turnover, all same lines I used to carry. Draw plenty customers... now if I get take-away counter, fit it in somewhere..."

That was Nanny over there, waddling towards the frenzy of a free-gift never to be repeated opening-day offer, specially reduced, only 3 per customer, hurry while stocks last. She prised apart a pair of henna-rinsed madams and clawed at the counter. While they glared at her and muttered.

Out past the row of cashiers, the music and the tinkle of their cash-registers, the magic adding up of numbers jumping bright on to digital displays, past the Leave Your Parcels counter, back to the main concourse.

Where files of dark-skinned children were being marched in through the main entrance. Flash-bulbs exploded on to blinks, on to apple-green and royal-blue tracksuits trim with twin white stripes down the sleeves, jaws all chewing, chattering, the girls ribboned by bows in their frizzles, the boys as noisy as they dared. "Stop, hold it, I said halt, can't you hear me?" thundered a Press Liaison Officer from the Department. A pamphlet, a mug, a smile, a few kind words were bestowed on each in turn, "Come along now, don't be shy, and what's your name?", while a camera panned the scene for the evening's background to the news. The official beckoned to a squad of policemen who hustled the children out again. "Quick quick, get a move on, off with you, clear off, back to your bus now-now-now or you'll find out what trouble means. Little bastards." Waving batons hurried them on. Balfour picked a crumpled pamphlet out of a litter-bin—'All That Is Being Done For YOU.'

He wandered, he wandered, under placards hanging down from strings, past posters, helium balloons, streamers, through a conglomerate of competing noises, with stumbles in the turgid stream, bumpings, no 'Excuse me', one yeasty hiccuped 'Sorry' from a drunk who staggered against him. Through the open door of the Manager's Suite, in a sanctuary of curtains, carpets and calm accentuated by the turmoil in the public spaces, there was a glimpse of Botha, the charming, the host sipping from bone china between the robes of Mayor and Town Clerk.

Mrs Balfour navigated through the crush towards her husband. "There you are. You've seen the others? They're absolutely lapping it up." She had to shout. "Look what I've managed to pick up, space-saving, exactly what we'll need. Heavens." she kicked up a heel, the frolic of a colt, and leant well forward. "I'm dripping", and licked round the edges of her Snofreeze cone.

A uniformed Security Guard swept between them and she was lost. Balfour felt himself being circulated by the pedestrian flow through the parts of the building, of a structure whose pipes he knew more intimately than his own veins and arteries, its frame of beams and columns better than the bones of his skeleton. A temporary, a number in the record turn-out, addressed as another of the 'Ladies and Gentlemen' by a voice that boomed out a public announcement. Dummies in shop-front windows, dolled up in the latest, greeted him with fixed grimaces of papier-maché; his reflection in the mirrors mimicked him.

He turned behind a screen wall, past a row of rubber dirtbins spewing a sour overflow of crushed cartons, crumpled wrappings and cigarette stumps, through a concealed opening few would notice, down a bare and narrow stairway so rough it was obviously private, into a bliss of quiet, the dim light restful. Now the echo of his footsteps kept him company. He halted at a landing. Almost silent, almost, only a faint hum from the ballyhoo above.

He advanced. Down again, no retreat, more exacting than a panic flight from menace, each step in the emergency exit was dangerously steep, probed deeper towards the foundations of the pomp and glitter overhead. No handrails, when he stumbled he had to press palms against the unplastered walls on either side to steady himself; they felt warm and rough with the coarse honesty of plain baked earthen clay. Solid. Full grout in every joint. Enduring. No fault here, nor would any appear during the maintenance period, nor in the generations to follow.

Down, further down, the descent brought him to the lowest level where the stairs opened on to the crypt of the low-beamed parking basement, almost empty except for the official cars from the procession and a few with Federal Investment stickers on the windscreen. Across the vehicle ramp, next to the central column, signs proclaimed RESERVED and PER-MIT HOLDERS ONLY.

An explorer's footsteps, his footsteps rang hollow in the space enclosed by bare grey concrete. It could have been a cavern carved from solid rock by centuries of waves and tides at the outer limit of the land. The gleam from a row of glass bricks flooded a pale green translucency over walls and floor and cars; the watery twilight gave them the look of being already submerged below the level of a wishing-well.

It was musty and smelt of damp, the only sound a drip drip drip of condensation from the ceiling as nature worked out her role. There was no appeal against the laws of physics on which a sound career, this structure itself, depended. Breath after breath, inevitable, he drew moisture into his lungs as the droplets gathered, hung suspended, clung, dripped, dripped. Slow, slower that the thump and blare of drum and bugle from the street above as the regiment marched off in triumph—not fast enough to strain the pump. No flaw in the construction.

He went round stroking and patting the surfaces. A fine powdery dust on the palm, bone dry, not a crack, nothing so far that could be found faulty, or could be made faulty, all too soundly executed, too solid, the Department's grand design seemed to be working; stable, in man-made balance. The cables were firmly caulked into the ducts in their altered positions, the waterproof patch over the original openings covered by a rough-cast block of concrete—not at all neat, not at all slightly but out of public view, serving its purpose, only one tiny peep of orange plastic where the membrane was exposed; well protected, a remote possibility. Not more than that, it would hold if nothing disturbed it.

A little roughness here and there, a few uneven places, petty blemishes only to an expert eye. Maybe in time those minor maladies would cure themselves, the public address wear out, the extravagance of tinsel ornaments corrode with rust, only the durable remain, the concrete, the same proportioned mix of sand and stone, cement and water, as used in schools and clinics. Patience and a lifetime were unlikely to confirm the vision. Walls dead plumb, the central column seemed solid despite its overload of decibels and flashing neon. The structure stood, as it was, for the multitudes above and for the man who had erected it, built to outlast any actuary's prediction of how many days still left for him to view it.

Balfour prostrated himself near the column to sight along the floor. His body lay still, eyes staring. Yes, yes there, right there at the column, under a RESERVED sign as though the notice itself was too heavy a burden for the floor to bear—a minute deflection. Definitely. Still too minor to be noticed by any official at the Final Inspection.

He bounced up. And even should one of them spot it, dared they admit that it existed? Nor could the contractor be blamed, there were enough protests on record in the file. Disregard of warnings bore a danger of its own.

It seemed the earth itself was yielding to the stress imposed, there was a limit to what each component of a structure could be forced to bear. Wreaking a slow revenge for the violation done to it, the affront of its distortion by the men who had dug into it? The sacrifice of its repose on an altar of greed?

Drip drip drip of condensation, drip and wait and drip, wait till the seconds added up to years, decades; wait for the subsidence to tear the waterproofing under the floor, the flood, short-circuiting of pump and cables that could have summoned rescue, the moment of collapse— reinforcement rupturing from shattered beams and broken bones from flesh, screams of the injured piercing the rumble of toppling masonry, sheets shrouding inert forms on stretchers laid out in rows on the parking area, the wailing of orphans and widows clutching pillows in the dark to soak them with the tears of loneliness. Why wait for that? Why? Each second added to the load, the load of hurt, of guilt, to the credits cash-registers were piling into computers. The loudspeakers and the advertising signs, they would be the first to fall and shatter.

He stood before the block cast over the patched membrane at the original cable inlets. Hardly visible in the gloom, a glimpse of colour, the only touch of brightness in a grey musty world.

They would have had to release retention, a routine; the future a routine released from tension, reputation retained. He shivered, it was cold here underground. Upstairs, outside, a pleasant sunny day; wife and children waiting to go back to the place they had grown used to calling home. An honourable career, the ease and comfort of tomorrow, all ripped by a pair of fingers forced into a gap.

No. Too narrow, too well protected. Sharp edges on the chips of stone rasped his knuckles. Shreds of skin on concrete. He scratched at the surface—a few grains of crumble, a tiny sliver of rock, a broken nail.

An idea. Carefully, trying to keep the garment clean, he groped inside a pocket and shook loose his bunch of car keys. This one, the ignition, the biggest, a sword, a weapon. He thrust it in to try and prise away a corner. It bent. He flung the keys away and hurled himself against the block.

Must, must. Deeper, deeper into the opening, now he could feel it at his fingertips, the plastic slippery against his lacerations. Nearly. More effort, more pain... and perhaps. More grit. Pluck. Blood on his hand and blood on his wall.

He kept on tearing his flesh on the concrete he himself had cast.